The LIFE AND DEATH of LAURA FRIDAY
— AND OF PAVAROTTI, HER PARROT

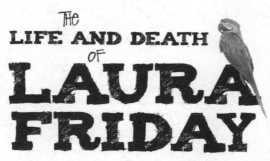

The LIFE AND DEATH of LAURA FRIDAY
— AND OF PAVAROTTI, HER PARROT

DAVID MURPHY

HarperCollins*Publishers*

National Library of New Zealand Cataloguing-in-Publication Data

Murphy, David, 1940-
The life and death of Laura Friday and of Pavarotti her parrot /
David Murphy.
ISBN 978-1-86950-700-8
I. Title.
NZ823.3—dc 22

First published 2008
HarperCollins*Publishers (New Zealand) Limited*
P.O. Box 1, Auckland

Copyright © David Murphy 2008
David Murphy asserts the moral right to be
identified as the author of this work.

All rights reserved. No part of this publication may be reproduced,
stored in a retrieval system or transmitted in any form or by
any means, electronic, mechanical, photocopying, recording or
otherwise, without the prior written permission of the publishers.

ISBN: 978 1 86950 700 8

Cover design and illustrations by Matt Stanton
Cover images courtesy of Shutterstock
Internal text design and typesetting by Springfield West
Printed by Griffin Press, Australia

50gsm Bulky News used by HarperCollins*Publishers* is a natural,
recyclable product made from wood grown in sustainable
plantation forests. The manufacturing processes conform to the
environmental regulations in the country of origin, New Zealand.

'If you only read one book in your entire life, this one's as good as any other!'

Bullock Telegraph

'Give me a break! Who gives a shit anyway?'

Mary Francesca Wilton

London Daily Chronicle

For Tricia Snell,
in memory of
fifteen good years.

Acknowledgements

Jane Judd in London lit the fire, many years ago. Ray Richards rekindled it. Barbara Else and Norman Bilbrough saw something flickering among the dead wood, but weren't sure what. Lorain Day at HarperCollins magically transformed a spark into a flame.

Kate Stone is a joy to work with.

Tricia Glensor critiqued the first draft and braved the ensuing storm. Tricia was and remains beside me with advice, encouragement and love.

To everyone who has helped me travel this long and winding road, I am eternally and immensely grateful.

Prologue

I was forty-six when I went back to Bullock to get rid of Laura Friday. I hadn't decided how she was going to die. A hit man most likely, with a bullet between the eyes after she'd suffered a while. If that sounds extreme, I make no apology. Laura had been driving me crazy for twenty years and deserved everything she got.

Solly said I was being unreasonable.

'Laura's been good to you, Fitz.'

Solomon Greenberg, Executive Producer on Laura's movies, from the back seat of his Mercedes limo somewhere in the hills above Los Angeles.

'If it hadn't been for her you'd still be translating Kraut sales manuals and living in that shit-hole in Himalaya Street.'

Which was all very well for Solly. He didn't have to live with Laura twenty-four hours a day. Laura *and* Pavarotti. A bullet for him would be a kindness. He was overweight and losing his voice.

'What am I supposed to be? Grateful or something?'

It was Men's Final Day at Wimbledon. The champ was teaching an American brat a lesson. I could have been there but I hate crowds, so I was on the terrace of my Richmond Hill home. Fifteen bedrooms. A priceless view over the river. Mick Jagger for a neighbour. Five hundred acres of Elizabethan parkland outside my back door. Deer, rabbits, squirrels, foxes. An Aston Martin DB9 in the garage, a Brazilian supermodel called Anaconda mixing the drinks, and one of my all-time favourites on the surround sound. Dire Straits: 'Money For Nothing'.

And I still wasn't happy.

'Don't forget, I made Laura what she is today. She'd have been nothing without me.'

'But what about her fans, Fitz?' said Solly. 'The websites? The blogs? There's a guy in Vancouver knows every word Laura's ever said, everyone she's ever fucked or killed.'

Solly sounded desperate. I could understand why. Laura had been good for him, too. A ten-thousand-square-foot house in titanium and glass on Mulholland Drive. Four wives, not counting the incumbent. Solomon Greenberg Street in downtown Tel Aviv. Greenberg Productions employed over a hundred people.

But all things must pass, as my old mate George Harrison once said, and Laura's time had come.

'I'm going to get rid of her in Bullock, Solly.'

'Where the fuck is Bullock?'

'New Zealand.'

'Where the fuck is New Zealand?'

I looked at the plasma screen. Match point to the champ on the brat's serve. First serve into the net. Second serve wide by a mile. The brat sank to his knees and began to sob. I took aim with the remote. Fired. The screen went black.

'It's where Laura was conceived. And it's where she's going to die.'

BOOK ONE

Chapter 1

When I was a kid in the late 1960s, Bullock was just another small New Zealand coastal town. It never made the news and had no wish to. Great events elsewhere mattered far less than small ones close to home. When I went back forty or so years later, nothing much had changed. Bullock was still small, still coastal. And the first thing people still wanted to know when they opened yesterday's *Bullock Telegraph* was not whether there was a war somewhere, but who'd died and who was doing the funeral catering.

We lived in a two-storey house on Wey Street, close to Bullock General Hospital. This reassured my mum, who believed that every minute, day and night, disaster lurked like a cat outside a mouse-hole. She made us change our socks and underwear several times a day.

'What will they say when you're brought in to A&E, Johnny, when you've been hit by a bus and you've a skid mark?'

It was never if, but when. A Terrible Accident was only a matter of time.

Like Bullock in general, Wey Street never aspired to anything. It was a no-exit road with a stream at the bottom that would rise whenever it rained, turning its bramble-infested banks into an impenetrable bog. In late summer, my sister Carmel and I collected blackberries and Mum made her Bullock Pie with apples, nutmeg, cinnamon and a sprinkling or two of Aunt Agnes's Mother Mary Irish Green.

There were twelve houses and everyone knew everyone else's

business. We shared a phone line with the Calloways, who lived next door. Whenever Marge or Roy Calloway was using theirs, ours would give a little click. Mum had an ear for it. She could be vacuuming, with the radio on and Dad mowing the lawn, but if that phone clicked she'd be there in a second. Lifting the receiver with a stealthy hand. Preserving the myth of privacy. Miming to Carmel to quit saying her Hail Marys and Our Fathers and put down her rosary beads. Later she'd give the report.

'Marge's mum's coming over from Gundry for the weekend, but her dad's staying at home. He doesn't like to keep stopping to pee. Otherwise it's a milk bottle and she has to hold the steering wheel. Her eldest's late again.'

Mum would blow the surveillance operation wide open the next time she saw Marge Calloway.

'Hi, Marge, how's your dad's prostate? When's the baby due?'

I was not especially tall for my age but I did have long fingers, so everyone assumed I'd become a pianist.

'Johnny's going to be rich and famous,' my Aunt Agnes said. 'Like that little Jewish bogger, Barney Boim. Look after us in our fockin' old age, so he will. Won't you, pet?'

The fingers were an embarrassment, protruding like lobster claws from my bony wrists and hillock-sized knuckles. These digital promises of future wealth and fame were brought out for visitors along with the Waterford crystal and Royal Doulton china, so they were a cross I learned to bear.

As it became apparent that my fingers were never likely to cause Daniel Barenboim any loss of sleep, my mother would look at them with reproach, as if they had failed her in some way. The fact that we did not possess a piano, and I had never taken a lesson, seemed irrelevant. The fingers had failed.

From my earliest years until she died I loved Agnes, my dad's sister, who lived with us when she was not enduring her novitiate in the Sacred Sisters convent. Like a bird seeking a mate, she would hear the Call each spring and disappear until the weather turned colder, when a taxi would arrive unannounced. I would wave to her from my bedroom window. She would blow me a kiss before coming inside and asking Mum to pay the driver.

'It was the bloody floors, Johnny,' she said to me one year. 'There's nothin' in the fockin' Bible about scrubbin' yer fingers raw at four t'irty in the fockin' mornin', now is there?'

Another year it was the toilet paper.

'There's nothin' in the fockin' Bible about penitential greaseproof, now is there, Johnny?'

I loved her brown eyes and how she held a cigarette and talked through the smoke like Lauren Bacall. I loved the way she cheated at poker. How she swore like a sailor, to my mother's tight-lipped disapproval. And I loved and envied her easy relationship with her God.

'Sure, He's always wid ye, Johnny. Sittin' on yer shoulder like a parrot, givin' ye fockin' what-for if yez steps out of line. But that's only because He loves ye. D'ye see that now, pet?'

I loved the smell of her hair against my cheek, the comfort of her generous bosoms when she gave me her special hugs. When we played hide-and-seek around the house, I would find her by the scent of her soap and she would find me by my giggles.

One thing about Agnes remained a puzzle for many years. If Agnes was Dad's sister, why did she have a thick Irish brogue when he didn't? It was one of those Dark Secrets like the Monthly Mysteries, and why my only sibling was Carmel when all my schoolmates had several. Secrets that had Dad averting his eyes and Mum giving her plate her undivided attention.

'Ask no questions, you'll hear no lies, Johnny. Now eat your greens and we'll have no more prying into things that don't concern you.'

Our house was a combination of Saint Peter's Square and Dublin Airport. Priests and nuns flitted in and out. Distant relatives arrived from Ireland, their faces alive with dreams and fantasy. Disillusioned ones departed. Aunts, uncles, cousins, came for a meal and stayed for a month.

I was seven when Agnes came back from the convent to find her room taken by a priest, and my sister doubling with a nun. So she dumped her suitcase in my room, and we topped-and-tailed. Night after night I would listen for the squeak of the door hinge, watch her silhouette kneel, hear her murmured prayer. Then she would withdraw the sheet, rest her feet on my pillow, brush my cheek with her toes and squeeze my fingers before sleeping.

Paradise is always fleeting. A few days later the priest flew back to Dublin and Agnes had her own room again. I was bereft.

Chapter 2

As a kid I never liked my sister. She was ferociously intelligent. An aggressive bundle of brains and glasses and always wanting the last word. She sailed through school without even trying, while I had to work like hell just to stay afloat.

Religion was her favourite subject. She never gave God a minute's peace. Her walls were awash with posters of Jesus, and religious books covered every square inch of bookshelf. There was a framed sign above her bed which said *The best exercise is walking with God*. She observed every Saint's Day and before she was ten had what Mum called 'God's callouses' on her knees from praying. I'd outgrown her by then, so I used to beat her up whenever I thought I could get away with it. Chinese burns. Kidney punches. Things that wouldn't show.

She'd run crying to Mum.

'Don't bully your sister, Johnny. If she got run over by a bus and went to Heaven, you'd be sorry.'

No, I wouldn't. I'd have been ecstatic. I tried dropping bogeys in her Rice Krispies when she was saying Grace and peeing on her toothbrush, but nothing worked. Her teeth gleamed. In fact she had the best teeth in the family, and since Dad was a dentist that was saying something.

The only time Carmel and I did anything together was when we were Little Crackers. Dad's brother, Tommy, used to run the Bullock Ritz cinema on Thames Street opposite Meggett's department store. Saturday mornings were for Ritz Little Crackers.

There'd be a Hopalong Cassidy film (*'fill that ornery critter full of lead, Hoppy'*), maybe a Gene Autry or a Tex Ritter or a Roy Rogers (the Singing Cowboy) and Trigger (the Neighing Horse), and a Laurel and Hardy or a Three Stooges.

The session would end with a serial where the hero was left hanging from a flagpole atop a tall building or from a rope over a cliff with the strands slowly snapping, so you'd have to come back the following week to find out whether he died. As far as I can recall, he never did. Next Saturday he'd be in a dark doorway lighting a cigarette, or in a smoky bar ordering a Jack Daniels, so he must have scrambled free during the week.

Uncle Tommy had this idea of staging a talent quest in the interval to minimise seat wreckage. Mum said Carmel and I should enter. Carmel wanted to play 'Ave Maria' on the clarinet. I could fart the first few notes of 'Onward, Christian Soldiers'. Mum said we should do something together, so while Carmel sang 'All Things Bright and Beautiful' I accompanied her on the paper and comb. But I couldn't resist ripping off a few bass notes and making a turned-up-nose face which got a huge audience response but pissed Carmel off so much she wet her knickers.

We were unplaced, but for me it was a moment of supreme triumph.

Chapter 3

Music ran in our family. Dad played tin whistle or fiddle and sang in the Mayo Brothers band each Friday at the Bullock Workingmen's Club, with Tommy on guitar and accordion, Jimmy Kelly on drums, and Ricky Flannery on bass. Fridays were Irish Night, and it was on one of those Fridays in 1957 that Dad fell in love with my mum, Moira Fitzgerald. She was celebrating her birthday, and had been persuaded to get up to sing 'My Blackjack Man'. The Kennedys came from Blackjack in County Mayo, and so did the Fitzgeralds. It seemed like Fate had brought them together.

There was music everywhere in our house. Mum crooned Irish ballads as she peeled the onions or vacuumed the floors. Dad was always singing or playing records, whether he was working in his shed or mooching around the house getting under Mum's feet. A Dublin shop sent the latest release each month and he'd open the parcel like an excited kid. He liked all Irish music, but his main man was Declan Maloney, a young folk singer from County Clare who released his first LP, *Travellin' Man*, in 1969. Dad wore it out and had to order another copy. From then on, every time Maloney released a record, Dad bought two copies. One he played, the other he kept in his shed in its wrapping. Dad's dream was to see Maloney perform, but since Maloney rarely left Ireland, and Dad never left Bullock, there seemed little hope that it would ever be fulfilled. Agnes was a Rolling Stones fan. 'I Cain't Get No Satisfaction' blared constantly from her room when she was supposed to be praying.

Carmel played clarinet in the school orchestra but was tone deaf. Each time she practised a piece it would be different. And wrong. I never took much interest in music until Abba blew my mind with 'Waterloo'. From then on I was hooked.

Except when he was on stage with the band, where he became a whirling dervish, Dad was slow and methodical. When he sought a philosophy of life he did so alphabetically, beginning with Aristotle and ending several weeks later with Zeno of Elea. He chose Epicurus, who espoused a simple, moderate, trouble-free life, more concerned with immediate pleasure than future redemption. Dad believed that everything in life was a finite resource, to be stored and rationed, lest at some future point it might become exhausted, leaving a Dank Void.

'Let's enjoy ourselves,' he'd say as we set off to the Working-men's Club for a family meal. 'But not too much.'

Dad's dental surgery was above Percy Cartwright's Family Funerals, which was next door to Murray's Barber Shop on Amazon Street. As a good Catholic Dad did not believe in aborting teeth.

'We're given them for life, Johnny. It's not a choice thing.'

Dad's careful husbandry was never more evident than on Sunday poker nights, which alternated between our house and Uncle Tommy's. Tommy lived on Tamar Street at the other end of town in those days, although he moved out to Passion Dale when my grandfather Sean died.

Every second Sunday we took the car, an immense Humber Super Snipe which came from the same production line as the Churchill tank. It had a bonnet like the prow of a supertanker, a bird in flight for a bowsprit, deep burgundy leather seats, sheepskin rugs to protect the carpets, a sheepskin cover to protect the steering wheel, and a sign in the back window that said *I Slow Down For Horses* although there was never any need.

Dad had bought the car from the proceeds of a legacy, and, like the woman he married and the teeth he cared for, he saw no sense in change for the sake of it.

'Warm her up in winter, keep her ticking over nice and slow, service her every six months, treat rust before it gets a hold, she'll last forever.'

In a town of slow drivers, Dad was the slowest. We were on our way to Uncle Tommy's one Sunday night, rolling down Thames Street at a steady twenty, when we were pulled over by Seth Nelson, the Bullock cop.

'You're causing a traffic jam six cars long, Joke. Where's the funeral?'

'Joke' was Dad's nickname from schooldays, an abbreviation of Joe Kennedy. He didn't mind being called Joke, but he hated it when people called him Joker. He always gave them fair warning — *'appreciate it if you didn't call me Joker. Joe or Joke's OK'* — but if they didn't take heed, next time they came in for a filling or some intricate work around a nerve he'd go light on the Novocaine, or his pick would slip. He wasn't a vindictive man. He just had his own perception of right and wrong and liked to ensure that on the playing field of life the score remained even.

'No funeral so far as I know. No point in rushing, Seth. Get there too early, could run out of conversation.'

'Couldn't you have left home a bit later?'

'Then we'd have had to repeat ourselves. I think we got it just about right.'

'Maybe you should try pulling over from time to time.'

'Then I'd be late.'

'Well . . .' Seth scratched his head, leaned on the roof. 'Wouldn't hurt to try going a little faster anyway, Joke. A little extra speed never hurt anyone.'

But Dad was never convinced about that.

'We're only given so much time in this life, Johnny. Go too fast, you run out. Then what're you going to do?'

From then on, if he saw Seth Nelson before Seth saw him, he'd speed up until Seth was safely out of sight.

Like most Bullock drivers, Dad was forever trying to teach others a lesson. At intersections he'd indicate a right turn, look to his left and wait until a car was approaching. Then he'd drop the clutch and roar into the junction. The approaching car would try to cut off Dad's manoeuvre. Dad would look in his rear-view mirror and smile.

'Guy tried to cut me up! No wonder there's so many accidents. Fellows like that on the road.'

On the other hand, if a car dashed from a side road in front of him, Dad would drop a gear, flatten the accelerator, close to within a few inches of the car's rear bumper, beep his horn and flash his lights.

'Fellow knows I've got priority. It's drivers like that that Seth Nelson should be after, not innocent motorists like me.'

The only other time I saw Dad speed up was when we came to a passing lane. If a car came alongside, he'd grip the wheel until the whites of his knuckles showed, plant his right foot and lean forward as if urging a carthorse into a gallop, while the other guy did the same. Usually the Snipe's monstrous cylinders would generate enough speed before the lanes converged to force the other guy to back off. Dad would give a grunt of triumph and slow right down again. If not, he'd hog the other guy's back bumper for miles, way beyond where we were supposed to be going, until Mum told him to cool down.

'All he did was overtake you, Joe.'

'What's his hurry? That's what I'd like to know.'

Dad was Bullock's worst driver, and its worst poker player. Everyone could read his cards by the expression on his face. In all the years he, Mum, Uncle Tommy, Aunt Bridie and Aunt

Agnes played together, I don't think he ever won a hand. Agnes was superb, though. It was only years later I discovered why.

Although Dad drove the car, Mum drove the house. Nothing happened without her say-so, but she always gave Dad the belief that his opinion was valued.

'Joe, are you going to mow the lawn this weekend?'

'I don't think so.'

'I think you should.'

'Well, then, I will.'

It wasn't that Dad was henpecked or under Mum's thumb. She simply ran things better than he did.

As soon as Carmel and I were old enough, Mum took a job behind the hospital's A&E reception desk where she kept track of patients, nurses, doctors and staff. She fed us, made sure we never ran short of clean underwear (*'Don't worry, I'll be there with a spare pair when you're admitted, Johnny, just in case you have an accident when you have your accident'*), supervised admissions and discharges at home, organised our lives, and knew when the lawn needed mowing.

But she never went into Dad's garage.

'Your father needs his little bit of privacy.'

Chapter 4

God was everywhere in our house. In the form of Father Martin Donovan, who used to call in on his parish rounds to top us up with devotion like bottomless coffee. In the living room, as Christ bleeding from his wounds. As a full-size Virgin Mary who gazed down from the upstairs landing. In our meal-time rituals. And in Mum's everyday speech, which was peppered with His Capital Letters.

'Have you done God's Homework, Johnny? Why are you jumping about like that? Do you need to visit His Bathroom?'

I was seven when I first took Christ's Body. As an incentive to a life of unquestioning faith I was force-fed the Catechism like a goose and offered the prospect of Eternal Damnation if I failed to confess to an Impure Thought.

Carmel took to religion as if it satisfied some atavistic need. She nagged Mum and Dad until they gave her a little nun's outfit. She'd run around the house singing 'Ave Maria' out of tune, pushing a toy pram with the baby Jesus inside wrapped in swaddling clothes. She couldn't wait to join the Little Daughters of Mary and later the Young Sisters of Holy Redemption.

She was eleven when she made her Announcement.

I'd been in my room reading the *Concise Oxford Dictionary*, which Agnes had given to me as a birthday present. Sitting on my bed inhaling its contents as I would later inhale Mother Mary Irish Green. Drinking its great words as I would later drink great wine. Drawing them into my mouth. Rolling them around my tongue. Closing my eyes. Tasting their ripe complexity.

Numinous. Arcane. Perspicacity. Uxorious. Usurious. Fundamental. There were thousands of them, they were free, and there were no harmful side effects.

Dad had been polishing his ports. He'd bought a Vincent Black Shadow motorbike, a thundering black-and-chrome beast with a kick-start like a bucking bronco and an exhaust that rattled windows and sent cats up trees. In all the years he had the bike he rarely went beyond the No Exit sign at the end of Wey Street.

He would roar back, lift his goggles and say, 'She's down on power, Johnny. Ports could do with a bit of a polish.'

Then he'd strip the engine on his pristine bench, grease every thread, label every nut, and set to work with his dentist's rouge. He loved his Black Shadow. He loved it most when it was in bits on his bench.

Mum had been cooking dinner while Agnes tended her small weed plantation. Everyone in Bullock grew their own weed. Had done so ever since the seeds had been washed ashore from the *Heavy Going* in an oilskin bag and dispersed among the survivors. A century later, enthusiasts around town had bred several hybrid varieties, including Bullock Gold, Special Curler and Crackling Rose. Weed sampling evenings were a Bullock tradition until television came along and people started watching *Coronation Street*.

Carmel asked if she could say Grace that evening. I groaned and she gave me her Look.

Bless us, dear Lord, and these, the gifts of Thy bounteous Grace . . .

As the words tumbled from her mouth and across the table, she sat with her fingers laced, her eyes squeezed shut, her pigtails tied with navy blue ribbons patterned with little white crosses.

She seemed oblivious to the congealing gravy.

> *. . . and give us the humility, Lord, as we enjoy this food, to remember those less fortunate here in Bullock and throughout Thy Earthly Kingdom . . .*

I stole a one-eyed glance around the table. Dad's face was noncommittal. He'd never been on close terms with God. He took Communion and said Grace and went to Confession and Mass in preference to the alternative, which was shopping.

'It pleases your mum, Johnny. Keeps the peace. And it's cheaper than Meggett's.'

Mum was ticking off each plea with nods of her head, as if they were ledger items. She'd studied bookkeeping and saw life as a balance sheet to be audited on Judgment Day. Agnes was reading the *Bullock Telegraph* racing page, quartered and tucked beside her plate. She sensed my look, and blew me a kiss.

> *. . . we are here, Lord, to serve Thee and to sup at Thy Feet in Everlasting Joy . . .*

Agnes looked up from her paper.

'That's very good, Carmel, but we're all fockin' starvin' here, so amen to everythin' ye said an' let's get on wid it before the Divil takes it from us.'

Mum had just served the apple crumble when Carmel coughed.

'I have an Announcement to make. I intend to become a nun. I have heard God's Call.'

'Ah, sure, there's many a time He's called me, too,' said Agnes. 'But it's a good idea to wait a while before you answer.'

Dad said, 'Have you considered dentistry? Looking after people's teeth's a noble profession. And it pays quite well.'

'Take no notice. We're all delighted for you, Carmel,' said Mum. 'God will regard this as a Great Investment and as compensation for our lack of Further Issue. What do you think, Johnny?'

'I think it's providentially perspicacious.'

I was never convinced about God. As my hormones ran berserk, as I discovered what an erection was for, and as I sank into a permanent state of Impure Thought, I developed the same doubts as Woody Allen in *Love and Death*.

'If I could just see a miracle, I'd believe,' said Woody. 'A burning bush, or the seas part.'

That would have done it for me, too.

But instead I got Father Donovan hefting his sack of Sin, Guilt and Purgatory through our front door like a black-clad Santa as he called in on his rounds or to prepare Carmel for her entry into the convent.

Chapter 5

I made my own Announcement at Sunday lunch in late November 1974. A delicious early summer day, everything green and fresh. I'd been in the garden most of the morning reading *The Great Gatsby*.

I was fourteen and reading everything, from the medical magazines my mate Merv Scunthorpe brought to school to Dad's Vincent manual. I'd known the shape and function of the vagina and how to replace a timing chain since I was eleven. I'd read the Bullock Library's entire catalogue of spy stories, romances, thrillers and whodunnits, and the town's complete history. There weren't too many non-religious books in our house, so I'd begun to raid Roy Calloway's shelves.

Roy was our next-door neighbour and my godfather. Editor of the *Bullock Telegraph*, he was a tall, rangy guy in those days, with a lantern jaw and a short-back-and-sides haircut, although later he went to seed.

Roy's hobby was sheep-shearing. He kept a mob of neurotic Romneys which would bolt at the sight of him clambering over the fence with his clippers. Earlier that year, he'd given me a book of W. B. Yeats's poems: 'Yeats was your abstract lover-man, Johnny. Loved Maud Gonne but couldn't have her, so he turned her into a vision and wrote love poems. The loss of love can be a terrible thing, but it can also provide the spark for great creativity.'

It would be another thirty-odd years before I learned that Roy's affinity with Yeats went deeper than appreciation of great poetry.

That he, too, had loved and lost. That my mum was his Maud Gonne. And that shearing sheep was his creative compensation.

Yeats was great, but I preferred American writers with their tight, no-nonsense style. Dos Passos, Hemingway, Steinbeck and Fitzgerald.

Once Mum had said Grace and Dad had carved the meat and extracted the bones with his usual precision, I coughed and said, 'I'm going to be a writer.'

Dad looked puzzled as he wiped his scalpel.

'That's not much of an ambition, Johnny. You can write already. So can everyone. You should try something more specialised. Have you considered dentistry?'

'And there's another thing,' I said. 'From now on I'm going to be J. Fitz Kennedy. It has a certain *cachet*, don't you think? Like F. Scott Fitzgerald.'

'Fitzgerald was a fockin' alcoholic, pet.' Agnes put her racing page aside and stubbed out her Rothman's. 'He died very young. Drinkin's all well and good in its place, but I'm not so sure it's a good idea to be modellin' yer life on someone such as himself.'

'He died of a heart attack.' I felt the thrust of my Announcement drifting away on an ebb tide. 'Which can happen to anyone.'

'I was reading about Fitzgerald in Murray's Barber Shop the other day,' said Dad. 'He suffered frequent bleeding from the oesophageal varices caused by advanced liver disease. It was his lifelong drinking that led to the coronary.'

'Which was what happened to Father Doyle,' said Mum. 'After Mass he'd get at the Communion Wine, saying that since it was now the Blood of Christ it could only be good for his gout.'

'Father Doyle could never write a decent sermon, though,' said Agnes, 'no matter how much he drank. Will ye be after passin' the salt, Johnny?'

'*Cachet!*' said Carmel. 'Is your own language not good enough for you now? You have to use French? Pride comes before a fall, Johnny.'

'Fitz,' I said. 'J. Fitz Kennedy.'

'Well,' said Dad, 'if you're going to become a writer, I'll take you to Murray's Barber Shop. You'll learn all you need to know about life if you just read what's on Murray's shelves and listen to what's being said.'

Chapter 6

We went one morning during the school holidays. The holidays were a chance for several fathers to introduce their sons to Murray's. Tony Scunthorpe was there with Merv, and Giorgio Scarlatti with Andy. Merv and Andy were my best mates.

There were two barber chairs, one for Young Murray who was learning the trade, and the main chair for Murray. Young Murray was the same age as me and in my class at Saint Benedict's. A quiet, likeable guy with an amazing thirst for knowledge, always close to top of the class. Young Murray could have been anything he wanted, but he never yearned for more than to move a few paces to his right and take over his dad's chair. There'd been a Murray's Barber Shop since Murray the First had been washed ashore on Bullock Beach when the *Heavy Going* foundered, clutching his scissors and comb. Young Murray had every intention of continuing the family tradition.

'This shop's a microcosm of the human condition, Johnny,' he said as he practised a few moves. 'Where better to pass a lifetime than at its very core? Would you like a little more off the top?'

There was a mirror the length of the back wall, so that customers would not be left out of the conversation simply because they were being shorn, and so that Murray could join in without causing a log-jam by turning from his work every few seconds. The two side walls were crammed floor to ceiling with books and magazines, each catalogued and in its rightful place.

There was a quick reference-card index system and a sign that said: *Please put me back where you found me. Then you'll know where I am next time.*

In the back corner beside Young Murray's chair and next to the passage that led to the toilet-cum-stockroom was a table on which there was a Pyrex jug of coffee on a hotplate, milk, sugar and a stack of mugs, some stuck with an Elastoplast on which the owner's name had been written in biro. There was another sign here which said: *If you're getting one for yourself, ask others if they'd like one, too.*

Two of the customers that day were local celebrities. 'Stuttering' Hutch Scandrett did the Breakfast Show on Radio Bullock from about five each weekday until he could be persuaded to give someone else a chance. Hutch (*'Goo-goo-goo-good mo-o-o-o-rning B-b-b-b-ullock!'*) looked older than he sounded, with long strands of dyed blond hair twirled around his scalp and fixed with a pin south-west of his left ear.

Genghis Punch had come to our house when he was canvassing for his fourth term as Mayor (*'Vote for me! You'll be as pleased as Punch'*), but hadn't impressed my parents.

'He's too smarmy,' said Mum, who liked her politicians open and honest.

'He has crossed incisors,' said Dad, 'which I've found to be a sign of a devious personality.'

I never met anyone who admitted to voting for Genghis, but he was always elected anyway. There was talk of a Punch dynasty because Genghis's father and grandfather had been Mayor and his son Septimus was being groomed. The Punches belonged to the Future Indicative Gospel, which believed that everything pointed the way forward if only you could read the signs.

When Young Murray had finished with me and begun working on Andy Scarlatti, I returned to my seat next to Dad.

'You fellows going to see the *Sound of Music*?'

Dad bent his head and whispered, *'Ray Stubbs. Two decayed laterals. Nice guy.'*

This was December 1974. The film had been released around the world in 1965, but hadn't arrived in Bullock until 1971. Uncle Tommy shared Dad's cautious philosophy and usually waited a few years to see how a film performed before booking it into his cinema.

Ray's question provoked puzzled looks.

'Saw it twice when it came through the first time.' Hutch Scandrett spoke without any sign of a stammer, my first exposure to the duplicity of the entertainment industry. 'Not sure I want to see it again.'

'Not the film,' said Ray. 'Bullock Operatic Society's putting it on.'

'Who's playing Maria?'

Dad leaned down. *'Howie Clifton. Three cavities. Drinks.'*

'Alice Mulvaney.'

'Good choice,' said Dad. 'She's in good shape. I gave her a filling only last week.'

'Bet she appreciated that, Joker.'

This from a tall, fat guy, who winked around the shop and sat back with a smirk as a few people laughed. Dad frowned. He didn't like clean or dirty dentist jokes, Irish jokes, Catholic jokes, or any joke that made fun of anyone. And he didn't like being called Joker.

'Cole Range,' said Dad. *'Lower left molar's giving him trouble. Just wait until the prick comes in to see me!'*

I'd never heard Dad use an expletive. Murray's Barber Shop was giving me a whole new perspective on life, and I'd only been there a few minutes. I sat back and relaxed, a boy among men, reading the *Journal of Cardiovascular Medicine*. Medical magazines were popular among Murray's customers. The shop was used as a reference library by the town's three doctors.

'That's Madge Mulvaney's daughter,' said Howie. 'Madge is secretary of the Heavy Going Ladies' Society.'

'Did you see yesterday's *Telegraph*? Page one banner headline?' said Genghis Punch. 'Madge Mulvaney in Mustard Seed Sensation.'

'What did she do?' someone asked.

'Came up with a new recipe for chutney. Seems if you combine mustard seed with lemons and a few other ingredients it takes on a whole new taste.'

'That's clever.' Hutch Scandrett looked up from his *Lancet*. 'Maybe she'd come on the show. We could do talkback, throw in a few commercials, take up most of the morning.'

'A stammer or two would spin it out,' said Ray.

Meanwhile Murray had been snipping away. Now he looked in the mirror and said, 'Talking about the HGLS. Often think about those people who came out on the *Heavy Going*. Hector Meggett kept a diary, you know. I was reading it in the Bullock Hall of Memories the other day. *This ship has been aptly named*, it said. *As we wallow from wave to wave, our vomitings are food for the fishes. Were it not for our daily ingestations of hasheesh this voyage would indeed be Heavy Going.'*

'As it was, those hundred and six days passed like a dream,' said Young Murray. He'd been struggling with Andy Scarlatti's thick Italian hair and paused for a breather. 'There's that bit where he says, *All measurements of time and space became a whirling void. When I drank it was as floods into an abyss which became engorged by the sea.'*

'Heavy Going Ladies' Society re-enactment meetings must be quite something,' said Ray Stubbs. 'Especially after they've ingested the hasheesh.'

'Put some in Madge's Mustard Seed Chutney,' said Hutch Scandrett. 'That'd finish everyone off.'

From then on Murray's Barber Shop became an integral part of my life. Dad dropped in there most days for morning coffee, and gave me an expurgated digest when I visited the garage after dinner to help polish his ports. I'd visit the shop after school if I needed something to read, and could soon hold my own whenever the dinner table conversation turned to urinary tract disorders, diseases of the gall bladder, or the Bauhaus school of architecture. I was a sponge. What I learned and heard at Murray's Barber Shop coloured my perception of the world, and years later helped transform Laura Friday into a superstar.

Chapter 7

Girls were an even greater influence. I had my first sexual experience at nine when I just happened to see Carmel through the bathroom keyhole as she emerged from the shower. As far as I can tell the experience did no lasting damaging to my sexual psyche, although I never repeated it. It seemed to me then that women were built pretty much the same as men but without a willy. Subsequent experience proved this to be untrue.

I fell in love many times. At least, I thought I did. It wasn't until I met Frankie that I knew what love was. Until then I had several years to discover what it wasn't.

It wasn't Betty Rice, whose parents ran Rice's Dairy on Orinoco Street. She was a plump girl who used to serve behind the counter after school. She and I never connected on an intellectual level, but it was hard to miss her immense breasts. Merv Scunthorpe, Andy Scarlatti and I used to line up in front of the ice cream cabinet and take our time choosing a flavour while Betty hovered, scoop in one hand, cone in the other, her left breast pointing at the Hokey Pokey, her right at the Peppermint Crumble.

Merv was always the boldest and so was the first to ask her for a date. He took her to the Ritz to see *Ben-Hur*.

'She's got cold, clammy hands,' he said when he made his report.

'Left or right or both?'

Andy always wanted specifics. I was happy with the overall concept.

Merv thought for a bit, then said, 'I only tried the right.'

'Hardly surprising,' said Andy. 'That's the one she holds the scoop with.'

When Andy took her out, he made sure he sat on her cone side.

If Merv's approach was frontal, and Andy's a steady progression, I preferred poetry, though I'm not sure Yeats would have been impressed by my first effort.

Betty Rice, don't think twice
Come with me to Paradise.
Failing that the Bullock Ritz
Here's my number. Call me.
Fitz.

But she never did.

Chapter 8

Love wasn't Maria Santos Almeida, either. Maria was a Portuguese beauty with creamy skin and huge, dark eyes and black eyebrows and perfect white teeth and the finest pair of breasts this side of Marilyn Monroe. I'd seen *Some Like It Hot* several times. The movie had come out in 1959 but had taken its time getting to Bullock. By the time it appeared, Marilyn had been dead for more than a decade but her breasts lived on.

Andy, Merv and I had spent many hours discussing the ideal breast, and Maria's met our stringent criteria. They were lemon-shaped. Proud Meyers with protruding nipples. We'd read that a woman's nipples went hard if you stroked or kissed them. We discussed what would happen to Maria's.

'They'd become gob-stoppers,' said Merv. 'Lemon flavour.'

'More like the cherry on a trifle,' said Andy. 'Squishy. With maybe a lemon liqueur inside.'

'Black olives,' I said. 'You remove the stone with your teeth.'

That night I had a wet dream.

'Never mind, Johnny,' said Mum as she changed the sheets. 'A Nocturnal Emission's nothing to be ashamed of as long as the Cause of it's Pure. Was it a Pure Thought, Johnny?'

'I was in an olive grove, Mum. Eating olives and spitting out the stones.'

'Like the Garden of Gethsemane?'

'Yes, Mum.'

'And what were you thinking about?'

'Heaven, Mum.'

'That's just fine, Johnny. Make sure you change your underpants before you go out.'

Maria's father was a wine-maker, one of the first in Bullock, and the family lived out of town at Casa Almeida, a cream hacienda with a Roman-tiled roof surrounded by a high stucco wall and enclosed by wrought-iron gates.

Maria went to Bernie's, Saint Bernadette's Girls', which was next door to Benny's, Saint Benedict's Boys'. Merv, Andy and I used to skip rugby, climb onto the cricket pavilion roof then into the branches of a massive oak tree, and watch the girls play netball. Maria played goal attack. As she stretched beneath the basket, hands high above her head, six testosterone-charged eyes would climb her long legs, linger for a glimpse of knicker, close for a prayer of thanks as they reached her twin lemons, and come to rest on her lips. She had a habit of opening her mouth slightly and poking out the tip of her tongue as she made the shot. A rhapsodic moment.

'Fantastic!'

'She can score with me anytime.'

'I think I'm in love.'

Maria's mother transported her to and from school in a huge Mercedes, and the only time I came close to her was at Sunday Mass.

'You've developed a new enthusiasm for your appearance lately, Johnny,' Mum said as we assembled one Sunday morning. 'But we'd all be grateful if you'd spend less time at it. We've only the one bathroom and your father's developing a Condition.'

'Fitz,' I said. 'J. Fitz Kennedy.'

But it made no difference how many times I said it.

The Almeidas sat in front of us that day. I watched them shuffle along the row. Father, mother, four sons and Maria. Father, haughty with swept-back silvery hair and several rings;

mother, an impressive woman in a grey suit and peach-coloured blouse; the sons, dark-haired and lithe, faces the colour of burnished copper. But I only had eyes for Maria, who followed her brothers and — *my heart leapt!* — who smiled at me as she took her seat. The nape of her neck was no more than two feet from my lips. I longed to part her polished black hair and kiss it. I could smell the soap she'd washed with that morning. I closed my eyes and sent her a message of love, but it might have gone astray because one of her brothers turned around and gave me a filthy look.

That night I wrote my first love letter.

Dear Maria
I sat behind you at Mass today. When you smiled at me, I felt as if the heavens had sent me an angel. I think you're the most perfect person I've ever seen. Can I share a minute of your life? There's a gap in the fence between your netball court and our cricket pavilion. Could we meet there at twelve when we break for lunch?
Yours always.
J. Fitz Kennedy xx

There was no sign of her on Tuesday, Wednesday or Thursday, but on Friday there was a rustle in the undergrowth and she emerged in her Bernie's uniform with her hair tied back and her tie askew. She gripped the chain-link fence.

'I can't stay long. I'm supposed to be at violin class. Thank you for your letter. It was lovely.'

We sat on the ground. The sun sent a cross-hatched shadow from the fence across her beautiful face.

'I saw you in church.'

'I saw you, too.'

'Can I see you this weekend? We could go for a swim.'

'I'm not really allowed out without my mother or a brother. They're very strict.' She bit her lip. 'Can you pick me up? Outside the hacienda. Tomorrow afternoon. At three. I have to go.'

Before I'd had a chance to say I didn't have a car, let alone know how to drive.

Dad went to Confession every Saturday afternoon. After a raucous Friday night at the Workingmen's Club during which his soul had been at the mercy of many forms of Temptation, and after a week of close proximity to the town's female teeth, tongues and upper torsos, Mum considered Dad's Spiritual Cleansing to be crucial prior to Sunday Mass.

That Saturday I went to morning Confession. Later, from my bedroom window, I watched Mum, Dad and Carmel leave in the Humber Super Snipe, wait at the Give Way sign before turning left in front of a sheep truck, and head towards Saint Mary the Grateful.

Mum always gave Dad a List of Sins because he was inclined to be vague when faced with the Grille, so his exculpations were brief and to the point. But Carmel and Mum were both Marathon Confessors. They would be gone for at least two hours.

I went into the garage and stood there, eyeing the Black Shadow as if it were a snorting stallion. I knew how to start it. Had seen Dad do it a hundred times. Turn on the fuel tap, turn the choke to full, turn the key, prime the compression by giving the kick-start a half-thrust. Then grab the handlebars, leap into the air and launch down with your right heel as if you wanted to drive it through the floor.

With luck the 1,000cc V-twin engine would belch blue smoke then rumble on its stand, rattling crockery in the kitchen and threatening to dislodge the house from its piles. Without it, the kick-start would recoil and break your ankle.

I took Dad's goggles from their hook and climbed aboard, shit scared. But love makes heroes of us all, as well as fools. For Maria Santos Almeida I would have faced Genghis Khan and his Mongol Horde armed only with Yeats's *Collected Poems*. I leapt, thrust. It fired.

With the care of a brain surgeon I squeezed the clutch lever, clonked the bike into gear, pushed it from its stand and allowed the clutch to engage. The bike moved forward under a terrible restraint, like a jumbo jet held on its brakes prior to its charge down the runway. Unlicensed, unprotected, unsure whether my underwear remained clean, I wove and wobbled my way out to Casa Almeida.

I'd been waiting fifteen minutes, parked out of sight beneath some trees, when she appeared. She was wearing a knee-length skirt, flat shoes and a white T-shirt, and had her hair loose about her face, blowing in the wind. I felt a knot in my guts as she came towards me. But it wasn't love. It was fear. That her father or brothers would catch us. That they would submit me to arcane forms of Portuguese torture or keep me captive in their wine cellar where I would die in chains.

'Hi, Maria.'

'What's this?'

'Dad's motorbike. It's a classic. They don't make them anymore.'

'I'm not surprised.'

Nonchalantly I straddled it, hauled it upright, switched on the ignition and launched my right leg down on the kick-start. It recoiled. I sailed towards the trees but clung to the bars, came down hard on the seat, crushing my engorged balls beneath my right thigh. I'd been dreaming about olive groves again and they hadn't yet recovered.

'*Unh!*'

Maria looked at her watch.

'I don't have much time. Is this thing going to start?'

'Sure. No problem.' I threw myself at the kick-start, felt it turn the massive pistons. There was a cough. A roar. Smoke poured from the exhaust. 'Let's go.'

Maria hitched up her skirt and clambered aboard and — *oh, Heaven!* — leaned her Meyer lemons against my back and put her hands on my waist. My balls were on fire. My right leg throbbed. The bike weighed a ton and was wrenching my arms from their sockets. I had no licence. The bike was not insured. I'd seen *West Side Story,* had read *Romeo and Juliet.* Maria's brothers would kill me if they caught us together. Dad would kill me if I crashed his bike.

But I didn't care. As we swept around bends and Maria put her cheek between my shoulder blades and her arms around my waist, I felt sure that love would conquer all.

That summer, Saturday afternoons became a weekly ritual. Dad at Confession, me on his Vincent with Maria's hands on my waist, her lemons nestled against my back. We'd ride out to the hot pools and swim beneath the waterfall. I was a good swimmer, and loved showing off my speed. After the hand-holding and cuddling routines had lost their thrill, Maria taught me how to French kiss and allowed my hands to roam.

Exploring Maria's body was like establishing the various camps on Mount Everest. Once a particular point had been achieved — her neck, say, or the second button of her blouse — it would become the launching point for the next date. Over several weeks I progressed from the outer extremities — toes and hair — towards the centre.

Her lips and knees were staging posts *en route* to Maria's breasts. I was fascinated by their shape beneath her wet swimsuit, but the pools were too popular for full exposure. Meanwhile, she was showing some interest in what was straining beneath my shorts, and I was desperate for a chance to expose it. So we looked for another location.

One Saturday we lay side by side in long grass on the edge of a paddock looking back to the town and beyond it to Apprehensive Bay. It was a perfect summer afternoon. Cows mooed. Sheep baaed. Birds sang.

'What are you doing?'

'I'm lifting your T-shirt.'

'Why are you doing that?'

'So that I can admire your breasts.'

'Just a minute.'

She sat up, pulled her T-shirt over her head, unclipped her bra, threw it aside.

And there they were. Two stupendous creations. Proud, independent, identical. I kissed the left nipple. It was neither gob-stopper nor cherry nor olive. More like Portuguese Delight. I tried the right. There was little if any discernible difference, so I browsed between them for a while, made mental notes, knowing that Merv and Andy would demand a full report.

Going All The Way or, to maintain the Everest metaphor, Knocking The Bastard Off, had supplanted breasts as a topic of oak tree discussion. But three male Catholic virgins with nothing but their imaginations and the contents of Murray's library to go on couldn't compare with the real thing.

A few weeks later, I put the idea to Maria.

'Sex is a Mortal Sin outside the boundaries of marriage, Fitz.'

'Is that a no?'

'We could do sixty-nine if you like. The priests and nuns do it all the time.'

'What's that?'

'Take your shorts off and I'll show you.'

After a brief induction course, I beavered with lips and tongue and found the experience strange but pleasant. Unable to speak with a mouthful of me, Maria positioned my head with both hands, and made the same precise adjustments I'd seen Dad make when setting the needle on the carburettor of his Vincent. Slightly too far to all points of the compass, nothing. Find a certain spot and Maria's ignition would fire with a string of moans and groans. She would dig her nails into my scalp and clasp my temples with her strong thighs, all of which I took as proof that I was on target.

Meanwhile she was treating my cock like one of Betty Rice's Double Chocolate Chips, licking, mouthing, and occasionally clasping with her teeth until I felt an overpowering urge to make a Nocturnal Emission even though it was only three-thirty in the afternoon.

'Don't come in my mouth,' Maria had instructed. 'I don't want to swallow your spunk.'

So I rolled away and fertilised the grass.

'I love your tongue,' said Maria as we lay side by side, holding hands. 'I had three orgasms.'

'Really? When?'

'You know the first thing I noticed about you? In church that day?'

'No, what?'

'Your fingers. They're very sexy. As soon as I saw your fingers I knew you'd do great sixty-nine. Do you play the piano?'

As if this weren't enough flattery, as we were getting dressed Maria made my mum's day.

'I love your underpants. They smell all fresh and lemony. Clean underwear really turns me on.'

I've often thought how proud Mum would have felt had she been there at that moment.

Over the next few months I saw my fingers in a whole new light. They'd been transformed from piano-playing failures into powerful sex tools, capable of inducing as much Ultimate Pleasure as my penis, which until then I'd assumed to be my body's Paramount Organ.

I'd long since learned the vagina's topography and the location of the clitoris. But there was nothing on Murray's shelves about the theory and practice of cunnilingus. Nor was this a topic for dinner-table discussion. My only other source was Andy and Merv.

Andy's pursuit of Betty Rice had culminated in an evening encounter among the dunes on Bullock Beach. Andy had spent too long kissing her neck.

'Stop pissing about and stick it in,' she had apparently said. 'And don't give me no fucking love bites, neither. I got shit from Mum last time.'

Unsurprisingly, Andy had learned nothing about the intricacies of sixty-nine.

Merv was stuck on square one. He had a thin, ferret-like face and had inherited his dad's crossed upper centrals, which my dad was doing his best to correct with wires and braces. These presented a hazard to pubic grazing, so he was no use either.

So I travelled alone, seeking new places with tongue and fingers from which to elicit one of Maria's gasps and sudden clutches of scalp. We would snatch furtive meetings. In the cricket pavilion. Among the dunes. In our favourite field if I could safely steal Dad's Vincent. And the furtiveness made our lovemaking all the more exciting.

We were in what we had begun to call Our Field one Saturday afternoon when Maria said, 'Do you love me, Fitz?'

'Of course I do.' I raised my head and kissed her inner thigh. 'Why?'

'Because I'd like to Go All The Way with you. But I won't unless you love me. And I'd like you to meet my parents.'

'Me, too.'

I wasn't sure about buying into the total package. GATW would have sufficed, but if telling her I loved her and meeting her parents was what it took, I was willing. I shifted around so that we were face-to-face and touched her neck with my exquisite fingers. She pushed me away.

'Not now, Fitz. You'll have to get some condoms.'

As Catholics we'd never discussed contraception in our house. We rarely discussed anything that contained a hint of controversy or potential embarrassment. But I knew the Church disapproved, and assumed this was the official Kennedy line.

Although I'd heard rumours that parents did it all the time, I also found it hard to believe that Mum and Dad indulged in sex just for the hell of it. So there was little hope of finding an unused condom just lying around.

Murray sold them. I'd seen him slipping little packets wrapped in brown paper from beneath his cash register into furtive hands following a series of Masonic winks and nods and enquiries about weekend supplies. But I hadn't nearly enough courage to brave the stares of his customers and put myself at Murray's mercy. I might as well have asked my dad and been done with it.

The only alternative was to brave one of Bullock's three chemist shops. One was O'Malley's on Thames Street. Mr O'Malley was a Knight of Saint Columba and would have reported me to Father Donovan. A second was Mackenzie's on Hudson Street. Mr Mackenzie was an elder in the Church of Everlasting Humility whose granite-faced philosophy of life was as far removed from Dad's Epicurean as was possible without falling off the edge of the planet. An encounter with Mackenzie was unthinkable. That left Stirrup's on Colorado Street. Graham Stirrup was a cheerful young chemist with a brightly lit shop, a sunglasses display and a perfume counter. I walked up and down outside until I saw him emerge from his dispensary, then made a dash for it.

'Hi there!' He greeted me with a broad, man-to-man smile. 'Can I help you?'

'I'd like some—'

Graham held up his hand.

'Just a sec, there's the phone. Better get it. Sandra! Can you serve this guy? I think he might want some Durex.'

Sandra came over from the perfume counter. She was a tightly constructed package with prominent breasts encased in a pink uniform smock, platinum blonde hair, fresh red lipstick. I saw Graham watching over the dispensary's opaque half-glass. He didn't seem to be on the phone.

'Would you like regular, form-fit or flared?'

She withdrew a tray from beneath the counter, racked with about a dozen different styles which swam before my eyes.

'Uh . . . regular.'

'Plain or ribbed?'

'Uh . . . plain.'

'Small, medium, large, or extra large?'

Hysterical laughter followed me as I fled.

The next day I asked Young Murray to arrange a supply via his dad. He agreed in return for a small commission.

The next Saturday, Maria and I added eleven to sixty-nine. We alternated, mixed and matched, made up our own variations. We loved both numbers. It was a perfect arrangement. We went to Our Field. I told Maria I loved her. She permitted penetration provided she was protected. Young Murray got rich. Ed Hillary would have been proud of me.

I'd been telling Maria I loved her for about three months when she reminded me about the rest of the package.

'It's time we came out in the open.'

This puzzled me.

'I thought that was what we just did.'

'I want you to meet my family, Fitz. In Portugal, a suitor must obtain the girl's parents' approval before he is allowed to be alone with her. In Portugal, if they knew what we'd been doing, my brothers would be obliged to kill you, as a matter of family honour.'

'A suitor? Is that what I am?'

'You do love me, don't you, Fitz?'

'Of course.'

At the time I meant it. At the time I always meant it.

'Well, then, there's nothing to worry about, is there?'

Our families met on the church steps after Mass. A formal meeting of Irish and Portuguese cultures. Polite compliments about hats and dresses. Maria's brothers sombre and stone-faced, bowing at the waist as they shook first Dad's and then Mum's and Agnes's and Carmel's hands. They ignored mine. Maria virginal in a white dress with a chunky pearl necklace and fine gold watch. Me in my best suit under intense scrutiny from the brothers' and from the father's disdainful eyes. Dad asking whether Senhor Almeida by any chance shared an interest in old motorbikes or teeth. Almeida's polite denial. And did Senhor Kennedy by any chance take an interest in Renaissance Art? He seemed impressed when Dad gave him a ten-minute exposition. Murray's Barber Shop had a pretty good Art History section.

Then came the expected invitation from Maria's mother for me to share their family lunch, after which I would be allowed to walk with Maria in the grounds of Casa Almeida followed by a brother or two, then be transported safely home in the Mercedes.

'So, John? You like to be called John?'

I sat in the back with two brothers, Almeida driving, another brother beside him, the car reeking of garlic and cigars. Maria, her mother and fourth brother were in the second car.

'My family call me Johnny, but I prefer Fitz. Short for Fitzgerald — J. Fitz Kennedy.'

'Sure thing, Fitz. And you can call me Paul. So Fitz, short for Fitzgerald, what you going to do with your life? You decide yet?'

He adjusted the rear-view mirror so he could see me.

'A writer.'

'What sorta writer?'

'Fiction. Haven't decided what sort yet. I'm trying all kinds. Short stories, film scripts, poetry, thrillers. Every writer needs time to find his voice.'

'Much money innat?'

'Money? Ah, well, Paul, there can be, if you write a bestseller.'

'Wassa chances adat, Fitz?'

'Not great.' I laughed. 'Thousands to one. No one takes up writing for the money.'

'Seems to me like you need to screw your head straight, Fitz. You gonna marry my daughter, you better have a solid career, cos if she's anything like her mother, she's gonna be high maint'nance, you know what I mean? You could come into the wine business. My boys'd teach you. But is hard work lookin' after dem fuckin' vines.'

Marry?

Through my suit and theirs, I felt the steel bands of muscle that were the brothers' shoulders.

Marry?

I gazed from the window at the orchards and paddocks sliding by.

Marry?

I wondered whether I would survive a dive onto solid tarseal at fifty miles an hour.

We dined *al fresco* beneath a vined pergola, the leaves rustling in a soft breeze. There were sardines, beef marinated in red wine and garlic, tomatoes in olive oil and herbs, goat's cheese and fresh fruits. Delicious no doubt, but to me they were cardboard.

Maria and I were separated by brothers and parents. I sat next to her mother, who insisted I call her Sophia.

'How long you known Maria, Fitz?'

'Uh . . . six months.'

She nodded her approval.

'She say nothing to us. Obviously want be sure her own mind. That's good, huh? After all, marriage is lifetime commit. Paul and me know each other from children. Engage he seventeen, I fifteen, marry he twenty-one. How you two meet?'

'Uh, at school. Dancing lessons. The only time Benny's and Bernie's mix. Otherwise half the boys would only learn how to dance backwards.'

No smile broke through her round, well-nourished face. Sophia Almeida was one tough cookie. So were her husband and sons. And for the first time since we'd met, I began to suspect that Maria might have a heart of steel beneath that delightful left breast.

'Of course the boys adore her,' Sophia was saying. 'She late arrival. How you say? A bit of afterthink. They kill anyone who hurt her.'

Sophia's eyes held mine. In them there was only sweetness and kindness. But the way she was slicing her meat made me shiver.

Aunt Agnes was in the kitchen smoking a joint when I walked into the house.

'Whatever is it, pet? You look as if you've seen Old Nick himself.'

'I'm in trouble, Aunt. Big trouble.'

'Is it Maria?'

I nodded.

'How far gone is she?'

'It's not that. Her family thinks I'm going to marry her.'

'Here,' she said. 'Have a fockin' drag o' this. It's a new strain. Pot of Gold. Tell me what ye t'ink.'

I inhaled, held the smoke, allowed the weed to work its magic, let it out in a long sigh.

'Fantastic, Aunt. Best I've tasted. How did you do it?'

'Human waste, pet. After I've said a prayer over it. Next time you need to go, I'd be grateful if you'd use the bucket provided. Come upstairs wid ye. We'll see if we can sort yer fockin' problem out.'

I'd never been inside Agnes's room. As a nun, if only part-time, she had a right to private contemplation that we all respected. There was a little table along one wall covered in a white cloth with a gold cross on a wooden stand, an alabaster statue of the Virgin Mary suspended from a picture hook, and a little shelf where burning candles gave off a sweet scent. There were shelves upon which Agnes had set out the souvenirs from her various pilgrimages. A statue of a Spanish peasant girl which shed tears when you pressed a little bulb. A stake to which Joan of Arc was tied, with red plastic at its base that glowed and flickered like real flames when a switch was pressed. A working model of the Virgin Birth.

There were also more secular expressions of my aunt's passions. *The Kama Sutra. How to Cheat at Poker and Live. How to Get Maximum Pleasure From Your Dildo. The Thoroughbred Yearbook. Maximise Flavour and Taste in Weed Hybrids.* There were shelves filled with magazines with titles like *Hunk, Big Boy* and *Hung!*

My aunt followed my amazed gaze.

'Just because I'm a nun, Johnny, doesn't mean I'm not a human being. Or a woman for that matter. Would you take a libation, pet?'

Agnes lifted the white cloth, took out a half-full bottle of Bushmills and two glasses, poured shots.

'*Slaintje!* There's no problem can't be solved with a whiskey and a prayer. Now tell me all about it.'

We sat on either side of the window looking beyond the garden to the paddocks where cattle grazed, and beyond the paddocks to the bush-clad hills. I rested my glass on a low coffee table.

'Do you know what sixty-nine is, aunt?'

'Of course, pet. In case you're wonderin', I'm not a fockin' virgin, but I've only ever had sex with a priest. I regard it as a merciful relief for two persons in dire need. I've never tried the sixty-nine, but I've heard good reports.' She smiled wistfully. 'It's very popular within the Church because it's not specifically proscribed by the Vows.'

'Maria and I—'

Agnes waved a dismissive hand. 'I don't need the graphic details, pet. Just give me the gist.'

'We progressed from sixty-nine to full-blown sex. And now she thinks we're betrothed.'

'Did you tell her you love her?'

'Yes, Aunt.'

'Ah.' Agnes shook her head. 'That's a shame. And you don't. Is that the fockin' nub of it, Johnny?'

'She's very pretty. I love her body—'

'Was she a virgin, pet?'

'That's what she said.'

'Hmmm.' Agnes seemed unconvinced. After she'd topped up our glasses, she thought for a while. 'When you think of her, what do you think about? Other than sex?'

'Nothing. We never talk. I can't get beyond her breasts and she—'

'That's not what love's all about. We must nip this thing in the bud, pet.'

'If her parents find out . . . or her brothers . . . '

'I'd put good money on them knowing already, Johnny. You've deflowered their daughter. In Portugal that's tantamount to a fockin' marriage contract.'

'What can I do?'

Agnes lit another Pot of Gold and put *Bridge Over Troubled Water* on her little stereo system. We sat in the twilight, the room lit by sputtering candles, listening to Art Garfunkel telling us he was on our side when times got tough. In the garage, Dad was stripping his Vincent. From downstairs I could hear the crash of crockery as Mum made dinner. From the room next door came the monotone of Carmel's muttered prayers. She was leaving for the Sacred Sisters convent in the morning.

'Get on your knees, pet. I'm after askin' a little favour of God.'

We knelt, blessed ourselves. Agnes entwined my hands with hers.

'Are ye there, God? Look, Johnny here's got himself into a bit of a fockin' mess. D'ye have any ideas as to how we might get him out of it wid'out getting his bollocks stuffed down his t'roat? Amen.'

There was a tap on the door.

'Dinner's ready, Agnes. Everyone's here.'

'Leave it with Him, pet.' Agnes rose to her feet and drained her glass. 'He'll give us a Sign when He's good and ready. Now we'd better send Carmel on her way rejoicing. And we'll hear not'in' at dinner about this little discussion or what you've seen in this room, is that agreed?'

I normally had a horse's appetite, but not that evening. It was Carmel's last meal. Father Martin Donovan had joined us together with Uncle Tommy, Aunt Bridie and Roy and Marge Calloway. My uncle was a quiet, unassuming little man until he got on the Bullock Workingmen's Club stage on a Friday night and became a Presley with a hip-swivel to rattle teeth. Aunt Bridie was short and dumpy and pregnant for the seventh time.

'I was mentioning you to the Bishop the other day, Bridie,' said the priest after he'd said Grace and asked God to keep a Special Eye on Carmel as she embarked on a life of Devotion and Duty. I hoped He'd have enough time left over to work on my escape plan.

Agnes must have been thinking the same thing because she gave me a wink.

'And he said what a wonderful daughter of the Church you were.'

'It's not me who deserves the praise, Father,' said Bridie. 'Every time Tommy sings "All Shook Up" it supercharges his sperm.'

My aunt and uncle now lived at Passion Dale, which my grandfather Sean had built in the 1920s at Back Bullock on rising land looking over the town and across Apprehensive Bay. Tommy allowed Nature to care for the land around Passion Dale while he practised his guitar and his hip-swivel, and searched for top-rating movies to show at the Ritz.

'Talking of which, I've been thinking of supercharging the Vincent,' said Dad. 'Give it a bit more oomph. But not too much. Don't want to overdo it.'

'You'll save a tenth of a second getting to the No Exit sign,' said Agnes. 'What fockin' good'll that do ye?'

'Johnny had lunch with the Almeidas today,' Mum said to Father Donovan. 'He's courting their daughter, Maria. Tell the Father how you got on, Johnny.'

'Fine.'

I toyed with the turkey from which Dad had extracted the bones with great precision.

'Johnny's right. They're a fine family,' said the priest. 'Very supportive of the Church. Very generous. But, unlike yourselves, they have yet to give us a son or daughter. No amount of money can equal the Ultimate Sacrifice that every Catholic family should make if it can.'

'Have you discussed it with them?'

Aunt Agnes had a glaze in her eye which might have been from the preprandial Bushmills.

'Many times with Senhora Almeida when she visits me for special devotions.' Father Donovan took his wine glass in both hands, held it above his head, then took a long drink. 'She says she's waiting for a Sign.'

'Is that so?' Agnes winked at me, pursed her lips, said nothing more. But as we were leaving the table and everyone was crowding round Carmel, kissing and hugging her and wishing her well, Agnes took me aside. 'He spoke to me, Johnny.'

'Who?'

'Fockin' God, o' course, who d'ye t'ink? Told me what to do. Come and see me for a nightcap and I'll tell you all about it.'

In the end, as with so many of life's problems, the solution was simple. A few days later I borrowed Dad's bike and went out to Casa Almeida. Once Maria, her parents and brothers had gathered in their oak-panelled living room, I clasped my hands between my knees and made my Announcement.

'I have heard the Call.'

'Call?' Sophia Almeida frowned. 'What call? From 'oo?'

'God's Call.'

'What He say?'

'He sent sixty-nine angels to kneel before me and eleven to welcome me with open arms. And I'm sure you'll understand, Sophia: I was unable to resist.' Aunt Agnes had enlightened me about the nature of Sophia Almeida's special devotions with Father Donovan. 'As soon as I'm of age I intend to enter a seminary, then spend my life in His Devoted Service.'

'Oh!'

Maria put her hands to her lips. Tears formed. She stood and ran from the room.

'You sure 'bout this, Fitz?' Maria's father looked solemn, but not too solemn, as Dad might have said. I thought I even detected a smile of relief. 'Last week you gonna become writer.'

'There's nothing to prevent me from doing both,' I said.

'Your parents must be concern,' said Sophia. 'Give daughter and son to Church leave them nothing. No grandchildren. It's sacrifice so far we not been ask to make.'

'We're 'appy for you, Fitz. Of course.' Paul Almeida rose and offered me his hand. 'An' of course we shall take great interest in your progress. Maria's very upset. She loves you.'

'As do I her.' I clasped my hands together. 'I love all God's children.'

They watched me leave. Mother, father, four brothers, together at the hacienda's double doors. Maria at her bedroom window. They waited while I hefted the bike upright and primed the ignition. I offered a silent prayer as I hurled my right leg at the kick-start, promising God if he made the engine start I'd give up sex before marriage. As it coughed and fired, I decided it would have started anyway.

As I thundered away from Casa Almeida for the last time, white smoke drifted among the trees, heralding a new era in my life.

Chapter 9

I had learned some powerful lessons. Be prepared to sacrifice sex for freedom. The immediate pleasure does not represent good value when measured against the long-term cost. Never tell a woman you love her unless you're prepared to face the awful consequences. If there's a God and He's in the brain, then the Devil is in the penis. Sixty-nine is a safe number. Eleven is not.

A white lie is better than a black truth.

Chastened and grateful to Agnes for my escape, I retired to my room to write. To my surprise I discovered that my experience with Maria and the Almeidas had provided me with inspiration for a short story. I recalled Yeats's inspiration for great love poetry. Perhaps like him and his Maud Gonne I was destined to fail at love but to achieve literary fame in compensation. The story went like this:

> Fritz Doyle, a young New York accountant with a bright future in auditing, has loved only from afar. He meets Carla Capelli at a disco. Carla has luscious breasts, full hips, thick dark hair, and four brothers. Fritz tells Carla he loves her, which at that moment, in his apartment, stripped of his clean underwear and extremely erect, he truly believes. Carla becomes pregnant when Fritz's extra-large Durex slips off. He has given his barber the impression that he is well-endowed. Carla introduces Fritz to her father and brothers, who know about her

condition. The Capellis control the Manhattan pitted-olive business. Fritz is given a choice between joining the business and marrying Carla, or a slow and painful death. His dismembered body is found floating in the Hudson River.

I called the story 'Too Small for His Boots' and entered it for the Bullock Literary Club's short story competition. It wasn't even Highly Commended. The critique said: '. . . and finally we were unhappy with the violent ending. A story should end on an up-beat, leaving the reader pleased to have undertaken the journey.'

If they'd thought 'Too Small for His Boots' was violent, they should have seen what I wrote later. None of my stories has ever ended on an up-beat.

The winner was a thing called 'My Dog Scruff'.

Chapter 10

I was now nineteen. My two best friends, Andy Scarlatti and Merv Scunthorpe, had gone their separate ways — Andy to Mainland University to study law, Merv to join his dad full-time at Tony's My T Motors.

Andy had put on a lot of weight in his final year at Benny's and was now Big Andy. Merv had assumed the used-car salesman's livery. White shoes, white socks, white shirt with stitched monogram on the breast pocket, gold chain, gold bracelets. Although Dad had done a good job of uncrossing Merv's centrals, they would protrude forever, so he had become known as Merv the Mink. Meanwhile Young Murray had joined Murray full-time at the Barber Shop.

It was early summer, so Agnes had sold her stereo and Simon and Garfunkel records and gone off to join Carmel at the Sacred Sisters. Dad still played at the Bullock Workingmen's Club every Friday night, and Mum sang 'My Blackjack Man' if the crowd needed quietening down. During the day, Dad rescued teeth. In the evenings, he spent quality time with his Vincent while Mum kept the hospital's A&E department under control.

The time had come to decide whether to waste the next three years in pointless study or to take the writer's solitary road.

'Roy Calloway says there's a job going at the *Bullock Telegraph*,' Dad announced over dinner one evening. 'Social Diary. Johnny, it's a piece of cake. Get all the gossip you need each morning at Murray's. Meet people, pick up ideas. Put business my way, too, if you notice someone's teeth need fixing.

Write your piece in the afternoon. Give Roy a call.'

By then I'd accumulated a thick portfolio of work, and was becoming used to rejection. Betty Rice had spurned my poem; the judges had spurned my short story; and at school I'd managed to have several stories returned by the editors of *The Benny*, the Saint Benedict's school magazine. A difficult task, because they were always desperate for material. They would willingly publish diatribes on the meaning of motherhood and 'My Top Ten Saints', but all I got was a snotty attachment to my returned manuscripts: 'The editors regret that this story contains gratuitous sex and violence and is therefore unsuitable for our magazine, but we would be interested in any future submission.'

At some stage, most would-be writers encounter someone they admire. Austen, Dickens, George Eliot, Henry James. For me it was Splint Macramé. Macramé was a *noir* pulp-fiction writer who'd created Troy Weeks. More hard-boiled than a sixty-minute egg and with a gossamer-thin shell, Troy took umbrage at anything. A look could do it. Or the way a barman handed him his change. Weeks's heart was in the right place, though. He cared for the environment, treated women as equals, had a Miniature Schnauzer called Jellicoe, and voted Democrat. Weeks didn't haunt the mean streets, but cocktail parties and art galleries, book launches and charity concerts, where the talk was highbrow and the martinis came with an olive. Women fell for him like pine trees at Christmas. A cocked eyebrow or a correctly identified perfume was usually enough.

Macramé never gave details about the sex act, preferring to allow the reader's imagination to run riot. *Troy took a firm hold of the bedroom doorknob* ... was about as far as he went, always with the three little dots. Macramé would just cut from the knob and the dots to the post-coital joint. ... *They lay side by side* ...

Weeks fell in love all the time, but the woman always died.

I read every Troy Weeks book and he never achieved a lasting relationship in any of them, although once his lady of choice, a girl-next-door type called Kate, made it to the penultimate page only to fall out of a window and be carried off by a garbage truck. Troy took it better than I did.

I made several attempts at creating my own hard-boiled detective, but the genre was overworked and filled with cliché. My bedroom floor was awash with failed ideas. I decided that a stint on a newspaper might provide the inspiration I needed. Maybe I'd meet someone on my daily round who could light my creative fire, as Maria and the Almeidas had for Carla and the Capellis in 'Too Small for His Boots'.

Chapter 11

Roy Calloway had bad halitosis, so I was seated upwind. The window behind me was open to admit fresh air, but with it came the noise from Thames Street. There were no traffic lights in Bullock, but there'd been talk for years. A crowd of six or seven had gathered to watch a team of engineers take measurements.

One wall of Roy's office was an array of cups and medals and little statuettes of a guy clipping wool. There was a framed photo of a sweaty Roy in black singlet receiving a cup from the Queen Mother. She seemed to be leaning backwards while maintaining her Royal Smile, her gloved hand extended as far as it would go. Otherwise the office was a mess of old *Telegraph*s and proof sheets, two phones and an upright Olivetti.

Roy was in shirt-sleeves and braces, damp patches beneath each armpit. Once a lithe, lanky guy, Roy had let himself go in the past few years. Lunches at the Workingmen's Club, a heady social life and a healthy disrespect for exercise had helped him put on a lot of weight. A second chin flowed over his open-necked collar and his breasts fell unfettered above his mounding belly. He flicked my portfolio open.

'What the fuck's all this?'

'My work, Roy. Everything I've written. I thought you might like to read it. So that you could see whether my writing style's right for your paper.'

He closed the file and pushed it back across the desk.

'Not interested, Fitz. Listen! *Telegraph*'s an easy read. No long words. No smart-arse quotes. You and I might love Yeats, but what two consenting adults read in the privacy of their own home's their business. *Telegraph*'s a family paper. No smut. No scandal. We don't shove sex down people's throats. Far as we're concerned it doesn't exist. Feel like a beer?'

Roy hauled himself to his feet and padded across the tattered carpet to a bar fridge concealed behind a mahogany door. He removed two bottles of Special Curd, snapped the tops, handed one to me.

'It's more a friend than a newspaper, Fitz. Takes us all day to get it ready. We send it out the following day around lunchtime. There's nothing so important happens in Bullock people can't wait to find out about it. If there is, they'll hear it from Hutch Scandrett on the radio. Names in print, son. That's all people want. Their name, wife's name, mates' names, and pictures. Loads of fucking pictures of people smiling, having a good time at the bowls or the rugby.'

He took a long suck on the bottle, wiped his mouth with the back of his hand, and let go a fart.

'Look at it this way. Russia invades Europe? Couldn't give a fuck. Spell someone's name wrong? You're in big trouble. Get the idea? Who's dead? First thing most people want to know. When's the funeral? Who's doing the catering? Start Monday. Brenda'll sort out the paperwork. Welcome aboard, son. Your old man does a good filling, plays a good tune of a Friday. And your mum's a saint with the voice of an angel. You do as well as them with your reporting, we won't go far wrong. This bottled stuff tastes like rat's piss. Let's go down the Club for a jug.'

The original Bullock Workingmen's Club was constructed soon after the survivors of the *Heavy Going* had realised they needed somewhere to drink their jugs of Special Curd. That building was destroyed in November 1918 when the Armistice Day celebrations got out of hand. Its successor collapsed in 1973 when an attempt was made to move it from Nile Wharf to Orinoco Street without closing the bar. The third building was an eclectic design of multi-coloured brick, patterned concrete block, pastel stucco and wrought iron.

Roy signed me in and brought a jug back to one of the height-adjustable drinking tables.

'See that guy over there?'

He nodded towards a table in the middle of the room where four men were standing.

'Which one?'

'One with the smoke coming out of his throat.'

I took a sip of beer and nodded. There was an old guy of sixty-five or seventy with a silvery beard, wiry hair, grease-encrusted fingers and a beige sweater. Every time he took a drag on his cigarette, smoke would seep from his throat when he inhaled and again when he exhaled.

'Henry Sackville. Sackville's Garage on Volga. Cancer. Just had his voice box removed. Used to hog the conversation. Now he writes notes. Time he's done that, people're talking about something else. Just goes to show.'

'Show what, Roy?'

'There's only so much any of us has to say in this life. Better to get it said when you're young.' I could see why Dad and Roy got on so well. 'See the fellow with him?'

'The guy in the black suit?'

'Percy Cartwright. Runs the funeral place next to Murray's. Looks like he's sizing Henry up. Once Percy gives you that Look, it's time to make sure he's got your plot reserved and to get Beryl Harper's Memorial Catering to pencil something in.'

Roy refilled our glasses, held up a finger and let rip with another sonorous fart.

'That's why we don't allow women in here, Fitz. Every man needs a place he can express himself.'

The doors swung open and my heart sank. I'd been doing my best to avoid Father Donovan ever since my Announcement to the Almeidas. Skipping Confession and Mass. Staying in my room when he popped in for his 'tea and pee' break. Now there was no escape.

'*Ave*, Johnny.' He threaded his way between the tables and stood there, his nose wrinkling like a deer as he picked up Roy's scent. 'How fortunate. I've been hoping for a little chat, but you seem to have been somewhat . . . elusive lately.'

'Like a drink, Father?' Roy took a clean glass from a wire tray and half-filled it from the jug. 'Been giving someone the Last Rites?'

'Ah, indeed. Poor woman. I'm in fearful need of a pick-me-up.'

Roy opened his wallet and gave me a note. 'Get the Father a double Bushmills, Fitz. It might help him to remember her name.'

Once the priest had downed the whiskey and given Roy the dying woman's details, he turned to me.

'Now, what's all this about entering a seminary, Johnny? Are you truthfully planning to follow your sister into a life of service and sacrifice, or was it a ruse to get yourself out of a hole you'd dug with your penis?'

'She was threatening marriage, Father.'

'After you'd told the young woman you loved her, I suppose, so that you could have your wicked way with her.'

'I'm sorry, Father. I meant no offence.'

'You've put me in a difficult position,' said the priest. 'Paul Almeida keeps asking me how you're getting along with your preparations. I can't lie to him, Johnny.'

'Oh, I think you can,' said Roy. 'You can tell him Fitz has

taken a job with the *Telegraph* to gain essential life experience prior to entering the seminary.'

Father Donovan raised his eyebrows.

'And why should I do that?'

'Is Sophia Almeida still attending the presbytery for special devotions, by any chance? A little bird told me what she does when she's on her knees.'

I seized the chance to capitalise on the priest's discomfiture.

'And by the way, my aunt is tired of scrubbing floors at four-thirty in the morning. I'd be grateful if you'd have a word with the Mother Superior.'

A strange look passed between Roy and the priest, as if they shared a Dark Secret. The priest took a swallow of beer.

'I'll see what I can do.'

Chapter 12

For the next six years I became both a would-be writer and a professional reporter. I would rise at five, write my own stuff until ten, then head into Murray's for morning coffee with Dad and whoever dropped by. I didn't say very much, just read the magazines, watched and listened, picking up snippets about who was pregnant, engaged or terminal.

There was usually a story, even from the most unpromising material. For example, here's something from my notes for 1981.

'Did you watch *The Odd Couple* last night?' Cuth Kelson sold insurance to people who had no need, and did pretty well. 'Walter Matthau and that violin guy. Jack Benny Lemmon.'

'You're a wee bit astray there, Cuth,' said Murray. 'Matthau was in the movie. Jack Klugman plays the same character in the television series. The other guy's Tony Randall. Benny's a comedian; Lemmon's an actor. Otherwise you're pretty much spot-on.'

'Did you see Benny in *Some Like It Hot?*'

This from a bald-headed guy called Matt Barnes.

'That was Marilyn Monroe.' Cuth came back in, trying to regain some lost ground. 'Played the ukulele. Married the oil millionaire.'

'That was Jack Lemmon,' said Murray.

'But Lemmon was a man,' said Barnes.

'That actually happened,' said a tall guy with a big Adam's apple which leapt up and down his throat like a tame seal begging for fish. 'Right here in Bullock. Steve Perry. Keeps racing pigeons out towards Gundry. Steve married late in life, eyesight wasn't too good. Five years later, he discovered his wife was a man. He said what the millionaire said in the movie: "Nobody's perfect." Just carried on as before.'

'They still together?' asked Barnes.

'Silver wedding this year. Steve came from a big family, always wanted one of his own. His wife couldn't have any, but his pigeons could. Won plenty of medals, too. He's as happy as Larry.'

Roy was running a *Telegraph* feature on Interesting Hobbies. That afternoon I went out to meet Steve Perry's pigeons. If I hadn't been at Murray's that morning or if the conversation had taken a different direction, I'd have missed one of the best stories of the week.

I became a member of the Workingmen's Club and dropped in from time to time for a beer with people like Percy Cartwright. Percy never became a friend. We were from different generations. I could never look at his hands without wondering where they'd been. And I never had anything in common with his sons, who bothered God each Sunday at the Lord Is My Shepherd Chapel on Colorado Street.

Percy was a useful contact, though, and for the price of a McCurdle's Special Brew he'd tell me who he reckoned might need his services next. Percy had an amazing prescience, which proved invaluable for the obituaries page.

'Sandra Carter's been on my mind lately,' he said one afternoon early in 1982.

Sandra was coach of the Bullock Silver Ferns netball team, a tall, strapping woman in her early forties who lived with a friend called Ronnie and a few chickens and geese on a block of land out towards Passion Dale. I called her that evening and said I'd like to do an in-depth profile interview as soon as possible. I'd never interviewed anyone before. All I had to go on was Troy Weeks's technique for interviewing suspects.

We published the interview in the Friday Sports section which came out on Saturday morning. On Saturday night she crashed her motorbike into a pine tree. On Sunday afternoon I did a quick rewrite, mostly changing the tense from present to past. We published the interview again as an obituary on Tuesday.

The job didn't pay well, but it gave me a stunning social life. I attended every event in Bullock, and as the person with the media muscle I was in huge demand. People would do anything to get their name and picture in the *Telegraph*. Invitations flowed across my desk for lunch, dinner, fishing trips, hunting weekends. Gifts would arrive. Bottles of wine, chocolates, and, once, a gift-wrapped box of twelve assorted Durex from Sandra on the perfume counter at Stirrup's Pharmacy, together with a little card saying sorry if she'd embarrassed me the first time I went in there.

She was delighted with her photo at the Pharmacy Ball. And we both agreed that the Blackberry Bubble was best.

I got more offers of sex than I could handle, but did what I could to oblige. However, whereas my keyhole encounter with Carmel had left no mark, my experience with Maria Almeida had left me scarred.

'What's wrong, Fitz? Is it me? Is there something you'd like me to do?'

'I need time, that's all. Time and patience.'

'But the cocktail party's tomorrow night.'

'Don't worry, I'll take your picture.'

'Can we get dressed then? I've got to pick up the kids from school. Oh, and thanks by the way. You've got lovely fingers and tongue. I had a good time even if you didn't. Do you play the piano, by any chance?'

Before Maria I was priapic. After Maria, my penis developed a persecution complex. It would cower between my legs until reassured there was nothing to fear. This might take several days. But every woman I knew during those trying times was patient and kind, encouraged by my promise that if she would only stick with it, in the end it would prove worthwhile. Even then things were inclined to go haywire.

'You know your trouble, Fitz?'

Her name was Sylvia. She was single, nubile, and had excellent breasts.

'No, but I've a feeling you're going to tell me.'

'You're afraid to commit. When we make love, I feel like you're holding back. Even when you come I sense a reluctance. You don't go *o-o-o-h*, you go *o-o-o-o-o-h no-o-o-o*. That really pisses me off. And there's another thing.'

I lay there, smoking a post-coital joint, knowing what was coming because it was a litany I'd become used to. So I saved Sylvia the trouble.

'I never tell you I love you.'

'You never tell me you love me.'

'I just said that.'

'Do you?'

'Do I what?'

'Love me.'

'Why is it so important that I say that word? What about the hundreds of other words? Like; enjoy; respect; admire; cherish; lust; drink. I drink you. There. I said it. I drink you like a fine wine. I uncork you. I allow you to breathe. I swirl you around. I nose you. I taste you. I swallow you. You are a very good year.

You are ripe, luscious and have the flavour of berry fruits and damp straw.'

By now I'd be inside her again and she'd be laughing, the topic forgotten. Until the next time.

Philip Larkin was wrong. It wasn't my mum and dad who fucked me up; it was Maria Santos Almeida. Because of her, my Afternoon Delight sessions were a disaster. The Sylvias who came along were seeking more than I could give. They were looking for love. It would have been so easy to toss the word out like an old cliché and be done with it. But after Maria, I'd resolved never to make that profession again unless I was prepared for the Awful Consequences.

There was more to it than fear. I had yet to meet someone who captured my entire being; someone who enraptured me; who set my pulses racing and sent my heart into orbit. But at the same time I wasn't looking for anyone. I was content to pursue my writing career; to submit my stories and wait for the rejection slip; to search my growing database of *Telegraph* acquaintances for an inspiring character in the mould of Troy Weeks. Everything was just fine.

And then Dick Worth cut his penis off.

Chapter 13

Dick Worth was a recently-married man in his late twenties, with a house not far from ours, on Severn Street. Dick was an electrician. Like most of his trade, he was forever forgetting to switch off the mains power, so he carried about him the smell of burnt flesh. He also had wiry hair and a twitch.

While rewiring an old cottage one day in February 1985, Dick took hold of a red lead in one hand, a red lead in the other, and was catapulted backwards across the kitchen into the dining room. Most of the furniture was covered in drop sheets. If he'd landed on a chair he'd have been fine and my life might never have changed as it did.

What Mum called the Hospital Finger of Fate had decreed that the owners should hold a house-warming party the night before and leave the glass-topped dining table bare. Dick played loose-head prop for Bullock and weighed over a hundred kilos. It was mid-summer and he was wearing shorts that were skin-tight around his crotch. As he fell, amid the explosion of glass a spear-shaped piece sliced at the point where his scrum bum met his thighs. And kept going.

When the news came through, I was in Murray's Barber Shop listening to a discussion about the forthcoming Garden Gnome Contest, trying to decide whether it merited a piece in the Social Diary.

'Who d'you think'll win it this year, Murray?'

'Norm Paget. Wins it every year.'

'Guess so.'

It wasn't much of a discussion, but then the Garden Gnome Contest wasn't much of a contest.

Norm Paget was Chairman, Treasurer, and Secretary of the Bullock Garden Gnome Club, which used to meet every first Tuesday of the month in Norm's living room (*6 p.m. sharp, bring a plate*). Not much happened from month to month in the garden gnome world, so meetings didn't last long. They'd fill the rest of the time with a discussion about God, recycling, or world peace. If there weren't enough members for a quorum, Norm would read and approve his own Minutes. As long as there wasn't Any Other Business, he'd declare the meeting closed and go outside to talk to his gnomes.

Norm lived in our street. His front garden was filled with elves playing tricks, little concrete men with red bobble hats fishing in a make-believe stream, and a miniature London bus. When you rang the front door bell a little man's voice said: *Hello, my name's Gerald the Gnome. Welcome to my humble abode*.

Most people used the back door.

Every November, Norm would surround his house with Christmas lights. They kept us awake, but Dad was too tolerant to complain.

'Moira, he's a Baptist, so he has little enough fun, and the gnomes seem happy enough.'

When the phone rang, Murray was busy on the nape of a customer's neck so he let it go for a while, but eventually he answered it.

'Fitz, it's your mum. Says there's something happening at the hospital. Might be an idea if you wandered up there sometime.'

Hospital day on the *Telegraph* was Wednesday, but if anyone was admitted with an interesting condition Mum would get all the information and give it to me over dinner. So I rarely went there myself. Roy ran a Schadenfreude column every Friday which gave gory details of traffic accidents, mishaps at home, life-threatening diseases and serious sports injuries. We ran it under the banner 'Rather You Than Me' and it was very popular.

'I'm right in the middle of an article,' I said. 'Can you ask her what it's about?'

Murray spoke for a while.

'Dick Worth the Sparks. He's cut his prick off. They're going to try to re-attach it. She thinks an in-depth interview might be called for.'

The last in-depth interview I'd done had been with Sandra Carter. There wasn't much demand for them in Bullock. Everyone already knew everything there was to know about everyone else.

'Is it life-threatening?'

'She doesn't think so.'

'I'll talk to Percy, see if he's got any thoughts. I'll be at the hospital in about an hour, maybe two, depends on what Percy has to say.'

I was buying Percy a beer at the Workingmen's Club when Sid the barman took a phone call.

'Fitz, it's your mum. The hospital switchboard's going crazy. Radio, newspapers calling from all over the country. Television news crew coming in from Gundry by chopper. She's lined Dick up for a *Telegraph* exclusive, but he's holding out for a deal.'

'What's his price?'

'A dozen Special Curd.'

I took an executive decision.

'Tell her to sign him up. I'm on my way. Call Roy, tell him we've got an exclusive coming in for the day-after-tomorrow's paper. Hold the front page. This could be big. Very big.'

I'd been wanting to say that ever since I'd started at the *Telegraph*.

By the time the hospital bus dropped me outside the main entrance, it was late afternoon.

'They've got him sedated,' Mum said as I pushed through the double doors. 'But I managed to sign him up on an exclusive contract. If he talks to any other paper you can sue him for everything he's got. Or hasn't got. You might not get much out of him, but his wife's with him so you could talk to her. Apparently they can't re-attach his thingy. It was shrivelled by the shock.'

'What shock? I can handle it, Mum. Give me the full gist.'

After Mum had told me how it happened, I wondered whether there was much more to know, but she'd arranged the interview so I felt obliged to see it through. She took me to Dick Worth's dimly-lit room. Before we entered, she took hold of my arm and whispered.

'He'd a skid mark, Johnny. You'd have thought being an electrician he'd have worn a clean pair of underpants.'

His wife, Paula, was beside the bed, holding Dick's hand. Dick lay there looking sleepy, his hair a little wirier, the smell of burnt flesh more pronounced. There was a mound in the middle of the bed which made a useful rest for my notepad. I pulled up a chair and tried to remember how Troy Weeks would have approached the interview.

'Paula, I guess this means there'll be no more sex, no patter of tiny feet. You feel bad about one, the other, maybe both?'

She dabbed at a tear.

'They said there's a chance of a transplant.'

'Could be a good thing. At Murray's they said Dick wasn't too well-endowed. Make you feel better about what happened, maybe?'

A ghost of a smile flitted around her mouth. I sensed I'd struck a nerve. She glanced at Dick's comatose expression, made a face, raised her right thumb. I nodded my silent understanding. Some things don't need saying.

'Do you get a choice? Like with a box of Cadbury's Continental?'

'Depends on what's available. Obviously we wouldn't want some old fart's clapped-out willy.'

'What about size?'

She drew a diagram using two pages of my pad. I was impressed by her ambition.

'Colour?'

She raised her eyebrows.

'I hadn't thought of that. Something in black would make a good contrast. Kind of stand out, don't you think?'

'Religion? What if the donor was Jewish?'

'Circumcised'd be interesting. Anything except Protestant.'

I nodded my understanding. It wouldn't have been right. The Worths were good Catholics.

'You know a possible volunteer?'

'It's not the kind of thing like a kidney where you have a spare you don't need. I think the guy would have to be dead.'

'I guess so.'

Dick was asleep, but he woke when I shook his shoulder.

'Dick, how you feeling?'

'It's a big shock.'

'Two hundred and forty volts. Could have killed you. Maybe you're immune. Your body's become accustomed.'

'I can still feel it.'

'You mean the pain when the glass sliced your penis off and nearly severed your femoral artery, in which case you'd have bled to death?'

'My prick. Feels as if it's still there.'

'Well, it's not. In fact it's there.'

I pointed to a stainless steel kidney-shaped dish where there was a shrivelled object like a barbecued cocktail saveloy. I reached into my bag, took out my camera, snapped a shot of the dish.

'This'll be front-page news. You're going to be a star, Dick.

At least, your missing prick is. You mind pulling back the covers so I can take a shot of your bandages? A smile would be nice. Maybe one of you and your brave wife.'

When I emerged from the hospital, all hell broke loose. The car park was a mass of cameras, mikes and screaming faces.

'Fitz! How much is Dick Worth's dick worth?'

'Fitz! Your paper can't handle this. Open up the story. Let's go.'

I waved the single sheet of paper Mum had thrust into my hand when I arrived.

'Sorry, ladies and gentlemen, but the *Bullock Telegraph* has an exclusive on this.'

They chased me to the bus stop, elbows and fists flying.

'Come on, Fitz, the country has a right to know.'

'Fitz, I'm from the Gundry Chronicle. *You can talk to me.'*

I was drowning in a sea of notepads and cameras when a car drew up, a door opened.

'Fitz, jump in.'

It was 'Stuttering' Hutch Scandrett from Radio Bullock.

'What a bunch of arseholes.' He stopped at the hospital gates, waited until a car was coming, then pulled out. 'Could be quite a story you've got there, Fitz. Think you can handle it? Want to do a deal? The station'll look after you. I hear you write stories. I could read one of them on-air. Throw in a stutter or two, might add atmosphere. What do you think?'

I turned my face away, gazed at the streets I'd known from birth. The setting sun was flaring on bedroom windows. From a nearby lawn came the lullaby of a motor mower. It was the end of just another Bullock day and yet I sensed that since its dawn everything had changed. The scrum at the hospital had stirred something that had lain dormant, and forced it into the world.

I turned and looked at Hutch as if for the first time, although he was a regular attendee for morning coffee at Murray's. He was all sham, from the hair twirled around his pate like a Danish pastry to his on-air stutter and his off-air expletives. He didn't give a damn about me any more than those reporters back there had been my friends.

'Thanks, Hutch, but I can handle it,' I said. 'If I need any help, I'll ask Roy.'

'You want to come on the programme tomorrow morning? Tell everyone in Bullock about your meeting with Paula and Dick?'

'They'll read about it in the *Telegraph* soon enough. This is my street. Thanks for the lift.'

'Change your mind, let me know.'

Roy was waiting when I walked into the house. Dad had poured beers and they were sitting outside on folding chairs watching the sun set. Mum had come back from the hospital and was flitting back and forth with plates of cheese, pâté, slices of salami, as if Roy would die of hunger if she slowed down. There were sweat patches around his armpits and his shirt buttons were under their usual strain, but there was an unaccustomed heaviness to his face. I poured myself a beer and joined them, told them what had happened at the hospital, and about the ride with Hutch Scandrett.

'Fitz, I don't know if you realise,' said Roy when I'd finished, 'but this is the story of the century. It's going to put Bullock on the map.'

'Mayor Punch'll be pleased about that,' said Dad. 'He's been trying to get the Lands and Survey people to do that for years.'

'Have you thought how you might write up the story?'

Roy took a swallow of Special Curd, wiped the froth with the back of his hand. But he didn't fart. He obviously respected Mum's proximity.

'I thought I'd talk to Murray about the medical background. Find out how many times they've done a penis transplant. The risks. The success rate. Talk to the doctors. Do a human interest feature on Paula and Dick: *Dick's new penis is in the surgeon's hands.* Find out who the donor was. Talk to his widow: "*Do you feel that Dick Worth making love using your late husband's penis is a form of adultery?*" I thought we could run it over the next week, every day a different angle.'

Roy shook his head, pursed his lips.

'Can't do that, Fitz. It's a nice idea, and maybe it would work somewhere bigger, but Bullock people don't want to read about penises when they're having their sausages and bacon. I don't think you're ever going to make a real reporter. You're missing the real story here.'

'What's that?'

'Safety angle. Don't mess with electricity. Make sure the power's off before you change a light bulb or a fuse. If professionals like Dick Worth can hurt themselves, so can you. If you're going to have a glass dining table, make sure it's shatterproof and covered with a thick cloth. A practical story people can read and go, "*Yeah, I guess that's true, I'll do that in future*".'

'But what about Dick's new penis?'

'Far as the *Telegraph*'s concerned, Fitz, Dick doesn't have a penis.'

'Well, at the moment that's true, but—'

'Only thing rarer than a penis is a vagina. Told you before: it's a family paper. If a batsman gets a bouncer in the nuts, or a front-row prop bites the other guy's balls off, groin's about as far as we go. *He took it in the groin.* Everyone knows what that means. And for women, there's nothing between the neck and the knee. No tits, no fanny. Another thing. People's sex lives are their own business. People don't want to know what Paula and Dick get up to in the privacy of their own home. No doubt about it, safety angle's the way to go with this. And I'm, sorry, Fitz, but you're not the man to handle it.'

'What about Dick's teeth?' said Dad. 'Sometimes a filling can come loose with an electric shock. That's an angle you might not have thought of.'

'But what about the exclusive contract?' I felt uncomfortable, knew there was more to this than Roy was allowing. 'The case of Special Curd.'

Roy looked worried.

'Yeah. To tell you the truth I'm pretty pissed off about that, too, Fitz. Deal like that, you should have consulted me. Do you think Dick will sue if we don't go through with it?'

'I just thought of something,' said Dad. 'Maybe you could just give him the dozen beers anyway. Gesture of goodwill. Could be a good PR move.'

Roy was thoughtful for a minute or two.

'Tell you what, Fitz. I don't want to see you disadvantaged over this. You thought you were doing the right thing. The paper will go fifty-fifty. You buy Dick half a dozen, I'll match it. How's that?'

Dad nodded at me.

'That's a good offer, Johnny. I think you should accept.'

'Just one more thing.' Roy drained his glass, held it at an angle as Dad refilled it from the flagon. 'I'll tackle the story from here. Nothing personal, Fitz, but you're fired.'

Dad took a thoughtful swallow.

'Seems very reasonable to me, Johnny. Do you want to give me a hand polishing the ports after dinner?'

After Roy had gone, I went up to my room, lit some of Agnes's Mother Mary Irish Green and sat there thinking. This wasn't right. Dick and Paula had a contract with the *Telegraph* to tell their story. It deserved to be honoured. I'd never read any other paper, but it seemed to me those reporters had made a hell of an effort to get over the Bullock Pass from Gundry and possibly places even further afield, and they weren't there for the safety angle.

I said nothing through dinner. After I'd helped Dad for a while, I went back to my room.

It was after midnight when Mum shook me awake.

'There's a phone call for you, Johnny. From London. Someone called Frankie. Should I tell her to call back when you're awake?'

'I'm awake now, Mum.'

I padded downstairs to the kitchen and picked up the phone.

'This is J. Fitz Kennedy.'

'J. Fitz Kennedy, this is Mary Francesca Wilton. Friends call me Frankie.'

'Friends call me Fitz.'

'Glad we got that out of the way.' She laughed easily, sounded warm and close. 'Fitz, I have a column on the *London Daily Chronicle*. Human interest. Tears and tissues. Nannies and nappies. I've just been trying to speak to Dick Worth, but he says your paper's got an exclusive contract.'

'That's right.'

'Fitz, I'm authorised to offer your paper one hundred thousand British pounds, that's about three hundred thousand New Zealand dollars, for the worldwide rights. You can keep the local story. We'll handle the rest of the world through our syndication network.'

I thought fast. Frankie should have been talking to Roy. I was off the story, off the paper. The contract Dick and Paula had signed had said nothing about exclusive rights outside New Zealand. In his drugged state, Dick had obviously forgotten that small point. I resented the way Roy had fired me the first time the *Telegraph* came across a decent story. This was my chance to get even.

'You can have the story, Frankie. The *Telegraph*'s only interested in Bullock.'

'Is that so?' From twelve thousand miles away I could hear Frankie's brain firing better than Dad's Vincent with its ports freshly polished. 'Bet there's a hundred other papers sniffing around, though.'

'They'll be onto it in the morning, I would think.'

'Tell you what, Fitz. You got a fax?'

'A fax? What's that?'

'A facsimile machine, Johnny. We've just installed one at the hospital.'

'Jesus, Mum, will you get off the phone!'

'No, it's OK,' said Frankie. 'If you give me the number, Mrs Kennedy, I could fax a contract for the worldwide rights through to the hospital. Fitz could get Dick to sign it and then you could fax it back.'

'Who gets the three hundred thousand?' said Mum. 'Dick and Paula or the *Telegraph*?'

'Dick and Paula. The *Telegraph* has nothing to sell.'

'It's a deal.'

We were easing Mum's car from the garage into the silent street when she smiled thinly.

'You see, Johnny, what goes around comes around. Roy had no right to fire you. Now he's three hundred thousand dollars worse off. God's always on your shoulder like a parrot, Johnny, watching every move.'

I remembered Agnes saying the same thing, many years before. And a few years later I would remember it again.

'I'm Fitz, Mum. J. Fitz Kennedy.'

'You'll always be Johnny to me.'

Chapter 14

The chopper came in like a hornet over Apprehensive Bay, hovered a few feet above Bullock Beach, kicked up a storm that got into every available orifice, then settled its skids on the sand. A few seconds later a door opened and a woman emerged. I blinked like a camera shutter and imprinted her image. Tall. Nice breasts. Not the equal of Maria Santos Almeida's but then very few were. Pale-blue cotton shirt, tan chinos, running shoes, a lightweight bush jacket, unbuttoned, copper-coloured hair tied into a ponytail with an elastic band.

She jumped to the ground, hefted a brown shoulder bag, bent beneath the rotors and ran like a hunchback until she reached me, when she stood straight, smiled and offered a firm hand.

'I'm Frankie. You must be Fitz.'

'How was your trip? What do you think of Bullock?'

'I'm shattered. Hadn't realised it would take so fucking long. This really is the end of the world, isn't it?'

'Not if you were born here.'

She touched my arm.

'Sorry. Didn't mean to be rude. I'm sure Bullock's a nice place. It's just very far from anywhere.'

'Some people think that's not a bad idea.'

She laughed again, the way she had on the phone two days before.

'Don't take any notice of me. I'm not very good at protecting other people's feelings. Oh, by the way, this is Pete. He goes everywhere with me. Vietnam. Afghanistan. Buy him a beer he'll tell you his life story.'

Pete was a weathered guy in a black shirt under a multi-pocketed jerkin. He had a two-day growth, frizzled grey hair, a fresh cigarette in his left hand as we shook with our rights.

'You're younger than I expected,' said Frankie.

We walked to the Snipe which Dad had lent me for the duration.

'I'm twenty-five,' I said. 'How old are you?'

'Twenty-seven.'

Pete smirked, but said nothing.

'Your kind of work must be tough on the system.'

'Thanks a lot.' She tossed her bag in the back, Pete loaded his aluminium camera case, I slammed the lid. We were already a team. 'Look, I'll agree to twenty-nine. But that's my final offer.'

She sat in the passenger seat, Pete in the back.

'Where are we staying?'

'The Yes Oh Yes Motel.'

'The *what?!*'

'It's sort of a pun on SOS. It's got a nautical theme.'

'*Jesus Christ!*' Frankie turned to me. 'Can't this heap of old crap go any faster?'

'We're already doing forty-five.'

'What's the speed limit?'

'Fifty.'

'Pete, you remember that time we were in — what the fuck was that place . . . ?'

'Gimme a clue.' Pete blew cigarette smoke, ignoring the *Weed only* sign on the dashboard, and spoke with a strange accent I hadn't heard before. 'Continent might help.'

'States. Midwest. Wisconsin. Idaho. Some shit-hole in the middle of nowhere. Guy sliced up his parents and fed them to the pigs. Everyone was related to everyone else. What the fuck was it called?'

'Hogs,' said Pete.

'No, wasn't that.'

'They're called hogs. Not pigs.'

'Whatever. That's what this place reminds me of. It's the arse end of the world. Maybe they should have called it Buttock.'

I pulled to the side of the road and turned off the engine.

'That's it. You've been here five minutes, you've done nothing but insult the place I've lived in all my life. Say what you like in private. But if you're going to get anyone in Bullock to talk to you, I suggest you keep your opinions to yourselves. I happen to think it's a damned nice place with some of the world's finest people.'

'But then you would, Fitz.' Frankie took Pete's cigarette, inhaled, let out the smoke in a long, thin stream between pursed lips, gave it back. 'You've never been anywhere else. I'd guess most of the people in Bullock haven't either. Now. Are you going to get off your high horse and take this exquisite piece of metal to our luxurious motel or are we going to get out and fucking well walk?'

'What time is it?'

We were in Frankie's room. She'd said nothing about the ship's wheel with light bulbs on each spoke and little sailor hats for shades. Hadn't mentioned the lifebuoy-and-knotted-rope wallpaper. Or the sea-blue shagpile carpet. I guessed, though she hadn't admitted it, that my outburst had struck a nerve.

She was stretched out on the bed. Pete was pouring duty-free scotch at a Formica mahogany table. I checked my watch.

'Eight-thirty.'

'Morning or evening?'

'Evening.'

'What's that in London?'

'Twelve hours behind,' said Pete.

'Deadline's what?'

'For pictures by wire, first edition, two, two-thirty latest.'

'So we've got, what . . . ?'

'Eighteen hours. Two o'clock tomorrow afternoon local time.'

'Let's have dinner. Fitz, you can tell me what makes Bullock such a fucking fantastic place. Give me some background I can use. I'll talk to No-Dick first thing in the morning. Fitz, you set it up. Two-hour sessions with a break while Pete takes his pictures. There's a press conference with the doctors tomorrow morning, right?'

'Right,' I nodded.

'Fitz, you cover that. Every motherfucker and his dog will be there, so there's nothing exclusive but we need to know what goes on. Takes us to midday, just after. Gives me an hour, maybe more, to write something up for the fax, otherwise I can talk it down the line to one of the copy-takers. How's that sound?'

'I'll need to work in a visit to Murray's,' I said, 'but otherwise it sounds fine.'

'What's Murray's?'

'Murray's Barber Shop. Murray'll know more about penis transplants than those doctors.'

Frankie looked at Pete. They both convulsed. I waved a dismissive hand.

'It's a long story. I'll tell you over dinner. Where would you like to go?'

'How the fuck should I know. I only just got here.'

'It's Irish Night at the Workingmen's Club. Everyone'll be there. And you can meet my mum and dad.'

Frankie smiled. She had brown eyes which seemed to light

up and a slight twist to her mouth. It was the sexiest thing I'd ever seen. She was lying back with her elbows supporting her, legs crossed, nipples prominent, laughing at me.

'So what's this, Fitz? I have to be on my best behaviour? Hope they'll like me? Then we get married? Have a family? Die of boredom in Bullock? That the way it works?'

'Something like that.'

The Mayo Brothers were playing 'Galway Races' when we fought our way through the doors. Dad on tin whistle, fingers flying, sweat streaming, shirt soaked. Uncle Tommy racing him on guitar, Jimmy Kelly rapping on the *bodhrán*, Ricky Flannery crouched over his bass, pushing the beat forward as if he were using the whip. The crowd loving it, urging Dad and Tommy on, like they were neck-and-neck heading down the home straight. The room was thick with weed smoke, people shoulder-to-shoulder, jugs swimming in table-top pools.

After I'd caught Sid the barman's eye and been served a jug of Special Curd and three glasses, we stood there, crushed together. Frankie put her lips to my ear.

'We'll never find your mum and dad in this.'

I shook my head.

'Not a problem.'

A four-way dead heat. Dad and Tommy, Ricky and Jimmy, hands above their heads in triumph as the crowd went wild, thumping tables, demanding more. There was a rumble somewhere, a shout, a crash of glass.

Dad gave a signal backstage, picked up his flute. Mum came from behind a curtain, looking good in her emerald-green dress, dark hair loose about her shoulders. People shushed, coughed, shuffled. The lights dimmed. Mum waited until Dad had played a couple of bars, then began to sing 'My Blackjack Man'.

I glanced at Frankie, half-expecting a sneer, but she seemed to enjoy the sentimental old song as much as everyone else. When it came to an end the crowd erupted again, but there'd been silence throughout and the fight seemed to have snuffed itself out.

'What did you think?'

'I don't go in for this diddle-diddle-di stuff, but she's got a sweet voice. And the old guy on the tin whistle was pretty good, too.'

'Would you like to meet them?'

'Sure. I'll say hello to anyone.'

They were taking a break, so we pushed through the crowd to a table in a corner by the stage.

'Frankie, this is Moira and Joke and Tommy and Jimmy Kelly and Ricky Flannery. Oh, and this is Agnes.'

Frankie shook hands all round and said, 'So let me guess. Moira, you're his mum, right? Joke, you're his dad. Fitz, you owe everyone a drink for taking the piss. And Agnes, I love your dress. Where did you get it?'

'Fifty cents at the fockin' Sacred Sisters charity shop, pet. Put that fockin' cigarette out. Don't you know tobacco's terrible bad for you? Have a Mother Mary Irish Green. It'll do you more good than harm.'

Chapter 15

Murray's was full the following morning, and I was lucky to get a seat between my dad and Andy. The only topic of conversation was Dick Worth's severed penis. Once everyone had got the obvious puns out of the way, someone asked Murray about the chances of a successful transplant.

'Rejection's going to be the problem.'

Murray was snipping at Father Donovan, who'd lost a lot of hair since Roy and I had discussed his relationship with Maria Santos Almeida's mother. We'd avoided each other ever since, but he'd secured a place for Agnes in the convent's herb garden, so some good had come of it.

'I can understand that,' said Giorgio. 'My wife wouldn't be too happy about being shagged by another man's dick. She might reject it, too. Least, I hope she would.'

'No, no, organ rejection,' said Murray. 'Dick will have to take a cocktail of immuno-suppressant drugs for the rest of his life. They're non-selective. So his defences will be down. His whole body will become vulnerable to attack by things he'd never normally know about. A cold could kill him.'

He turned from the priest, comb in one hand, scissors in the other. 'There are three types of rejection: hyperacute, acute, and chronic. Hyperacute's only usually a problem if the organ comes from another species.'

'Such as a donkey,' said Hutch Scandrett, who'd recently enthralled his listeners with a detailed account of his visit to an Istanbul nightclub.

'Acute's more common,' said Murray. 'It's caused by a mismatch of proteins, or by destruction by toxic cells. How would you like your nape, Father, square or tapered?'

'I'll leave it to you, Murray,' said the priest. 'You're the expert.'

Over the next half-hour the discussion ranged from the possible graft of one of Dick's fingers (*'Too small, Paula would never agree'* — *'No problem keeping it up, though'*) to the possibility of conception, since Dick's testicles remained unharmed (*'A* Playboy *centrefold might do it'* — *'Or an Eartha Kitt record'*).

I had to leave at that point to get to the medical press conference. Dad followed me outside.

'Didn't want to say anything in there, Johnny, but I had an idea how this rejection thing could be overcome.'

'What's that, Dad?'

'Your mum and I, we really liked Frankie. She's quite something. Agnes thought she was terrific.'

Sometimes Dad could take a while to get to the point. If you rushed him, it just made him worse.

'She enjoyed meeting you, too. She really liked Agnes.'

'That set me thinking about something Dick Worth told me when he had a decayed molar. You know, people tell their dentist a lot of things when they're in pain. Brings out the desire to confess. That's why they torture people.'

I looked at my watch.

'Look, Dad, I'm sorry but I have to go. Can we talk about this at dinner?'

'It's about Dick's family.'

After Dad had told me, I forgot all about going to the press conference.

Chapter 16

The road from Bullock to Gundry takes a while to get going, but once it begins to climb it doesn't give up until it reaches Look Out Point, so called because that's what most passengers say when they're being driven around Head-On Corner.

It goes down like a lead balloon with signs at various stages until it reaches flat land. Then the signs begin to encourage people to keep going. *A fair bit yet to Gundry. Less now. Nearly there.*

It was early afternoon when I cruised down Wild Boar Street. Whereas Bullock streets had been named after rivers by the surveyor, Thomas Cropper, after a long night of Special Curd, Gundry streets were named after meat cuts and hunting.

I watched the car's reflection in shop windows, saw a black cat amble across the prow of Dad's Snipe. Heat bounced from painted iron roofs, from black tarseal. Parked cars baked. Front doors were wedged open to allow a breeze. I indicated a right turn although there was nothing in front to see the signal, nothing behind but a dead cat.

Offal Street. Wooden telephone poles wearing aluminium sleeves to deter late-night revellers. Concrete power poles. Little weatherboard bungalows painted blood-red. I parked outside number nineteen and walked up the cracked concrete path, used the brass skull knocker. After a while the door eased open on its safety chain and a face appeared.

'Yes?'

'Gloria? I'm J. Fitz Kennedy. Representing the London *Daily Chronicle*. I phoned. Can I come in?'

'Just a minute.'

The door closed and I could hear the chain being removed. Then it opened again. We went into a small living room with a big television in the corner. A chat show presenter was holding a book to camera: '*Available from all good bookshops. Just mention my name for a ten per cent discount.*'

Gloria sat on a dark brown moquette sofa. She was nearly six feet tall. Curly blonde hair covered her forehead and most of her cheeks. She was fleshy around her arms and shoulders, wore a cotton dressing gown, nothing on her feet, the toenails painted red. Strong bone structure, face heavily made-up, mouth slashed with red lipstick. A solid figure beneath the dressing gown, which she folded across her legs as she sat. She lit a cigarette. Held it loose between the fingers of her left hand.

'So what's this all about?'

'You and your brother.'

Her dismissive laugh became a cough. She hacked for a while, fist at her mouth. There were hairs on the backs of her fingers. I always noticed people's fingers. And their teeth.

'Yeah, I heard about him. It's all over the news.'

'We think you could help him.'

'Me?' She took a sip from a dirty wine glass. 'Why the fuck should I help him? We haven't spoken for twelve years. I hate the bastard.'

'Our paper's prepared to offer you one hundred thousand dollars if you do.'

She put the glass back onto a chipped mahogany table.

'Say that again.'

'You've got something he needs. And you're the only person in the world who can give it to him.'

'Oh yeah? What's that?'

'A penis. You don't need it. In fact you'd like to have the op to get rid of it, but you can't afford it. We'll pay for that, too. Just agree to the transplant and give us exclusive worldwide rights to your story.'

Gloria dragged on her cigarette and studied my face.

'How do you know so much about me and Dick?'

'Sources,' I said. 'I can't tell you who they are.'

I'd looked at her teeth. They were in good shape. Dad's dental work was meant to last.

'You want a glass of wine? It's crap, but it's cheap and it gets you pissed.'

'Thanks, you made a sale.'

She laughed and coughed, went into the kitchen. I turned to the television. The presenter was discussing female orgasms with an American woman.

'And where exactly is the A Spot?'

'Tania, I promise, when I find it you'll be the first to know.'

Gloria came back with a smudged glass half-filled with warm white wine.

'Chateau Cardboard,' she said. 'Now then, Mister Moneybags, what's your very best offer?'

'Where the fuck have you been?'

'Gundry.'

'Don't play games with me, Fitz. You missed the fucking press conference. I had to get the gist from Paul Sacker of the *Mail* who's a prick. Unless you've got a bloody good story, I can't work with you any more. I'd rather work alone.'

I tossed a piece of paper on Frankie's motel room table.

'What's this?' She picked it up. Read it. Looked it me with a face as cold and white as marble. 'One hundred and fifty thousand dollars? Gloria Melling? Who the fuck is Gloria Melling?'

'Dick Worth's sister.'

'Let me get this straight. You've been to this shit-hole. Gunshy. And you've committed the *Chronicle* to pay No-Dick's sister — *what?* — fifty thousand pounds in proper money. Without my authority. Why, Fitz? Is it Bullock? Has everyone here got shit for brains or what?'

'She's also his brother. She's a transsexual. Used to be George Worth. Changed sex about twelve years ago.'

'So what? Transsexuals are ten a penny. There's no story in that.'

'She's also Dick's monozygotic twin. Genetically, they're identical. They can transplant Gloria's penis onto Dick and there'll be no allergic reaction. No rejection. No immuno-suppressant drugs. He'll have a perfect working part. Plus Gloria will have her sex change. She'll be able to live a normal life. Plus, they haven't spoken for the past twelve years. Dick went all phobic when she told him what was happening. This will reunite them. Don't you think that's worth fifty thousand pounds?'

'How do you know all this if you weren't at the press conference?'

'Murray's Barber Shop. Plus my dad. You made a hit with him and the rest of the family last night. He thought he'd do you a favour. Bullock people are like that. Not sure whether London people are. As you said yesterday, I've never been anywhere but here.' I took the contract back. 'Of course, if you don't want this, I expect Paul Sacker would be happy to talk.'

'*Jesus, Fitz!*' Frankie poured two slugs of duty-free scotch, pushed one across the table. 'Is this true? This mono-whatsit stuff?'

'There are two types of twin. Monozygotic and dizygotic. Monozygotic is when one fertilised egg splits into two in the womb, and that gives you identical twins. Dizygotic is when there are two eggs. The foetuses develop independently, and although the babies are born at the same time, they're not identical.'

'How do you know all this?'

'Most of the guys who go to Murray's would have read the medical literature and known about monozygotic and dizygotic twins, but they didn't make the connection with Dick and Gloria. When people sit in Dad's chair, they have an irrepressible urge to confess. Twelve years ago Dick had poured his heart out about his transsexual brother/sister. Dad remembered, and made the connection between Dick's severed penis and Gloria's desire for a sex change. You still mad at me?'

She looked at me with that twisted smile. 'What do you want, a medal?'

When she gave me that smile again I felt a stirring in what Roy Calloway would have called my groin.

'I'll think of something.'

Frankie came to dinner that night. She travelled light, just the one cotton dress which she'd worn to the Workingmen's Club the night before and washed out in the motel room basin. A touch of make-up. And that was about it. No jewellery. No hairspray or fancy styling. Most local girls would have taken an hour to get ready, but when she emerged from the motel room after about ten minutes she looked terrific. Hair like filaments of polished copper. Eyes bright. And she seemed happy. For the first time since she'd arrived, she seemed pleased about where she was, what she was doing and who she was with. She got into the Snipe and turned to me.

'I've just been talking to London. They're holding an editorial conference to confirm, but it looks like they're going to want eight pages. Everything. Dick, Gloria, Paula, their families, childhood, friends from school, the day Gloria broke the news, how Dick felt, how she felt, how they used to be close but for twelve years they've carried the hurt . . . How come Dick never mentioned any of this to the doctors, by the way?'

'I think he must have blotted Gloria from his mind. Like she didn't exist.'

'The paper's lawyers are tying up deals in Europe, the States, Australia. This is going to be the biggest story of the year. Worldwide. We're talking Pulitzer Prize. Megabucks. This is the break everyone dreams about but never happens. Let's go. I could eat a horse. You want to let me drive?'

'Dad wouldn't let anyone but me touch his Snipe.'

She looked at me with that quizzical smile. 'What's the matter? Did I say something?'

'Thanks might have been nice, Frankie. Or sorry. Both would have been even better. "Thanks for the Gloria deal. Sorry I hit the roof." Doesn't cost anything.'

'I told you, Fitz. I'm not much good at protecting people's feelings. I'm sorry. And thanks. That make you feel better?'

'Much.'

We parked on the concrete pad. The garage door was up and Dad was working at his bench, wearing his faded blue overalls, thin rubber gloves, goggles, dental mask. He removed the protective gear when he saw us arrive, wiping his hands on a cheesecloth. Frankie ran from the car, threw her arms around his neck and kissed his cheek.

'Joke, you're my hero.' She stepped back, holding both his hands. 'Thanks so much for what you did today. I'm really grateful. If you and Moira ever come to London I'll make sure you have the time of your lives.'

'London?' Dad scratched his head, looking more confused than I'd ever seen. Not too many people had thrown their arms around his neck and kissed his cheek. Certainly no pretty young women. And the next second he'd been thrown a question he'd never considered. 'Don't know why we'd want to do that. What's London got?'

'Restaurants, theatres, the Tower, Buckingham Palace, history,' Frankie shrugged. 'Everything.'

'I can read about all that or see it on the television. The people. They any better than Bullock people?'

Frankie gave Dad her smile, took his hand to walk into the house.

'Not better, Joke. Different.'

But Dad wasn't prepared to let go until he'd extracted the root.

'In what way different?'

'Twelve million people,' said Frankie. 'Infinite variety. Colours, creeds, languages, cultures. Most people in Bullock come from the same place. In London they come from everywhere on earth.'

That seemed to satisfy Dad. He nodded.

'Good point. I can see that would be interesting. Let's have a beer.'

He didn't let go of Frankie's hand until he absolutely had to.

There were five of us for dinner, Agnes being home for one of her sabbaticals. We rarely saw or heard from Carmel, though. She'd sailed through her novitiate. We'd attended the ceremony when she'd wedded the Church and taken her vows, but we'd lost her since. Though we'd hardly ever spoken an unnecessary word, I missed her at dinner time, sitting there with her know-all look, never letting anyone have the last word, getting my back up with her brilliant brain. I didn't know whether Mum and Dad missed her, too. We didn't expose our thoughts for general scrutiny. We rarely mentioned her, but whenever we did I saw a look come across Mum's face. She'd glance at the photo on the sideboard and at Carmel's empty chair.

Frankie was in that chair now, telling a story about the time she was caught short in New York and the Yellow Cab driver gave her his bottle. She'd peed going down Fifth Avenue and he'd slowed for the potholes.

Dad was drinking it all in. Loving Frankie's outrageous conversation and her self-deprecating laughter. He seemed to have abandoned his usual concern that he might be in danger of enjoying himself too much. But Agnes was strangely quiet. When everyone laughed at the conclusion of Frankie's story she just smiled and kept her thoughts to herself, hardly saying a word until the meal was over and we were alone in the kitchen, making coffee.

'Listen to me, Johnny.' She fixed me with her dark brown eyes, took both my hands in hers. 'She'll break your heart if you allow it. When this business is all over, she'll be off somewhere else and that'll be that. Keep your distance, pet. I'd hate to see you hurt.'

'Don't worry, Aunt,' I said. 'There's nothing between us. We're just working together, that's all.'

'Johnny,' said Agnes, 'I believe in Immaculate Conception. I believe that Christ rose again on the third day. And that He walked on water. But I do not believe a word of what you just said.'

Chapter 17

There's something I've been meaning to ask you.'

I ran a finger across Frankie's left nipple, felt it go hard.

'What's that?'

'When you met my parents. At the Irish Night. How did you know who they were?'

'I like to do my homework before I go on assignment.'

I passed her the post-coital joint. As far as both Troy Weeks and I were concerned it was *de rigueur*, although I didn't know that phrase at the time.

'Do you always sleep with the people you work with?'

'Only if I like them. And not if they're married. Why?'

'I just wondered.'

She sat up, rested on her left elbow, passed the joint back.

'Give me a break! You're not a virgin, Fitz. Nor am I. I enjoy sex. So do you.'

'That's it?'

'What more do you want? Who gives a shit, anyway!'

She slid out of bed. I watched her walk naked across the carpet and into the bathroom. She left the door open. I heard her pee, flush, get into the shower. Then she brushed her teeth, messed around with brushes and things for a few minutes. Came back.

'Hey, come on, big day today, work to do. I'll call London while you have your shower. Is there somewhere we can get a coffee? How about this Murray's place you're always talking about?'

'It's men only.'

'You're kidding.'

'It's a barber shop. Murray's wife runs the female side of the business. *Hair Today, Gone Tomorrow*. Combined hairdresser's and travel agency.'

'So what do we do about breakfast?'

'Meggett's café. First-floor balcony. We can watch the traffic on Thames Street.'

Frankie laughed.

'That'll really make my day. When's Gloria getting here?'

'Taxi's picking her up in Gundry at nine-thirty. It's a three-and-a-half-hour drive. Should be here about one this afternoon.'

'*Shit, Fitz!*'

The anger that was always just below the surface erupted.

'That's no good — London deadline's two. How the fuck am I going to do a big interview, brother and sister reunited after twelve years, if she doesn't get here until one?'

'I told you last night what time she was being picked up.'

'But you didn't say how long it would take to get here. We're talking a real paper here, Fitz, not the arse-wipe *Bullock Telegraph* where if it doesn't go in today it can go in next week. There's people all around the world waiting on this story. If I miss this deadline I'll have editors tearing my face out through my arse.'

She stomped around the room, threw her hairbrush at the table, lit a cigarette, looked at her watch.

'Forget coffee. Give me her number. I'll call her while you have your shower. We'll pick up No-Dick and Paula, meet halfway. *Shit!* I wish I'd arranged this myself. Is there somewhere between here and Gundry? A place with a phone?'

'The Head-On Café. At Look Out Point.'

'How far's that from here?'

'About an hour and a half.'

'That's at your speed. I'll phone the story through from there. What's Gloria's number?'

I turned the shower mixer into the red zone, clenched my eyes and allowed the water to scald my skin. Who the hell did Frankie think she was, talking to me as if I was her slave? Treating me like shit. Last night, when I'd dropped her off at the Yes Oh Yes Motel and she'd invited me in for a nightcap, she'd been funny and tender and full of good things to say about my family. In bed she'd been fantastic, her lips soft, her body responsive to the slightest touch. She'd made me feel like Alexander the Great with the world at his feet. This morning she was a shrew.

I'd never known anyone like Frankie. Someone so entirely her own person. Who said what she thought and you could take it or leave it. Who could exude charm and sex and warmth one minute, become an Ice Maiden the next. She was fascinating, fantastic, outrageous and devastating. And I was sorry I'd ever set eyes on her.

By the time I'd dried with her wet towels, used her toothbrush and run her brush through my hair, she was already in the car, the motel room door open, the engine running. I leapt into the passenger seat still buttoning my shirt.

'Take it easy. I had a better idea. No-Dick's in no state to travel. If the phone lines are down at Look Out Point, or we have a puncture, or anything else goes wrong we're in deep shit. I've ordered a chopper to pick Gloria up, bring her to the hospital. We've got forty minutes. Let's see what Meggett's can do breakfast-wise.' She kissed my cheek. 'Sorry I got mad. It's gone. Look. Sun's out. It's going to be another glorious Bullock day.'

I couldn't imagine how I could ever live without her.

As the Twins Transplant storm raged around the rest of the world, Bullock became calm. One or two bought outside newspapers, but most Bullock people relied on the radio or television for their foreign news. Although the bare facts were available to everyone, all comments by the stars of the show — Dick Worth, his transsexual sister/brother, and his wife — were restricted to the London *Daily Chronicle* and its international affiliates. And the *Chronicle* never reached Bullock.

So the drama that was being played out within Bullock General Hospital — Gloria's donation of her penis, her full sex change, the re-attachment and subsequent progress towards full recovery, how Dick's wife, Paula, felt about it all — came to the people living within sight of the hospital via London in expensive snippets on the nightly television news.

Meanwhile the *Bullock Telegraph* forged its own path. As the television headlined '*Gloria parts with private part*', the *Telegraph* banner screamed, '*Accidents Will Happen. A&E Receptionist advises, "Always wear clean underwear"*'.

At Murray's, the Twin Transplant became part of the barber shop's rich history. The issue had been debated, Murray's expertise had proven priceless, the outcome pronounced satisfactory. It was time to move on.

'Stuttering' Hutch Scandrett had been running a contest on his Breakfast Show to compose a town song. Frank Kedgley's winning entry, 'I'm Sold On Bullock', stimulated some concern:

> *As long as there's a Meggett's where the coffee's on the boil*
> *As long as Carter's Gardens have the very best topsoil*
> *As long as Nigel's Menswear's giving fifty per cent off*
> *As long as Graham Stirrup's got a mixture for your cough*
> *As long as Bullock Hardware's got a special deal on seed*
> *I'll be sold on Bullock, it's got everything I need.*

'No mention of Murray's,' said Tony Scunthorpe of Tony's My T Motors. 'Your coffee beats Meggett's. And they don't do haircuts.'

'Frank runs Radio Bullock advertising,' said Murray. 'Said it was a hundred dollars a line, one-fifty if Percy Cartwright and I did two lines together. *"Murray's Barber Shop is where the coffee's strong and black. Right next door to Percy's — go in there, you won't come back."* Percy and I don't need to advertise. There'll always be a need for barbers and burials.'

'Good song, though,' said Tony. 'If the crowd gets behind it, should put the fear of God into the Gundry Butchers when they play the Bullock Bulls in the Super Two Rugby Championship.'

The Twin Transplant story hogged the international headlines for a while. There was no reality television in those days, otherwise Frankie would have taken a film crew into Dick and Paula's bedroom. But once Dick had achieved his first erection (*'Proud Dick Stands Tall'*), with before and after photos of the happy couple, the story detumesced.

I was never more aware of the passage of time than during those hectic days. Every minute with Frankie was a priceless treasure. Every minute apart, I was a condemned man fearing the dawn. We met with Dick and Paula for breakfast every morning. By lunchtime Frankie would have filed her story from the fax she'd installed in her room at the Yes Oh Yes Motel. Once it had been eaten by the machine, Frankie forgot about it.

'Don't you wish you could see your story in print?' I asked one morning.

'Once it goes to bed there's nothing I can do.' She shrugged. 'I might catch up with how it looked when I get back to London, but I'll more likely forget about it. No point in looking back.

Keep moving. Stay alive. That's my philosophy.'

'Will you forget about me, too?'

I knew as soon as I said it what her reaction would be.

'Oh for Christ's sake, Fitz, give me a break. I like you a lot. Most of the time you're funny, great company, good in bed, and you have a brain. I won't forget you. But life goes on. Let's get to work.'

I tried to give Frankie the space she needed. I'd sit in my room trying to write a short story that didn't include a tough woman who spoke her mind and had the sexiest smile anyone had ever seen. But there was no room for anything or anyone else. Frankie had overwhelmed me.

I knew she needed nights alone, but I couldn't help thinking about the thousands of lonely nights after she'd gone. So I'd walk through Bullock's cemetery streets at one or two in the morning, tap on her motel room door and slip into the warmth of her welcoming body.

'You should ring before you come round,' she said one night. 'I could have a strange man in my bed.'

'What? Like Pete?'

I laughed, knowing I had nothing to fear from the seedy little photographer.

'Or Dick Worth.' Frankie laughed, too. 'I'm always up for a new experience.'

We both knew why I never called first: I was afraid she'd tell me to stay away.

It was early autumn when Frankie left Bullock. She came to Wey Street the night before for a farewell dinner. We spent her last night at the motel.

'You need to get out of Bullock,' she said as she undressed. 'You're wasting your life here. Come to London. I'll get you a job on the *Chronicle*. With what you've done on this project, you stand a good chance.'

'I don't want to be a journalist. I want to write books.'

'Give me a break! You have to earn a living, Fitz. Starving for your art is deeply uncomfortable.'

'Do you love me?'

I knew I shouldn't have asked but I couldn't help myself. As we kissed, I knew the taste of her, the smell of her would stay with me forever. She moved on top of me, eased me inside her. We lay still. When she moved her face close to mine her hair enclosed us.

'I love your tongue, and your fingers, and your cock, and the way you touch my breasts and stroke my hair.'

Kissing me as she spoke.

'You drive me crazy,' I said. 'Sometimes you're the most exasperating person I've ever met. But I love you very much.'

'You'll get over it,' she said. 'Let me know when you get to London. You can stay at my place until you get yourself sorted. Hey, slow down! What kind of a gentleman are you? Don't you know ladies should always come first?'

The next morning we stood on the beach watching the chopper come in over the bay. In the weeks since it had brought Frankie into my life she had taken hold of my life like a terrier, shaken it, and now was about to drop it. We hugged as the sand-storm erupted, then, as the rotors settled, she and Pete ran beneath them, hunchbacked, and climbed aboard. The chopper lifted off, hung above the sand for a few seconds, then swirled off across the water and quickly became a speck.

I turned and walked back towards town, wondering what the hell I was going to do.

Chapter 18

There was an oak tree at the end of our street with a huge trunk which took four of us to encircle with our widespread arms. It had been planted in 1870 by a man called Sparrow who'd carried it as a sapling in a wheelbarrow all the way from Gundry to mark the opening of the mountain road. Its leaves began to fall every year in early April, and for us that was the end of summer.

A chill wind was tossing the first of them across the street when they brought Agnes home. Although no one said as much, I knew this was not just another of her peregrinations. This time there was no taxi driver for Mum to pay, but instead Father Donovan in his black Rover with the Mother Superior beside him and Carmel beside Agnes in the back. They fussed and clucked around her until she slumped into a chair in the living room and shushed them away.

'Johnny, would you be after bringing me the Bushmills and a glass, and one for yourself, pet?'

She looked pale and thin and very tired. She saw me looking at her wig.

'It's the chemo, Johnny. I've lost all me fockin' hair. Now away and get the drink before I die of thirst.'

I hadn't been in Agnes's room for years, but it hadn't changed. The Bushmills was where I remembered, beneath the table that served as an altar. When I went into the kitchen for the glasses the others were gathered around the table, drinking tea and eating Mum's Bullock Cake.

'She can't have that,' said Carmel when she saw the Bushmills. 'It'll make her sick.'

Although most of the nuns wore pale grey dresses, Carmel was in full fig with a starched white collar from shoulder to shoulder, forming a crescent across her chest.

'She'll have whatever she likes,' I said. 'If she's sick, I'll clean it up.'

I took the glasses into the living room and poured two shots.

'*Slaintje.*'

Agnes sat back, entwined her fingers in her lap and closed her eyes.

'So, Johnny, how's it going? Are you writing?'

'Every day, Aunt.'

'Any success?'

'I've papered one wall with rejection slips. I'm starting on another.'

'Do you get downhearted?'

'Sometimes. But I don't have a choice. I have to keep going.'

'I admire your determination, Johnny.' She nodded as she took a sip of Bushmills. 'You're like a dog at a bone. Whereas I've always had a terrible weakness for Distraction and Temptation.' A dreamy smile crossed her face. 'It's been a year now since Frankie left. How's the heart? Mended yet?'

I thought about what to say for a while, and decided there was no future in prevarication. 'There's not a day goes by I don't think about her, Aunt. She's my last thought at night and my first when I awake. I can't help it.'

Agnes reached forward, took hold of my hands, and fixed her eyes on mine.

'Johnny, I'll tell you a little secret. I've a wee bit put aside. Not much. Winnings from poker and the occasional flutter when

God answered my prayers with a winner. I won't be needing it now. I want you to have it. I want you to go to London and see Frankie and sort this thing out one way or the other. You'll be no use to anyone unless you do. Don't worry about me. I'll be well looked after. Go as soon as you can.'

'I can't leave you like this, Aunt,' I said. 'I need to be with you until . . .'

'Do you remember, pet, when you were about seven, the few days we topped-and-tailed? How you used to lie awake while I was saying my prayers?'

'I'm sorry. I never knew—'

She shushed my apology.

'I'd say a special prayer for you every night. That God should look after you. He gave me a Sign the other day. He's promised me He'll be like a fockin' parrot, screeching in your ear if you start to go wrong.'

'What sort of sign?'

'A parakeet. I was sitting outside and it shat on my shoulder.'

BOOK TWO

Chapter 19

You can sleep under the kitchen table. Forty quid a week, due Friday. Nick gets up at six, so mind he doesn't kick your head when he has his porridge. Sorry, but that's all there is. We've got fourteen in at the moment. House is four bedrooms. You're bottom of the list. Someone moves out, you move up. You could have a room of your own in six weeks, six months, who knows?'

Alex made it sound like a career move, but I had no ambitions about scaling the Himalaya Street heights. I hadn't told Frankie I was coming to London for the same reason I'd never asked if I could come round to her room at the Yes Oh Yes Motel. But I'd called as soon as I arrived and discovered she was in Vienna on assignment.

So I told Alex, 'I'll only be here a few days. Soon as a friend of mine gets back from Vienna I'll move in with her.'

'You got a sleeping bag?'

'No.'

'I've got an old one you can rent. Fiver a week. You want anything? Weed, coke, poppers, ecstasy, whatever pushes your trolley? See me. I'll do you the best deal in town.'

'Thanks.'

'Gotta go. I'll take the first week's rent now if you like.'

I fished in my bum bag, found my wallet and took out two twenty-pound notes.

'Word to the wise, mate.' Alex nodded towards the wallet. 'Keep that well hid. This place is a den of fucking thieves. Just cos they're Kiwis or Aussies don't mean they're your pals.

There's lockers in the passage. Chuck your bag in there. Two pounds a week. Take care.'

I'd found Alex through a freebie paper when the Airbus dropped me at Victoria Station. *KiwiNewZ*. Ads for bars and clubs and cheap travel with a big sports section and classifieds for flats, Kombis, backpacks. The ad had caught my eye: *Cheap crash-pad Kilburn, no druggies, no piss-heads, no fuckwits*. Judging by the mountain of cans and bottles outside the front door, the piss-head ban seemed negotiable.

Alex was a big guy with wild red hair, freckled skin and a ripe odour. He was studying hotel management at the North London Polytechnic, but I didn't think he had much to learn. Fourteen people at forty or more a week. He was raking in at least six hundred tax-free plus whatever he made from ancillaries, and paying the landlord a couple of hundred at most. I'd never encountered anything like that in Bullock.

I decided to explore London.

It was a late May morning, summer on the near-horizon, when I found myself on Fleet Street outside the *Chronicle* building. This was faced with bottle-green glass panels with black trim, the masthead in stainless steel above double doors. On impulse I went into the reception hall where three girls were handing out badges and signing people in, and a huge black security guy was watching a console of mini screens, one of which was showing a football match.

'Hi,' I said to one of the girls, whose glossed black hair was braided and threaded with tin foil. 'My name's J. Fitz Kennedy. I'm from Bullock.'

'You what?'

She glanced at the girl next to her, who was examining her fingernails.

'Bullock.'

'You taking the piss?'

'You ran a story. The Twin Transplants. Dick and Gloria. Dick was an electrician. Got a shock, cut his penis off. Gloria was his transsexual sister.'

'Arthur!'

The girl called the security guard.

'Wassup?'

'Frow this fucker out, willya! He's come in 'ere, talking filf about penises and sex on trains 'n' stuff.'

Arthur rose from his swivel chair and did something with his neck and shoulders, like a rugby prop preparing to crouch.

'Wass your problem, sunshine?'

He came around the reception desk and invaded my personal space. I took a step back.

'No problem,' I said. 'I was just wondering if you had a library where I could look up old copies of the paper. There's a story you were running. I was involved.'

'Wass your name?'

'Kennedy — J. Fitz Kennedy. I was working with Frankie Wilton.'

He stuck out a banana hand. 'Got some ID?'

He took a year to examine my passport, handed it back, nodded across the lobby.

'Frew dere. First sign of trouble you're on your fuckin' wossname, unnerstan'?'

'Sure,' I said, 'I unnerstan'.'

The woman behind the library desk was no friendlier. She was fiftyish, hair in a bun, Betty Rice breasts spreadeagled across her chest. I approached her cautiously, and chose each word with special care.

'Do you have stories filed by subject?'

'Who are you?'

'I worked on a story with Frankie Wilton. About a guy called Richard Worth, who had a transplant. You ran it as an exclusive. I've never actually seen any of the reports. I wondered if you'd be very kind and let me see them.'

'Your name?'

'J. Fitz Kennedy.'

'Just a minute.' She tapped at a keyboard, frowned, tutted, sighed. 'There's nothing by that name here. If your name had appeared anywhere we'd have it on our system.'

'I didn't actually write the reports,' I said. 'Frankie did that. But I did all the background research. I was the one who found the transsexual sister which made the transplant possible. There must be something about that.'

She tapped again, went through the same ritual of disapproval, seemed to reach a Samaritan decision. 'Go and sit over there. I'll bring you the file.'

I sat at an oak table beneath a neon strip light. I counted eight chairs on each side, and there were six tables. Ninety-six chairs. Ninety-five were empty. There were high windows along the wall facing the street. Closed, begrimed, begrudging the muffled sound they allowed through. A clock struck eleven. If I'd been in Bullock it would have been coffee time at Murray's. Heads hunched over magazines. Murray holding forth. Young Murray providing back-up. Was there any barber in London, I wondered, who knew more about urinary tract infections and the Bauhaus school of architecture than Murray? Somehow I doubted it.

I looked around the room; bare except for the library racks that stretched its length from floor to ceiling. No sign of a coffee jug. No sign saying *If you're getting one for yourself, ask others if they'd like one, too.*

'Here you are.' The woman thumped a box file in front of me. 'I'm not supposed to do this. The library's for staff and authorised people only. You've got twenty minutes until I go for my break.'

'You've been unbelievably kind,' I said. 'I'm immensely grateful.'

She nodded and emitted a grunt of agreement. A flake of dandruff fell onto her shoulder. I did not brush it away, but opened the file instead.

It was all there in screaming headlines and graphic pictures.

'*Electrician Loses Manhood in Shocking Crash*'. '*No More Urinals Sobs Brave Kiwi*'. '*My Pain. A Wife's Story*'. '*Found! Sex Change Twin Sister*'. '*How I Saved a Worthless Marriage by star* Daily Chronicle *reporter Mary Francesca Wilton*'. '*It Works! My Delightful Afternoon by star* Daily Chronicle *reporter Mary Francesca Wilton*'.

The last headline caught my eye. I read the first paragraph:

Your intrepid reporter can categorically confirm that Dick Worth's new penis is in excellent working order. Following negotiations involving a new car with transplant hero Dick Worth's wife, Paula, I spent a delightful afternoon at the hick town of Bullock's Yes Oh Yes Motel with a bottle of champagne and the strong arms, hands, whatever, of her husband. All in the line of duty, you understand! But I can assure you, readers, this motel is aptly named.

Until that moment I had never known deep, visceral, mind-numbing hatred. This was cynical treachery. With a trickle of sweat running down my spine, I read each report. There was no mention of me. As far as the world was concerned, Frankie had discovered Dick's transsexual twin sister by using her own detective skills. It was Frankie who had realised there'd be no rejection problems with a penis from a monozygotic twin and had broken the news to Dick, Paula and the doctors. She'd even devoted a paragraph to an explanation of the difference between monozygotic and dizygotic. A difference which *I* had explained to *her*, for God's sake.

Like opening a Russian doll, as I read each report the kernel of truth became clearer. No one at the *Chronicle* knew I existed. The pitiful money Frankie had given me each week in lieu of my wages at the *Bullock Telegraph* had almost certainly come out of her own pocket, more probably her *Chronicle* expense account.

Then there was the infidelity. Or was it adultery? Could it be adultery if the wife was complaisant? Was it even infidelity? Frankie had made no commitment to me. And then I remembered her throwaway comment: *'You should ring before you come round. I could have a strange man in my bed . . . Dick Worth. I'm always up for a new experience.'*

As far as Frankie was concerned, sex was a currency. It had kept me in line, kept me running, kept me coming up with useful contacts. And when she had needed a story with spice, she'd found a fellow mercenary in Dick's wife, Paula.

And the final doll? She had charmed my mum and dad into believing she was the girl-next-door.

'Come back and see us anytime,' they'd said on her last night in Bullock. 'Don't stay at a motel. There's always a bed for you here in Wey Street.'

I could never forgive her for that.

But she hadn't charmed Agnes. Agnes had seen Frankie's satanic core. Had known I needed to see it, too, before I could be rid of her. Had perhaps even suspected that what Frankie had written was far removed from the sweet persona sitting at our dinner table. Which was why she'd given me her life savings so that I could come to London.

'I'm going for my break now. I have to close the library. You'll have to go.'

I looked up at the hard-faced woman looming above me.

'I'm very grateful.'

As she stood at the door, something inside her must have softened, because she said, 'I'm sorry to push you out like this. If you didn't find what you were looking for I suppose you could come back.'

'Thanks,' I said, 'but that won't be necessary. I found precisely what I was looking for.'

Chapter 20

I walked back to Himalaya Street. Around Trafalgar Square. The length of Piccadilly. Through Hyde Park to the Bayswater Road. Its length to Shepherd's Bush. And into the run-down streets of north-west London. Boarded-up shops, burned-out cars, wind-blown rubbish, houses galloping towards collapse with ours leading the charge. The exercise was good for my anger. By the time I arrived, the worst of it had gone.

The house seemed deserted apart from a body in a sleeping bag. My sleeping bag. Under my kitchen table. I kicked the body. Not hard. Just enough to make me feel better.

'*Hey!* What the hell do you think you're doing in my sleeping bag?'

It stirred. A muffled voice muttered from the depths.

'I'm J. Fitz Kennedy. You're in my spot. In my sleeping bag.' I kicked again. Harder.

'I'm talking to you, you prick.'

The body spun. The head shot up and hit the underside of the table.

'*Ow! Shit! Fuck! Jesus Christ!*'

As the sleeping bag fell away, I saw a green Dartmouth College T-shirt beneath which were breasts every bit the equivalent of Maria Santos Almeida's, the enduring gold standard.

'Oh God, I'm sorry!' I squatted alongside. 'I thought you were a bloke. Are you OK?'

'No, I'm not! You asshole! I just got in from Los Angeles, I'm tired, you hurt my back, and now my head hurts.'

'Do you want me to rub it?'

'Piss off!' She turned towards me. 'What the hell do you mean? Rub what? And stop looking at my tits. Christ! This is all I need. A body on the plane and a pervert kicking shit out of me.'

'What body?'

'A guy died in the seat next to me. Mexican. Fat guy. Heart attack. Win some, lose some. They upgraded me for the remainder.'

I offered my hand.

'I'm Fitz — J. Fitz Kennedy.'

'Yeah, you told me. I'm Cheryl. Cheryl Cole. Anyway, you've been upgraded, too. You get the sofa with no springs and a duvet. Some guy moved out this morning.'

'Look,' I said, 'I feel really bad about this. Can I buy you dinner? There's a Thai place on the main road. Fat Long Nosh. Alex says they do great things with ginger.'

'Wake me at seven. A tap on the shoulder will do it.'

The ambience at Fat Long Nosh was Bangkok Basic. Scrubbed wooden floors, chipped Formica tables, rickety chairs, a greasy, steamy, sweaty smell mixed with unfiltered cigarette smoke. A tiny woman in an electric-blue sheath dress clearing crockery, wiping plates with a thick rag, wringing it into a bucket, a thin fag dangling from her mouth. A red-faced old guy in a corner muttering into a mug of tea which he held to his face between woollen mitts. A spotty young couple committed to the All Day Breakfast. A bald-headed guy with a gut and a mangy little terrier with a line of frayed string tied to its collar waiting at the back for a takeaway. From a wide range of options, we chose a table against a side wall with Cheryl facing the door, giving me a view through the plastic slats of the chef with a chopper. He was dismembering a chicken.

'You won't find this place in the *Time Out Restaurant Guide.*'

I picked up the menu, a single sheet of paper in a protective plastic cover, wet from the table.

'They don't want the publicity,' said Cheryl. 'Otherwise half of London would be outside, demanding a table. What do you recommend?'

'This is my first time,' I said. 'I'm a Fat Long Nosh virgin. Be gentle with me.'

Cheryl laughed and put the menu aside.

'I'm not really hungry. When they upgraded me I pigged out. I'll share some of yours. Help with the budget.'

I'd shaken Cheryl's shoulder at seven. Watched her emerge from the sleeping bag like a chrysalis, stretch and scratch, and run a hand through her tousled blonde hair and wipe her sleepy eyes. She was taller than I'd imagined. Excellent legs. Perfect frame slung from wide shoulders. An open, outdoors, fresh face. Wide blue eyes, thick eyebrows, wide mouth. Dad would have given an eight for her teeth, but then he always kept something in reserve. She'd grabbed clothes and a toilet bag from her backpack. Shuffled off to the bathroom muttering something about a shower. Returned a few minutes later cursing British hygiene. The Himalaya Street bathroom was for the desperate and the brave.

She had a cheetah's grace as we walked the few hundred yards to the main road. An easy, flowing movement that seemed effortless and yet restrained, as if she could, if she wished, chase down prey at immense speed.

The lady in the sheath dress stood between us, smiling with half-closed eyes and a thin mouth. I asked for the twenty-seven with a thirteen on the side. She said something in Thai and went into the kitchen screeching her orders.

'So,' I said. 'What are you doing in London?'

'Looking for work.'

'What kind of work?'

'Stage. I dance, sing, I can act. I've been performing since I was six. My daddy was an actor, but he mainly produces now. So I kind of have it in my blood, I guess. How about you?'

'I'm a writer.'

Cheryl looked around the restaurant. The young couple had demolished their All Day Breakfast and were preparing to leave. The old guy was staring into his mug. The guy with the dog had gone.

She leaned forward and whispered: 'Is the rest a state secret?'

'Anyone can say they're a writer. I haven't had anything published. Until I do, it's all bullshit.'

'And in the meantime you wear this constipated face and suffer. Is that how it goes?'

'What do you want me to say? I'm looking for my voice? I haven't found my genre? Pretentious crap like that?'

'Nothing's pretentious if it's what you truly believe, and not what you think you should say to look good. I'd like to know about your writing. But if you don't want to tell me, we'll talk about something else.'

So I told Cheryl about my poem to Betty Rice, and about Troy Weeks, and 'Too Small for his Boots' and the dozens more short stories I'd had rejected, and about the *Bullock Telegraph* and Murray's Barber Shop and the Almeida family. Because somehow it all seemed connected and relevant.

'It's called life,' said Cheryl. 'You need to find a way of distilling it into a story. What's the most important thing that's ever happened? Love, hate, birth, death?'

After the twenty-seven and the thirteen had arrived I told Cheryl about Frankie and the Penis Transplant and the Great Betrayal.

Afterwards, we drank green tea out of thick white bowls then decided to walk for a while. There was a small square just off the main road with a few hardy perennials struggling for space between crushed beer cans, dried vomit and dog shit. We picked our way along its cracked paths to a kids' playground where there were swings shaped like rubber nappies, seesaws, and a slide on the end of a wooden fort. We sat on a bench seat and ate ice creams for dessert.

'What are you going to do about Frankie? Can you hold this while I do my exercises?'

Cheryl gave me her ice cream, stood, and did some stretching exercises, placing her palms on the ground bending forwards, then bending over backwards and doing it again. Then she put her weight on her hands and did a perfect backwards somersault.

'I . . . er . . . I . . . sorry, but what you just did is impossible.'

She laughed, spread her legs wide, placed her hands on her hips and bent her torso until it was horizontal. Then she did the splits, reached for her toes, did a limbo dance with her back horizontal and about three inches from the ground. She stood up, hands on hips.

'Does this bother you?'

'Bother me? No. It's . . . just . . . a very, very warm evening, that's all.'

'No, it's not. I'll stop.' She retrieved the ice cream. 'You didn't answer my question. About Frankie.'

'I'm going to confront her. Have it out. Tell her what I think of her.'

'Do you think that's wise?'

'What else can I do? It's why my aunt paid for me to come here. Deal with the situation. Put it behind me. Get on with my life.'

Cheryl took a couple of bites, leaving a white smudge on her lips.

'That's one way of doing it. What most people would do, I guess. But you've got another.'

'What's that?'

'You remember you told me about that story, what was it called — "Too Small for his Boots"?'

'Yeah. So?'

'You wrote that after your experience with that Portuguese girl, right?'

'Maria Santos Almeida. I turned her family into the New York mafia. Carla and the Capellis.'

'Didn't you feel better afterwards? Like you'd achieved your own brand of victory?'

'You think I should do the same thing with Frankie?'

'It's just an idea. Might be worth thinking about, anyway. Better than a fight you're not going to win. Because if I was Frankie and someone like you came halfway around the world to pick a fight with me, I know what I'd say: *Fuck off back where you came from*. So she did the dirty on you. So what? You're a big boy now, Fitz. You can take it. She's a tough lady in a tough profession. She gets what she wants and she doesn't care how she does it. Put her in your creative mixing bowl. Add a few of your own special ingredients. Let her cook for a while. See what comes out.'

Chapter 21

There was never more than a few minutes' quiet in the Himalaya Street house. Although I'd grown up amid domestic traffic, I'd always had my own room. Now I had a dusty sofa, constant interruption, and the thumps of several stereos.

I retreated to the Kilburn Public Library, a tired old Victorian building hidden behind plane trees. Lonely old men slept over the *Daily Mail*; widows borrowed Georgette Heyer in large print. There was a quiet corner I made my own. Psychology to the left of me, Philosophy to the right. Browsers rarely came near. I spread papers and notebooks and a brown paper bag with my morning doughnut from Mr Bun the Baker, and colonised the table without opposition.

For three weeks I spent each day there until the library closed. I covered my corner with notes about Frankie. The way she spoke, dressed, made love. It was easy enough to distil her personality. Cheryl had said it: '*She's a tough lady in a tough profession. She gets what she wants and she doesn't care how she does it.*' But it was harder to create a fictional biography, harder still a profession where Frankie's ruthlessness would prove priceless. I considered law, advertising, politics, accountancy. They offered plenty of scope, but lacked life-threatening excitement. I needed something where my character could emerge victorious in the last chapter, just like the heroes at the Ritz Little Crackers Saturday-morning movies.

When I came to a dead end, I talked it over with Cheryl

one evening as we shared spaghetti bolognaise in the Himalaya Street kitchen.

'She has a heart of steel tempered by a hard childhood. She was a hooker's unwanted child, brought up in an orphanage, shuttled around religious foster homes. Scrubbed floors at four-thirty in the morning before being forced to ask God to forgive her sins.'

'But she rises above it all,' said Cheryl. 'Works hard at school, works her way through college — but she's always in trouble.'

'What kind of trouble?'

'Fights. She has a very short fuse. She hurts someone, gets arrested. A cop gives her a break. Tells her to take out her aggression in the gym. She learns martial arts. Karate. Kung fu. Judo. Gets her black belt.'

'Falls in love.' I picked up Cheryl's thread, enjoying the back and forth inspiration. 'He's murdered. She exacts revenge. Discovers she's good at it. Decides to become a professional assassin.'

Cheryl looked at the disgusting mess in the kitchen. People had come and gone, leaving unwashed dishes, pots, pans, an overflowing rubbish bin.

'Yeah.' She laughed. 'Cleaning up the world's garbage. I can see a potential problem, though, Fitz.'

'What's that?'

'A lone character could become tiresome. She needs a partner to spark with.'

Over the next twenty years there'd be interminable discussions about the genesis of Pavarotti the parrot. Highbrow television talk shows, Sunday magazines, the literary media, the summer book festivals. They would all offer their own theories. Pavarotti had been inspired by the Monty Python 'Dead Parrot' sketch. I'd kept a budgerigar as a child and wished to recreate it in fictional form. It was a corruption of the word *Pierrot* meaning Little Peter. I was a lapsed Catholic. So my heroine was a pastiche of the Virgin Mary, and Pavarotti was parroting the Word of God.

All rubbish.

Aunt Agnes had undoubtedly lodged the parrot metaphor in my unconscious. But Pavarotti was not God. He was neither my moral conscience nor my heroine's. He was a pub sign.

Our local pub was the Long John Silver. I went there sometimes with Alex or some of the other guys from the house. The sign outside showed the peg-legged and eye-patched pirate with a parrot on his shoulder.

When I went there one evening with Cheryl, my memories from childhood must have connected with my unconscious, which had been toiling away, trying to find a partner for my heroine. I was carrying two pints of Guinness back to the table when it hit me. I slumped into the chair and stared at Cheryl.

'What's up?' She supped at her pint. 'Have you just seen a ghost?'

'Sort of. That's it. That's fucking *it.*'

I stared at Cheryl.

'What's that that's fucking *it*?' she said.

'A parrot. It sits on her shoulder. She goes everywhere with it. She uses it to help her kill people.'

'How does it do that?' Cheryl laughed. 'Peck them to death?'

'I'm not sure. It just seems like a really good idea.'

'It could fly over to the victim, I guess,' she said. 'And distract them while your heroine does the business. What's her name, by the way?'

'Haven't got one yet.'

'What about the parrot?'

'Haven't got a name for him, either. I've only just come up with the idea, for God's sake.'

'I had a friend who had a parrot called Stalin. Does that help?'

'Not really.'

'Parrot,' said Cheryl. 'Just call it Parrot. Or Carrot. Carrot the Parrot.'

'Don't like it. Too vegetarian.'

'Claret?'

'Too alcoholic.'

'Something more parroty, then. Papa Parrot. He's got a wife, kids, a mortgage.'

'Sounds like a guy I used to listen to on Radio Bullock. What about Parachute?'

'It'll never fly,' replied Cheryl.

'Paradigm, then?'

'Too academic.'

'Pavane?'

'Old dances are out of fashion.'

'Pavlova sounds good,' I said. 'Pavlova the Parrot.'

'What about Pavarotti?' said Cheryl. 'Pavarotti the Parrot. It's the word parrot. Plus a few extra letters.'

'Pavarotti.' I said the name a few times. 'That's fantastic! Now what about a name for the heroine?'

'She's a spider,' said Cheryl. 'Squashes men like flies. Sucks them dry, spits out the husk.'

'Tarantula? Tara for short?'

'Don't like Tara,' said Cheryl. 'She sits in her first-floor office with a neon sign outside flashing off, on, off, on, off, on . . . '

'Or maybe she's a sort of Jekyll and Hyde character. Or something to do with food? A chef. Puts poison into the dessert.'

'Crimes of passion fruit,' said Cheryl. 'And all this time she has this parrot on her shoulder? I don't think so.'

'All day long Pavarotti squats on his perch, thinking. The

heroine comes home, talks her problem through. Pavarotti squawks the answer.'

'Which side of the law is this woman on? Is she a detective or a killer?'

'Both. She offers a total package. One-stop shop. Solves the crime, then delivers the punishment.'

'How about Dostoyevsky?'

'Too gloomy.'

'Pavarotti has to be involved,' said Cheryl. 'Maybe what I said before. She uses him as a distraction. So that she can get in close with—'

'—a Bowie knife. She stabs people in the back. Just like Frankie.'

'The parrot sings to the victim,' said Cheryl. 'Flutters its wings and sings.'

'Sings what?'

'Opera.'

'Too highbrow. What about Abba? She teaches Pavarotti the words to every Abba song.'

'You know, that's pretty good,' said Cheryl. 'Professional female assassins are ten a penny. But no one's had a parrot who sings "Dancing Queen" before.'

'I could write a Spanish story. Pavarotti flies in front of the victim. Sings "Can You Hear The Drums, Fernando?" Fernando shakes his head: *I cannot heer no dru*— as the knife goes in.'

We sat in the Long John Silver all evening tossing ideas back and forth. It was a fantastic session. Ninety per cent of the ideas were rubbish, but occasionally a gem would pop up and I'd write it on the back of a beer mat.

Just before they threw us out at closing time, Cheryl said, 'We still haven't given this woman a name.'

'I've been thinking about that,' I said. 'What about Beryl?'

'Too close to Cheryl.' She laughed. 'And we can't have that.'

Then it came to me from nowhere.

'Laura,' I said. 'Laura Friday.'

'Why Laura Friday?'

'When I was about twelve I fancied a girl called Laura. I wrote her a poem.

Laura, Laura,
I adore ya
I'll explore ya
Friday night.'

'And did you?'

'She sent me one back.

Johnny Fitz
Loves my tits
But he just
Gives me the shits.'

Cheryl laughed. 'All the same, I like the name. When she comes to someone's rescue, they can say, "*Thank God! It's Friday!*"'

I drained my glass.

'Maybe we should call it a night.'

That's the truth about how Laura was born. Two people in a pub with their brains on fire drinking bottomless Guinness. She'd been conceived at the Yes Oh Yes Motel in Bullock, but she might have been stillborn if Cheryl hadn't suggested a better alternative to a face-to-face confrontation with Frankie.

Frankie had morphed into a ruthless female killer who does whatever she must to get what she wants, leaving a trail of broken men in her wake. For me the story would be the perfect catharsis. Creativity inspired by rejected love. Just like Yeats and his Maud Gonne.

I was on a personal journey of closure. When I typed *THE END*, I'd have put Frankie behind me. I'd be free. Free to write other books. Free to live the life I chose. At least, that was the idea. It just didn't quite work out that way.

Life rarely does.

Chapter 22

Once I'd developed Laura Friday and Pavarotti as characters, it didn't take long to write the synopsis for the first novel, *When the Fat Parrot Sings*. I gave it to Cheryl to read, and a couple of nights later we sat in the little garden which had become a favourite meeting place.

'What do you think?'

She riffled the pages, then watched a kid slide down from the fort.

'I love it. Laura's tough. Kind of life she leads she has to be. But there's a soft, vulnerable side, too. She loves Pavarotti. He's the one thing in her life she can depend on. I'd like to send it to my daddy.'

'What does he do?'

'I told you before. Produces movies. He wants to get into the mainstream. He's looking for a project.'

'Would I know anything he's made?'

'I doubt it. His movies don't get national exposure. But he knows a lot of people. If he liked your idea he could pull a few strings. That's how it works.'

'I haven't written the book yet.'

'Doesn't matter. I already faxed some of your other stuff to him. He was very impressed. Thinks you write very well, have some great ideas.'

'When did you do that?'

'Soon after we met. You remember? You gave me those stories to read. About the guy who gets in trouble with the olive oil

Mafia. And the one about the hospital receptionist? And about the barber shop? You don't mind, do you? I did it for you, Fitz. Right now you need all the help you can get.'

In fact I felt invaded, but I didn't want a fight with Cheryl. She was an attractive, bright, funny American. We were becoming great friends and I'd heard Yanks were pushy, so I was prepared to make allowances.

'The book will take time to write. Eight or nine months. And that's just the first draft. Then there'll be rewrites. Could be a year before it's finished. My money's going to run out. I need a job.'

'So do I.'

Cheryl was watching a couple of kids bouncing up and down on the seesaw, but her voice sounded distant. Since we'd met, all we'd talked about was my writing career. Her first question had always been '*How's it going?*' and I'd told her at great length. But she'd told me almost nothing about herself.

I felt guilty. I'd been self-obsessed. But also manipulated by her silence. As if she'd been accumulating credits to be redeemed with interest at some unspecified date.

'How's it going with you?' I touched her shoulder. Tentative. Unsure of her response. 'Anything happening?'

'They're auditioning for a new World War Two musical. All the old songs plus a few new ones. Good-looking fighter pilots, pretty girls in overalls and headscarves with axle grease on their cheeks. Fantastic sound and lighting effects, and a genuine bomber. That's what it's called. *Bomber!* They'll try it out in Plymouth then bring it to the West End. I went yesterday.'

'How did you get on?'

She shrugged.

'Hard to say. I sang "White Cliffs of Dover". Showed them my tap. And my high kick. Gave them a few lines. They just said thanks. There were hundreds of girls.'

'What's the attraction of London? Why not New York? Chicago? Any other big city in the States?'

'My mom died when I was a kid. She was jogging near our house in Malibu, got hit by a drunk driver. My daddy brought me up. Made sure I had everything. Took me to school, brought me home, never let me out of his sight. Put me through stage school, dance classes, singing lessons. I don't think he ever believed I had much talent, but he always said hard work would compensate. It got to a point where I just felt I had to get out from under. London seemed like a good place to strike out on my own.'

'But if you want to send him my stuff you must still be close.'

'Oh sure.' A little girl fell over on the rubberised concrete. Cheryl half-rose but the mother got there, picked the girl up. Cheryl wiggled her fingers as the little girl peered over her mother's shoulder. The girl smiled through her tears. 'I love my dad. He can be a pain in the ass at times. Pushy, aggressive, likes to get his own way. Hard to say no to. I know he loves me, too, but I'll always be his little girl. He needs to let go of a few heartstrings. Get married again. But I think he's afraid.'

'Why did you choose Himalaya Street?'

'Dad wanted to pay my way. Set me up in a nice apartment. I said no. I just had my savings, and this was all I could afford. I'm not worried. If I don't get this part, I'll get a job. Waitressing. Bar work. Whatever. Soon as I do I'll move out, get a room somewhere. I can live anywhere.'

'Look, Cheryl, I just want to say, I'm grateful for what you're doing.'

She took my hand from her shoulder, held it.

'I like you a lot, Fitz. I think you have talent. I'd like to help. And the bruises have gone.'

'What about us?'

'You're still dealing with Frankie. Let's see how the writing project goes. Take it from there.'

'Sounds good to me. Fancy a pint?'

'At the Long John Silver?'

'Where else?'

As we walked arm-in-arm from the playground, Cheryl's head on my shoulder, I knew everything was going to work out. She must have been thinking the same thing, because as we reached the pub she said, 'This reminds me of Bogey and Bergman. *Casablanca*. We'll always have Paris.'

'We'll always have the Kilburn High Road.'

She laughed and kissed my cheek.

When we got back from the pub, Alex was pegging a message to the noticeboard.

'Your mum's been trying to call you. Said you should call her back soon as you got in. Reverse the charges.'

Chapter 23

Ever since I'd seen them bring her home from the convent, I'd known it was coming. I'd feared it, tried to forget it, as if my denial would prevent it. Each time I'd passed the noticeboard, I'd averted my gaze. Whenever the phone rang, I'd prayed it would not be for me.

'Your aunt is as well as can be expected,' Mum had said in her last letter. 'Under the circumstances.'

The family motto. A white lie was better than a black truth.

Agnes had never shied away from the truth. She'd have looked death square in the face, and gone to meet it with a Bushmills in one hand, a Mother Mary Irish Green in the other. As she'd gone off to the Sacred Sisters each spring, to return when the weather cooled, with a blown kiss to the boy watching from the upstairs window and a plea for the taxi fare.

I could imagine what she'd say if she came back: *'They had me scrubbin' that fockin' Stairway to Heaven, Johnny. There's nothin' in the fockin' Bible about it stretchin' to infinity now, is there, pet?'*

But this time she would not come back. This time she had left a Dank Void which could never be filled.

'She's at peace now, Johnny,' Mum said. 'In the Better Place. She mentioned you just before she died.'

'What did she say?'

'Something about a parakeet. She said you'd understand.'

'Yeah, I do. Was she in much pain?'

'The Irish Green was a big help. She was chain-smoking

towards the end. I don't know what she'd have done without it.'

'Should I come back for the funeral?'

'She'll be upset if you do. We're having a big wake. Beryl Harper's doing the catering so there'll be a big turn-out. Agnes was very popular, you know, Johnny. The Mayo Brothers will play a few jigs and reels. Carmel will sing "Ave Maria". You'll be there in our thoughts. Are you wearing clean underwear?'

I went back to the Long John Silver and got drunk with Agnes's money. Before they threw me out, I treated the bar to 'I Cain't Get No Satisfaction'. It was not a patch on the original. But it was what Agnes would have wanted.

Chapter 24

A handwritten sign said *Hire-A-Hack 1ˢᵗ Floor.*
I stepped over a black cat and climbed a moth-eaten staircase lit by a single bare bulb. Came to a door on which another handwritten sign said *Reception Ring and Enter.* There was nothing to ring and the door was open so I entered.

Reception was four chipped oak-veneer desks, a carpet whose twin was on the staircase, and the décor a continuation of the bare-bulb theme. Behind reception were two semi-partitioned offices. A pale-faced woman was clacking at an IBM golf-ball typewriter amid a mountain of papers, squinting through cigarette smoke which rose in a thin stream from a metal ashtray and clung to the yellow ceiling. A few lank threads of hair hung across her face, which was half-turned to the right. She was reading from an upright copyholder.

'Just a minute. Must finish this. Chair over there. Haven't seen Naples, have you?'

She spoke without averting her eyes and her fingers seemed to move independently of her body. They were long and thin, and their red nail polish needed a touch-up. With Dad, the first thing he'd always noticed about people was their teeth. With me, once I'd grown out of my adolescent breast phase, it was fingers first, teeth second.

'Not yet. Haven't been anywhere except London. I might do Europe some time.'

I sank into a wooden armchair whose fabric had been shredded and whose arms needed a repolish. The entire room had a sad, resigned feeling, as if it had accepted the inevitability of old age and now awaited the end.

'Naples is the cat,' said the woman. 'It's His Lordship's little joke. See Naples and die. The cat's black. Bad luck. Geddit? That's what a fucking public school education does for you.'

'It's downstairs. I stepped over it.'

'Pity you didn't step *on* it. Mind you, it'd have torn you to shreds if you had. There. Sorry. Now then.' She looked up, gave me a thin-lipped smile. 'What can I do you for?'

'I'm J. Fitz Kennedy. I've got an appointment to see John Carnforth. About a writing job.'

'Really?' She took the hair between two fingers and tucked it over her left ear. It fell back. 'Never said a fucking word to me. Mind you, that's about par for the course. His Lordship's at lunch. What's it now? Two-thirty. Be another half-hour yet. Far left stool, lounge bar, Rising Sun. Roger and Nigel are there, too. I'm Jane by the way. If it wasn't for me this place would fall apart.'

'I can see that.'

'Mind you, it's doing that anyway. Due for demolition, see. Nine months, a year at most. Hilton, Sheraton, some fucking monstrosity. Don't let him get you pissed. Or make you pay for every round. I'll be serving afternoon tea when you get back.'

The Rising Sun was down a side street between Tottenham Court Road and Charlotte Street. Black paint, frosted windows, wooden bench-tables chained to a concrete pad, and a pair of fold-back steel flaps for dray deliveries. Inside was mock Victorian. Tasselled lamps, flock wallpaper, old Pears' soap posters in oak frames, burgundy padded banquette seats between etched glass dividers. A guy in a Next suit was feeding coins into a fruit machine. Elvis was singing 'Love Me Tender' to no one in particular.

Two guys were standing in the far left corner of the bar near the toilets, flanking another on a stool.

'You must be John,' I said to the guy on the stool.

'Must I? And who the fuck are you, coming in here, telling me who I am?'

'J. Fitz Kennedy. Jane said I'd find you here. I rang yesterday. About the writing job.'

'What writing job?'

'The one you advertised in the *Evening Standard*: *Hack wanted. No prospects, crap money, guaranteed tedium.*'

'How do you spell "innocuous"?'

'I-n-n-o-c-u-o-u-s.'

'Where does the apostrophe go in the phrase "the people's favourite"?'

'Between the *e* and the *s*. Unless you're talking about several different peoples, in which case after the *s*.'

'What about "it's people I can't stand"?'

'Between the *t* and the *s*, and between the *n* and the *t*.'

'It's also true. You're hired. This is Roger, this is Nigel. I, as you so emphatically claim, must be John. Buy us a round and you can start when we get back. Mine's a double Johnny Walker, Nigel's on pints, and Roger's got a meeting so he's on the Stolly.'

Roger was tall, heavily built, fortyish, with sandy hair, and mottled skin that appeared sensitive to sunlight. Nigel looked like a dormouse disturbed during hibernation. Eyes that took seconds to blink in a conscious movement. He looked desperately tired as he clung to a cigarette for support. He swayed back and forth, balanced on the knuckles of his left hand, which were resting on John's stool. John himself was mid-forties, perhaps more, wearing an ash-stained double-breasted suit, striped tie, with an owlish grey face, and small, rheumy eyes.

'What does Hire-A-Hack do?' When the drinks arrived I

pocketed the remnants of a ten-pound note. 'What will *I* be doing? Exactly?'

'Anything and everything,' said Roger, who seemed to have a faint Scottish burr. 'Plus this, that and the other fucking thing.'

Nigel nodded.

'Just about sums it up.'

'Take no notice of these idiots,' said John. 'Hire-A-Hack's the shit-hole of the advertising, PR and corporate communications industry. Brochures about road haulage, leaflets on pest control, annual reports for fertiliser companies, press releases for the sewage industry, instruction manuals on how to use your new cooker, or how to wank in your new shower. When an advertising agency picks up a big account they do the flashy stuff. Television, magazines, press ads, whatever. We do the shit work. They pay us a pittance. Charge the client a fortune. You know anything about the pharmaceutical industry?'

'Well, yes, I do as a matter of fact.'

'How come?'

'There was a barber's shop I used to go to. Had a huge library of medical magazines.'

'Speak German?'

'Just what I learned at school.'

'Ever heard of a company called Eingeheimer-Fossblatt?'

'Sure. They make Xzylenol, Prolactate, Moxichlor, Supracholest. Why?'

'Their Sales Manual needs to be rewritten in plain English. Someone in Bremen or Hamburg or wherever the fuck they are has translated it. *"Before on ze Herr Doktor one calling is, ze E-F representative his shoes clean ensure will, and of the utmost politeness at all times be."* Crap like that.'

'How much does it pay?'

'Three quid an hour.'

'How many pages?'

'About two thousand.'

'And when it's finished?'

'There's the Operations Manual, the Factory Manual and the Administration Manual. Roger, it's your round. Fitz looks as if he needs a double Johnny.'

'What do you guys do?'

I was beginning to feel light-headed. I looked at my watch. Ten to three. With any luck the pub would be closing in ten minutes.

'This is Nigel's day job,' said John. 'He's a sub-editor on the *Chronicle*. Paper goes to bed at two, Nigel gets home at three, comes in at ten, works till six. Three wives, six kids to support.'

'Do you know a reporter called Mary Francesca Wilton?'

Nigel looked at me with spaniel eyes, swaying. 'Frankie Amazon.' His laugh became a cough. He hacked at it before hauling himself more or less upright. 'Sounds like Frankie Anaconda. Or Frankie Avalon, see? Remember them? Frankie Avalon and the Four Seasons? That's her. Eats men spring, summer, autumn and winter. She's just been appointed to the editorial board. Not offending you, am I, sunshine? Not a mate by any chance?'

'She was once. Or at least, I thought she was.'

'You and ten thousand other poor bastards,' said Nigel. 'Got any paper experience?'

'I worked on the *Bullock Telegraph*.'

'What's that, some sort of cattle paper?'

'The Sex Change Twins Penis Transplant story. Started out with me. In Bullock, New Zealand.'

'Always thought that was Frankie's.' Nigel rubbed his chin. 'She nick it off you, did she? Won several awards with it, too. That's how she got her promotion. What a bitch, eh!'

We supped on that idea for a while, then John said, 'Better

get back. Jane'll get her knickers in a twist if we're late for after-noon tea.'

As we were walking back to the office I asked Roger, 'Why does Jane keep referring to John as His Lordship?'

'He's the third son of the Earl of Carnforth. Doubt if he'll ever inherit, though. Elder brothers are both in rude health. Whereas John's doing his best to kill himself before he's forty.'

Chapter 25

'Good news.' Alex waded towards me through a sea of backpacks when I walked into the Himalaya Street living room that evening. 'Four people left today. There's a single room spare if you want it. With a view. Back of the house, overlooking the railway line. Fifty a week. You up for it?'

I did a quick calculation. Three pounds an hour, twenty-four pounds a day times five was one-twenty a week. After paying the rent I'd have seventy pounds to live on. I'd never intended to stay at Himalaya Street more than a few days. It was a noisy dump. An overnight oasis for colonial nomads. But it had a kind of masochistic charm, and I couldn't face the idea of packing up my stuff and going room-hunting. Not in my condition. I was pregnant with Laura Friday.

'I'll take it. Have you seen Cheryl?'

'She's having a drink with a mate at the Long John Silver. Said you can join them if you like.'

The drink was Veuve Clicquot in a silver ice bucket, and two flute glasses. The mate was a bronzed god wearing a tailored jacket and a slim watch. He had a square jaw, sparkling blue eyes, faultless teeth, hairs on the backs of his fingers and mile-wide shoulders. He and Cheryl were sitting close at a round table, their knees touching. He'd just said something funny and she was laughing. She looked up.

'Oh, hi, Fitz. You got my message. This is Brad. Brad

Comstock. Brad, this is Fitz. The guy I was telling you about.'

'Glad to know you.' When Brad stood, he blocked the light. Six-four at least, with a grip that crushed my hand like a paper cup. His voice came from somewhere near his polished brown brogues. 'You're living in that crap-hole, too? You wanna drink? *Hey!*' He snapped his fingers at the barman. '*You!* Bring another glass. And another bottle of champagne.'

'What's this, a celebration?'

I dragged a low stool across and sat facing Brad, trying to figure out how it was possible to dislike someone so intensely on such a brief acquaintance.

'I got the part in *Bomber!*' said Cheryl. 'I play Suzie. I fall in love with Chuck, an American bomber pilot.'

'That's me.'

Brad gave Cheryl a performance with his perfect teeth and smouldering eyes.

The barman brought the champagne and another glass, ripped the foil away and popped the cork. Froth spurted from the bottle and splashed onto Brad's creased twill trousers.

'Hey, what the fuck!'

'Terribly sorry, sir!' The barman offered a tea towel. 'That's thirty pounds.'

'It was only eighteen last time.'

'That was non-vintage, sir. This one's the Brut '78. More to your liking, I would think.'

Brad produced a tan leather wallet from the inside pocket of his jacket and removed five five-pound notes from a thick wad.

'I'm taking five for the dry cleaning. You have a problem with that?'

'Not at all, sir. Most understandable. Thank you, sir.'

From the smirk on the barman's face as he turned away, I guessed he'd come out of the exchange well ahead.

'*Asshole.*' Brad wiped his thigh with the tea towel. 'Teach him to fuck with me!'

'So, you're the star of the show, then, Brad?'

I took hold of the bottle, took my time pouring.

'Yeah, I guess you could say that. Before this I was a great Curly in *Oklahoma!* Not too happy about the ending of this one, though.'

'Why's that?'

'Chuck gets shot down in the final scene,' said Cheryl. 'I sing "My Man's Missing in Action".'

'Too downbeat,' said Brad. 'Should be me up there at the end with a rousing number, sending them home happy.'

'We're going out to dinner,' said Cheryl. 'Do you want to join us?'

I remembered a poker game I'd watched at my Uncle Tommy's house one Sunday night. Tommy, Aunt Bridie, Agnes, Mum and Dad. Agnes had lost hand after hand until Tommy had suggested they raise the stakes, then she'd scooped the pool.

'It's not who wins the fockin' battle that matters, Johnny,' she'd said later. 'It's who wins the war.'

'Thanks, but I'll have an early night. I've got a room now. First floor back. I'll get a good night's sleep, get up early. Big day tomorrow. Good to meet you, Brad.' I emptied my glass and stood. 'Look forward to seeing you in *Bomber!* I'm sure you'll be a great Chuck.'

I avoided the handshake and kissed Cheryl's cheek instead.

'Have a great evening.'

I sauntered back to Himalaya Street trying to sort out how I felt about Brad and Cheryl. Why did I care whether anything happened between them? Cheryl was a free agent. We were just good friends, weren't we? Or was it just the threat, the challenge, of another male that was making me feel so pissed off? I liked Cheryl, no doubt about that. She was kind, generous, eternally positive and happy. Most guys wouldn't have thought twice.

I had two problems with her.

First, there was nothing to get my teeth into. Nothing to get angry about. Nothing to dislike. Why was that important, I wondered as I turned into Himalaya Street and skipped around a pile of dog shit? Because no one was perfect. There had to be a flaw in Cheryl's make-up. Something I hadn't been allowed to see, or hadn't identified.

Second, there was someone else. Frankie. But not Frankie. An amorphous, incoherent, part-formed character, part Frankie, part bits and pieces of people I'd known or imagined. A tough, no-nonsense, hard-bitten character I both loved and hated. As I climbed the stairs to my room, I felt as if she was waiting for me to bring her to life. A brief firework of a life. Laura Friday would die in the final chapter. So would her parrot.

Chapter 26

Cheryl moved into an attic flat in Notting Hill and I settled into my first floor back at Himalaya Street. I bought an old desk and chair from a Kilburn junk shop, and an even older Olivetti upright typewriter with sticky keys and a missing *N*. I oiled its moving parts, treated it to a new ribbon and set it up in a corner by the window. If I turned to my left there was a view of the railway, but if I looked straight ahead at the blank wall I could see my characters, and every detail of their lives.

I learned to cope with my transitory neighbours. There was no one around at five in the morning so I had the bathroom to myself. The shower was no more than a dribble above the grimy yellow bath, but at that time of day it didn't run hot and cold whenever someone turned a tap. By the time I heard the first slam of the front door I'd have been writing for three hours.

I reprieved an old bike from a skip, gave it new inner tubes and tyres, oiled its chain, adjusted its saddle and used it for free transport to and from Hire-A-Hack. I zipped through traffic, hurled abuse at motorists, scattered pedestrians and jumped traffic lights. By the time I cruised down the cobbled mews my mind was clear of Laura, and I was ready to attack the Eingeheimer-Fossblatt Sales Manual.

This was a ring-bound tome with a solid black cover. It had its own glowering presence. A Beethoven of a book. As it loomed at me from my desk, I would grab any opportunity for distraction.

Jane at eight-forty-five with doughnuts.

Roger a few minutes later with the overnight bulletin on his six-month-old daughter, Rose, which sounded like the BBC Shipping Forecast. '*Two o'clock feed fine, some wailing after the six, gale force wind from the south before morning.*' Roger produced in-house newsletters for companies no one had ever heard of.

Nigel at ten, clinging to a fag as he heaved his skeletal frame up the stairs and cupped his hand for Jane to insert his first coffee. '*Christ! I can't take much more of this! We got anything on today? Be a love and top it up with some heart-starter, Janey.*' Nigel edited commercial press releases and slipped them into the late editions of the *Chronicle* when no one was looking.

Although he lived two hundred yards away, in a flat above a laundrette, John usually arrived last, looking half-asleep.

'He's a night person,' Jane had explained on my second day. 'Don't expect much sense out of him until he's had his liquid lunch. Or after, come to that. They tell me he's at his best at about two in the morning, but I wouldn't know.'

Nigel would disappear into John's office, close the door and sink into a deep conference.

'New business?' I asked on my first morning.

'Newmarket more like,' said Jane. 'They sort their bets out between ten-thirty and ten-fifty-five. Only time of day they can't be disturbed.'

'Why ten-fifty-five?'

'Gives them five minutes to get to the Rising Sun.'

At ten-fifty-five John's office door opened and he came out rubbing his hands.

'Three bets today, Jane, all good. Better get there before the rush. Coming, Roger?'

Roger had his head bent over a block of type which he was pasting onto a brochure layout.

'I'll just finish this. See you there.'

'Fitz?'

'Um, bit early for me, and . . . er . . . I need to earn a bit of money, so . . .'

'Don't worry about that.' John waved away my concern. 'You get three quid an hour, eight hours a day, twenty-four quid a day. Doesn't matter how you spend your time. I charge you out at twelve quid an hour. Agency charges the client twenty-five. Long as we make some sort of progress everyone's happy.'

'All the same . . .'

John checked his watch.

'Must go. Rush'll be starting soon. See you there.'

'He says the same thing every morning,' said Jane once John and Nigel had gone. 'Always has three bets. They're always good until they cross the line behind some other bugger.'

I went with John and Nigel once or twice, but my hourly rate bought one round. John's four-hour lunches cost me a day's pay, so I brought Marmite sandwiches and kept working. By the time I'd biked back to Himalaya Street it would be after six, nearer seven once I'd made baked beans on toast. I would eat in my room, reviewing what I'd written that morning, then settle down to another four hours with Laura Friday.

From time to time Cheryl took me to a movie or a meal. I never had any money, but she was getting paid well for her part in *Bomber!*, so after a couple of protests I accepted her charity. But I didn't feel good about it. Each time she paid for the cinema tickets or called for the bill I felt as if another obligation had been added to the ledger.

Her place was much more comfortable than mine, too, with its own bathroom and a spiral staircase from the bedroom to the living room. At the end of the evening Cheryl would press a five-pound note into my hand, kiss my cheek and call a cab.

She treated me to coffee and croissants each Saturday

morning at Cerise, a little café in Holland Park. Cerise was run by two gay guys in silk shirts and dyed blond crew cuts who danced between the tables and cooed to each other like wood pigeons. If the weather was fine, we sat outside at a wire-brushed aluminium table. We usually talked about work. Laura's character was evolving all the time. Early in the morning when my brain was at its freshest, I'd often discover a new aspect of her character. One morning it was fish. She loved flat, bottom-feeding fish, especially Dover sole. Another, it was cheating at poker.

Cheryl was a terrific listener, taking in every word with her wide-awake eyes and sexy mouth, nodding her understanding as I explained the plot twists, asking sensible questions, coming back with ideas. Then we'd talk about *Bomber!* She'd explain the intricacies of preparing a new musical, which seemed to concern where people stood and which way someone was facing when they delivered a line and the trouble someone was having finding the right key.

One Saturday morning I was reading the magazine section of *The Times* when she said, 'How's progress?'

I put the paper aside and gazed at her. She looked terrific in a loose sweater, her hair tied back in a ponytail, teeth in great condition. I could hear my dad. '*Cheryl Cole, Johnny. Perfect incisors, molars, gums. Never get rich on her teeth. Nice lady, too.*'

She was. A very nice lady.

'About a third of the way through. Should have the first draft finished in about six months.'

'Daddy called during the week. He wants to see what you've written so far. If he likes it, he'll help you find an agent. He says publishers get thousands of unsolicited manuscripts. Most of them never even get read. You need someone whose opinion publishers respect, who knows which publisher is most likely to be interested, who can get the best deal for you.'

'Sure,' I said. 'And who'll take fifteen per cent of everything I earn.'

'What's better? Eighty-five per cent of something or a hundred per cent of nothing? After all that hard work. You need to be more professional.'

'And I suppose you're going to tell me your daddy knows someone.'

'No need to be so touchy, Fitz. He knows dozens of agents. Schmoozes with them all the time. He said there's an agency called Philip Bedford International. PBI. Offices everywhere. They represent sports stars, movie stars, rock stars, the celebrity speaking circuit, best-selling authors. You get someone from PBI to look after you, you're as good as made.'

'But someone like that's never going to talk to me,' I said. 'I'm just another unpublished writer. Catch-22. You have to be famous first.'

'Let me send what you've written to Daddy. Can't do any harm, can it?'

It didn't seem important. I'd had so many rejection slips over the years, I didn't really believe *When the Fat Parrot Sings* would ever be published. Or, even if it was, that it would sell many copies. In any case, that wasn't why I was writing it. Laura Friday was a personal journey. To erase how I felt about Frankie Wilton.

When we met at Cerise three weeks later, Cheryl had a look on her face. The kind of look Mum would have said, '*It was as if she'd lost a penny and found sixpence.*'

'He's done it.'

'Done what?'

'Daddy loved your story. Called someone at PBI in LA, who called their London office. Helen Valentino heads up their UK

Literary Division. She's agreed to look at what you've written so far. If she likes it, she'll take you on as a client. If she doesn't, she'll tell you why. Either way you've got nothing to lose. Isn't that just great?'

'Yeah,' I said. 'Just . . . great.'

Cheryl's face fell.

'I thought you'd be pleased.'

'I am. Really. It's just . . . come out of the blue, that's all. Here I am, rewriting a German pharmaceutical sales manual at three quid an hour, single room in a Kilburn squat. Suddenly I'm offered the world. I'm not ready.'

'You mean you'd rather suffer? Struggle? Let the world discover you in twenty years' time or after you're dead? Haven't you got enough rejection slips yet?'

'It's my first novel. Hemingway, Forster, Waugh. They all had their first novels rejected.'

'Is that what it's all about? Failure? You can't handle success?' Cheryl did something angry with her teaspoon and her half-full coffee cup, like she was taking it out on the sugar. 'You're writing this book so it can be rejected and you can feel sorry for yourself, spend the rest of your life suffering for your art?'

'No, of course not. It's just not as simple as all that.'

'I don't know what life's like in Bullock, Fitz,' said Cheryl, 'but this is the real world. A chance like this comes along, you grab it. That's what Frankie did with the Twins Transplant story. It's what anyone in their right mind would do.'

'I need time to think about it.' A gust of wind caught the Saturday newspaper, sent its pages flying across the pavement. I scuttled after them and brought the scrunched-up mess back to the table. 'When does this Valentino person want to see my stuff?'

Cheryl passed a slip of paper across the table. 'This is her home number. She's expecting your call. She'll look at it this weekend, then let you know one way or the other.' She covered my hand with hers. 'Please don't let Daddy down over this, Fitz. He's doing you a very big favour.'

'I know,' I said. 'I'm very grateful.'

Just like I was grateful for the free meals and the free movie tickets and the little pots and pans Cheryl bought for me to cook with, and the shirts and socks.

'There's a phone inside the café. You could call her now.'

I did as I was told, came back a few minutes later.

'She lives in Islington. Wants me to put the manuscript in a cab.'

Cheryl bit her lip and thought for a few seconds.

'Best we do it in person. Make sure it doesn't get lost. And she can put a face to the name. Let's take a cab back to Himalaya Street, pick up the manuscript, and go over to Islington.'

There were no rubbish bins in sight, so I left the newspaper on my seat and threaded between the tables to the kerb where Cheryl was hailing a black cab. Who said anything about we? Whose book was this, anyway?

An hour or so later the black cab swept past the Sadler's Wells Theatre, turned into a side street, then entered a square which looked as if it had recently featured in a Disney movie. Black lacquer reproduction gas lamps etched with gold paint were spaced at intervals along a pristine pavement. The houses were three-storey terraced Georgian with perfect symmetry, newly-pointed pale brown bricks, freshly-painted doors with big brass knockers and bold brass numbers. Through the ground floor windows there were spacious rooms with chandeliers and ornate fireplaces. Black fleur-de-lis railings ran around all four sides and if there'd been a boy in breeches on a delivery bike and Julie Andrews selling lavender '*Cor blimey, duckie, buy a posy for the*

lady? Only a farthin',' I wouldn't have been surprised.

Only the Porsches, Ferraris and Mercedes angle-parked around the central garden spoiled the impression. We stopped outside number thirty-seven and double-parked next to an Aston Martin. Cheryl delved into her shoulder bag and produced a ten-pound note which she gave to the driver.

'There's an antique market at the Angel,' she said. 'I'll meet you there.'

She kissed my cheek. I watched her walk away, swinging her shoulder bag. Watched her tight arse do its little rumba, the stride of her long legs encased in tight blue jeans, the bob of her ponytail. Once again I reminded myself how lucky I was to have friends like Cheryl. And Cheryl's daddy. I tucked my manuscript under my arm and climbed the steps to the front door.

The woman who answered was short and wide. She had olive skin and was wearing a black ensemble beneath a white lace pinafore, with a white lace tiara pinned to her black hair.

'I'm J. Fitz Kennedy,' I said.

'I Consuela. You com' thees way. Miss Wal'tino òn phone. She see you som' minutes.'

I followed Consuela across a deep blue carpet between walls lined with softly-lit paintings in gilt frames, into a room which I guessed must be the library because the walls were crammed with more books than Murray's Barber Shop. There was a Chesterfield setting of club chairs and sofa around a coffee table on either side of a white marble fireplace. I chose one of the club chairs.

'You make self comfor'ble. I bring coffee.'

I submerged into a leather bath. Rested my nape on soft calfskin, my arms on padded sides. Gazed at the rug beneath the carved teak coffee table and wondered how many years at three pounds an hour it would take to buy it. Wondered how many of the books Helen Valentino had read, and concluded all of them.

Heard the rattle of fine china. Watched Consuela deposit a heavy silver tray on the table. When she poured coffee from a silver jug and blessed the biscuits with a wave of her hand, I felt as if I had just been crowned King of Spain.

'*Gracias, Consuela.*'

'*De nada, señor.*'

Consuela retreated, smiling.

The coffee was exquisite. The sponge biscuits dissolved on my tongue.

I wanted this. Wanted all of it. The Aston Martin. The biscuits. The house, the books, the Spanish maid. The special smell of money, oozing from everything in the room. The figurines on the mantelpiece, the paintings, the rugs. I felt like Aladdin, transported by the genie from his single room in Himalaya Street to the place of his dreams and desires.

Was it possible? Was the genie a parrot called Pavarotti? Was my manuscript a magic carpet?

The door opened and a woman entered. She was tall and thin, wearing a floral dress that hung from her shoulders with little deviation. A long face, nose too large, mouth too small, eyes heavy, as if resigned to the *ennui* of the everyday world. She had thin, bare arms, tanned and freckled. As I stood to greet her, I realised she was older by maybe ten years than she had at first appeared. She extended thin fingers.

'Mister Kennedy. I'm Helen Valentino. Awfully sorry to have kept you waiting. I see Consuela has been looking after you. Please. Do sit down.'

Her voice had a velvety lowlands Scottish accent. She sat on the sofa, crossed her legs, and folded her dress over her knees as if the sight of them might excite or offend me.

'It's very good of you to see me.'

'I don't know him personally, but Mister Cole is a contact of a Los Angeles colleague.' She looked at me as she might a piece of furniture at auction, appraising my worth, deciding whether I merited closer inspection. 'When asked to help under such circumstances, one does what one can. One never knows when one might need a favour in return.'

No indeed, I thought, one certainly doesn't.

She poured coffee for herself and topped up my cup.

'Now I must warn you, Mister Kennedy. As an unknown writer, your chances of being published are very remote. I do hope you understand.'

'I do,' I said.

Solemnly. As if I had just taken a marriage vow.

'And even if you do become published, it's highly unlikely that you'll earn more than a few pounds. Two hundred perhaps. Possibly five. Will you please keep that in mind at all times?'

'I will.'

'Good.' She took a delicate sip of coffee. 'Now then, do you have something I can read?'

I gave her my part-finished manuscript. She flicked through it in about three seconds, peering through half-spectacles suspended from her neck by a silver chain.

'An interesting idea.' She looked at me over the top of her glasses. 'Whether you can successfully convert it into something people will wish to buy is another matter. How much is here?'

'About sixty thousand words. It's still very rough. Just a first draft.'

She tossed the pages aside as if they were drivel.

'Very well. My assistant will give you my card as you leave. Give her your contact details. She will call you when I've made a decision. It's been a pleasure to meet you, Mister Kennedy. I don't expect I shall see you again, so may I wish you the very best of luck. Keep writing. Don't give up. That's the main thing. Please. Finish your coffee.'

'She said keep writing. Don't give up. And she doesn't expect to see me again.'

We were in a small Italian bistro on Islington High Street. Fake washing strung from wall to wall. Mandolin music. An overripe waitress breastfeeding a *bambino* between customers.

'Well, what did you expect?' Cheryl toyed with a twist of spaghetti. 'That she was going to leap at you with open arms? She's doing you a big favour. You should be grateful.'

I was fed up with being grateful.

'What do you want me to do, Cheryl? Grovel? I didn't ask for this. All it's done is make me realise I'm wasting my time with this fucking book. I might as well go back to Bullock.'

'Maybe you are. Maybe you should.' She helped the spaghetti into her mouth with a spoon, bending low over the plate so as not to splash sauce onto her shirt. 'But isn't it better to find out now? Anyway, Helen Valentino isn't the only agent in town. You might have to go through this a dozen times before you find one who'll accept you. Write a dozen books before you get one published. That, or give up writing altogether. Go back to Bullock if that's what you want to do. The world doesn't care either way.'

I caught the waitress's attention. She waddled across with the baby at her breast and looked at me with dark, hostile eyes. As if she hated all men for what one had done to her. Cheryl said she didn't want any dessert, but I was pissed off so I ordered tiramisu and coffee. The coffee came first. Stale from the Pyrex jug, dropped onto the table one-handed, a small puddle in the saucer. Then the tiramisu from the cabinet in the window. The waitress got cream on her fingers which she sucked then wiped on her apron before dropping the bowl beside the coffee.

At that moment all I wanted was to get back to my room

and the safe arms of the only woman I'd ever been able to handle. But Cheryl seemed to have other ideas. She looked at me, reached across the table and took hold of my hand.

'Let's go back to my place,' she said. 'I think it's time I gave you something special.'

As we left, the waitress said something in Italian which sounded like a curse on me and my offspring. It certainly wasn't '*Have a nice day.*'

Chapter 27

We edged past the buggy and babywear blocking the shared entrance, climbed four flights of stairs to a landing where there were two bedrooms and a bathroom. Then up a spiral staircase into the converted loft where there was a kitchen, another bathroom and an open living space with a balcony overlooking the street. There was a chaise longue along one wall. Cheryl pointed at it.

'You sit there. Make yourself comfortable.'

She went across to the French doors opening onto the balcony and drew the curtains, then moved to the bookcase, took a cassette from its case and snapped it into the stereo. Gentle Hawaiian guitar music filtered into the darkened room, mixed over the sound of lapping waves. Smiling, Cheryl put a finger to her lips then pressed it to mine.

'Close your eyes. Relax. Don't open them until I say. I'll just be a second.'

I lay against the cushions, allowed the music to wash over me, and felt far from London. Behind my closed eyelids I could see Bullock Beach, smell the sweet breeze coming in from Apprehensive Bay, taste the smoky air from a midnight barbecue. I hadn't appreciated how good life had been amid people I'd known since birth, who loved and cared about me and what I might become. Here the air was cold and uncharitable and nobody cared if I lived or died.

A voice began to sing about tropical nights, moonlight and palm trees. I remembered a farewell party for Big Andy. Skinny-dipping in the glimmering sea. Could see the silhouette of a girl, dancing to the seductive beat, rustling her . . .

'Open your eyes.'

She was in the middle of the room, wearing a wicked smile and little else. A necklace of coral. Dried-grass tassels on each nipple. A dried-grass skirt. The music was lilting and soft and she was weaving her body in time to it. Hips from side to side. Hands down each side of her torso and thighs. Fingers splayed coyly across her face, so I could see only her laughing eyes.

'You like?'

'I like.'

The music changed. Drums beat out a driving rhythm. Now Cheryl's arms were spread wide and she was moving her bare feet across the rug in small steps while swivelling her hips at an impossible speed.

'Come on,' she said. 'Dance with me.'

For a while I tried to match my cumbersome body with hers but it was impossible, so I put my hands on her hips and swayed.

'Take something off,' she said.

I laughed. 'There's not much left.'

'Not me, you.'

I stripped off my shirt.

'More.'

Her fingers were at the buckle of my belt. I hopped on one leg, removed trousers, socks and shoes. She put her arms around my neck and kissed me, searching inside my mouth with her tongue. Her dried-grass tassels tickled my chest. Her dried-grass skirt rustled against my groin.

'More.' She slipped off my underpants with both thumbs, fondled my cock until it was bursting at the seams, then unhooked her skirt which fell around her ankles. 'Lie on the rug. Close your eyes. Here comes the special treat. I call it my Horizontal Hula.'

And all the while her hips kept swaying to the beat of the drums.

'Where did you learn to do that?'

We lay on the rug sharing a post-coital joint.

'I used to be a dancer in a Hawaiian floor show.'

'What about the finale?'

'That wasn't part of the act.'

'Did you give private encores?'

'Does it matter? I think you're a terrific guy who's going to be a great success. We make a great team. And I think I'm in love with you. Isn't that enough?'

Yeah, I thought. A great team. You, me and Daddy. But my overriding thought was Cheryl's Horizontal Hula. For that at least I was genuinely grateful.

'I love you, too.'

At the time I meant it. At the time I always meant it.

Two weeks later, when I had heard nothing from Helen Valentino or her PA, I'd resigned myself to getting another rejection. *Bomber!* was opening in Plymouth on a trial run prior to the West End, so I went with Cheryl to Paddington, waved as the train rolled out of the station, then made my way back to Himalaya Street. But I couldn't face its squalor and the loneliness of my single room, so I took the Tube to Marble Arch. As we rocked beneath London I remembered the trouble I'd made for myself when I'd confessed love to Maria Santos Almeida in return for Going All The Way. Was I falling into the same trap with Cheryl?

The trouble this time was, if love equated with obsession, with absorption, with a complete preoccupation, then I loved someone else. It didn't matter whether I was sitting at my chipped oak desk at Hire-A-Hack trying to turn a garbled translation into plain English or making love with Cheryl, she was always there. Laura Friday. With a bloody parrot on her shoulder.

I'd emerged at Marble Arch into bright sunshine and begun to walk through Hyde Park alongside the Bayswater Road when a hand grabbed my arm.

'*Fitz!*'

'*Frankie!*'

'*Fuck!*'

We went into an impulsive hug. With her hair against my cheek, London disappeared. I was in a room at the Yes Oh Yes Motel with a suspended ship's steering wheel, lifebuoy-and-knotted-rope wallpaper, making love on a shagpile sea.

'How amazing! I was just thinking about you. I'm always thinking about you.'

'Crap!' She laughed. 'You always were full of Irish blarney. I heard you were in town. Why haven't you been to see me or even called?'

With the blink of an eye the scene changed. It wasn't me but Dick Worth who was undressing her, carrying her to the unmade bed, his second-hand penis rampant.

'How did you hear?'

'One of the subs on the paper. Said you were working at Hire-A-Hack. What are you doing here? Where are you living?'

'You're why I'm here. Aunt Agnes gave me the money to come and see you. When I got here, you were in Vienna.'

'But why didn't you let me know you were coming?'

'I was afraid you'd tell me to stay at home.'

'That's utter crap,' she said. 'I told you before I left Bullock I'd be happy to see you in London any time. Why haven't you called?'

'I was passing the *Chronicle* offices. I went into the library.

Looked up the Penis Transplant story. There was no mention of me. You took all the credit.'

'*Chronicle* readers don't know or care about you, Fitz. How I get my stories isn't news.'

'There was a big splash on you spending an afternoon with Dick Worth, though.'

'You shouldn't believe everything you read in the papers, Fitz.' Frankie's face was granite, her voice blue steel. A storm was brewing and in Hyde Park there was no shelter. 'You're not the only person who writes fiction. The Afternoon Delight story never happened. I agreed the idea with Dick's wife. We spent that afternoon shopping. We concocted the story together. It made the front page, added to my reputation for being a hard-hearted bitch. No one got hurt. Except you. I thought you'd never see it. I'm sorry, but sometimes these things happen.'

As the storm broke around me, all I could think of was the old Buddy Holly classic. 'Raining in my Heart.'

'But why would you want that kind of reputation?'

Frankie laughed.

'You really don't get it, do you? Mary Francesca Wilton is a face I wear for the public. A character I play. The tough female reporter who'll do anything for a story. It gets me the top assignments. I'm the first woman to join the *Chronicle* editorial board. Next stop, the Editor's chair. Where nice girls don't get to sit.'

'What are you saying? Underneath that tough exterior there's a woman who cries when she cuts her finger? I'm not sure she even bleeds.'

'If that's how you choose to see me, that's your problem. It's time you learned to face up to situations, Fitz. You think I should have given you credit for the transplant story? Well, I did. Behind the scenes. My editors got glowing reports. If you'd called me, I'd have got you interviews other people would cut off their right arm for. You could have walked into a job at the *Chronicle*. But instead you went off and created your own scenario.

'I have to go,' she said. 'They're giving me an award for the transplant story at the Grosvenor House tonight. I have to get ready and I haven't written my speech yet. Do you want to come? Anyone who's anyone in the media will be there. I'll make it up to you. Give you a big mention. You could stand up and take a bow.'

I was torn. My head was saying I'd lost the fight, was hurting, and in no mood for Frankie's crumbs of compassion. There was a new woman in my life. I couldn't let Cheryl down. My heart was telling me the opposite. Then Frankie gave me that twisted smile and I had no choice.

There were twelve at the round table. I knew two. Frankie, stunning in a backless number that left just enough to the imagination, and Pete the photographer, all wrong in a tuxedo and combed hair. I'd been introduced to the others when we sat down, but they'd given me that English look. I was a nobody. I didn't belong. I wasn't worth their time.

I tried to make conversation with a woman on my right, but she kept turning her shoulder and I found myself talking to her mole. Frankie was on my left. She kept squeezing my hand, saying nice things.

'Thanks for coming, Fitz. So good to see you again. Having a good time?'

I reminded myself not to be fooled. This was the Frankie who'd wooed my mum and dad. The Frankie I'd fallen in love with. If her public face was a performance, this was too. For me, and for anyone who might be watching. But it didn't make any difference.

She'd done a twirl for me on the pavement outside her flat.

'What do you think?'

'I'm speechless.'

'That bad, huh?'

'No, that good.'

We'd touched hands a lot. In the cab. Beneath the table. Held each other's eyes. The flame still burned. At least, it did for me. Frankie was more worried about her speech.

'I'm sure you'll be fine.'

I must have said it a thousand times, but she didn't seem to hear. Just kept looking at her notes. All the same, I guessed she'd invited me to provide reassurance. I couldn't help wondering who'd have been in my chair if I'd turned the invitation down.

When she was in Bullock, Frankie had told me how impossible it was to sustain a relationship with a job like hers. Maybe that was why she was so hard on herself and other people. To protect herself from the inevitable.

We were into the coffee and liqueurs before they started the presentations. I'd been to plenty of Bullock Personality of the Year Award dinners for the *Telegraph*'s Social Diary, and although this was glitzier the speeches were no better. After about half an hour a guy with bad teeth and fat fingers got up and told everyone how terrific Frankie's story had been for the *Chronicle*, its international affiliates and the whole wide world.

'That's Jimmy Eckford,' Frankie whispered before she stood up to head for the platform. 'Owns the paper. I'll introduce you to him later.'

'Good luck.'

I squeezed her fingers as she brushed past.

After she'd kissed Eckford's cheek and taken hold of her award, Frankie turned to the microphone.

'There are a thousand people I could thank,' she said. 'But this isn't Oscar Night and you've all got homes to go to. So I'm just going to thank one. His name's J. Fitz Kennedy. Without Fitz I wouldn't be standing here. When Fitz realised that Dick Worth's sister had a redundant penis he grasped it—'

The audience erupted. Frankie grinned and relaxed.

'He grasped the implications. Saw just how big it could become.'

Frankie paused for a full minute to allow the convulsed audience to settle. Then she went on.

'Fitz deserves the credit for making the Dick Worth Transplant story such a huge success. In my opinion he's got a great future in journalism. He's here tonight. And he's looking for a job. Fitz, would you stand please so that everyone can see you.'

The woman with the mole spoke to me after that.

'Do you want to come up for coffee?'

I'd kissed Frankie in the cab. Guilty kisses. Now we were hugging outside Frankie's front door. Guilty hugs. Coffee didn't mean coffee. Troy Weeks knew that, and so did I.

'Frankie, there's something I have to tell you.'

'You've found someone? Already?'

'Cheryl Cole. She's an actress. She's in Plymouth trying out a new musical.'

'Wow!' Frankie stood back. Her eyes widened. 'Not exactly dying of a broken heart, then, Fitz.'

'She's a kind, generous person. I owe her a lot.'

'You in love with her?'

'I told her I am. Right now I'm not so sure.'

Frankie sighed. 'Fitz, here's the deal. We've had a great time tonight. I got my award, you got God knows how many offers of job interviews. When you're not in one of your sulks, you're great company. I'm having a terrific time and I don't want it to end. I'd like to sleep with you. No strings. You can piss off back to your actress in the morning if that's what you want. Or not. It's up to you.'

I looked into Frankie's eyes. And reached for the doorknob.

Chapter 28

I left Frankie's place on Sunday morning before the sun was up, went back to Himalaya Street, tried to work, but for once found the page staring back. I decided my body needed exercise and my brain a rest, so I got the bike out and pedalled west to Hammersmith, then along the towpath, following the Boat Race course to Putney, Barnes and Mortlake.

A crisp mist hung above the water. A crew of four dipped its oars in unison, pursued by an outboard motor and a megaphone ('*Rhythm, gentlemen, rhythm. Follow stroke, dip, don't plunge!*'). A swan on its long take-off run lumbered into the sky like a 747.

Into Richmond then up the hill to the park, its main gates closed but a side gate open for bikes and joggers. The sun was just rising, the fresh air filled with new promise. I was the day's first human. I saw a fox slink home. Saw a grey carpet of rabbits flow like mercury over glass at my approach. Saw a herd of fallow deer trot among the bracken. And as I crested the hill, I saw all of London, laid out before me. Waiting to be conquered? Or scornfully dismissive?

I fantasised Helen Valentino, apologising for not calling sooner, but excited about giving me the good news. Then a cloud covered the sun and there was nothing but toil, tears and sweat. Years of Himalaya Street squalor. German pharmaceutical sales manuals, forever seeking *Lebensraum*. A raddled middle-aged Hire-A-Hack supporting the bar at the Rising Sun, wondering if he could afford to pay for the next round. Beyond that? What Dad would have called the Dank Void of old age.

I'd always wanted to be a fiction writer. But what if fiction writing didn't want me? I'd never considered an alternative. Now I was being offered one on a plate. Wouldn't a reporting job be a sensible career move? Big salary, expense account, all the toys. Wasn't last night what life was all about? Using people to get what you wanted? Wasn't that what Frankie Wilton had done?

And what about Cheryl? Could I shrug off sex with Frankie as an aberration or should I tell Cheryl everything? Now that she'd done her Horizontal Hula for me, were we beyond friendship? Committed to each other? How would I feel if she slept with Brad in Plymouth? Would she tell me if she had?

The answers, I decided as I rode back down Richmond Hill, lay elsewhere and with another woman. It was time to give my heart a break, and use my brain for a change.

I decided to let Helen Valentino make my decision for me.

If she took me on as a client, my writing career would take off and I would stick with Cheryl. We were a great team. She would inspire and motivate me, which Frankie never would. If Helen turned me down, my writing career would struggle, maybe for a short time, maybe forever. In which case I'd be better off taking up one of the offers from last night's dinner. I'd almost certainly lose Cheryl. And as for Frankie? I'd see her from time to time whenever our paths crossed. I didn't hold any greater expectations or hopes than that.

If and when the phone rang I'd have my answer. Meanwhile my night with Frankie would remain my secret. I was used to keeping secrets. I'd grown up in a house where a white lie was better than a black truth and within a religion where blind faith was better than clear-eyed questions.

I was in my room that Sunday evening when Alex pounded on my door.

'Fitz, phone!'

My gut took a wrench. Could it be Helen Valentino? I didn't dare hope. I took the stairs three at a time, paused to gather my breath before taking hold of the dangling receiver.

'Hi! This is Fitz!'

'Darling, it's me.'

'Oh!'

'What's the matter? Did you think I might be Helen?'

'Sorry. How are the dress rehearsals going?'

'Dreadful. The show's running far too long. Brad's about as exciting as a broom handle. Everyone keeps forgetting their lines. One of the flats fell over. The conductor gave us three wrong cues . . . '

I leaned against the wall, half-listening to Cheryl's litany of woes. I knew I should care. Knew I should take as much interest in her career as she did in mine. But Laura Friday's voice was too dominant, too demanding to allow me to focus on anyone else.

'Look, I just called to say I love you and I miss you. I have to go, there's someone waiting to use the phone. Wish me luck?'

'Of course. All the luck in the world.'

'Let me know what happens with Helen. What did you do last night, by the way? I called but they said you were out.'

'Oh, nothing much. Went to a movie. My favourite. *Some Like It Hot.* Everyone in the audience sang along with Marilyn Monroe. *Boo-boop-ee-doo.* Great ending. "Nobody's perfect." See you soon.'

I replaced the receiver feeling like the world's biggest shit.

Chapter 29

Ten-forty-five the following morning. John and Nigel had been meeting for fifteen minutes. Roger was fussing over a layout. I'd been stuck for twenty minutes on page 362, *'How to Handle the Confrontation With Herr Doktor'*, my mind a million miles away.

Jane took a call.

'Hire-A-Hack, how may I help you?' She covered the mouthpiece. 'Fitz, it's for you.'

I wiped a sweaty hand on my jeans and took hold of the receiver.

'Hi! This is Fitz!'

'Mister Kennedy, this is Carol Wellesley. Helen Valentino's PA.'

'Yes.' My heart felt fit to burst through my chest. My tongue hit the roof of my mouth. 'Good morning.'

'Helen has read your manuscript.'

'Good, yes, uh-huh.'

'Are you free for lunch today? One o'clock at Le Gavroche?'

'Er, yes, wonderful, great, certainly.'

'Good. Helen will see you there.'

'Did she like—'

But Carol was gone. I gave Jane the receiver.

'She wants to take me to lunch.'

'Who does?'

'Helen Valentino. When I saw her she said she didn't think she'd ever see me again. Now she wants to take me to lunch.

Helen Valentino. Wants to take me to lunch. Helen does. Helen Valentino. When I saw her—'

'Fitz, I got that bit. Where?'

'Place called Le Gavroche.'

'Upper Brook Street,' said Roger. 'Albert Roux. Top-notch grub. You'll need a tie.' He began to fumble in his drawers. 'Sure I've got one somewhere.'

He found it underneath a pile of papers. A yellow background, spotted with Winnie the Pooh characters. When the morning meeting broke up, John and Nigel joined the ad hoc J. Fitz Kennedy Luncheon Organising Committee.

'They won't let you in without a jacket,' said John. 'We're about the same size. Borrow mine. Can't wear those filthy trainers, either. Swap shoes with him, Nigel. They're open. We've got two hours. Better get there before the rush.'

'Three good horses today, too,' said Nigel. 'One's called Beans On Toast. Seems like a good omen to me.'

They poured me out of the Rising Sun and into a black cab at ten to one. John, Roger and Nigel on the pavement, swaying and waving. Me waving through the back window clutching John's loan for the fare. The driver spoke out of the side of his mouth.

'Where to, guv?'

'Le Gavroche.'

'Lovely jubbly. Taking out a mortgage?'

'What for?'

'Pay for it. Fucking Albert, Gavroche is.'

'Albert?'

'Albert Speer. Dear. Mate of mine had his twenty-fifth wedding anniversary there. Him and his old woman. Cost him three nuns.'

173

'Nuns?'

'Tons. Hundreds. I says to him, "Fred, mate, you'd a bin better orf givin' her a right good seeing-to and a packet of crisps." But he says, "Nah, she'd a just thrown a Fagin".'

'Fagin?'

'Moody. Ron Moody. Don' choo speak English? Where you from then?'

'New Zealand.'

'My daughter lives in Australia and New Zealand. Sydney. You might know her. Sheila Stubbs. Mind you, everyone's called Sheila over there, 'n't they?'

'Only the women. The guys are all called Barry.'

'You pulling my Watney's?'

'Watney's?'

'Watney's Keg. Leg. Here you go, guv. Posh.'

'Let me guess. Posh nosh. Gavroche.'

'Nah, mate, this place. It's posh.'

The *maitre d'* let his eyes hover over my makeshift ensemble just long enough to let me know I should have used the tradesmen's entrance before leading me to a table by the window.

Helen Valentino was wearing a cream dress and pearls, and looked ready to launch something.

'*I name this book* Laura Friday. *God bless all who read her.*'

'Mister Kennedy.' She rested her glass on the linen and looked at me with sharper intent than she had on Saturday. 'How good of you to come at such short notice.'

'It was either this or Marmite sandwiches.' The restaurant was awash with celebrity, so no one took any notice of me. I sat back to allow the waiter to pour me a Perrier. 'Do you mind calling me Fitz? Mister Kennedy makes me feel about a nun. That's a hundred, apparently.'

'What is?'

'A nun. Rhymes with ton. Ton means a hundred.'

'What on earth are you talking about, Mister Kennedy?'

'I've no idea. Shall we start again?'

'I'd like to know more about you. How old are you?'

'Twenty-six.'

'I can't place your accent. Where do you come from?'

'Little town called Bullock. New Zealand.'

'Oh dear.' She shook her head. 'And what sort of a childhood did you have? Unhappy, I hope. What about your parents? Did they divorce when you were very young? Were you abused as a child?'

'Mum's a receptionist at the hospital. Dad plays and sings at the Workingmen's Club every Friday. Mum joins them occasionally. My sister Carmel's a nun. I had a very happy childhood. My parents are still together. And quite happy as far as I know.'

'No, no,' she said. 'That won't do at all. I'll ask our creative people to come up with something.'

'Why? What's wrong?'

'Fitz,' she said, leaning forward, 'I think you've created something powerful with Laura Friday and Pavarotti the parrot. I like what you've written so far. I spoke to my people this morning and I've sent them copies of your half-finished manuscript. My guess is we'll be looking at offers before the end of the week. But that's just the beginning. It's my task to make you a marketable commodity. A brand. When we launch you, it must be as a complete package. When someone's browsing in a bookshop we have eight seconds in which to make a sale. Cover design. Title. Blurb. Biography. First page. Get those right, add in a hard-hitting publicity campaign, and we stand a good chance. Bullock? Sorry. I'm sure it's a charming place, but no one's ever heard of it. What's that New

Zealand bird? The kiwi? It doesn't fly. Nor does Bullock.'

All this as Helen sipped at her Perrier and fixed me with her unsmiling eyes. This restaurant felt like a foreign country, a million miles from Frankie Wilton and my catharsis. As far as I was concerned, Laura Friday was redundant. When I'd left Frankie on Sunday morning I'd left my nemesis behind. I'd already begun to think about other characters, other stories. I wanted to talk about my long-term future as a writer. But I couldn't tell that to Helen Valentino. Not yet, anyway.

'Anything else?'

'I don't like your name.'

'J. Fitz Kennedy?'

'No, no, no.' She shook her head. 'That will never do. You're not a literary writer. Not F. Scott Fitzgerald. You'll never win a Booker. Your name's too . . . too . . . we need something harder-hitting. To reflect the genre you're writing in. The brand name must always reflect the genre. Otherwise you're likely to get cognitive dissonance, and that can have a disastrous effect on sales.'

'Are you saying I've got to use a pen name?'

'A *nom de plume*, yes.' Helen frowned. 'Is that a problem? Because if it is, say so now and we'll forget the whole thing.' She looked at her watch. 'I've got a very busy schedule.'

I've never been able to hide how I feel. It must have been obvious to Helen that I was unhappy. Her face softened. She laid a bony hand on top of mine.

'Look, it's not the end of the world. It's far more common than you might think. Look at all the movie stars who've changed their name. Michael Caine, John Wayne, Cary Grant, Bob Hope, Marilyn Monroe. Who are your favourite authors?'

'John le Carré.'

'His real name's David Cornwell.'

'George Orwell.'

'Eric Blair.'

'Splint Macramé.'

Helen's laugh sounded like a triumphant trumpet.

'A perfect example. Splint Macramé was actually a woman. Jenny Weston. She was one of our clients. Jenny had always wanted to write hard-boiled detective fiction, but her real name didn't suit that genre at all. You wouldn't have bought a Troy Weeks book if it had been written by Jenny Weston. English romance would have been fine, but not tough American gangster stuff. She was a nurse in the Orthopaedic Unit at the Surrey General Hospital. That's where the Splint came from. And her hobby was arts and crafts.'

I felt betrayed. One of the foundations upon which my adolescent life had been built had just been kicked away.

'What do you suggest, then?'

A thin smile of victory passed across Helen's face.

'Something strong, easy to remember, slightly unusual.'

I had a bizarre fantasy of Helen as my pregnant wife, discussing baby names.

'Tell me more about your background. Your father. What does he do?'

'He's a dentist.'

Helen winced, gritted her perfect teeth.

'Mmm. Nothing there. Hobbies?'

'He spends most of his time dismantling and reassembling an old Vincent motorbike.'

'Yes, yes.' Helen pouted as she thought. 'Vincent's good. Suggests invincibility, success, triumph. Now what about a surname?'

I remembered the wonderful old car Dad used to drive.

'How about Humber? Vince Humber?'

Helen gave me a surprised smile.

'You really do come up with some original ideas, don't you?

I like it. Vince Humber. We'll go with that. I'll consult with my people of course, take a straw poll, but that's what we'll go with.'

'So what happens to J. Fitz Kennedy?'

Helen looked impatient and checked her watch again.

'You're not changing your name, Fitz. This is just a marketing exercise. Whenever you appear in public, on television, in newspaper and magazine interviews, you'll be in your role as the creator of Laura Friday, so you'll be Vince Humber. On contracts, and in private, you'll remain J. Fitz Kennedy. You'll soon get used to it. In fact it can be a huge benefit that people don't identify you everywhere you go. You'll be able to put your name in the phone book, for example, and people won't bother you. Now we've got to decide where you come from. Kennedy. I don't suppose your people are from Ireland by any chance?'

'Yes, as a matter of fact. A little place called Blackjack. County Mayo. I've never been there.'

'Perfect.' Helen gave me her triumphant smile again. 'Ireland says vigour, humour, energy, madness, music, and a great literary heritage. I'll get my people to do some research on Blackjack, and we'll develop a biography based on your Irish roots. Then you'll be able to talk convincingly. No pun intended.' She glanced at the menu. 'I can recommend the *ris de veau*, by the way. You're a very lucky man, Fitz. I never consider unsolicited manuscripts. If it hadn't been for your contact through our Los Angeles office, I'd never have looked at you. She's your girlfriend, is she?'

'Who?'

'Cheryl Cole. Martin Cole's daughter.'

'Yes. I guess so.'

'You don't sound too sure.'

'Cheryl's terrific. We met soon after we'd both arrived in London. She's in Plymouth at the moment. Trying out a new musical. Tonight's the first night.'

'Her father's Los Angeles connection could be important,' said Helen. 'I'll be talking to our movie division about setting up bids for an option. I've been wondering whether we might market Laura Friday as the female James Bond.'

I felt as if I was being swept downstream towards the Victoria Falls. Unless I threw out an anchor I'd be crushed by overpowering forces.

'Look, Helen. This all sounds terrific,' I said. 'But *When the Fat Parrot Sings* is strictly a one-off. Once the book's finished I want to move on to other ideas. I'm planning to kill Laura and Pavarotti off in the final chapter.'

'*You can't do that!*'

Helen put down her glass and stared at me as if I'd gone insane.

'I'm not going to put myself and my people to all this time, trouble and expense for just one book. Laura Friday's a potentially highly lucrative brand. It can sometimes take two or even three books before an idea really takes off. This is a long-term investment, Fitz. If you try something else it might be rubbish. In fact it almost certainly will be. Laura's what you're good at. Which means you'll almost certainly not be as good at anything else. It's up to you, of course. You're the writer. But if you want my help, and the total resources of the Philip Bedford International organisation, which is something most writers would give their eye teeth for, you'll have to commit to at least six Laura Fridays, with a renewable option for another six after that.'

'Laura's not someone I want to live with for the next ten years,' I said. 'She's ruthless. She doesn't care who she hurts. She's got no charm. And she's a killer.'

'Which is precisely why she's perfect for the 'eighties,' said Helen. 'Thatcher. Falklands. The Me Generation. Everyone out for themselves. Preying on the weak. Money. Power. Laura's a symbol for the women of our times. That's why Vince Humber is so perfect. And the parrot Pavarotti is a stroke of sheer genius.'

I smiled, thinking about the inspired evening at the Long John Silver. Cheryl's face aglow, excited as hell when she came up with Pavarotti's name. We'd only just met, but we were already a great team. I must have been crazy to go to the awards night with Frankie. Insane to have spent the night with her. Cheryl was perfect. I wished she could have been beside me. She wouldn't have had any doubts about my future.

'What sort of money are we talking about?'

'It will depend on the bidding,' said Helen.

'For what? Exactly?'

'An advance on the first six books. Royalties once the advance has been breached. Then there'll be the film rights. Other media. Serialisation. Video's becoming important. Talking books. Merchandising. PBI will handle everything. Publicity, signings, contract negotiations. We take twenty per cent. It's more than some agencies, but you get a far higher figure through us so you end up better off. Plus the PBI name opens doors all over the world. Asia's a very big market these days. We have offices in Hong Kong, Singapore, Bangkok.'

'And what do I have to do now?'

'Finish the book. Our editors will polish it, in consultation with you, of course. Once everyone's happy we'll market it, and leave you to get to work on your second Laura Friday. We'll be looking for one book per year, eighteen months at the most. So that we can keep the Laura Friday brand fresh and in front of your public. We should be able to get an immediate retainer to you by some time next week. Ten per cent, the remainder payable on delivery of the finished manuscript. I'll ask you to come in to sign as soon as they're ready.'

I couldn't believe this was actually happening. Maybe it

was all a big practical joke. I took a long drink of Perrier and examined Helen's serious face for a telltale twitch.

'Do you have any idea how much we might be talking about?'

'One, perhaps one and a half. Two would be exciting.'

'Two what?'

'Million.'

'Are you pulling my Watney's?'

Chapter 30

I walked from Mayfair to Belgravia. I hadn't had the nerve to ask Helen Valentino for the money for a bus, let alone a taxi. Anyway, I liked the irony. Broke today, tomorrow a millionaire. One day I'd write a story about it.

What with walking on air, skipping into gutters like Gene Kelly in *Singin' in the Rain*, dancing backwards, bumping into people and doffing my imaginary cap, it took me an hour. Jane was alone in the office, preparing afternoon tea, when I tripped over Naples and fell at her feet.

'No need to grovel,' she said. 'Flowers'll do. How'd it go?'

'She said whoever thought of a parrot called Pavarotti's a genius. Going to look for bids of around two million pounds. Wants six Laura Fridays with six more after that.'

'She liked it, then.'

'Loved it.'

'Suppose you'll be leaving us now.'

'Suppose I will.'

'We'll miss you.'

'Miss you, too.'

'Told Cheryl yet?'

'Not yet.'

'Don't you think you'd better?'

'I was going to call her. Tell her the news and wish her luck for her first night.'

'Just a phone call? That's not very romantic. Jump on a train. Take her out after the show. Here.' She reached into a drawer, took out her petty cash tin. 'Two hundred quid. Pay us back when you're rich and famous. Now bugger off.'

As I slipped into my seat, the orchestra was playing an overture of World War Two tunes to overpower the rustle of chocolate wrappers and the last-minute gossip. Then the auditorium went black, cowing the audience into silence.

A sound came from behind us, distant at first, then nearer and louder. A sputtering aircraft engine, coughing and cracking, the dull crump of gunfire in the background, flashes of bright white light from all sides. The sounds became deafening, and there, right above our heads, was a bomber on fire, flames licking its wings. We could hear the calm voices inside: *'Steady, Jack'*, *'Think we'll make it, skipper?' 'Sure thing, bud.'* A woman in the next row screamed, but most of us held our breath. Then the bomber was gone, the curtain rising, chorus and orchestra crashing into the opening number, 'Coming in on a Wing and a Prayer', the audience on its feet cheering its ovation.

The trouble was, the thing with the bomber before the curtain went up was the best part of the show. If they'd saved it until later, perhaps it would have kept the audience interested. There was some good ensemble stuff with hammers and spanners on 'String of Pearls', and 'Boogie Woogie Bugle Boy From Company B' had the audience clapping along, but most of the show was one soporific ballad after another about boys far from home or meeting again some sunny day. There were empty seats after the interval and, as the show dragged to an overdue end, it became clear there'd be no surprises for those who'd stuck it out. The Yanks won the war.

Nobody cried when Chuck failed to come back, and when Cheryl as Suzie sang 'My Man's Missing in Action' half the audience cheered.

I'd spent most of the show watching Cheryl. She looked good, even in a boiler suit and headscarf with black grease marks on both cheeks, and she danced well enough, but her singing voice sounded thin and she had trouble staying in tune. She'd have had a good reception on Talent Night at the Bullock Workingmen's Club, but the Plymouth audience had paid good money. All she got when she took her bow was a scattering of applause and a big cheer from a guy at the back who rose to his feet and whistled. I took no notice of the puzzled stares.

'Did you ever read "The Indian To His Love?" *Here we will moor our lonely ship / And wander ever with woven hands*?'

'Who wrote that?'

'Yeats.'

'Who's Yeats?'

'The world's greatest ever poet.'

'Never heard of him.'

Cheryl blew smoke at the ceiling, passed me the roach. I took it between thumb and forefinger, sucked, inhaled. My smoke joined hers beneath the yellow plaster.

'Only poet I know's Robert Frost. We did him at school. I learned some Shakespeare at drama school. I was never into poetry. Except for maybe Bob Dylan, John Lennon, Joni Mitchell. Why? Are we going to stay in this crappy hotel room forever? Spend the rest of our lives doing what we just did?'

I rolled over, caressed Cheryl's cheek.

'I was just lying here thinking. I feel as if you and I have sailed to a new land. We've come ashore. And now we're going to explore it.'

'What's this new land called?'

'Togetherland.'

'That's nice. Is that what you want? Or are you just saying

that to make me feel good? Because you don't have to, you know. I'll get over tonight. There'll be other shows.'

Backstage had felt like a morgue when I'd tapped on Cheryl's dressing-room door. After I'd lied about her performance and told her my news, we'd skipped the First Night Party. Cheryl said it would be a wake and we should look for somewhere to eat. But at eleven on a Monday night everywhere in Plymouth was closed, except for a 24/7 corner shop where we'd bought bread, cheese, ham and chilled champagne and gone back to Cheryl's room.

'I'm not just saying it. I want us to be together. We're a great team. If it hadn't been for you, I wouldn't have created Pavarotti the parrot, wouldn't have met Helen Valentino, would never have had this break.'

'Gratitude's not much of a foundation for a relationship, Fitz. It could become a burden. You could end up resenting me.'

'It's more than that. You're sweet and kind and funny. You have a smart brain, a terrific body. And I love you.'

'I love you, too. I'm very proud of you. I guess this means you'll be moving out of Himalaya Street.'

I sucked my teeth, pursed my lips.

'Tough decision. But I guess you're right. Why don't we look for somewhere together? If this all works out, we might even be able to buy somewhere.'

'You're sure about this, Fitz?'

'Hundred per cent.'

'Then yeah, I'd love to.'

'I told Helen I only want to write one Laura Friday book. I didn't tell her why I created her in the first place. About Frankie. Coming down here on the train I was thinking. I don't want to be tied down to a long-term contract. Helen's talking about six Fridays with an option for another six after that and changing my name to Vince Humber. In my head I'm over Frankie now.

I'm not sure I even want to write one Laura Friday, let alone twelve.'

'What did Helen say?'

'It's Laura Friday or nothing. She's not interested in anything else I've written, or might write in the future. What do you think?'

'I think you'd be crazy to turn Helen down. After all your hard work. After everything Daddy and I have done to help you. This is a golden opportunity. If you let it go, Fitz, you could be stuck in Himalaya Street forever. I'm not sure I could handle that. How come you're over Frankie all of a sudden, anyway?'

'It was your Horizontal Hula. How could I think about anyone else after that?'

Cheryl laughed. 'So what are you going to do?'

'Take you with me across the ocean of life to Togetherland.'

'Do you really love me?'

'Of course I do.'

At the time I meant it. At the time I always meant it.

Chapter 31

The Signing Ceremony was low-key. No speeches, no handshakes for the cameras, no exchange of pens. We met in the PBI boardroom on a wet Friday morning. PBI had offices in Covent Garden, overlooking the cobbled square where magicians and fire-breathers made more money from the tourist trade than made sense. Helen Valentino was in charcoal pinstripes, a single string of pearls, tight smile, perfect hair. Beside her was Tom Prescott-Jones, PBI's contracts maestro, who'd whittled offers down until he was happy with the form and size of the winner. Carol Wellesley, Helen's PA, was dishing out documents like fine china plates at a corporate lunch.

'This is the agreement between you and PBI.'

Helen's thin fingers slid it across the table. I wondered if she played piano. If she'd taken it up as a kid, she might have given Daniel Barenboim a run for his money. But then, so would I. Out of a thousand paths, we choose only one.

I flicked through the clauses, codicils, definitions and footnotes, clicked the pen Carol had placed at my right hand.

'Aren't you going to read it, Fitz?'

Tom looked crestfallen. As if his distended sentences packed with more riders than the Grand National merited more than a passing glance.

'You take twenty per cent of everything,' I said. 'What else do I need to know?'

'Terms and conditions,' said Tom. 'Notification of intention to terminate. Parameters of responsibility.'

'I write the books. You sell them,' I said. 'Isn't that how it goes?'

'Not quite, Fitz,' said Helen. 'Remember what I said at lunch the other day? Think of us as Vince Humber's Brand Managers. We devise marketing strategies and implement them. Packaging. Promotion. Advertising. PR. In conjunction with third parties, of course. From now on, you won't have to worry about a thing. Tax? We have people who'll ensure you never pay a penny more than you absolutely have to. Bills? We'll pay them for you. Health? You're covered through us. Travel? Carol will take care of everything. If the PBI Learjet's free, you're welcome to use it. Our objective is to give you the freedom to do what you do best: write Laura Friday books.'

I looked at the three expectant faces, pen poised. This was it, then. The Faustian moment. I remembered those old Saturday-morning movies at the Bullock Ritz when a grizzled cowboy and an Indian brave would seal their brotherhood by slicing open a finger and mingling their blood. Maybe Helen and I should do the same. Maybe I should sign with a bloody fingerprint. J. Fitz Kennedy: his mark. Or was it Vince Humber?

'You initial the bottom of each page,' said Carol. 'And sign the last.'

'If you're happy,' said Tom.

Happy? The country's best literary agent was about to take me under her wing. Sitting alongside the agency agreement was a contract to die for. My fortune stretched before me like the Yellow Brick Road. In Cheryl, I had a beautiful friend, lover, partner. Of course I was happy. Only a fool wouldn't be.

I did as I was told and earned Carol's languid praise as if I was a kid on a potty.

'Well done, Fitz.'

We shook hands all round. Carol offered a fragrant cheek. I gave her twenty per cent of mine.

'Now for the Laura Friday contract,' said Tom. 'It's with Langford's. Top international publishing house, part of the Berthold media empire. You have until May next year to complete *When the Fat Parrot Sings*. They want six Fridays over a maximum of nine years, option for a further six after that on negotiable terms, excellent royalty sequence. One-point-eight on acceptance of *Fat Parrot*, royalties kick in once the advance has been breached. Ten per cent up front. I've got their cheque for one-eighty. Less our commission there's one-forty-four sitting in your account. As long as you're happy.'

That word again. What the fuck did it mean? What was I supposed to say? Why was everyone so concerned about my happiness?

'Very,' I said.

And initialled wherever Carol pointed her manicured finger.

'I think we should celebrate,' said Helen. 'Let's go to lunch. Fitz, you choose. Where would you like to go?'

'Maxim's of Paris, I think. If the Learjet's free.'

A few days later, Cheryl and I flew to Los Angeles. *Bomber!* had struggled through the first week of its Plymouth run under a barrage of critical flak, then ditched. With time on her hands, Cheryl had begun to look for somewhere for us to live. Meanwhile I'd no sooner told Alex I was leaving Himalaya Street than a biltong-chewing South African in tight shorts and safari boots was sticking lion posters on the walls of my room and everyone else was moving up a notch.

A Mercedes took us the VIP way into Terminal Four. Through a gate, down a ramp. A guy in a British Airways blazer took our tickets and passports, someone else our bags. Suddenly we were sharing a lounge with the Foreign Secretary, who gave us a glance, decided our votes weren't worth so much as a smile, and returned to his papers.

'Before we go any further I think I should tell you about Daddy.'

Cheryl had asked for a Bloody Mary. It came on a trolley with a supporting cast of sauces, spices and raw oysters. They'd never heard of McCurdle's Special Brew, but promised to have some next time I flew. I had a Heineken instead. I glanced around the room.

'What do you mean, before we go any further? You think I might want to cut and run?'

'Maybe. Have you ever heard of a movie called *Once, Twice, Three Times I Laid Her*?'

'Can't say I have.'

'How about *A-Lamma-Lamma Big-Dong*?'

'Nope.'

'*Foreskin Foray*?'

'You're kidding me.'

My coughed laughter blew the froth off the beer. The Foreign Secretary looked up and frowned, as if wondering whether to call security.

'Daddy makes porn movies,' said Cheryl. 'It's not glamorous. Most of the time, it's not much fun. But it's a living. A very good living. He makes a movie a month and each one makes a big profit. Not too many Hollywood producers can say that.'

I didn't know what to say. From the thousands of questions buzzing in my brain, one emerged.

'Is it legal?'

'Of course it's legal.' Cheryl swizzled her drink, sucked an oyster from the stick. 'Porn's big business. Sex sells. Hotels, motels, clubs, bars, private homes, specialist movie theatres. It's a big market and it can never get enough good product. Daddy's is the best. Quality merchandise. Commands a premium price.'

I'd never watched a porn movie. I could never see the point.

'I don't understand,' I said. 'Why would anyone want to pay good money to watch other people have sex?'

Cheryl laughed.

'That's very sweet. Anyway, what's the difference between reading about Laura Friday doing it and watching it on a movie screen?'

'There's nothing wrong with describing two people having sex if it's part of the story. But not if it's the entire story. That would just be very boring.'

She shrugged.

'Well, that's not how it is in the real world. Thing is, Daddy wants to get out. Wants to make mainstream stuff. He's looking for a vehicle. That's why he's interested in Laura Friday.'

'He'll need to talk to Helen about that.'

'Daddy can be very determined about getting what he wants.'

'I thought we were taking a break.'

'We are. Daddy has a big pool and Southern California has sunshine most days of the year. Once you've talked to Daddy, you can forget about Laura Friday until we get back to London.'

When they called the flight, we were taken down a deserted corridor. It was only when we passed through yet another security door into the departure lounge that we came face-to-face with four hundred other passengers. If I hadn't known before, I knew then that from now on I'd be living in a different world. A rich man's world.

Chapter 32

'Hey, hey, hey, how's Daddy's little girl?'

Cheryl ran into the widespread arms of a bear with a beard and dark glasses. Much less hair than his most recent photo. A round face with moisturised skin. Wearing a rumpled cotton jacket, open-necked shirt, chinos and slip-on shoes. A fine gold necklace, a gold bracelet, chunky rings on two fingers. He'd have looked good on the forecourt at Tony's My T Motors.

'Daddy, this is Fitz.'

'Marty Cole.' He offered a total package. Banana hand, chunky chronometer, tanned right arm covered in black hair. 'Heard a lot about you, Fitz. Hope it's all true. Cherry thinks you're pretty special.'

Cherry? It made Cheryl sound like a fruit. With a hard kernel.

'I think she is, too.'

I retrieved my hand and flexed away the pain. He waved at a burgundy-and-cream Cadillac limo. A black guy in a uniform was stowing our bags into its cavernous boot.

'Let's ride. We can talk turkey in the Caddy. Good flight?'

'We slept most of the way.'

'Sorry to hear about the show, Cherry. That's how it goes sometimes. Just gotta pick yourself up and start all over again. Ain't that right, Fitzie?' Martin punched my arm. It hurt. 'You know all about rejection.'

Cheryl and Martin sat facing the front, me opposite, the black guy behind a glass partition. As the car eased away from the no-parking zone I wondered how I was going to tell Cheryl's daddy how much I hated being called Fitzie. About as much as Dad had hated Joker. Slightly more than I hated the name Cherry. And slightly less than I hated Vince Humber. But right then didn't seem to be the moment.

'I had a rejection wall in my bedroom. But I don't think you ever get used to it. Cheryl's keeping busy looking for somewhere for us to live.'

'That right?' Martin gave Cheryl a grin. 'Something you want to tell me, hon?'

'Like what, Daddy?'

'You two?'

He made a circle around the ring finger of his left hand, pursed his fat lips.

'We're just going to live together for a while, Daddy. See how things work out.'

Martin frowned.

'Without getting married? What happens if you have kids?'

'They're not on the agenda. We've got plenty of time. Fitz hasn't even got his first book finished yet. And I've got to look for another job. Can't get work if I'm pregnant.'

I sat there, trying to tune in to a conversation which would never have occurred in our family. I couldn't remember the word 'pregnant' ever being uttered at the dinner table. Overdue. Fallen. Half-term. Full-term. The Four Stages of Childbirth. Pregnancy came a close second to menstruation for euphemisms.

Something else was bothering me. Cheryl and I had never discussed children. Never discussed anything about the future. It was enough keeping up with the present. But here she was, five minutes after meeting her dad, expressing attitudes I'd never known she possessed.

'Doesn't seem right,' said Martin. 'Two people living together without being married. Not as if you're hippies.'

I tried to look through the dark glasses to see whether there was a hint of irony in his eyes. How could a porn filmmaker take a moral stance on cohabitation? But the glasses were opaque.

'I think that's a matter for Cheryl and me, Martin,' I said. 'If and when we decide to take things further, you'll be the first to know.'

'Maybe so.' There was a new hostility in his voice. Cheryl was frowning at me. But I didn't care. I wasn't going to spend my well-deserved break walking on eggshells. 'But if you're staying under my roof, and you ain't married, you'll be in separate rooms. Cheryl's got her old room. You can stay in one of the guest rooms, Fitz. Hope that's clear. Unless you want to check into the Beverly Wilshire. Up to you.'

I looked at Cheryl for support. But she came out on Martin's side.

'It's only for a week, Fitz. It doesn't matter, does it?'

'I suppose not.'

Martin Cole was sitting back, a victorious smile flickering around his mouth. First round to the bear. I hadn't even put up a fight. Maybe because I hadn't realised until then that this was a contest.

'So, Fitzie, the Laura Friday movie option. What's the latest?'

We were stuck in traffic on an eight-lane freeway. I hadn't felt this trapped since my back-seat ride with Paul Almeida.

'You'll have to talk to Helen Valentino and Tom Prescott-Jones. Helen said something the other day about sitting on the first movie for a year or two, watching its value increase along with the Laura Friday brand. Like the stock market. She might not do anything about a movie until we've consolidated book sales. But it's all beyond me. I don't get involved in the business side.'

At which Martin's face fell.

'Hey, it's your baby, Fitzie. You should be calling the shots.'

'PBI take twenty per cent of everything I earn. I pay them to take that kind of decision.'

'That's another thing. You should maybe think about bringing your business in-house,' said Martin. 'I have a great network here in LA. I've arranged for you to meet a few guys while you're here. Cheryl could represent you back in England. Whaddya need those assholes at PBI for? By the time they've creamed off their percentage and you've paid taxes on the rest, all you've got left is small change. We could set up an offshore company. Bermuda. Grand Cayman. Make tax a distant nightmare. I know some people could make it all happen. What sort of a contract you got? Never mind. Whatever it says, I know people can get you out of it.'

'I couldn't do that,' I said. 'Helen put me on the map. She liked what I was doing with Laura. If it hadn't been for her, I'd still be writing pharmaceutical manuals and living in a room in Himalaya Street.'

'Wrong,' said Martin. 'Wasn't Helen who put you where you are today, Fitzie. It was me. Cheryl sent me your work. Basis of which I contacted PBI in LA. Who contacted Helen. Hadn't been for me, she wouldn't have seen you in a million years. You owe me. If you don't want Cheryl and me to save you millions, least you owe me the movie rights.'

'Like I said. You'll need to talk to PBI.'

'Bullshit.' Martin was all aggression, as if he'd been stewing for weeks and was ready to boil over. 'I'm sitting here talking to you, fella. I'll make you a terrific offer. Make payment offshore so the taxman never sees it. You're happy with it, you tell Helen it's a done deal. End of the day, Laura's yours, Fitzie. No one else's.'

Which was probably the least convincing thing anyone had said to me for a long time. Laura Friday was a brand, Vince

Humber was a brand. And a lot of people were involved in their management. My work on *When the Fat Parrot Sings* was a solo effort. But Laura's second book would be written in collaboration with the PBI editors. Which explained why the magic had gone out of my writing. The routine of sitting at my typewriter each morning with a jug of coffee and several slices of toast had been transformed. Once it had been something to look forward to. Now it was becoming a drudge. And I had a six-book contract to fulfil with an option on another six. A fifteen-year sentence. The longest I'd ever write.

I looked at Martin and his daughter and wondered. Had we come to LA for a holiday and a family introduction? Or to negotiate a deal? Maybe jumping from a plane straight into a confrontation was routine procedure if you lived in Hollywood, but it wasn't the way things were done in Bullock.

Cheryl was just sitting there, saying nothing. Whose side was she on? Weren't we all supposed to be on the same side? What did she and her father talk about during those long transatlantic phone calls? Was this all a Cole conspiracy? Or was it just my mind, stuck in Laura Friday mode?

'I'll talk to Helen,' I said. 'You can make your offer. If she thinks it's fair, we'll have a deal.'

'You're the main man, Fitzie. That's how you want to call it, that's how we'll play.'

Second round a draw, but the contest wasn't looking good. I was on foreign soil and the referee's neutrality was in doubt.

Whose side Cheryl was on became clear the first time we were alone. We'd driven to Martin Cole's house in a strained silence, all three of us gazing bleakly at the slow-moving traffic as if we were strangers on a bus. When we reached Malibu we exited the freeway and took a series of turns until we reached a quiet street, its houses hidden behind trees, walls and gates, one of which opened at our approach. The house was a pink fortress perched on a rock looking out to sea, its windows reflective glass. The Stars and Stripes fluttered from its roof.

When the driver took our bags, Martin muttered his need to make some calls. Cheryl said she'd show me around, but she didn't do much showing. We went through an open living space and down a flight of stairs to a self-contained apartment. Kitchen, living area, bedroom, bathroom.

'This is where I grew up.' She unlocked a sliding glass door and stood on a deck, resting her palms on a rail. 'There's a private path going down to the beach. I used to swim every morning before school.' The driver appeared from below, carrying my bags across a deep green lawn watered by a sprinkler system. 'Your quarters are behind those trees. Fully stocked bar. Everything you need.'

'Cheryl,' I said, 'this is ridiculous. This is more like a bloody resort hotel than a house.'

She turned on me.

'This is Daddy's house. He makes the rules. You might not like it, I might not like it, but that's how it is, Fitz. And I'd be grateful if you'd show him a bit more respect. That was a pretty shitty thing about the movie rights. After all Daddy's done for you. Don't you think you could have been a bit more generous?'

'What did you expect me to do? Helen's going to put the rights out to tender when she thinks the timing's right. I've offered him the inside running. No one else will have the opportunity Martin's getting.'

'Big deal,' said Cheryl. 'Why couldn't you two just sit down together and agree terms? Isn't that what being family's all about?'

'Maybe it is in your family,' I said, 'but in mine we don't

expect or ask for anything. We're grateful for whatever we're given.'

'Well, I'd be grateful if you'd make sure Daddy gets the rights.' Cheryl turned to me and smiled. Her hand went to my crotch. She unzipped my fly, felt my rising cock. We moved inside to a couch, Cheryl on top with her skirt around her waist, doing that hula thing with her hips. 'You will, won't you, darling? Please. For me?'

Although the weather that week was unremitting California sunshine, a dark cloud settled into a fixed orbit over my head. That first evening Martin took us out to a restaurant. When Meryl Streep walked in he leaned across and whispered, *'Great Laura Friday.'* He waved at Streep but she didn't wave back.

When he wasn't pointing out movie stars — *'There's Jack. Make a great bad guy, wouldn't you say, Fitzie?'* — Martin expounded on everything from the Reagan presidency — *'Makes you feel like everything's under control. He and Thatcher make a great team. World's safe in their hands.'* — to abortion — *'I pray to God every day for the souls of unborn children.'*

I disagreed with virtually everything he said, but I kept silent. I wondered if he was just goading me when he said, *'There's a gun in every room, Fitzie, locked and loaded. Any black fucker comes through my window, he goes out feet-first and horizontal.'* By the end of the evening, two things at least were clear in my confused mind. I couldn't stand the guy. And I couldn't wait to get back to London.

I kept reminding myself that Martin Cole lived six thousand miles away and that I wasn't in love with him but with his daughter. But each time I had that sunny thought, the dark cloud of the movie rights obscured it. If Martin acquired those rights, he'd become an inextricable ingredient in the Laura Friday marketing mix. In my life. In my face. Forever. And yet I didn't see how I could deny him and retain Cheryl's love.

That night I lay in bed and watched a big moon rise over the Pacific Ocean. I looked across the shimmering water and wondered how the hell I was going to keep everyone happy. Cheryl, Martin, Helen. I seemed to be in everyone's debt.

There was a soft sound outside. I heard the door, knew it wasn't an intruder. I could see Cheryl's silhouette in the moonlight. She padded on bare feet into my bedroom, reached over her head to slip off a garment, withdrew the sheet and slipped into bed beside me.

'If I'd known where the gun was I could have sent you out of here feet-first.'

I kissed a cold shoulder.

'You mustn't take any notice of Daddy.' Her face was close on the pillow, her breath sweet and fresh. 'Once you get to know him he's really a sweet man.'

I wondered whether I'd live long enough.

'What's he going to say if he finds out you're here?'

'He knows. We had a little talk. He's all bluff and bluster. I know how to handle him.'

After we'd made love I lay awake, wondering whether Cheryl said the same thing to her daddy about me. And watching the moon disappear behind that cloud.

Next morning I was doing a few easy lengths of the thirty-metre pool, Cheryl relaxing on a lounger, when Martin dived in. He swam half a length underwater, then ripped into a powerful crawl, creaming through the water, doing racing kick turns. He surfaced near me like a seal, water streaming from his beard and melon face.

'Wanna race?'

'No thanks. I'm not much of a swimmer.'

'Six laps. Give ya a one-lap start.'

'I don't have much speed.'

'Ten laps, then. Two-lap start.'

'What does the winner get?'

Martin laughed and glanced at Cheryl as if they both knew something.

'How about the movie rights? They're as good as mine anyway. Might as well make it official.'

'Sure,' I said. 'Why not?'

We stood side-by-side at the deep end. Cheryl called out, 'Ready, set — go!' I dived in, settled into a slow, steady crawl down to the other end, turned, came back. As soon as I touched, Martin dived in, did his underwater start, then ploughed after me. Each time I turned for a breath I could see Martin swimming further ahead, his kicking feet punching him through the water, his huge body creating a bow wave. When he made his first turn I was several strokes behind, and was only halfway into my fourth lap by the time he'd completed his second. In three more laps he'd be beside me. I kicked harder, worked with my arms and shoulders, picked up some speed, turned just ahead of him on lap eight, could feel the churning water as his arms thrashed alongside my feet. We touched together for the final lap.

'Come on, come on!' I could hear Cheryl's excited voice. 'You can do it, you can do it!'

Thirty metres to go. I reached out in a racing rhythm, could feel stroke after stroke pulling me ahead, sensed that Martin was tiring. He was on my shoulder, then my feet. I touched two strokes ahead of him.

'I was hustled.' He hauled himself out of the water and snatched a towel from a pile on a low table beside the pool. 'You're a better swimmer than you gave out, Fitzie. I was cheated out of those goddamn fucking movie rights.'

'I only just made it,' I said. 'You're a much better swimmer than I am.'

I thought I was in the clear, but Cheryl stepped in.

'Fitz didn't say you couldn't have them if you lost, Daddy. Only that you could if you won. He'll talk to Helen back in London, won't you, darling?'

'Be glad to.'

What else could I say with Cheryl looking at me like that? Martin grunted and waved a hand at the table setting.

'Let's have breakfast.'

Cheryl poured coffee. Martin and I wrapped ourselves in white robes and sat around a square hardwood table sheltered by a huge sun umbrella, watching hummingbirds drink nectar from submissive flowers.

I sat back, turned my face to the sun and felt better. The fight wasn't over yet, but Martin and I were even. Only one thing bothered me as I sipped my coffee. Who had Cheryl been cheering for?

'So, Martin,' I said, 'how's business?'

'I don't talk about my business at home, Fitzie.' Martin spread peanut butter on a pastry and fed it between his whiskers. 'Like to leave my work behind when I leave the office. But I can tell ya this. I run a tight ship. Strict shooting schedules. One movie a month. Regular distribution network waiting for every product that comes off the line. Big mailing list. We work about three months ahead from original concept to completed product.'

'Who comes up with the ideas?'

'I have a team of writers. Been with me for years.'

'What about the . . . er . . . actors?'

Martin shrugged, took a swig of coffee.

'They come and go. It's just a job, like any other. They do a good job, they get well compensated. First priority, a guy's got to be able to get it up on demand and keep it up while we do a take. They can't do that, they're shown the door. We don't have time to waste with losers.'

'But you want to get out of the porn business, is that right? Go legit?'

Martin poised his knife above his plate and looked at me as if he was wondering whether to stab me with it.

'Don't like the word "porn", Fitzie. Sounds like there's something sleazy about what we do. Adult. That's the category we're in. There are all kinds of categories. Thriller, Sci-Fi, Comedy. Adult's no better or worse than any other. Don't like the legit insinuation, either. What I do's legit. I'm a well-respected man in this town. The money men love me. We have the set-up and the know-how to make much bigger pictures, make much more money. I want to turn Hot Cole Productions into a major facility. Maybe win an Oscar or two. Something for Cherry to inherit. That's why I want the Laura Friday rights. For Cherry's sake.'

Martin had resumed his dark glasses and I was wearing mine, so it was impossible to see what he was thinking. All I was sure about was that the more he pushed, the more I resisted.

I'd been thinking about it all week. Lying beside the pool, waiting for time to pass. On the drive up the coast to Hearst Castle. At interminable lunches with people Martin insisted were dying to meet me but whose sole interest seemed to be the Laura Friday movie rights. Their eyes would glaze if I talked about anything else. Whenever I asked about their lives, they described a dream world where everyone was wonderful, money grew on trees and the only thing lacking to make it Paradise was a big opportunity.

We were forty thousand feet above Greenland when I

reached my final decision. It wasn't clear-cut, but Martin, the major negative, was falling further behind with every thrust of the jumbo's engines, and now that I knew who I was up against, I was confident I could deal with him. I nudged Cheryl.

'You awake?'

'I wasn't. But I am now.'

'Can I ask you something?'

'What?'

'Will you marry me?'

'Yes.'

'Don't you want to think about it?'

'I talked it over with Daddy before we left. I told him whenever you asked I'd say yes.'

'What did he say?'

'He's very happy. I keep telling you, Fitz, he really likes you.'

'Should we celebrate?'

'We'll have champagne with breakfast.'

A few minutes later, Cheryl nudged me.

'Fitz, I've been thinking.'

'What about?'

'Maybe we should celebrate now.'

'What have you got in mind?'

She made wavy movements with her hands.

'Do I have to spell it out for you?'

I rose from my seat, padded across the cabin to a vacant toilet. I reached for the doorknob . . .

BOOK THREE

Chapter 33

One damp day in February 1987, Cheryl, Henry Fawcett and I rested our bums against Fawcett's Jaguar and gazed across a gravel drive at a rambling old building. Fawcett was the 'son' of Fawcett & Sons, estate agents of Cirencester. Fat, bald, with a purple nose and matching handkerchief in the breast pocket of his hacking jacket. His shifty eyes reminded me of Tony Scunthorpe of Tony's My T Motors, with an overlay of English snobbery.

'Don't you just love it, Fitz?'

'Barton Lodge is Elizabethan, madam.' The estate agent blessed it with a wave of his hand. 'But the land goes right back to the Domesday Book. The Bartons were devout Catholics. Both the original Barton Hall and the Lodge that was attached to it were destroyed during the Dissolution. Some say the Virgin Queen stayed up at the big house once it had been rebuilt, but there's no proof . . . ' He inhaled, let it all go with a long sigh. 'Aah, that country air. Just look at those ivy-covered walls, those perfect windows. Two receptions, four bedrooms, two bathrooms. Grade II listed. You said you're a writer, sir. Well, you can shut yourself away here. No traffic. Wonderful views to inspire the imagination. I've often thought of writing a book myself. People I meet. You wouldn't want to read about some of them.'

'Not much point in writing a book, then.'

'Let's go inside.' Cheryl took my hand. The agent had anticipated us and gone ahead to stand at the front door beneath a coat of arms. 'Calm down, Fitz. He's only doing his job.'

'Snotty-nosed prick.'

'Ssh, he'll hear you. Don't you think the house is lovely, though?'

I had to admit, I liked the look of Barton Lodge. It was two miles from the village of Higher Stoughton and part of an estate which included a number of tenant farms plus Barton Hall's two thousand enclosed acres.

'It's a big step up from a single room at Himalaya Street.'

'Be a bit more positive, Fitz.'

'The brochure said something about a library. Where's that?'

'In here, sir.' Fawcett opened a door and stood back. 'A lovely spacious room. Twenty by seventeen. My favourite, if I may say so. With a wonderful view of the grounds.'

I walked between oak bookshelves, past a marble fireplace to the window, stood with my hands in my pockets and tuned out the estate agent's burble. Beyond the clipped hedges bordering the gravel paths, the perfect lawn, the tall trees, was a sublime English landscape of rolling fields and distant spires.

I saw a Spitfire chase a Messerschmidt across a summer sky. Could hear Cromwell's cavalry, the tramp of Cranmer's destructive army. Perhaps there was a priest's hole. Perhaps Mass had been celebrated here in whispered Latin, by sputtering candlelight.

Turning from the window, I looked around at the empty shelves and saw them crammed with books. A rug in front of the fire beneath a hardwood coffee table. A suite of sofas and chairs. I'd felt a visceral desire in Helen Valentino's library. What I'd wanted more than anything was now within my grasp.

'I'll take it.'

'Sorry, sir?' Fawcett was standing by the door. Cheryl had wandered off somewhere. 'What did you say?'

'Talk to Helen Valentino at Philip Bedford International. Her people will take care of everything. How soon can I move in?'

'But . . . but don't you want to look at the other rooms? The grounds? A building such as this . . . surely a survey would be a good idea? In your own best interests.'

'Helen will take care of that. Why? Is there anything wrong with it?'

'Of course not, sir, the entire building's been fully restored, but all the same . . .'

'Are you saying you don't want to sell it to me? Afraid I won't fit in. Is that it?'

Cheryl appeared behind Fawcett.

'Whatever's the matter, Fitz?'

'I've just told this guy I want to buy the place and he won't sell it to me.'

'That's not at all the case, sir,' said the agent. 'I'll certainly make all the arrangements as soon as I get back to the office. And congratulations, sir, madam. I'm sure you'll be very happy here.'

We went outside for fresh air. Walked hand in hand down a gravel path towards a grotto framed by a bower of climbing roses.

'Fitz, I can't understand what's wrong with you at the moment.' We sat on a stone seat. 'Is it me? The movie rights? Daddy? Surely you're not worried about the book? The contract?'

How could I tell Cheryl it was all that and none of it? That it was all Laura Friday's fault. She'd become an albatross around my neck. The only reason I'd created her was as a catharsis for Frankie. I'd achieved that while Cheryl was in Plymouth. Now I was stuck with Laura Friday for the next fifteen years. Her and Vince Humber. I invented an explanation.

'It's nothing. I'm sorry. I've never had much money. Nor have any of my family. If Mum or Dad had any to spare they'd give it to charity. I feel guilty. As if I've played a con trick. As if I don't deserve it.'

'That's silly, darling.' Cheryl kissed my cheek. 'Of course you deserve it. You're a brilliant writer. What was it Helen said? Pavarotti is a genius of an idea. We make a great team, don't we?' She laughed and clutched my arm as we walked on. 'You'll soon get used to all this.'

I turned to look back at the house. Its shuttered windows blazed with reflected light. In them I could see *al fresco* Sunday lunches under a vine-covered pergola. Afternoon teas beneath a willow. Could hear classical music drifting from the house. 'Dancing Queen.' 'Can You Hear the Drums, Fernando?' 'Money, Money, Money.'

'It's going to be tough,' I said. 'But I'll do my best.'

From the moment we moved into Barton Lodge four weeks later, Cheryl took command.

'You need a clear mind to work on your book,' she said. 'No distractions. Leave everything else to me.'

I would emerge from my study after a morning with Laura Friday to discover people up ladders. Wander into the kitchen for a coffee to find a man beneath the sink, or installing a new fridge. Trucks came and went. Curtains went up. Paintings appeared. Men in cheap suits peered down Cheryl's shirt and pretended they were studying floor plans. Although no one touched a forelock, everyone called me squire, stood back as I passed, and agreed with whatever I said.

'Turned out nice again.'

'Tha's right, squire.'

'Shame about the weather.'

'Great shame, squire.'

Occasionally Cheryl would tap on my study door and seek my opinion.

'Sorry to bother you, darling, but we can't make up our

minds. Which do you prefer, this colour or this colour for the third bedroom?'

Laura hated interruption when she was about to orgasm, or was killing someone, or teaching Pavarotti a new song. I'd point to something.

'I thought the other one, darling. But if that's what you really want . . .'

'Well, then, the other one.'

I now knew how Dad must have felt when he was busy polishing his ports and Mum asked whether he planned to mow the lawns.

Our Wedding Day was set for Saturday, the twenty-fifth of July. I'd have been happy with the Cirencester Register Office and a few drinks on the lawn, but Cheryl wanted a church service, marquee, string quartet, rock band, two hundred guests. Daddy from Los Angeles to give her away. Two bridesmaids from New York. The caterer a minor royal.

On my side, my best man would be John Carnforth from Hire-A-Hack. Alex from Himalaya Street would be an usher since he was so good at finding places for people. And Helen was bringing a small team from PBI.

We were in Cheryl's office, which overlooked a hole in the ground. This would soon become a swimming pool. The floor was awash with wallpaper samples, the sofa drowning in bits of fabric. Cheryl was going through the invitation list.

'What about your parents and sister?'

'They'll never come.'

'Have you asked them?'

'No.'

'I think you should.'
'Well, then, I will.'

When Dad answered the phone we spent the first few minutes dealing with the time difference. We did this every time I called, but Dad could never come to terms with it.

'So it's last night in England.'

'Yes, Dad. And tomorrow morning in Bullock.'

'Doesn't seem right, small place like this being ahead. You'd think with all this new technology they'd find a way to catch up. Leap Year'd be a good time to do it. Extra day. Anyone tried that?'

'Not as far as I know, Dad. How's everything?'

'Pretty much the same. Had a tricky upper frontal last week. Hutch Scandrett. Was worried if I extracted it he'd develop a lisp. "Lisping *and* Stuttering" Hutch wouldn't sound right, and he's pretty much wedded to his stutter. Sorted it out, though.'

'Talking of being wedded, Dad—'

But there was a delay on the line, so Dad didn't pick up the interruption.

'Murray's always asking how you're getting along. That's Young Murray's dad. Young Murray's not ready to take over just yet. Got a bit more work to do on alimentary canals and the Pre-Raphaelites, but he's coming along just fine.'

'Dad, the reason I rang—'

''Part from that, Irish Nights are going well, your Aunt Bridie's not too good, put the bike back together yesterday but it's still not right, Norm Paget won the Garden Gnome Contest—'

'Could I have a word with Mum?'

'Can't stand here talking all morning, Johnny. You'd better have a word with your mother. Have to get to work. But of course you don't, do you? There was a good show on television last night. Make sure you watch it when it's last night over there.'

'Thanks, Dad. I will.'

Mum came on the line.

'Mum, Cheryl and I have decided to get married. We want you, Dad and Carmel to come to the wedding.'

'Is she a good Catholic, Johnny?'

'She's not religious, Mum. Neither am I. We're getting married in the local church, that's all.'

'What is it?'

'How do you mean?'

'Is it a Catholic church?'

'No. It's Anglican.'

There was a long pause. I wasn't sure whether the connection had been cut.

'Mum? Are you there?'

'Yes, I'm here. What about your children?'

'What about them, Mum?'

'Will you bring them up in the One True Faith?'

'Mum, I stopped being a Catholic when I was a teenager. We'll bring them up as best we can, like anyone else.'

'You never stop being a Catholic, Johnny. It's a good wife's duty to bring her husband back into the Fold. I'll pass you back to your father.'

'Nothing to worry about, Johnny,' said Dad when he came back on the line. 'We'll come, but Carmel's in the Solomon Islands. It'll just be the two of us.'

'You won't have to worry about a thing,' I said. 'Stay as long as you like. Take a trip to Blackjack.'

'I've always wanted to visit where we all came from,' said Dad. 'Might get a chance to see Declan Maloney. He rarely leaves Ireland, you know. Doesn't see the point. I know just how he feels.'

Chapter 34

Two weeks before the wedding we gathered in the PBI boardroom. Cheryl on one side of a lozenge-shaped rosewood table, with a lawyer named Sam Quercy on her left and Martin Cole on her right. Me on the other with Helen Valentino and Tom Prescott-Jones.

Over the past few days Quercy and Tom had hammered out a Heads of Agreement on the prenuptial contract which Helen had said I needed.

'If things don't work out between you and Cheryl, the divorce settlement could drag on for years, ruin your career, and cost you a fortune. This way, everyone knows where they stand.'

I'd protested.

'Two people in love don't need a cloud of legal negativity.'

I'd had enough clouds in my life already, but Helen didn't need to know that.

'You have to do it,' Helen had said. 'Otherwise if the worst comes to the very worst, Cheryl could strip you cleaner than a piranha.'

It was a metaphor Laura Friday used all the time in *When the Fat Parrot Sings,* along with 'hug like an anaconda' and 'sting like a scorpion', so it had the desired effect. When I'd mentioned it to Cheryl, she'd agreed with Helen. It was a Sunday morning and we were breakfasting in bed.

'It's for your own protection, darling. I was going to suggest it, but was worried you'd think I was only marrying you for what I could get. You don't think that, do you?'

'Of course not.'

Once Helen's PA had handed everyone copies, Quercy and Tom spent a quiet few minutes going through the legalese while I drank my coffee and remembered where all this had begun. With Frankie, Dick Worth's penis, and the Yes Oh Yes Motel. I rarely thought about those days, although Frankie was forever embedded in Laura. Whenever I did I felt a twinge of regret, like embedded shrapnel in certain kinds of weather.

I looked across the table and reminded myself that I was grateful for everything Cheryl had done. I owed this to her. Then I looked at Martin and shuddered. I'd been stalling on the movie rights ever since we'd got back from LA and I'd run out of excuses. He was face to face with Helen, Tom and me. I was sure he wouldn't let this opportunity pass.

'Everyone happy?' Tom looked around the table.

'Might be a good idea to run through the main points for Cheryl's and Fitz's benefit.' Quercy had removed his jacket and seemed in no hurry. There were sweat stains on either side of his breasts and he'd loosened his tie although the air conditioning was on cool.

'Sure,' said Tom. 'No problem. What it all boils down to is this. If the marriage remains healthy, the prenup has no value. It sits quietly in a drawer. If the marriage gets sick, and of course everyone here hopes that never happens, we open the drawer and have a look at what we all agreed. That clear to you both?'

Cheryl and I nodded.

'Agreement activates upon signature of marriage. Soon as you both sign the register, you're legally bound. That clear?'

We nodded again.

'Grounds for activation of the contract. One of you is unfaithful. That is, has sexual relations after marriage with another person. Physical cruelty. Mental cruelty—'

'We've got definitions of sexual relations in the preamble,' said Quercy to Cheryl. 'Happy with those.'

'—and by mutual consent,' said Tom. 'That is, if you both agree for whatever reason that the marriage cannot continue. Divorce is not crucial. Separation which you both agree is permanent is sufficient.'

'Everyone fights a round or two,' said Quercy to Cheryl. 'This only kicks in if it goes the full distance and you need a points decision.'

She nodded. Tom flipped a page and took a sip of water.

'Let's assume the worst happens. The agreement says the parties share current and future assets and liabilities equally. These shall constitute all net proceeds from the Laura Friday brand, in all media, and in all forms, such as property, company shares, retained profits, cash, and negotiable assets, such as paintings, vehicles, furniture and so on for the lifetime of both parties and whether or not either party subsequently remarries.'

'My client made and continues to make a substantial contribution to the conceptual development of Laura Friday,' said Quercy to Tom. 'As a specific she came up with the name Pavarotti, but there's plenty more contribution over and above that, plus all the work she's doing in support of ongoing projects. Half's her legal right. Don't need a prenup for that. Goes further, though. My client's family connections also made this possible. Martin here made direct contact with PBI in Los Angeles, who in turn contacted Helen here. That right, Martin?'

'Right.'

Martin Cole grunted and looked over to Helen for confirmation.

'That's correct,' Helen said.

'And if it hadn't been for that contact, Helen would never have looked at one of Fitz's unsolicited manuscripts. That right, Helen?'

She nodded.

'So if it hadn't been for my client, Fitz would be nowhere. She made him what he is today and what he'll be in the future.'

'We can't assume that,' said Tom. 'There's no knowing what might have happened. Fitz could have been discovered without Cheryl's or Martin's help.'

'Happy to debate that in a court of law, Tom,' said Quercy. 'We'd ask Helen to say how many unsolicited manuscripts she gets each year and what she does with them. We'd call every literary agent and publisher in London and ask what he or she does with them. Don't think we'd have too much trouble convincing a judge.'

'What's your point?'

Tom made a show of looking at his watch.

'Point is, half's not enough. We take into account the trauma involved in a marriage break-up, the psychological damage, the total disruption of an entire life, given the powerful influence my client has had over your client's success. Has to be worth seventy-five per cent. At the very least.'

'That's outrageous,' said Tom. 'You can't be seriously suggesting that my client is only allowed to retain twenty-five per cent of his entire net worth? Sam, we've already reached Heads of Agreement on this. Why haven't you raised this matter before today?'

'Don't see that it matters when it comes up, so long as it's before the parties sign,' said Quercy. 'This prenup's damned important.'

I looked at Cheryl, wondering whose idea this had been. Hers, Quercy's, or her father's? She was frowning, as if as unhappy and embarrassed as I was, but she didn't intervene.

Quercy must have known his eleventh-hour proposal would create havoc. Just when everyone thought the deal was done, he'd thrown a hospital pass.

'I've got a proposal might help resolve this.'

Martin Cole laced his fingers together, rested them on the table and smiled. While we were in LA I hadn't seen Martin smile much, so hadn't noticed his teeth. They were too perfect. Two rows of gleaming cuspids, laterals and molars. What Dad would have called 'eleven out of ten'. Expensive fakes. Dad had always said you could tell a lot about a man from his teeth.

'What's that?' asked Tom.

'Why don't we settle on fifty per cent?'

Quercy frowned, but it was ham acting. Like something he'd rehearsed.

'We'd certainly be happy with that,' said Tom.

Martin Cole held up a pudgy hand.

'Plus. Helen, Tom and I come to an agreement on the Laura Friday movie rights. Which should belong to me in any case.'

Everyone was looking at me. It was my call. I looked down at my hands, wondering what Aunt Agnes would have done. I shuddered at the consequences of a Martin Cole victory. Helen came to my rescue. She fixed Martin with an ice-cold stare.

'That's a fucking shitty suggestion, Martin, and you know it. How can you use your daughter's marriage as a business leverage? Fitz won't sign anything other than a fifty-fifty split. At the appropriate time I'm going to call for tenders for the movie rights. As I've told you already, the best I can promise is that you'll be included in the shortlist. The rights will be awarded to whoever submits the most attractive proposal, and that's not just the most money, but who can do the best job for the Laura Friday brand. If that's not acceptable, that's too bad. We're here today to sign a prenuptial agreement. Now I'm late for a lunch appointment. Cheryl, are you happy to sign or not?'

'Of course,' Cheryl said. 'This agreement's for Fitz's benefit, not mine. I'm sure Daddy was only trying to come up with an acceptable compromise. Right, Daddy?'

'Right.'

Martin had gone down under a barrage of blows from Helen. He'd taken a count. It wasn't a knockout. But we'd won the round.

Once we'd signed, Cheryl and I walked together from the boardroom and got into the lift. 'Darling, we weren't on opposing sides. We're in love,' Cheryl said as she unzipped my fly, hitched up her skirt, and pressed the emergency stop.

Courgette was a discreet Michelin one-star restaurant in Mayfair run by Antoine Lacour, who'd worked with Paul Bocuse in Lyon. The burgundy-painted door opened as our black cab pulled up outside. Georges, the *maitre d'*, stood there, smiling.

'Mister Kennedy. Madam. Good to see you again. And congratulations. A Dom Pérignon '77 is waiting for you at your table. From all of us at Courgette.'

There was a hush as Cheryl and I were shown to our table, a double in the centre with an ice bucket alongside. Cheryl looked gorgeous in an ice-blue suit, white wide-collared shirt, her hair pinned back off her face. Her engagement ring flashed beneath the spotlights and she gave everyone big smiles and winks as if we were all having the time of our lives. She sat opposite me, put her tongue between her lips, and did a little wriggle. Men at the other tables looked at me with a mixture of envy and hatred. I reminded myself once again how lucky I was.

'Let's forget about that stupid prenup,' I said. 'The only thing that matters is that we love each other.'

Which was true. But the nagging thought remained like a sore tooth. How involved had Cheryl been in her daddy's attempted hijack?

Chapter 35

A week before the wedding and I was looking forward to spending a few days with Mum and Dad. Since I'd left Bullock, my entire life had changed and I wanted them to see things as they now were. *When the Fat Parrot Sings* was in the final stages of editing, and I'd decided to dedicate it to Cheryl. As soon as the manuscript had been accepted, I'd received my full advance. The book would be launched in early November into the Christmas market with a major publicity drive. I, or rather Vince Humber, was booked to appear on the BBC's *Wogan* talk show and my face would be spread along the sides of London's buses. That wouldn't impress Mum and Dad. Money and fame had never meant much to them. But I was sure they'd be pleased with what I'd achieved, and would love the woman standing by my side.

The limo came through the gates of Barton Lodge and crunched up the gravel drive to the front entrance where Cheryl and I stood waiting. When it stopped, I opened the passenger door. Dad got out, hugging a yellow duty-free bag. I frowned.

'Where's Mum?'

'Got sick at the last minute, Johnny. Giddy spells. Doctor advised her not to fly. Ear infection. Nothing too serious.'

Dad had never been good at concealing the truth. His eyes gave him away, which was why he'd always lost at poker. He looked everywhere but at me, and mostly down at the ground. Something was wrong. I put my arm around his shoulders. He seemed to have become thinner and smaller since I'd been away.

'That's a damned shame. Good to see you anyway, Dad. This is Cheryl.'

Dad offered his hand, but Cheryl bypassed it and gave him one of her best hugs, the full treatment, cheek-to-cheek, wrapping him up like a Christmas parcel. When they broke apart she held both his hands.

'Fitz has told me so much about you, Joe, I feel I know you already. It's a shame Moira couldn't make it. I was really looking forward to meeting her.'

'Few days' rest she'll be fine. You're quite something. Johnny's a lucky man.'

'No-o, I'm the lucky one. You must be tired. Come inside. I'll make some tea.'

'You two go ahead,' I said. 'I'll join you in a minute. Just have to make a quick phone call.'

'What do I call you?' I heard Dad say as they walked away, arm in arm.

'My daddy calls me Cherry, but Fitz hates it. And just between you and me, so do I. So Cheryl's just fine. How about you?'

'Joe or Joke. But not Joker. Never could stand it. Don't ask me why. Just one of those things.'

When I joined Cheryl and Dad a few minutes later they were drinking tea on the terrace. Cheryl gave me a puzzled look as I sat and poured myself a cup.

'Everything OK?'

I nodded.

'So how are things in Bullock, Dad?'

'Oh, pretty much the same. Hutch Scandrett had a cold the other day. Over the radio people couldn't tell whether he was stuttering or getting ready to sneeze. Tony Scunthorpe died. Heart attack. Got his figures wrong on a trade-in, made a loss on the deal, ticker couldn't take the strain. Merv's inherited his dad's white socks and gold bracelets. Young Murray's taking over the main chair next year. Murray's going to provide back-up for when things get hot around morning coffee time. Andy Scarlatti's got his law degree. Spends most of his time at Murray's eating doughnuts. Says he's decided to specialise in maritime law. Shipwrecks. Salvage. That kind of thing.'

'But there hasn't been a wreck in Apprehensive Bay since the *Heavy Going* went down in 1863.'

'I said that. And he said he didn't want to be overloaded. Ask me, he's doing just that with the doughnuts.'

'How are things at the *Telegraph?* Roy Calloway still running things?'

'Ran into him the other day,' said Dad. 'He was asking about you. Sends his best wishes for the wedding. Said he was always sorry he fired you, and you can have your old job back any time you want. It's a generous offer, Johnny. Maybe you should think about it.'

'I don't think so. Dad, what's really wrong with Mum?' He looked at me like a rabbit caught in headlights. 'I just checked with my agent's PA. She only booked one seat on the plane. Yours. Mum was never coming. What's the story?'

Dad gave a long sigh, glanced at Cheryl.

'Shouldn't we talk about this some other time?'

'There's nothing you can say to me that Cheryl can't hear.'

'It's this fucking Church thing, Johnny.' A normal enough expletive from anyone else. From Dad it was nitroglycerine. His face was working as if there was an intense battle raging inside. 'I sometimes wonder if it does more harm than good.'

'How do you mean?'

'She was concerned when you called with the news. But she thought you might change your mind. Then the wedding invitation arrived. She saw the name of the church. Saint George's. Anglican. Your mum said she'd never set foot inside a heathen church and she didn't intend to start now.'

'Not even for her son's wedding?'

'I'm sorry, Johnny. Really sorry. But your mum's dyed-in-the-wool Irish Catholic. Always been a black-and-white kind of person. She has her principles. And she sticks to them. She's upset you've lapsed from the Faith. And that you'll be bringing your children up outside the Church. And that you're marrying a . . . '

'Heathen.' Cheryl laughed. 'I've been called a lot of things in my time but never that. Sounds like something from the Dark Ages.'

'It is,' I said. 'It's completely fucking ridiculous. And what about you, Dad? How come you're here?'

'I'm an Epicurean, Johnny. Quiet life. Keep things on an even keel. Don't go looking for trouble, chances are you won't find it. I've loved your mum ever since she got up at the Workingmen's Club and sang "My Blackjack Man". She's a good, kind, decent woman with a heart of gold. Until this, I've always gone along with whatever she wanted. But this time I felt she was wrong. I said to her, "It's Johnny's life. Not up to us to interfere or make judgments. Long as he's happy, that's all that matters. God's not going to condemn you to everlasting damnation if you sit in an Anglican church to watch your son get married."'

'And what did she say?'

'You know your mum, Johnny. Once she gets hold of something she's like a bulldog with a bone. You'd have to kill her to make her let go. And even then . . . '

'You stood up to her, Dad.'

'I said, "I'm going, Moira, even if you're not." Things got a little overheated. She hasn't spoken to me since.'

Dad looked old and tired and miserable. And it was all my fault.

'Sorry, Dad,' I said. 'I didn't mean to cause all this trouble.'

'We didn't, Fitz.' Cheryl stepped in. 'Your mum did. She's in the wrong. Not you. Joe, can I just say, from the bottom of my heart, thank you. It's not what people say that matters, but what they do. And you've done a wonderful thing. You've made us both very proud.'

Dad shrugged and looked away. I sensed there was more. Perhaps I should have given him the chance to say it, because we'd never talked like this before and might never again. But he looked so tired from his enormous journey, I didn't have the heart to press him further.

'I'll show you to your room,' I said. 'Take it easy. Come down whenever you're ready.'

'Traffic on the way here was insane, Johnny,' Dad said as he climbed the stairs behind me. 'What's the rush? That's what I'd like to know. Sorry I said the F-word. Hope Cheryl wasn't offended.'

'I think she's heard it before, Dad.'

'Guess so. Nice lady, Johnny. Good teeth. Eight out of ten. Maybe even nine. I'd need a closer look to be sure, though.'

'Did you bring your tools?'

'Carried 'em onto the plane just in case. Forty thousand feet. Gravity takes over. Pilot's fillings could drop out.'

I left Dad in his room and went back downstairs, seething with hurt, anger, frustration.

'The bloody, fucking Catholic Church,' I said to Cheryl. 'Was there ever a more evil institution? How can it condone this kind of bigotry?'

'Maybe she'll change her mind,' said Cheryl. 'Turn up at the last minute. There's still time.'

I shook my head.

'My mum's never changed her mind about anything. I don't think she'll start now.'

Chapter 36

I'd kept in touch with Jane and the guys at Hire-A-Hack. Whenever I was in London between eleven and three, I'd drop into the Rising Sun for a pint or two. John Carnforth hadn't taken much persuading to become my best man.

'What time's the wedding?'

'Eleven in the morning.'

'When does the drinking start?'

'About one in the afternoon.'

'And finish?'

'Should still be going strong at Sunday breakfast.'

'Fair enough. What about a stag party?'

'I thought we might have it here on Thursday night. Nothing special. Just a few close friends. And my dad.'

It began like that.

John, Jane, Roger and Nigel from Hire-A-Hack. Alex from Himalaya Street. Tom Prescott-Jones from PBI. Dad and me. John holding forth from his corner about the joke of life, the perfidy of thoroughbreds, the charms of betting shops, and the decline and fall of pubs in general and the Rising Sun in particular. Nigel hanging onto a fag for life-support. Roger offering snapshots of his new offspring with very few takers. Jane there to keep everyone in check, although a drink in each hand looked ominous. Alex telling everyone how many times love had blossomed among his transients. Dad discovering a fellow vintage motorbike fanatic in Tom, who owned an Ariel Square Four and a Triumph Thunderbird.

Things were on an even keel until Ava arrived. Ava was a large woman with barbed-wire hair, a vermilion slash of lipstick and yellow teeth.

'I've just got out of Holloway,' she said to John. 'Where's the fifty quid you owe me? Plus interest.'

'Ava, my love,' said John, 'you'd only give it to the barman. So why don't I save you the trouble. Have a bottle of bubbly. Have two. Join us. Fitz here's getting married on Saturday.'

She looked at me as if I had a terminal disease.

'You poor, sad fucker. Want one last fling? Ten quid. Bergman's delivery entrance is just around the corner. Deep doorway. Cardboard boxes. No kissing, mind.'

'Sounds like a good deal to me, Johnny,' said Dad. 'I think you should accept.'

'Thanks,' I said, 'but I'll decline on this occasion.'

'How about you, Granddad?'

When Dad seemed to be considering the offer I took him aside.

'You can do better, Dad.'

Dad nodded.

'Thought so when I saw the colour of her teeth.'

Ava shrugged off his smile of regret and turned her attention to a bottle of vintage Lanson. Then a bloke in a black leather jacket walked across.

'Reg's bearing up,' he said to John. 'He was wondering why you ain't been to see him.'

'Thought he was in solitary.' John drained his glass and waved it at the barman. 'Clobbered a screw with his shoe.'

'They let him out last week. What's everyone drinking? I'll have a pint.'

'What of?'

'Anything. Whisky for preference.'

News that free drink was available to anyone claiming

acquaintance with John's corner rippled across the bar and flowed into the street. Three Australians who swore they'd known me at Himalaya Street came from nowhere. A man in a stained suit who said he'd been in Dad's class at school, or someone very much like him, was handed a large Guinness. A guy in a blazer Tom had once played squash with invited Jane to sit on his knee. A woman in a tight plastic skirt who said she was writing John's unauthorised biography leaned against me like the Tower of Pisa.

As the hero of the hour I was toasted and cheered and before long was sitting on the bar singing 'As I Roved Out' with Dad beside me on his tin whistle. Then Dad was doing the 'Sligo Reel' and Ava was jigging with the black leather jacket after she'd come back from a quick visit outside with the stained suit.

They threw us out a little after eleven. We milled around until John said, 'Let's go to a little club I know.'

Three taxis left the Rising Sun in line astern as if we were *poilus* heading for the Western Front. We piled through a Soho doorway sandwiched between a dirty bookshop and a juice bar. Up several flights and into a room with a disco floor and people sitting around a dimly-lit bar clutching cocktails. A woman who said she was a friend of Jane's cracked a capsule with her thumbnail and stuck it up my nose. Alex came by and suggested we do a few lines. He set out the white powder on a closed toilet lid with an Amex Gold Card and gave me a rolled-up ten-pound note. I inhaled.

'You're Alexander the Great,' I said.

'And you're Fitz Perfect.'

Which at the time seemed hilarious. When we returned to the bar, there was no sign of Dad.

'I wouldn't worry.' John handed me a salt-rimmed margarita. 'Last time I saw him he was getting into a cab with Jane. He's in good hands.'

A taxi dropped me at the Savoy Hotel. The driver called to the guy in the frock coat and top hat who was on the door.

'Poor bastard's gettin' married termorrer. I says to 'im, "I'll take you to Eef Row if you like. Fuck off while you got the chance if I was you."'

The commissionaire gave me a gloved salute as he held the door open. 'Take no notice of him, sir. I've been married thirty-five years, never regretted a minute. Thank you very much, sir. Very generous.'

I set an unsteady course for the reception desk, grasped it and held on, as if a sudden gust might carry me away.

'Good morning. Kennedy. Room 501. Any messages?'

The guy behind the desk tapped his keyboard.

'Nothing, sir.'

'Did my father come in yet? Room 503?'

'No, sir.'

'Would you please let me know when he does?'

'Certainly, sir.'

Clutching my room key I set sail for the lifts, tacking between tables and chairs. On the fifth floor I eventually married the key to its lock with both hands, fell into my room and went out for the count.

A distant ringing brought me back. Became louder until it pierced my thick skull. I grappled for the phone.

'Mnumph.'

'Johnny, it's me.'

'Dad? Where are you? What time is it?'

'A little after eleven. I just got back. Do you feel like some breakfast?'

'Sure. My place or yours?'

'Yours.'

A couple of minutes later I let Dad in. He looked as if he'd just returned from a health farm.

'Great night, Johnny. You look terrible.'

I drew the curtains, winced as daylight stabbed my eyes, pulled them back.

'Order something, Dad. Whatever you want. Just coffee for me. What happened to you?'

Dad ordered a full English breakfast, then stood by the window looking across the river to the South Bank.

'You know, Johnny, ever since I can remember I've loved playing in a band. When I get up on that stand, the music flows through me like an electric current. I feel alive. Powerful. Special. I can make people feel every kind of emotion. Happy one minute, tears the next.'

'You become a different person when you play,' I said. 'You really come alive.'

'I wish I'd done more with it, Johnny. A guy offered us a recording contract once, and the chance to go on tour. Soon after I'd met your mother. I'd only just qualified from dental school. "You can't throw it all away," she said. And "I don't want to marry a gypsy." Tommy was game. But your mum put her foot down. So I told the guy we were happy just doing gigs around Bullock. Weddings, wakes, Fridays at the Club. She was right, of course. Your mother always is. Almost always.'

'What happened last night, Dad?'

There was a tap on the door. Breakfast came in on a trolley. A waiter set it up, took his tip and left. Dad sat down to bacon and eggs. I sat in a tub chair nursing my coffee and my headache.

'Jane took me to a club in Shepherd's Bush. Slattery's. The band had finished their last set. By the time we got there they were just fooling around. I pulled out my tin whistle, played a few bars. One of the guys lent me his flute. I played "Blackjack Man". Next thing I know we're all jamming away, having a hell of a time. Jane sang a few tunes. She's got a good voice, you know. About six this morning we went to one of the markets where the pubs are open early, got stuck into the Guinness. Broke up about half an hour ago.'

'Who was in the band?'

'I didn't get most of the guys' names. But one of them was Declan Maloney. Johnny, I got to play with Declan. And he said I was good. "You're the main man on that flute, Joe," he said. "We're back across the water this afternoon. Do you want to come along?" I said I had a wedding to go to, but I might catch up with them later.'

'I'm glad you had a great time,' I said, knowing how much a meeting with Maloney would have meant. 'Did Jane get off to work OK?'

Dad suspended his knife and fork in mid-air.

'Not exactly.'

'How do you mean?'

'She's . . . er . . . next door . . . having a bit of a rest. She said no one'll be at work this morning anyway. They never are after a late night.'

'I see,' I said. 'Well, you really did have a good time, didn't you?'

'It's not what you think, Johnny,' said Dad. 'We've just been talking. I've talked more in the past twenty-four hours than the whole of my life. I wish I'd done all this thirty years ago. We only get one chance. Never took mine. Make sure you don't make the same mistake.'

'I always thought you were happy,' I said. 'With your Vincent, your dental practice, Mum and your music.'

'We did our best to give you a good home. Make you feel loved. No need for you to know what was really happening. Hell of a lot can go through a man's mind when he's working in his shed. Every night when I was polishing the Vincent's ports, I couldn't help wondering what might have been. But there's no going back. All we can do is make the best of what we have. You happy, Johnny? Doing what you're doing?'

'You mean the writing?'

'Everything.'

'If I hadn't met Cheryl, we wouldn't be sitting here now, having breakfast in one of the most expensive hotels in London. I've got a contract most writers would die for. And a fiancée, too. Who wouldn't be happy?'

'You ever see anything of that girl who came out to Bullock for the Dick Worth story? What was her name?'

'Frankie.'

'Agnes said you were hooked.'

'I saw her once. It's over and done with.'

'I'll leave you in peace,' said Dad. 'Jane wants to take me to a place by the river for lunch. I'll find my own way back.' He paused at the door. 'I'm very proud of you, Johnny. Proud to call you my son. Ever since . . . '

'Ever since what, Dad?'

'I talk too much, that's my trouble. I'll see you later.'

I sat by the window finishing my coffee and wishing Dad wasn't such a terrible liar.

On our wedding day, Dad sat behind John Carnforth in the second row on my side of the aisle. When John read out the telegrams, there was one from Murray's Barber Shop, and another from the Calloways next door, but our house in Wey Street maintained its stubborn silence.

Chapter 37

*W*hen the *Fat Parrot Sings* launched on the second of November 1987 and became an instant hit. People needed something to cheer them up after the Great Storm and Black Friday, and *Fat Parrot* was perfect timing. Three weeks before Christmas, Helen Valentino called.

'Fitz, it's time to call for tenders for the movie rights. The studios are falling over themselves. We'll be in cinemas across the States and worldwide within twelve to eighteen months. By which time we'll have the second book ready.'

'What about Martin Cole?'

'He's bitter about the way we're handling this. No matter how many times I tell him otherwise, he still thinks we're under a moral obligation to award him the rights. How is Cheryl?'

'Martin's putting her under a lot of pressure. Calls every week. It's an impossible situation.'

'It'll all be over by Christmas,' said Helen. 'Once the rights are assigned, he'll either be a happy man or he'll have to accept that he's lost and get on with life. He can't brood forever.'

Helen was right about most things, but she was wrong about Martin Cole. On the twenty-first of December he discovered Greenberg Productions had won the Laura Friday movie rights. Martin didn't call Cheryl. He called me.

'You asshole. You think you can fuck with me? If you weren't married to my daughter, I'd fucking kill you. As it is, I'm just gonna break you. Merry Christmas, my friend!'

I didn't tell Cheryl about the call. It was our first married

Christmas and I didn't want to spoil it with a black cloud.

We decided to spend Christmas Day at Barton Lodge. On Boxing Day we'd fly to Zermatt for a week's skiing. Cheryl was still looking for theatre work, but a house deep in the Gloucestershire countryside wasn't an ideal base, so as soon as we got back she'd look for a little flat in town.

Throughout that autumn Cheryl had cultivated a growing circle of local friends, mainly through the church where we'd been married, which Cheryl went to for the social contact. Each Sunday morning she snared a widow and brought her back for lunch. Occasionally she'd catch a male and present him at the front door like a cat with a sparrow.

The village seemed full of them. Whenever I walked to the pub for a quiet pint they'd look up from their weeding, haul themselves upright to return my greeting, or watch me pass from a gloomy living room and wave if I waved first. Harmless old souls, painfully polite, who'd accepted Cheryl's invitation to Christmas Day lunch with little notes on headed paper, written in ink with shaky hands.

Twelve of them arrived late on Christmas morning, including Sir Edward Carbrook, who'd long since retired as Permanent Secretary at the Ministry of Transport. Once a club champion at tennis, he was hunched over a stick as he stood at the door, removing his brown leather gloves. He had mottled skin, a cadaverous face and a right eye with a mind of its own.

'Good to see you, Sir Edward. Merry Christmas.' I shook his skeletal fingers. 'You're looking well.'

'It's a recording,' he said.

'What is?'

'The bells. They can't afford to pay the ringers any more. Not even at Christmas.'

'I said you're looking well.' I raised my voice and aimed it at his hearing aid. 'Let me take your coat. Come in. The others are having sherry in front of the fire.'

'Has she really? I thought she didn't have one.'

'Who, Sir Edward? Have what?'

'Cheryl. A mother. Sent her a wire. Isn't that what you said?' He tapped a little plastic box attached to his waistcoat. 'Damned thing's playing up again.'

In the living room our guests were standing in little groups, clutching crystal glasses and mince pies. Miles Short, Economics Editor of *The Times* in the pre-Murdoch years. Six-feet-four when young, with broad shoulders, large ears sprouting hairs like old potatoes. Millicent Hart-Davies, in her late seventies but still flirtatious. Milly had been an It Girl, forever in the gossip columns as The Other Woman. The eyes that had once caused so much trouble still offered their sleepy invitation as I refilled her glass. Brigadier-General Sir Giles Heathcote 'Stony' Mason stood At Ease in front of the fire. Right hand tucked behind his back. Cup and saucer clamped between the thumb and finger of his prosthetic left hand. Stony had lost his right leg at Monte Cassino, along with a hand, an eye, and most of his face. By rights he should have died a soldier's death, but there he was, well into his eighties, inspecting the state of my uniform. Sally Sargent, who'd never been a star but had appeared in dozens of films in the 'forties and 'fifties, usually playing the woman crying as the train leaves the station. She lived alone at Hollyhock Cottage with several cats and an overweight Jack Russell.

There were others whose names I couldn't remember. A sclerotic surgeon who'd once been at the beck and call of the Royal Family. An overweight chap wearing a polka-dot bow tie who'd long ago appeared as an occasional guest on the Sunday night panel game, *What's My Line?* A woman with a loud voice who'd been a nurse during the Blitz, and then governor of a prison. She had white hair, set in stiff curls, a masculine face, a heavy body in a Laura Ashley dress.

'I was in Prague earlier this year,' Milly was saying. 'For the Music Festival. Too much Dvorak and Smetana for my liking.'

'Did you see the Old New Synagogue?' asked Miles Short. 'The Holy Ark?'

'Ark? Ark? What ark?' Carbrook offered his glass and took a mince pie from a dish Cheryl was passing around.

''Ark the 'erald angels sing,' sang Milly in a mock-Cockney voice.

'*Raiders of the Lost Ark.* That was a good film,' said the surgeon. 'I liked Harrison Ford.'

'Ford?' said Carbrook. 'I used to have an old Ford Model A. Tough as old boots she was. No one could match her.'

'She certainly is,' said Mason.

'What?' said Carbrook. 'Who?'

'Thatcher,' said Mason. 'Best Prime Minister since Churchill. Gave the miners their comeuppance.'

I caught Cheryl's wry glance, smiled. She blew me a kiss.

Earlier in the day, Cheryl and I had exchanged presents. I'd arranged to have hers delivered that morning, wrapped in a gigantic bow. A pale blue Lotus Esprit. Cheryl's favourite colour. She'd been ecstatic. Cheryl had given me a video recorder and a complete set of Woody Allen tapes.

Dad had sent me his Vincent manual. The letter with it said he didn't need it any more, and it might bring back happy memories. As I turned the oil-stained pages I could see his workshop, hear the thunder of the huge engine, smell white smoke as it belched from the bike's twin exhausts, feel Maria Santos Almeida's Meyer lemons press against my back when she climbed aboard for the first time.

There was nothing from Mum. I hadn't heard from her since before the wedding, although I'd called several times. If she answered the phone and heard my voice she'd pass it to Dad. I'd written. Dad said she never opened the letters. Just tore them up and threw them in the rubbish.

There'd been a small gift-wrapped present without any details of the sender. I'd grinned at Cheryl, given it a shake.

'Wonder if it's a time bomb.'

When I'd opened it there'd been a movie tape inside. *Some Like It Hot.* My all-time favourite.

'It's probably from Daddy,' Cheryl had said. 'You remember you told him how much you liked the movie when we were over there? He's doing his best.' Cheryl gave me a kiss. 'He suggested I give you the video recorder. He was obviously thinking you'd be able to enjoy the movie any time you felt like it. I keep telling you, darling, Daddy's really a very kind man. You should make more of an effort.'

I wondered whether I should tell Cheryl about the last time we'd spoken. *If you weren't married to my daughter, I'd fucking kill you. As it is, I'm just gonna break you.* If that was being kind, what would unkind be like?

We finished our Christmas lunch in time to watch the Queen, then sat around wearing our silly hats making desultory conversation. It seemed unkind to kick everyone out into the cold, so I said, 'Let's watch *Some Like It Hot.* A great Christmas Day movie.'

I slotted the tape into my new player. We all sat back with our glasses of port and cognac. Cheryl said she'd seen the movie a dozen times, wanted some exercise, so she and the sclerotic surgeon went for a walk.

Tony Curtis and Jack Lemmon were aboard the train to Miami when the scene cut to a rough title. *Some Like It Even Hotter.* Then to a tropical beach. A good-looking guy was lying back on a sun-lounger wearing a skimpy pair of swimming trunks. Hawaiian music began to play. A girl appeared, wearing tassels on her nipples and a grass skirt. She began to dance in front of the guy, who was resting on his elbows, enjoying the performance. She beckoned to him to join her. They danced for a while, then she hooked her thumbs into his trunks and slipped them down to reveal a huge erection. She sank to her knees and took it into her mouth, then unhooked her skirt and sat astride him. A close-up showed his cock sliding into her as she continued to move her hips to the rhythm. The camera lingered on the girl's face, went into an extreme close-up of her tongue between her teeth, her closed eyes, her arched back, her ecstatic expression.

'I don't remember this,' said Sally Sargent.

'They seem to be enjoying themselves, anyway,' said Milly.

'Well I'm sorry but I think this is utterly disgusting. And not at all the sort of thing for a Christmas afternoon.'

The prison governor stood and glared down at me. With her paper crown and her handbag, she looked like the Queen.

'If you think this is funny, you are a very sick and wicked man, Mister Kennedy. I accepted your hospitality believing it to be in the true spirit of Christmas. But you have lured me here so that you could play a cruel practical joke. I shall be speaking to my solicitor. Good afternoon.'

'Not cricket, old boy,' said Mason as he followed her. 'All very well in the Mess. Not with ladies present, though.'

'I presume you knew nothing about this?' said Milly.

Everyone else had gone and I'd switched off the video player.

'Of course not.'

I gazed at the blank screen.

'Oh dear,' said Milly. 'You poor man. Whatever are you going to do?'

'I don't know.'

'Did you know she'd done this kind of thing?'

'I knew her father made porn movies. But Cheryl said she'd never been in one. I believed her.'

'And her father sent you this? What on earth did he think he was playing at?'

'Doing his best to destroy our marriage.'

When Cheryl came back I was sitting in the living room reading Waugh's *A Handful of Dust*.

'Where's everyone gone? I was going to make coffee.'

'They couldn't wait for the film to finish. Mason decided to go home and sleep off the lunch and everyone followed him. How was your walk?'

'Chilly. There's a biting east wind. Good, though. Helped clear away the cobwebs. Do you think everyone enjoyed themselves?'

'I'm sure they did.' I closed the book. 'It was a wonderful lunch. Tell you what. You've done enough for one day. You sit down. I'll make coffee. There's something we need to discuss.'

'Really? What's that?'

'An idea for my next book. Laura discovers something about her lover's past. A fraud. He went to prison for it. It wasn't so much the crime as the fact that he lied to her. She feels betrayed. She teaches Pavarotti to sing "Una Furtiva Lagrima" from Donizetti's *L'Elisir d'Amore* as she stabs her lover in the back.'

'Sounds interesting. It'll make a nice change from Abba. What are you going to call it?'

'*Weep No More, My Parrot*.'

Chapter 38

Cheryl broke her right leg on the first day. An icy piste, a momentary loss of control, *crack!* A clean break. Within two hours she was back at the hotel, splinted and crutched, ensconced in the lounge with a cognac, waiting for the ambulance to take her to the airport. We'd agreed I should stay for the rest of the week.

'I'm not sick, Fitz. I don't need you fussing around me.'

I was still coming to terms with Cheryl's perfidy and Martin's attempted coup. I felt sorry for her, but a few days alone would give me time to think. I'd decided not to give Martin the satisfaction of provoking a split. I knew what Cheryl would say. I'd written the script in my head while she was on her Christmas Day walk.

Cheryl: *I lied about my past because I didn't want to hurt you.*

Fitz: *But how could you debase yourself like that?*

Cheryl: *It didn't mean anything. I needed the money.*

Fitz: *You looked as if it meant something.*

Cheryl: *It's called acting, Fitz.*

Fitz: *Is that what you do when we make love? Act?*

Cheryl: *Of course not. I love you. I love making love with you. I'm sorry you saw it. It was a mean, rotten trick. I'm very angry with Daddy. What are you going to do?*

That was the question I hadn't yet answered. I loved Cheryl. Loved her and needed her. We were a team. Roped together for life. A mountain of Laura Friday books loomed above me like the Matterhorn. But was that a sufficient foundation for a marriage? What about trust?

I'd told myself it would return with time. As the memory of that Christmas Day afternoon faded and our marriage, our children, brought us ever closer, the significance of Cheryl's lie would fade. A white lie was better than a black truth.

Two days later the crisis went beyond my control when I made the mistake that cost me my marriage.

I'd gone into the lounge bar after a solitary dinner and was minding my own and my fourth Courvoisier's business. The skiing had been good. I was tired, and ready for bed. A woman slid into the leather banquette seat, tossed her shampoo commercial hair away from her face and gave me a film star smile. A nine out of ten on the Joe Kennedy Scale.

'*Bonsoir, monsieur!*'

'*Bonsoir.*'

'Would you like to go to a party?'

'Where?'

'Your room. Just *nous deux*. Or I could call a friend. A guy. Or another lady. How do you say? Whatever rocks your trolley.'

In the cold light of day I'd have declined with a smile of regret. But right then, right there, warmed by the fire and the cognac, the prospect of simple, uncomplicated sex with an attractive professional appealed to my sense of symmetry. It might, if only in my head, balance the scales of justice. Just like Dad with his drill if someone called him Joker.

'The two of us seems like a great idea.'

After I'd given her my credit card, she asked me to unzip her sheath dress, as if we'd been together for years. She stepped out of it, and placed it carefully on a chair with her bag on top.

We started with a spell in the Jacuzzi. After she'd explored my body for a while, she spread her long legs, and took my cock inside her. Occasionally she used an endearment. Baby, honey, *chéri*, sweetie. I could understand why. In her line of work you wouldn't want to use the wrong name.

Once we'd gone into the bedroom, she took two phials of amyl nitrate from her purse, and I ordered a bottle of champagne. Although by morning the precise details were unclear, my overall impression was that we'd had a fantastic time.

She slid from bed and went to the window, drew back the heavy curtains and stretched her arms above her head.

'It's a beautiful morning. Come and take a look at the view.'

She turned and came back, holding out both hands. As I stood up, she cupped them around my balls and cock and led me across the room, walking backwards, both of us laughing. We stood side by side looking across the car park to the snow-capped mountains, the rising sun like raspberry icing. I tried to concentrate, but her fingers were making it impossible. She turned, her bare breasts against my chest, kissed my neck.

'Let's go back to bed.'

A while later she said, 'What are you going to do today? Are you going skiing?'

'Later. I might read for a while. There's a good bookshop in the lobby. They have the latest translation of Cervantes' *Don Quixote*.'

'We studied Cervantes at The Sorbonne. It's a great book, especially Part Two. I loved the story of the Knight of the Mirrors.'

'You went to The Sorbonne?'

'I majored in Mediaeval European writers. What? You think I'm just a dumb prostitute or something?'

'No, not at all. I just . . . never thought . . . '

'It's OK. What are you doing all alone here in Zermatt anyway? Are you married? You don't have to lie. It doesn't bother me.'

'Yes, I'm married.'

'And where is your wife?'

'She broke her leg. She went home.'

'And while the cat's away, huh?'

'Not exactly. I've got my own reasons for being unfaithful.'

She laughed.

'If you pay for it, I wouldn't say that's being unfaithful. Perhaps if we had more time we could have a philosophical discussion. You seem like a nice man.'

'Thanks. You're a nice lady. Would you like some coffee? I could order breakfast.'

'I have to go. Unless . . . '

'Unless what?'

'Look,' she said. 'We can talk if you like. But it's two hundred an hour. I'm sorry. I can stay for two hours.'

'That's OK,' I said.

She filled in the credit card voucher, gave it to me to sign, returned beside me.

'I'm Annette.'

We shook hands.

'I'm Fitz — J. Fitz Kennedy. Professionally I'm Vince Humber.'

Her mouth dropped.

'The writer? *When the Fat Parrot Sings?*'

'That's me.'

'I loved Laura Friday and the parrot. So tell me, Fitz: why did you decide to be unfaithful? If that's how you wish to regard it.'

'Well, it's a long story.'

'You're paying for my time. I'm happy to listen.'

'It all began when a woman called Frankie Wilton arrived in Bullock to report on Dick Worth's penis transplant . . . '

'This sounds like a Laura Friday story. Do you think Cheryl knew about the movie? Was it coincidence she was out of the house when you played it? Or did she go for a walk on purpose?'

Annette was snuggled beneath the covers, just her face showing, her right hand interlaced with my left. The bedside clock said our time was almost up.

'I don't know what to think. I know she lied to me.'

'Maybe you're being too hard on her and yourself,' said Annette. 'If I met someone and got into a relationship, I'm not sure I'd tell the truth about what I do, or did, for a living. He might not understand that, for me, it's just a job. Cheryl might have lied to you to protect your feelings. Why didn't you confront her when she came back from her walk?'

'I almost did. But it was Christmas Day. We were going away for a week's holiday. I thought it would be better to talk about it, calmly and quietly, when we got back.'

'Meanwhile you'd be spending a week here with her, with this black cloud you keep talking about always in your head.'

I nodded.

'I know. It doesn't make sense. But the Kennedys have always avoided confrontation. I grew up in a house where there were things we never discussed.'

'Like what?'

'Like why my Aunt Agnes had an Irish accent and her brother, my dad, didn't.'

'I really do have to go soon. Another client. I have to shower and change.'

'You can do that here.'

Annette gave my hand a squeeze.

'He likes me to wear special clothes. I didn't bring them with me.'

'Ah. I see. So what do you think?'

'I think you're looking for an excuse to get out of this marriage. You said Cheryl helped you with the development of Laura Friday, came up with the name for the parrot. You feel obligated. And scared.'

'Scared? About what?'

'You think you need her. That you can't write your books without her. You feel grateful. And you hate it. You resent her for it. Now that you've discovered her dark secret, you'll keep coming back to it, like a dog to a bone. No matter how rich and famous you become. Maybe you even *blame* her for your success. You're stuck with Laura Friday. You feel trapped. But you only have yourself to blame. So maybe you'll keep on doing things like this. Getting your revenge. But hating yourself for it.'

'What do you think I should do?'

Annette laughed as she slipped out of bed and back into her sheath dress.

'I'm not going to tell you what to do, Fitz. It's your life.'

Chapter 39

Three days later I was breakfasting in bed when the phone rang.

'Fitz! It's Helen. Have you seen this morning's *Chronicle*?'

'No. Why?'

'You're on the front page. A long-range picture of a naked woman and a naked man standing at a hotel bedroom window with their genitalia fuzzed out and a headline that reads: "*Vince Humber Evens Score on Porn Star Wife Cheryl*". There's a byline. "*A Mary Francesca Wilton exclusive*".'

'*Jesus Christ!*'

'Sam Quercy's just been talking to Tom Prescott-Jones. Cheryl's invoking the prenup. Taking half of everything. Your entire current and future income and assets. High eight, possibly nine figures. Is this story true?'

'I'll get a copy from the shop in the lobby. The headline's true enough.'

'The office has been going crazy,' said Helen. 'Phones ringing their heads off. Barton Lodge under siege. Cheryl's in the Cromwell Clinic. We're flying her out to Los Angeles tomorrow. What are you going to do?'

'Do?'

My muscles ached. My face glowed. I'd just finished a perfect breakfast. I was looking forward to the hotel's New Year's Eve party. I was damned if I was going to allow anyone or anything to spoil my day.

'I'm going skiing. That's what I'm going to do.'

I came down from the mountain that afternoon feeling as if my entire being — mind, body and soul — had been refreshed. I'd hired an instructor for the day, an Austrian called Pieter, who'd taken me places I'd have feared alone. Down near-vertical faces, swinging knee-deep through virgin snow, at speed down long runs. When I clomped into the hotel lobby as the sun was setting, I realised I hadn't given a thought all day to Laura Friday, Cheryl, Frankie or the *Chronicle*.

So when a voice from a tub chair said 'Hi, Fitz!' it took a second or two to register the face.

'Frankie! I should have known. You here for the skiing?'

She took a long drag, stubbed out the half-finished cigarette, blew smoke from the side of her mouth.

'I'm not into winter sports, Fitz. Summer either, for that matter. Did you see today's *Chronicle*?'

'Helen read me the headline. That was enough. You happy, now that you've fucked up my marriage?'

'Feel like a drink?'

I looked down at her, remembering when we'd last seen each other, the morning after the awards dinner. Frankie sprawled face-down across the rumpled bed in a torn T-shirt, fluttering her fingers on the pillow as I left, grunting something which might have been goodbye. Now she was giving me a look that said she knew what I was thinking. Frankie had always been at least one step ahead of me.

'You owe me one,' I said. 'Maybe more than one.'

We went into Harry's Bar, just off the lobby. Dim wall lights, a little candle at each table in a glass dish, dark oak furniture. We sat at a table for four amid the early drinkers, mostly groups in sweaters and jeans. The guy behind the bar was polishing glasses. He came across to take our order.

'Lagavulin,' said Frankie. 'Straight. No ice.'

The barman nodded, turned to me.

'Courvoisier. Double.' The barman walked away. 'How did you know I was here?'

Frankie smiled.

'You always want to know how I do my job. I told you before. Good reporting's all about doing your homework. A couple of phone calls was all it took.'

'Why bother, Frankie? What have you got against me? I thought we were—'

'Friends? Lovers? You know your trouble, Fitz? You want it all. Cheryl and sweet domesticity. Me and the wild side. Annette for a simple, no-strings, professional fuck. Well, I'll tell you something. You can't have it. You can only travel one road at a time. I'm not saying the one you chose is right or wrong. It's going to make you rich. From where I sit, that makes you a target.'

'How did you know about Cheryl?'

'Simple.' The drinks arrived with a dish of pretzels, nuts and olives. Frankie took a swallow. 'Great malt. You should try it some time. I've got a contact in LA. Asked him to do a little digging. Wasn't difficult. You could have done the same thing yourself.'

'I didn't need to. I trusted Cheryl.'

Frankie laughed.

'Big mistake, Fitz. You're not in Bullock now. You can't go around believing everything people tell you. Life doesn't work like that.'

'My life does.'

'You mean to tell me you don't have any secrets? OK, Mister Holier-than-thou. Did you tell Cheryl about the awards night?'

'Of course not.'

'Case closed.'

I've always been amazed at how the brain works away at a problem, without conscious effort. Like when I'm stuck for an hour on a crossword clue. If I leave it for a while and come back to it, the answer pops up in a second. Like when my brain took a creative leap at the Long John Silver and the parrot idea popped out. Like now.

'You sent me that tape. It wasn't Martin Cole. It was you.'

Frankie sat back and clapped, as if I'd won first prize.

'A story's like a box of fireworks. Sometimes one spark can set it off in all directions. I had an idea what you'd do. You didn't let me down.'

'You followed me here.'

'Not me. Pete. A story like this is no good without a picture.'

'Pete took that bedroom window shot? How did he know . . . ?'

Frankie was sitting there, sipping her malt, having the time of her life. Watching my brain churn.

'Annette. She set me up.'

'I set you up, Fitz. Annette just did what she was paid to do. Stood at the window with you until Pete gave her a signal.'

'But afterwards. We talked all morning. She seemed so . . . '

'Warm? Tender? You thought she was your friend? She's a hooker, Fitz, not a therapist. We put a bug in her bag. Taped everything. When your book came out, I wondered about the Laura Friday connection. Good to have it confirmed. Should make great copy.'

'You really are one hell of a fucking bitch, Frankie.'

'Thanks. I do my best. What are you doing tonight?'

'There's a New Year's Eve party here at the hotel.'

'Sounds good. I feel like celebrating. Do you want to help me choose a new frock?'

Chapter 40

'Tom wants to fight,' said Helen.

We were at lunch the following week. Our usual table at Le Gavroche. I gazed bleakly at a gloomy London, the rain at forty-five degrees, street lamps already lit, and yearned for Zermatt. And Frankie.

'He says because Cheryl concealed her past there's a fifty-fifty chance the prenup's invalid.'

'I bet he does,' I said. 'I can see millions disappearing down a black hole called Legal Fees, being dragged through the courts for years and the papers having a field day. I want a settlement.'

'If you're sure?'

'I'm sure.'

Helen reached for her mobile phone and called Tom Prescott-Jones.

Tom rang me at Barton Lodge that evening.

'Sam Quercy opened at two hundred million. I beat him down to eighty. It's a great result.'

'It's daylight robbery, Tom, and you know it.'

'It's your call, Fitz.'

'How long will it take me to earn that much money?'

'Current estimates, taking into account book sales, profit percentage on movies, brand merchandising, I'd say eight to ten years.'

'Can I pay Cheryl over that time? Instalments?'

'Quercy's given us twenty-eight days. Otherwise he goes to court for an order to seize fifty per cent of everything. I've spoken to the merchant bankers. They'll advance the money in return for your movie profits.'

'You mean on *When the Fat Parrot Sings*?'

'No, on every Laura Friday movie.'

'You must be joking. For how long?'

'Forever. It's not as if you're going to starve, Fitz. You'll keep full royalties on book sales and other merchandising. You just won't make any money on the movies. That's not too bad, is it?'

'What if Laura flops? What if we succeed with a couple of movies but people grow tired of Laura and we only manage to pay back a percentage?'

'Ah,' said Tom, as if pleased I'd foreseen a potential hazard. 'There'll be a reversion clause. If we fail to make payments on time, they'll lock into your book sales royalties, other income and, if necessary, your assets. You've got to maintain Laura's popularity. That's the key. Drop that ball and you're fucked. Big-time bankruptcy.'

'There's no need to sound so cheerful about it, Tom.'

'Could be worse,' he said. 'All this publicity's doing wonders for sales. *Fat Parrot*'s going through the roof.'

'Send me the papers,' I said. 'Tell Quercy he has a deal. Do you know "The Rime of the Ancient Mariner"? *Instead of the cross, the albatross / about my neck was hung?*'

'I do, Fitz, and a sorry tale it is.'

'Well, mine's a fucking parrot. And I'm stuck with it for the rest of my life.'

Chapter 41

Early February 1988. One of those fake spring mornings England does so well. A warm sun, daffodils out, as if winter had ended early. People sat on benches around Covent Garden Plaza, their faces turned upwards like sunflowers, making the most of whatever crumbs the sunshine gods allowed them.

It was all gloom and open hostility indoors. We faced each other across the same lozenge-shaped table we'd used for the prenup agreement. I sat between Helen and Tom. Cheryl arrived a few minutes later flanked by Sam Quercy and Martin Cole. It was like a second take of the same scene, except this time the script would be different.

Cheryl looked corporate in a dark suit and white blouse, her hair tied back from a face that looked tired and strained. Her eyes said it all. I'd seen eyes like that once before. We'd gone to Longleat to look at the lions. One of a long line of cars crawling through the reserve. A female had padded towards us, stopped and looked at me with the coldest, greyest, most terrifying eyes I'd ever seen. If the window had been open, I'd have been lioness lunch. Cheryl's eyes were just like that. She fixed them on me like radar. No matter which way I turned or what I did, they were always there.

Sam Quercy looked nonchalant as he dumped his briefcase on the table, took out copies of the papers Tom had sent him, gave a set to Cheryl and Martin.

Tom coughed.

'Well, thanks for coming. I realise this isn't a pleasant

occasion, but it's best to get things clear in one face-to-face session, rather than backwards and forwards through third parties. Before we get down to details, can I ask Cheryl whether there's any chance of a reconciliation?'

'You must be kidding.' Martin Cole half-rose, a fleck of spittle on his beard. 'After what that asshole did to my daughter, he's lucky to be alive.'

Tom raised both hands, palms outwards.

'Let's try and keep this civilised. Cheryl?'

'I have nothing to say.'

'Fitz?'

'I'm sorry, Cheryl, but—'

Tom held up one hand this time.

'A straight yes or no will do.'

'I suppose not.'

'Very well. Sam and I have hammered out a settlement. I have here a bank draft for eighty million pounds, in return for which Cheryl agrees to relinquish all current and future claim to Fitz's earnings and assets. Cheryl, if you're happy, I need you to initial the bottom of each page and sign and date at the end.'

'Happy?' Cheryl looked at me with venomous eyes. 'I'm fucking ecstatic.'

We crowded into the one lift back down to the lobby. This time there was no need for the emergency stop button. As we emerged from the building, a burst of applause sent a flock of pigeons fluttering above our heads. It wasn't for us. A guy on a unicycle was taking a bow. I watched Cheryl climb into a black cab, followed by her daddy and by Sam Quercy. She did not look back then, or as the taxi drove away. I never saw her again.

Chapter 42

When the Fat Parrot Sings was released as a movie in the UK and across the world in March 1989. Greenberg Productions had paid fifty million dollars for the all-time movie rights. Solly Greenberg recouped his investment within a month of its release.

The film had been given a light touch by Charles (*The Unimaginable Polly Curtain, Three Men and a Bum-Bag, Nicely Does It*) Knowles. Everyone agreed the photography, editing and music were stunning, but Laura herself, played by Jane Lloyd Wright, lacked what *The New Yorker* critic Langoustine Briggs called 'the brittle disaffected cynicism and ruthless brutality' that was the quintessential Laura Friday.

Solly asked Castanet, Hollywood's top talent agency, to search for an unknown to play Laura in the second movie, *Weep No More, My Parrot*. Everything clicked when Castanet secured the release on parole of Razoria Somme, one-time lead singer for the punk rock group SmashYerPhaceIn. Razoria was halfway through a five-year stretch for armed robbery.

Solly also hired whizz-kid director Pow-Lo (*Bush Baby, Mac Attack*) Cortez to give the movie attitude. Released in October 1990, *Weep No More* grossed over forty million dollars in its first weekend and went on to earn over two hundred million.

I was earning nothing from it, so I took little interest in the Laura Friday movie franchise. I churned out a Laura Friday novel every year. Helen sent it to Solly to arrange the screenplay. My *nom de plume* got a credit, but that was as far as it went. But, so long as the movie profits kept the merchant bankers' fingers out of my book royalties, I was happy.

As the franchise grew, audiences wanted more. More effects, more stunts, more nudity, and above all more of Pavarotti the parrot. They loved him so much he began to get more screen time and to upstage Laura. As a result, Razoria's tantrums became legendary. Relations between Razoria and the parrots who played Pavarotti took a dive. They stopped speaking except during a take.

The fifth movie was *Nuns Shall Sleep*, based on my story about Laura's contract to assassinate a crooked Mother Superior. It had seemed a good idea for Pavarotti to sing something operatic, so he screeched 'Nessun dorma! Nessun dorma!' as Laura slid the Bowie knife through the black habit.

By then the screen spark between assassin and parrot had died. Solly decided to buy Razoria out of her contract and send her back to prison to finish her sentence.

'Which is more than she could ever do for me, Fitz,' he said during one long transatlantic phone call. 'We had cue cards all over the set. We'll be better off without her. Parrots cost — and eat — peanuts. And they don't snort cocaine before every take.'

Meanwhile my problem remained. I hated being tied down by Laura Friday and her parrot. Day after day I gazed out of my window at the foxes playing on the lawn and envied them their freedom to roam, then looked down at the page in my typewriter and wondered how I was ever going to write another word. Then the spectre of the merchant bankers loomed, and somehow I forced the words out. I didn't have writer's block. I had writer's constipation. Fear was the laxative.

I tried to write other stuff as J. Fitz Kennedy. But Helen rejected it all.

'Laura Friday's your genre. When women go into a bookshop

and see a new Vince Humber on the shelf, they know what they're getting. Laura gratifies their praying mantis desire to eat the male after mating, and Pavarotti satisfies their mothering instinct. I've told you many times: Vince Humber's a brand, Fitz. When you buy a bar of Cadbury's Dairy Milk, you don't want to unwrap it and discover it's a cake of soap. People couldn't care less about J. Fitz Kennedy.'

That was another aspect of the strange phenomenon that was Laura Friday. Women bought my books and went to see Laura's films. When I created Laura I'd never given a thought to her readership, but there'd been no mistaking the gender queuing for Vince Humber's signature whenever a new book was launched. Women of all ages, only occasionally interspersed with a grey-bearded man in an anorak.

And always the same two daft questions. *How did you get the idea for Pavarotti? Who is Laura?*

Even the great Martin Carboys, Lord Carboys of Cleckheaton to his peers, couldn't resist it. Helen said it was a great honour to be the special guest on his *For Art's Sake!* programme on Channel 4, unkindly dubbed *For Christ's Sake!* by jealous critics. Carboys was God, and those who stayed up until eleven-thirty on a Sunday evening were forever complaining about his time-slot. For me its only benefit was an excuse for a day away from the typewriter.

'Vince Humber,' he said in his flat Yorkshire accent as the screen showed clips from Laura's movies. 'Born Blackjack, County Mayo, into a loving and devout Catholic family. Aunt a nun. Sister a nun. Father a Catholic dentist. A surprising background, you'd have thought, for one of the most successful popular fiction writers of the past twenty years and for the creator of one of the century's most brutal female characters. His Laura Friday books sell in their millions, and his parrot Pavarotti has become one of the great icons of the literary and film world.'

And then, as the screen cut to the studio where he and I were sitting in near darkness:'Tell me, Mister Humber, there have been many women in your life. Which of them is Laura? Or is she a distillation of them all?'

On his Radio 4 *Mind and the Gap* programme one Saturday morning, the psychiatrist Jonathan Hess had come at the question from another direction. By delving into my Catholic psyche.

'You were born guilty,' he said, 'surrounded by powerful women. I'm thinking of your mother, your aunt, and your sister. But there may have been others. You chose to expiate that guilt by creating a fictional character, a *femme fatale*, and give her the freedom to assassinate whomever she chose without fear of reprisal. Pavarotti is, of course, the voice of God which in your real life you have chosen to deny. Isn't that who Laura is, Vince? Haven't those women exerted the predominant influence upon your creative expression?'

A thought came to me as I sipped my BBC coffee.

'No,' I said. 'I think it was Murray.'

'Murray?' Hess flipped through his notes. 'But your father's name is Joe.'

Chapter 43

Dad died in March 1997. For his seventieth birthday, the Workingmen's Club had organised a parade. Dad was perched on his Vincent on the back of a truck, the bike facing backwards. As Dad reversed down Thames Street a parade of marching girls, brass bands and a special Murray's Barber Shop float with Father Connolly beneath the scissors made its slow procession through the town.

Most of the time Dad sat there and waved, but as he reached Meggett's department store he couldn't resist the urge to twiddle a lever or two, leap out of the saddle, and launch his right leg down on the kick-start.

It was the accident Dad had striven all his life to avoid, and Mum had always predicted. The investigating mechanics said the inlet and exhaust ports were so highly polished that when he primed the ignition they had allowed an enormous build-up of gases. When Dad leapt onto the kick-start the compression backfired and hurled him over the handlebars. As he soared, his left shoe caught on the gear lever. The engine started. The bike roared off the back of the truck. Half a ton of highly polished metal fell on Dad's head.

I flew back to Bullock for the funeral, the first time I'd returned since I'd left with Agnes's blessing to resolve my feelings for Frankie Wilton. At thirty-seven that seemed a ridiculous quest, but at twenty-six it had been all-consuming. I was prepared for a cold reception. Although my marriage had been over for nine years, Mum and Carmel would never forgive me for marrying outside the One True Faith. Far from healing the wound, my subsequent divorce had deepened it.

You made your bed, said Carmel in a letter she wrote from Zimbabwe soon after she heard the news, *and you should lie on it. Whether or not you attend Mass, you were born a Catholic. In the eyes of God you will always remain married to Cheryl.*

I'd written back. *I can't be held responsible for the circumstances of my birth. Anyway, it's all academic. I have no intention of ever marrying again.*

I hadn't heard from Carmel since, although I'd written to her care of the Sacred Sisters convent. Dad had said she spent much of her time in remote places. I could never be sure they redirected my letters.

Mum had maintained her hostile silence. When I parked the rental car outside our house in Wey Street she came to the door, but there was no welcoming smile.

'Hello, Mum.' I dropped my bag and gave her a hug. She felt cold and unyielding. 'I'm sorry about Dad.'

'You can't stay here,' she said. 'Go back where you belong.'

'I've come to say goodbye to him. And I thought you might need some help.'

'Carmel's here. We don't need you. Your dad's at Percy Cartwright's.'

'Can I see him?'

'I can't stop you.'

I stood there looking at the ground. I felt like a kid again, Mum warning me about the Dire Consequences of whatever mortal sin I'd committed and enquiring whether my underwear was clean.

'Look, Mum,' I said. 'There's just the three of us now. You, me, and Carmel.'

'You're wrong, Johnny,' she said. 'The three of us is Carmel, me, and the Church. When you married outside God's Grace, you cast yourself out. There's only one way back into this house, and that's through the Confessional.'

'I see.' I hefted my bag onto my shoulder. 'I'm sorry, Mum. But I'm not into that kind of hypocrisy. I was hoping Dad's death might have brought us together. I'll stay somewhere else.'

For old times' sake I checked into the Yes Oh Yes Motel. The Neptune Room where Frankie had stayed was taken. I was given the Mars Room. A starlit ceiling. Planets for lampshades. Outer space wallpaper. A welcoming Mars Bar on each pillow. Once I'd dumped my bags and showered, I drove downtown to Percy Cartwright's.

I'd forgotten how to drive in Bullock, so I was pulled over almost as soon as I left the motel. The cop parked behind me. I could see him approaching in my offside mirror. There was more belly, and the face was heavier, but it was unmistakably Seth Nelson. He leaned against the driver's door.

'Where's the fire, chief?'

'Sorry, Seth,' I said. 'I just got in from London. I wasn't thinking.'

He frowned.

'Do I know you?'

'Johnny Kennedy. Joke's boy.'

'Oh, yeah, sorry about your dad, Johnny. He was a good man. Everyone in Bullock respected him. Great dentist. Terrible driver, though. Must run in the family. He drove too slow, you drive too fast. Guess it just about evens things out. Take it easy. I'll see you tomorrow. I'll be leading the funeral procession.'

I angle-parked outside Percy's and went into reception, a small space with two G Plan chairs, an unoccupied desk, a vase of flowers and a framed certificate stating that Percy Cartwright was a Licensed Funeral Director. I rang the bell. Percy came through a door marked *No Entry, Authorised Personnel Only*, and offered his hand.

'I was having a drink with Joke in the Club the day before he died,' he said. 'Had one of my premonitions. Didn't say anything, though. Didn't want to spoil his birthday.'

We went through to a dimly-lit room where Dad's coffin rested on a velvet-covered bier.

'He wasn't wearing a helmet,' said Percy as I looked down at Dad's peaceful face, his crossed hands interlaced with rosary beads. 'When we were having a beer, I said he should. But he said the law didn't require it if you were sitting on the back of a truck. People wouldn't want to wave at a helmet. He was always one for caring more about other people than himself.'

'Was there any chance he could have been saved?'

Percy shook his head.

'He'd gone by the time he arrived at A&E. Father Connolly administered the Last Rites, though, despite still wearing the shaving cream. Who'd have thought the bike would do that to him, Johnny? After all the love and care Joke gave it over the years. Just goes to show. Doesn't pay to get too close to anyone or anything. Next thing you know it turns around and bites you in the bum. Guess I don't need to tell you that. I'll leave you two in peace.'

I sat beside Dad's coffin and allowed a thousand memories to flood my brain. The morning Dad reversed the Humber Super Snipe out of the garage and into the letter box. His only attempt at gardening, when he'd pulled up Mum's natives, thinking they were weeds. Dad at Mass, a half-beat behind everyone else in his Responses. Always in trouble with Mum. He had a motto which he whispered to me after one of Mum's tirades. '*Semper in Excretum*, Johnny. Always in the shit.'

Dad had been absent-minded in everything but his dentistry, his music and his Vincent. It was only when he came to London, escaping Mum's omnipresence, that I had understood why. His mind might have been absent, but it had not been vacant. It had been touring the country and the world with his band. Gigging in Irish pubs and clubs. Making records. Writing songs. Living his dream. At least his dream had come true when he met Declan Maloney.

I remembered taking him to Heathrow's Terminal Three. After the wedding he'd been to Blackjack to look up the Kennedy family and had gone on to meet up with Maloney for a folk festival. He'd returned with a sparkle in his eyes. As we sat in the lounge, I saw that his eyes had dimmed, like the lights in the room where I now sat. When they called the flight I hugged him and said, 'Thanks for coming, Dad. I hope you're not in too much trouble.'

'I wouldn't have missed it for the world, Johnny,' he said. 'The stag party, the wedding, the trip to Ireland. Jane.'

I'd never asked whether he and Jane had become lovers. It was none of my business. But when he spoke her name a wistful look had come over his face, and his eyes had briefly regained their spark.

'You don't have to go back, Dad.'

He'd shaken his head.

'It's too late. I made my decision thirty years ago.'

I'd watched him walk away, turn, wave, walk on. He'd braced his shoulders. As if steeling himself. It was the last time I saw him alive.

I remembered a kind and decent man who'd never intentionally hurt a fly. Who had welcomed Maria Santos Almeida and Frankie Wilton and Cheryl Cole into his life and would have welcomed Lucrezia Borgia or Mata Hari if he thought they'd make me happy.

I stood. Looked down at his body. Bent and kissed his cold forehead.

'Goodbye, Dad. I love you.'

The following day a lone piper preceded Seth Nelson, who had draped his flashing lights in black. People stood in silence as the funeral procession passed, many running tongues across their teeth. Over the years Dad's gentle hands had touched most mouths in Bullock.

There wasn't enough room in Saint Mary the Grateful, so the funeral was held in the Bullock Workingmen's Club with Dad's coffin perched on two height-adjustable drinking tables, the bar closed and the lights over the pool tables turned down low.

The Club was packed, so they relayed the service into the car park where people sat on bonnets with their heads bowed.

Chapter 44

It was a flying visit, but I couldn't leave Bullock without a visit to Murray's Barber Shop. Everyone had been at the funeral. The shop had closed for the day and its customers had retired to the Workingmen's Club where the bar had opened once Dad had left.

Murray was back in business the next morning looking a little heavy-eyed. Once everyone had greeted me with murmurs of condolence, the talk was all about Dad.

'He had a way with teeth, Fitz.'

'Stuttering' Hutch Scandrett was wearing a wig that made him look twenty years younger from the eyebrows up.

'I remember once. I had a rogue molar. A total pain. Couldn't stutter on the radio, just judder a little. Your dad touched it, talked to it in that soft voice of his, drilled a little, nothing violent, and, you know, I didn't feel a thing. As if I wasn't there. Just Joe communing with my teeth.'

'The Teeth Whisperer,' said Septimus Punch.

Septimus had replaced his father, Genghis, as Mayor. Genghis had resigned rather than face impeachment following the Stain on the Chain scandal, but the Punch Mayoral Dynasty had proved unshakable. Septimus was about to complete his second term. He had spoken at the funeral about Bullock's Proud Sons who were Always There when the votes were being counted, and had taken the opportunity to remind everyone that the mayoral elections were only four months away.

'It's not something you learn. Some people are born with an

instinctive empathy. Like me and leadership. Joke had a special affinity with teeth.'

'Nature nurture,' said Murray.

In the eleven years since I'd seen him, Murray had morphed into his father's shoes. He had the same stoop as he stood at the chair, the same way of looking at you in the mirror with his head slightly cocked, the same way of using scissors and comb as extensions of his body.

'It's the fundamental debate. How much of what we do, say, think, is predetermined and how much is free will?'

'How does it go? *A devil, a born devil, on whose nature Nurture can never stick*,' said Merv the Mink. '*The Tempest*. Act Four, Scene One. If I remember correctly.'

Murray had the *Complete Works* on his shelves. Merv had always been fond of them. He hadn't changed much over the years, either. Same white shoes, white socks, white trousers and shirt, gold necklace, gold bracelets, gold filling to his right upper frontal. The business might now be called Merv's My T Motors, but it was still the same car yard that had been Tony's My T Motors when I was a kid. With the same old cars.

'Fitz.' Hutch Scandrett stroked his wig as if it was a pet rabbit. 'You got any stories about your dad you might want to share with my listeners?'

'Not really. Dad kept pretty much to himself. Him and his bike. I used to ride it when I was seeing Maria Santos Almeida. Scared the shit out of me.'

'Not half as much as her brothers did, though.'

Big Andy laughed and munched a doughnut. Andy Scarlatti, Merv and I had been best mates in our Betty Rice Years. He'd gone off to Mainland University to read maritime law at about the same time as I'd gone to work on the *Bullock Telegraph*, and then to London, so we hadn't seen each other for nearly twenty years. He'd always been big, but now he was huge. He occupied most of the bench beneath the window with a milky coffee in his left fist, a jam doughnut in his right, his face a pumpkin. There was a brown paper bag between his feet. Andy had become a chain doughnut-eater.

'She taught most of the boys in Bullock how to do sixty-nine. Maybe one day they'll erect a plaque. Or a statue.'

He munched for a while.

'Statue'd be interesting.'

'Is she married?'

'No-o-o,' said Big Andy. 'Beautiful body and face like that, she had plenty of chances. Brothers were a big problem. Did wonders for recruitment into the priesthood, though. Word got out about how you'd escaped, Fitz. Every subsequent suitor did the same thing, although some didn't understand how it was supposed to work. They ended up in the seminary. I sometimes wonder whether it might all have been a scam between the Almeidas and the Church to boost numbers. Brothers went back to Portugal a few months ago to look after the family estates. You've got a clear field, Fitz, if you want to try again.'

I remembered a clear field of soft summer grass. *'Sex is a Mortal Sin outside the boundaries of marriage, Fitz, but we could do sixty-nine if you like.' 'What's that?' 'Take your shorts off and I'll show you.'*

The finest breasts I'd ever seen. The finest thighs. The finest adjustments with her lips and teeth to produce a sky-rocketing ignition to rival anything Dad's highly polished ports could muster. There was no doubt about it: when it came to breasts, Maria Santos Almeida's had always been the gold standard.

'I don't have the time,' I said. 'Got a plane to catch. Thanks for giving Dad such a terrific send-off. You made us very proud.'

'He was a great man,' said Murray. 'It was the least we could do.'

Chapter 45

In an interview for *The Times*'s *Saturday magazine* I'd been described as *'more prickly than a cactus ... approach with caution'* and accused of misogyny. *'Isn't it true, I ventured, that you use Laura Friday to express your hatred of women? That following your acrimonious divorce you have vowed never to allow yourself to become close to another woman? Aren't fear and hatred one and the same thing for you? Vince didn't say a word. Instead he ate a biscuit. Answer enough, methinks.'*

The answer, had I given it, would have been that I didn't know. I knew I'd created Laura as a means to an end, and when Helen had offered me wealth in return for Laura's immortality I'd sold my soul. But how can you tell that to an interviewer? The only place for such revelations is the therapist's couch.

By then I was seeing Jonathan Hess once a week.

My Mid Life Crisis began at six-forty-five on the morning of 30 December 1999. I was back in Zermatt, staying with a Florentine supermodel named *La Giraffa*. As I slithered out of bed she called to me. *'Tesoro amore!* You go *pipi tutto il tempo*. You 'ave *problema?* You go see *dottore. Subito.'*

The bathroom mirror was surrounded by halogens which highlighted my receding hairline. I tugged at a grey hair. Dropped it into the waste basket. There were more. Sprouting from my nostrils and ears. Growing tendrils among my eyebrows. My overnight stubble had flecks of grey.

The urge to pee was undeniable. I waited for the stream. As teenagers, Andy, Merv and I had played Fire Hose against the dividing wall between Benny's and Bernie's, pinching the ends of our penises until the pressure built, then releasing on the count of three. My stream had always scaled the wall. Now it was barely horizontal. In a few years it would be the trickle of a leaking washer, in the centre of the bowl one minute, spraying my left ankle the next. Then what? Incontinence. Padded underwear. Talcum powder. Dank Void.

I tried to read the sign beside the shaving socket. The type was too small. This was something I'd noticed everywhere. I rested my palms on the vanity unit and confronted myself. My back ached. There was a pain in my left hip. The first signal for a replacement?

'Fitz,' I said, 'you'll be forty next year. The first half of your life is over. You've achieved everything. From now on it's a downhill slide to the grave.'

When I got back into bed, *La Giraffa* took hold of my flaccid penis as if she were examining *salsiccia bianco* at a market stall and said, '*Possibilmente* you ask him for Viagra also, *caro*.'

Restless and scared, I sold Barton Lodge, bought and sold several more times, and finally came to rest on Richmond Hill, near the Royal Star & Garter old soldiers' home, and among ageing rock stars. I bought fast cars and dated younger women. Nymphets attracted by my C-list celebrity. From time to time I was offered marriage and children, but I'd been bitten twice and shied from any entanglement. There was a sort of yearning look I'd learned to identify. At the first sign of it, I fled.

My sessions with Jonathan Hess continued. My struggle now was not so much with my past as with my future. The inescapable fact that I was mortal had a profound effect. It was, said Hess, a common trauma in men of my age. It was called Ticking Clock Syndrome.

In 2002, Hess recommended an intensive week at his Self-Transformation Centre where I would learn how to overcome my fear of commitment with the aid of punch-bags, mattresses, and a special mantra. It didn't work. All I got for a thousand pounds were two sore fists and the word *'Ommmm'*.

I was settling into a resigned middle age. Moderately rich, immoderately miserable.

In 2006, Helen Valentino called.

'Fitz, the last six-book option on Laura Friday is due to expire. Do you want to renew it? I've got a feeling you and Laura need some time apart. A year or two. I could negotiate a hiatus.'

The end of the life sentence. Freedom spread before me like a summer meadow. Perhaps, even at forty-six, it was not too late to begin again. To take up life where I had left it behind.

'I agree. In fact, I think it's time Laura and Pavarotti met their Maker.'

'Do you want me to talk to Solly?'

'No,' I said. 'I'll do it.'

Before I left London, I went to see Jonathan Hess.

'Fitz,' he said at the end of our session, 'you need much more help. You can keep in touch via my website. Pay by credit card. Have a nice trip. See you when you get back.'

'Johnny,' I said. 'From now on I'm just plain Johnny Kennedy. No one in Bullock's ever going to know anything about Laura Friday or that I was Vince Humber. That chapter in my life is closed.'

BOOK FOUR

Chapter 46

It's late morning when I drive over the pass from Gundry. Earlier in the day, after an overnight at the Medium Rare Motel, I'd driven about five kilometres out of town until I saw the signpost to *Sturm und Drang Kennels*. I turned down a serpentine track to a cattle grid, then up a circular drive to an open square of tumbledown stables. When I rang the bell, an old guy of about eighty, with battered corduroys, a nicotine-stained moustache, toothbrush hair and a moth-eaten cardigan, came to the door.

'*Ja?*'

'*Sie sind Herr Sturm oder Herr Drang?*'

'*Herr Sturm. Was ist los?*'

'I'm Johnny Kennedy. From London. About the dog.'

'You speak good German.'

'Mostly pharmaceutical words.'

'My dogs know only German. Before you go I will you a manual give, with all the commands. *Komm!*'

I followed him into the stable block where there was a play area in the centre with tunnels, ladders, seesaws, concrete-block walls and a smoke-blackened circular contraption. Sturm waved at it.

'I send some of my dogs to the Fire Brigade. They have many babies saved. *Halt!* Here. This one.'

We stopped at a stall and peered over the stable door. A young black-and-tan German Shepherd had heard our approach and was sitting, its head cocked to one side, a quizzical expression on its face.

'This is Prinz Karl-Heinz von Hohenzollern aus Mecklenburg und Sorgen. His lineage goes back to Bismarck and the foundation of the glorious German Empire. If he human was he'd be the next King of England.'

'Could be an improvement.'

The old man looked at me with pale grey eyes that gave no indication of what was going on behind them. After a while, he decided he agreed and grunted what might have been a chuckle.

'*Ja! Wirklich!*' He opened the half-door and snapped his fingers. '*Komm!*'

The dog trotted from its stall. I knelt down, stroked the dog's neck and throat, then his head and ears, ran my hands over thick fur from the dog's shoulders to his chest and down his back. He was a fine animal, with clear black eyes and a wet nose.

'My dogs are *sehr* intelligent,' said Sturm. 'If you tell him his new name, he'll get it immediately.'

'Jerry,' I said. 'I think I'll call him Jerry.'

The dog's ears pricked up, and he licked my hand.

It's a fine summer's day. Jerry by my side. The windows down. 'Thank You for the Music' on the stereo. The car rounds one last corner and there's Bullock, arcing around Apprehensive Bay. I feel a knot in my gut. Like I'm about to write more than a new chapter in my life. It's a whole new book.

We've just passed the town sign — *Welcome to Bullock. You sure you're on the right road?* — when I pass the cop, hidden behind a rhododendron bush. A few seconds later, I see his flashing blue and red lights in my rear-view mirror.

'*Scheisse,* Jerry. *Polizei!*'

Jerry cocks his head and gives a sympathetic whine. In my wing mirror I see the cop get out of his car and stroll towards me in the simian manner they're taught at training school. As the window whines down, Jerry gives a growl.

'Good afternoon, sir. Did you see the sign?'

'Bullock? Yeah, I did. Thanks very much for asking.'

A smile flickers across the cop's mouth. He might have smiled the same smile as a kid when pulling the wings off a butterfly.

'I meant the speed restriction sign, sir. This is a fifty zone. Do you know what speed you were doing?'

'Fifty-five. Maybe sixty? I was slowing down.'

'My computer says sixty-two. You're allowed a margin of ten. You were two over the limit. Your name, sir?'

'Kennedy. Johnny Kennedy.'

'May I see your driving licence, Johnny?'

I produce it.

'And may I know your name?'

'Nelson. My friends call me Tea.'

'Well, Tea, if you're ever my friend, which is highly unlikely, you can call me Johnny. Until then, it's Mister Kennedy.'

The smirk disappears. A fleck of spittle arrives at the corner of his mouth. He goes back to his car, comes back a few minutes later with my speeding ticket, grips the door frame with both hands.

'If you're planning to stay in Bullock, Mister Kennedy, I'd drop the smart-arse drama if I were you. A bit of respect might be a good idea. In the meantime it's a hundred-and-twenty bucks and three points on your licence. Now piss off and keep out of my sight.'

There's a persistent whine from the passenger seat, so I let Jerry out. He rushes to the nearest patch of grass and cocks his leg. I smile at the cop.

'Couldn't have put it better myself.'

My first port of call is Murray's, where half a dozen guys are sitting around sipping coffee, engrossed in magazines which are stacked from floor to ceiling along the two side walls. The table's still in one corner with a coffee jug on a hotplate, milk, sugar, a stack of mugs.

After thirty-odd years of snipping and combing, Murray is slightly stoop-shouldered, with the same relaxed, quietly confident look he's had ever since school. He's in his place behind the chair with a comb in one hand, a pair of scissors in the other, snipping at an old guy's neck. The customer seems asleep, but there's nothing unusual about that. One of Murray's haircuts can take an hour or more, depending on how many times he pauses to join in the conversation. Most guys welcome the opportunity to recover their strength. Murray looks in the mirror.

'Fitz! Hi there! You been somewhere? Haven't seen you for a while.'

'London, Murray.'

'Really? What were you doing there?'

'Newspaper reporter. On the *Daily Chronicle*. Last time I was here was nine years ago for my dad's funeral. By the way, it's Johnny these days. I dropped the Fitz when I left London.'

'Seems like only yesterday your dad's bike turned feral.'

'You're a bit astray there, Murray.'

There's a guy in the corner. His face is familiar, but I can't place the name.

'Yesterday was when we were reading through the death scene from *King Lear*. Merv was Lear. I was Cordelia.'

'Thanks for the correction, Lloyd,' says Murray, without a tinge of irony, 'but I meant the statement whimsically. I realise it wasn't actually yesterday. Take a seat, Johnny. Dog can go under the table. Put some water in that old shampoo basin. Don't do shampoos any more. It's cheaper if people wash their hair before they come in. Help yourself to coffee. Your old mug might still be there. Could need a rinse, though.'

I look around the shop. Big Andy's looking older and wiser, taking up most of the bench beneath the window, clutching his coffee in one fist, a cream doughnut in the other. Merv the Mink's in the corner. He's taken on his dad's used-car salesman's lined pallor. He's reading *Othello*. A few guys I don't know are sitting around reading magazines.

'Hi, Andy! How's the maritime law business?'

'Steady, Johnny,' says Andy. 'No ships have gone down since I qualified, but when one does I'll know what to do. Have to be ready, so I keep my desk clear. Send people over to Gundry if they want some conveyancing or a will. There's a fellow over there's always hungry for work.'

'What's been happening in Bullock since I left?'

The guys look at each other, trying to think of something.

'Marge Calloway died,' says a small guy with cracked fingernails, tombstone teeth and a monotonous voice. 'She and Roy were celebrating their Golden Wedding anniversary. "This is the happiest day of my life," she said. They were cutting the cake. Maybe the flash-bulbs got her confused. She dropped the knife and kind of keeled over. Never seen anything like it. On the TV they take minutes. Clutch their chest, choke, stagger. But Marge just dropped like a stone.'

'Never said a word, either,' says Merv the Mink. 'That wasn't like her. Marge usually had something to say.'

While everyone absorbs this, the guy with the tombstone teeth comes back with yet another event.

'Speaking of lights. The traffic lights went in at the junction of Thames and Rhine Streets about a year ago. Did more harm than good. Motorists created havoc, pausing to watch the lights go through their cycle. Red, green, yellow, red again. Lloyd here's panel-beating business did well out of it. And the pedestrians couldn't decide whether the buzzer meant everyone should cross, or stay back and wait for the buzzer to stop. Had them doing a sort of hokey-cokey dance, some people putting their right legs in while others were taking them out. Everyone's become accustomed now, though.'

'That's it?'

The guy with the tombstone teeth glares at me.

'Isn't that *enough?*'

'Murray, I'm reading this article in *The Lancet* on the definition of obesity,' says Big Andy. 'And I'm thinking, maybe I have a problem.'

'No-o-o-o.' Murray combs a clump of hair between two fingers and snips. 'What's obese, anyway, Andy? It's like saying someone's tall. Tall in relation to what? Obese in relation to what? How we see things is based on Yin and Yang.'

Murray turns from the chair, allowing his customer's head to droop.

'From the *I-Ching*. Stands for the sun, the moon and the universe. The light area is Yang for sunlight, the dark area Yin for the moon. Yang is man, Yin is woman. Yin is born at the summer solstice, Yang at the winter solstice. There's a Yin circle within Yang, and a Yang circle within Yin. If you didn't have fat people, you wouldn't have thin people.'

'Billy Connolly.'

'What's Billy Connolly got to do with anything, Merv?'

Big Andy sounds peeved that the conversation has taken a tangent.

'The Big Yin.' Merv the Mink's wearing a Merv's My T Motors shirt with the slogan *Take our finance for a test drive* on the breast pocket. 'Went through to Gundry to see him once. Afterwards I said to Betty, "Can you remember any of the jokes?" And you know what? We couldn't. That's great comedy. When you piss yourself laughing and you can't remember why.'

'You're a bit astray there, Merv, with the Big Yin,' says Murray. 'Yin in that instance is the Scottish corruption of the word "one". *The Big Yin* was a Billy Connolly television stand-up show which first went to air in Scotland in 1985.'

Murray looks at a powerful young guy in the other corner with prominent cheekbones and a cauliflower ear. He's wearing Lycra longjohns and a fleece top and reading a *Ballet World* magazine.

'How's the training going, George?'

'Pretty good.'

Merv the Mink looks up.

'Who are you playing next?'

George puts his magazine aside, keeping his thumb inserted so he doesn't lose his place.

'Siegfried.'

Merv frowns.

'Don't think I know that team.'

'In *Swan Lake*.'

'Who's Odette?' asks Murray.

'Sharon Pollock.'

'Bit tall for that, isn't she?' asks Merv. 'Doesn't she play goal attack for the Bullock Silver Ferns?'

'Which is precisely why she was chosen.' George sounds impatient, which is understandable. Merv's always had that effect on people. 'She's the best jumper in Bullock, and I'm handy at lifting our locks in the lineout, so we thought it'd be a good combination for the *jetés* and the *pas de deux*.'

'Makes sense.' Murray has been distracted from his task and has turned to face us, using his scissors and comb as gesticulatory tools. 'You realise of course that the Petipa–Ivanov version was created after Tchaikovsky's death. Vladimir Petrovich Begichev commissioned the score in 1875, but there's some debate about whether Vasily Fedorovich Geltser wrote the libretto. Most experts believe he was just the copyist. The story's as old as time, of course. The legend of the Swan Maiden as a symbol of purity in women. The Ancient Greeks revered the swan, and great events were celebrated by flights of circling swans. Then there's the *Tale of the Thousand and One Nights* where Hassan of Bassorah visits a place inhabited by bird-maidens who are transformed into beautiful women. There's a Slav tale called *Sweet Mikhail Ivanovich the Rover,* and a Celtic legend called *The Children of Lir* in which a wicked woman turns the king's children into swans.'

Murray turns back, places the palms of his hands on his customer's temples and tests the symmetry of his work. He seems satisfied, turns back to face us.

'There were other influences as I'm sure you know, George. Johann Karl August Musäus's *Der Geraubte Schleier,* for example; Hans Christian Andersen's *The Wild Swans*; and Alexander Pushkin's *Tsar Saltan,* the prince who saves the life of a wounded swan who later reappears as a woman. And you mustn't forget *Lohengrin,* the Swan Prince.'

'OK,' says George, 'I won't.'

'As you were talking, Murray, I was just looking at that dog lying there. You remember Charlie Weston?' A middle-aged guy with teeth that have known plenty of pain looks up from his *New England Law Journal.* 'Poor bugger died last week. Had a dog called Roger. Slept on Charlie's bed. When Charlie got a girlfriend, Roger refused to budge. She put her foot down. Either the dog goes or no nookie. Charlie didn't think twice. "Had this dog eight years and it's never once demanded anything other than two walks and a feed each day," he said. "In return it's given me unquestioning love and loyalty. We've known each other five minutes and already you're trying to blackmail me."'

'Good man, Charlie,' says a bald-headed guy whose centrals

are in dire need of attention. Things have obviously slipped in the Bullock dental department since Dad died. 'Had a prostate problem. Stood next to him in the men's at Meggett's once. The one that's hidden behind ladies' hats. He'd already been there a while when I unzipped, and it looked like he had a way to go yet when I zipped up, although I didn't get a close look, of course. I said to him as I was leaving, "Charlie, don't you get bored, standing there waiting for something to happen?", and he said, "No, I just let my mind roam free."'

'Charlie had Benign Prostate Hyperplasia.' Murray snips and trims a few wisps of white hair. 'Which is pretty common in men over fifty.'

'What about women?' asks the guy who made the snide comment about *King Lear*.

Murray checks him out in the mirror.

'Women never have a prostate problem, Lloyd.'

Then it comes back to me. Lloyd Webber. Webber Panel Beaters on Mekong Street. His dad had had the same abrasive personality. It had always prevented his business from realising its true potential. People would rather keep the dent than risk a Webber sneer.

'That so? Must be a gene thing. Think I'll have a smoke. It's tobacco, so I'd better go outside.'

As Lloyd lights up in the street, Murray smiles.

'Biology was never Lloyd's subject. How he ever managed to have three kids beats me. Great with a spray gun, though. You can't have everything.'

'His brother Norm married Rachel Carstairs,' says Big Andy. 'Rachel's big in the Gloaming Gospel. She stopped me in the street the other day and said, "You'll know when the end of the world has come because it shall be light in the night and dark in the day."'

'And what did you say?' asks Merv the Mink.

'I said a guy in the Old Testament must have written that after too many mugs of honey mead.'

'Talking of which,' says Lloyd, who has finished his cigarette and resumed his seat, 'they're putting a roundabout on the junction of Thames and Nile.'

Merv the Mink sucks his teeth, shakes his head dolefully as if he's saying why he can't offer more for a car trade.

'I can see problems there, Lloyd. Bullock drivers don't like giving way at intersections. What they'll do at a roundabout doesn't bear thinking about.'

'What's that got to do with honey mead, Lloyd?' asks Murray.

'It'll be quicker to take the short-cut through the Woolies car park. That's where I always get my honey.'

'As long as Sunny Riverbank's not trying to park his Land Rover. Takes him all day to find reverse.' Murray goes to work with the dry razor, skimming the hairs from the nape of the old man's neck. 'There, that'll do him, I think.'

Murray unties the smock, whips it away and brushes a few strands of hair from the old man's shoulders. The old man doesn't move, but Murray seems unconcerned. He picks up his phone and punches a button.

'Percy, hi. He's ready for you.'

A couple of minutes later, two muscular guys in black suits, white shirts and black ties come in through the back door. They swing the chair around. While one lifts the feet, the other thrusts his hands into the armpits.

'Nice haircut,' says the guy at the feet. 'He'd have appreciated that.'

Murray has been following my curious stare.

'Old Reg. Been coming here since my dad took over the shop fifty years ago. His widow wanted him to look his best for friends and family.'

'So . . .' Murray ties the smock, looks at me in the mirror. 'You back for good this time, Johnny?'

'Maybe. I'm not sure yet.'

'You staying with your mum?'

'I'll stay there for a while. But we don't get on too well anymore. Ever since I married a Protestant. She's never forgiven me. And I've never forgiven her for not coming to the wedding. I might look for somewhere to buy.'

'Passion Dale's for sale. Your Uncle Tommy's place. Needs a lot of work, though. It'd be a great thing for Bullock if you restored it. Passion Dale's part of the town's heritage.'

'You guys remember Tommy Kennedy's wife, Bridie?' Big Andy replenishes a few lost calories with a doughnut. 'She died without the Last Rites because Father Connolly was out training for the Bullock Triathlon. She was in the John Rowles Flickering Twilight Home getting ready to establish Base Camp in Purgatory before attempting the assault on Heaven. But in any case he wouldn't have had his cassock or his holy water. It wouldn't have been the same, him standing there in his Lycra shorts with his tackle bulging, anointing her forehead from an H_2O squeeze bottle.'

'There was a full-page obituary in the *Bullock Telegraph*,' says Merv the Mink. 'Her great-grandmother, Annie, came out on the *Heavy Going*. Raised the first flock of sheep in Bullock. Put a ewe in her arms and walked twenty miles to the market, sold it, then walked back with a load of cabbages. And found time to have thirteen children. They don't make 'em like that anymore.'

'Annie's husband, Finbar, opened the Shipwreck Arms,' says Big Andy. 'Brewed *potcheen* in a shed out the back. Blew himself to pieces when he forgot to damp the fire.'

'He'd not have had the Last Rites, either,' says Merv. 'I wonder if he's reached Heaven yet.'

'Strength of that *potcheen*, I'd say he got there within a few seconds.' Murray whips the smock away. 'There you go, Johnny. You've a tidy thatch there now. Should give your brain breathing space.'

'How much do I owe you?'

'That's what we call the Welcome Home Haircut. On the house. Mind if I give the dog a biscuit?'

I call Jerry from beneath the table.

'Komm'! Setz'!'

Murray opens a drawer and removes a chocolate sultana sandwich bar which Jerry devours in one swallow. The guys sitting around the perimeter of the shop wave as we leave.

Chapter 47

Bullock Real Estate is a couple of doors along from Murray's Barber Shop and Percy Cartwright's Family Funerals. A guy in his late thirties or early forties is sitting behind a desk. He wears a floral bandanna, a black-and-grey ponytail and a pair of Art Nouveau Lalique-style earrings in silver. Sideburns flow from his temples and across his cheeks. His Bullock Real Estate T-shirt is in black and there's a slogan across the chest in white: *Buy or sell through BRE, satisfaction's our guarantee.*

'Hi there! I'm Sunny Riverbank Kennedy.'

'Johnny Kennedy.'

We shake hands.

'Must be a relationship somewhere, but I wouldn't like to say where exactly.'

'And this is Jerry.'

'Great dog, man!'

Sunny waves at a chair. I sit. Sunny takes a pack from a drawer, removes a machine-rolled joint.

'Try one of these. Early crop. Young leaf. Low on hallucinogens, but you still get that sweet aftertaste. I call it Bullock Lite.'

I drag, inhale, nod my appreciation.

'Mmm, tastes good, like a good weed should.'

Sunny takes out an order pad.

'Want me to put you on the mailing list? Five dollars a pack of twenty, twenty dollars a five-pack. And you go in the draw for a new car.'

'Put me down for a weekly five-pack. Good to see the weed business doing well. It was in its infancy when I left.'

'How long ago was that?'

'Twenty years.'

Sunny nods reflectively.

'First plants were brought out in 1863 on the *Heavy Going*. Captain's log said it was the sweetest crossing a man could wish for. Lost his way a couple of times, but everyone was cool about it. Even when the ship foundered in sight of land. Town's had a relaxed approach ever since. No crime. No violence. No drugs.'

'That's the way I remember it. Good to know nothing's changed.'

'I'm also Bullock Weed Cooperative's Marketing Manager. We keep prices low so there's no room for a black market. Return profits to the community. Built the BWC Little Theatre a couple of years ago. BWC swimming pool for the kids is next. Long as we keep a low profile, don't get greedy, Nelson turns a blind eye.'

'Who's Nelson?'

'Tea Nelson. Bullock cop. Seth's son.'

Jerry gives a growl at the mention of Tea's name.

'Yeah!' I laugh. 'We met him earlier on. He gave me a speeding ticket. I remember his old man. Seth seemed much more laid-back.'

'Tea's got a lot on his mind,' says Sunny. 'A&P Show's coming up soon. He breeds Red Setters. Wins gold each year. If he wins again this year, he gets to keep the Cup. They're not the greatest dogs in the world, but the judges are on the BWC Board, and all the other entrants know the story. It's a small price to pay for peace and quiet. And he's got woman trouble. Girlfriend's just dumped him. Everyone's trying to keep out of his way until it all blows over. Mostly he just hides behind the rhododendron bush and sulks. What can I do for you?'

'I'm interested in the Passion Dale property out Back Bullock way. Sean Fitzgerald Kennedy built the place when he got back from World War One in the early 'twenties.'

Sunny ponders this, tugs at an earring.

'War finished in 1918. He took his time.'

'Took demob leave in Paris. Called in at a Left Bank café. Hemingway was there with Pablo Picasso and Igor Stravinsky. Pablo bought Sean a beer. Got to talking about art, music, books. Next thing he knew it was 1923.'

'Oh man, that can so easily happen. Let's go. We'll take my wagon.'

Sunny's transport is a tattered Land Rover with a crash gearbox and a transmission whine if he exceeds sixty. He leans his arms on the wheel, keeps a joint between his lips, and drums his fingers in time to a Britney Spears CD.

'What brings you back to Bullock, Johnny?'

I know I'm going to be asked this question a thousand times, so I have my little speech ready. It's not the full story or even the true story, but it's near enough.

'Had enough of the bright lights and the big city. Time to get back to my roots. Mix with some real people.'

'I know what you mean.' Sunny waves at a passing Toyota Land Cruiser. 'That's Terry Foreman. Good guy to know if you like courgettes. You married?'

'No.'

'Kids?'

'No. But I've been doing some thinking. Maybe it's time I stopped kicking over the traces and settled down.'

'You don't mind me asking, how old are you, man?'

'Forty-six.'

'That why you've come back to Bullock? Start a family before you get even more decrepit?'

Jerry's lying at my feet, his face resting on my right shoe. His ears are cocked and he's listening to every word. But he doesn't understand English, so I don't feel inhibited. I gaze out of the window, my mind racing over the good and bad times Laura and I shared. She saved the planet twice, prevented three presidential assassinations, killed a hundred scumbags and fucked a hundred more.

'Something like that.'

'What were you doing back in London?'

'Newspaper reporter. On the *Daily Chronicle*.'

I wonder why I keep telling these lies. It doesn't matter now if anyone finds out I'm Vince Humber, the author of all those Laura Friday books, the guy responsible for all those movies. Mainly it's just a deceit I've grown used to over the years. But also I want to get back to the way things were before I left, when I was just a reporter on the *Bullock Telegraph*. If people think of me as a multi-millionaire international superstar with Learjets and supermodels at my beck and call, they might not be so inclined to take me at face value.

'You mind if we make a small diversion?' says Sunny. 'My sister called earlier, said she's got something to show me.'

'Sure. No problem.'

We turn off Back Bullock Road and bump down a rutted track to a clearing where there's an old corrugated-iron-clad building, a couple of outbuildings and the sweet smell of weed.

'Bullock Weed Cooperative headquarters,' says Sunny as we come to a halt. 'This is where growers bring their weed to dry before it's crushed, blended and put through the rolling and packing machine. Three staff. Lester Judd does the grading, stringing, crushing and blending, Lois Wilson does the rolling and packing, and Jill Stubbings runs the little office at the back — accounts, answers the phone, knows everything there is to know about weed.'

We get out of the Land Rover and begin to walk towards one of the outbuildings.

'Grower arrives with a trailer, or a truckload,' says Sunny, 'Lester runs a leaf or two through his dehumidifier then through his hand-operated roller. Lois, Jill, Lester and the grower light up a sample, pass judgement on a score sheet. On busy days, things don't progress much beyond that point. People know if the phone's unanswered or the accounts are late, Jill and Lois are helping Lester with his grading.'

A woman emerges from the outbuilding. She's tall and slim, pretty, mid-thirties, wearing jeans and a white coat. She shares Sunny's fine features and has her hair tied back in a similar ponytail.

'Johnny, this is my sister Thunderclap Cornfield.' Sunny smiles at my puzzlement. 'Mum and Dad named us after the weather conditions and location of our conception. I'm Sunny Riverbank, I have a brother Cirrus Clouds Backseat and another sister, Shower Pinewoods.'

'Nice idea. What sort of work do you do, Thunderclap?'

'Research and development.'

She smiles and cups a thin hand to her forehead to shield her eyes from the sun.

'Do you like it?'

'It sucks.' She throws her head back and laughs. 'I love it when I get a chance to say that.' She reaches into a bag. 'Do you want to try our latest idea? Fluoride weed. Cleans your teeth as you smoke.'

Sunny takes a long, expert drag, holds it for a few seconds, exhales.

'Not bad. How does it work?'

'I've added a whitening agent,' says Thunderclap. 'Each time you exhale you swill the smoke around in your mouth for a couple of seconds. Kills all the bacteria. No more plaque, no more decay. I might add a breath freshener, too. You smoke one first thing in the morning, last thing at night, after a meal, that's it. No more brushing. Think it'll take off?'

Sunny nodded. 'I can see a big demand.'

'Haven't got a name for it yet.'

I have a sudden inspiration.

'How about Bullock White? Goes with Bullock Lite. And what about *Mellow teeth, not yellow teeth* for an advertising slogan?'

'Hey, I like that!' She turns to Sunny. 'This guy's cool.'

'Where did you study, Thunderclap?'

'California mostly. Did my weedology doctorate at Berkeley.'

'You back here for good?'

'Probably. We're doing some interesting work on the conversion of weed into gas. Significant benefits over petrol. Happy drivers, less competitive. Means fewer accidents. Fill the atmosphere with weed emissions, may even have implications for world peace and global warming. I'm writing a paper for the *California Journal of Weed.*'

At the sound of a siren, we turn to see a police van slew into the clearing and come to a halt amid a dust cloud. Tea Nelson gets out, slams the door and comes towards us, taking in an extra notch on his trouser belt.

'Looks like trouble,' says Sunny.

'Belt's always a bad sign,' says Thunderclap.

'Morning, Tea.' Sunny offers the cop a cigarette. 'Want to try this? First batch of Bullock White.'

Tea stands there, legs apart, thumbs in his belt. He narrows his eyes.

'My information is, you're processing and selling weed from here, Sunny. That correct?'

Sunny blinks.

'Come again, Tea?'

'Sources tell me you're running an illegal operation. Gonna have to close you down. Impound everything. Take you two back to the station for questioning. Anyone else on the premises?'

'What do you mean, "sources"?' Sunny is aghast. 'BWC's been operating out of here the past five years, Tea. You made a speech at the Opening Ceremony. About how Bullock weed's always been an integral part of the community. Keeps the crime rate down, hospital beds free for those in real need, finances the Bullock Little Theatre, keeps domestic violence at zero, allows you to concentrate on your Red Setters. What's brought this about?'

'I'm the one asking the questions.' Tea produces a pair of handcuffs. 'Hands behind your back, Sunny. You, too, Thunderclap. I'm taking you both in.'

He turns to me.

'You again, Kennedy. What are you doing here?'

'We were on our way to look at Passion Dale.'

'Well, you'd better get going, then, before I take you in, too. Who's inside?'

'Lester, Lois and Jill,' says Thunderclap. 'They're batch-testing.'

'They're always batch-testing.'

Tea looks back at the dog van, from which has come a pathetic whine.

'Bruno's overdue for his walk. You'd better arrest yourselves. Lock the place up. Bring me the key. Don't touch anything. This is a crime scene. Going to have to come back with my forensics kit, check for traces of weed.' He sniffs. 'Looks like I caught you green-handed.'

'Can't drive with these handcuffs on, Tea,' says Sunny.

Tea rubs his chin, looks at Sunny's Land Rover. 'You never change gear in that bloody thing anyway.'

'I'll drive.'

The cop looks at me as if I've just crawled out of the ground.

'Keep your speed down. Go more than sixty, you won't need a ticket. This shit-heap'll explode.'

Half an hour later, Sunny's Land Rover draws up outside the Bullock Police Station. Lester, Lois and Jill tumble from its canvas-covered rear, Sunny and Thunderclap from the front. They lean against it for support, gaze up at the azure sky.

'Wow,' says Lester. 'Daylight. Far out.'

'Massive,' says Lois.

'This is going to put me behind with my bought ledger,' said Jill. 'Did you bring any ciggies with you, Les?'

Les pats his pockets.

'Got some somewhere.'

News of the arrest has raced through town. A small crowd has formed on the footpath. Someone has made a sign. *Free the Bullock Five*. A chant breaks out. *'What do we want? Bullock Lite. When do we want it? Now.'*

Before the Bullock Five can reach the door, a Bullock Radio van screeches to a halt. 'Stuttering' Hutch Scandrett tumbles out, microphone in hand.

'Listeners, we're live at the cop shop where a big d-d-d-drama is about to unfold. Sunny Kennedy, what's this all about?'

'I think Tea must have got out of bed the wrong side, Hutch,' says Sunny.

'Word is, his girlfriend dumped him,' says Hutch. 'Think that might have something to do with it?'

'Could be. That plus the dog show.' Sunny clenches his fist, turns to the crowd. 'People of Bullock! Never despair! We shall soon overcome this pernicious injustice. We shall soon be free! Bullock weed shall soon once more come dropping into the letter boxes of this great town. And look out for new Bullock White, available through the usual channels very soon. Bullock White gives you mellow teeth, not yellow teeth.'

When Sunny, Thunderclap, Lester, Madge and Jill disappear inside, Hutch signs off.

'This is "Stuttering" Hutch Scandrett returning to the studios of Radio Bullock which should take about five minutes. Meanwhile, here's John Rowles . . . '

And the small crowd continues its chanting.

'*What do we want? Bullock Lite. When do we want it? Now.*'

Chapter 48

I came back to Bullock for a quiet life. Yet my first day has included a dead body in a barber's chair, two clashes with a cop, and the arrest of the Bullock Five. And it's not over yet. As I turn into Wey Street the sun's going down and I wonder what sort of reception is waiting for me.

When *Fat Parrot* became a best-seller, I'd offered to buy Mum and Dad a bigger house, but they'd been puzzled by the idea. Where was the need? They were perfectly fine where they were. A man only had so much allotted time. Waste it moving somewhere else could cause trouble. And in any case it was close to the hospital.

Jerry and I go around to the back door. No one but Mormons and Seventh Day Adventists uses the front. Once, Mum had come home to find a pair of earnest young men in starched white shirts seated in the living room with a sheaf of brochures spread out on the coffee table and Dad on the sofa looking as if he was in a lifeboat, adrift in mid-ocean. After that she'd answer the front door clutching a *Vatican News*, which she'd press into a horrified hand with a command to seek the True Faith.

Mum has breast cancer. It's under control with Tamoxifen. She's not on chemotherapy and at her age it could take years to develop. When he heard I was coming back to Bullock, Roy Calloway brokered a truce by persuading Mum that the stress of conflict would exacerbate her condition. The prospect of prolonged life had achieved what no amount of pleading ever could. She'd agreed I could stay in the house until I found something of my own. But she hadn't agreed to make me welcome.

She's in the kitchen making dinner. Seventy-five, but looks older, thinner, her skin lined and waxy, her hair wispy and white. When I kiss her cheek she doesn't stop scrubbing potatoes.

'I'll put the kettle on. If you want to wash your hands, there's a clean towel in the bathroom. Your bed's made up. The dog can sleep in the kitchen. I'll not have his hairs all over my furniture.'

'It's good to see you, Mum. How are you?'

'As well as can be expected.' I remember she said the same thing shortly before Agnes died. 'The house stays tidy now that your father's not here to mess it up.' Her eyes are watery. I wonder if she cries when she's alone and why she has to pretend she's not missing him. 'How long do you intend to honour us with your presence?'

'I've come back to write my last Laura Friday book. I might go back to London afterwards. We'll just have to see how things work out.'

'Roy Calloway wants to retire from the *Bullock Telegraph*. He always says how sorry he was that he fired you. You could buy the paper. Petty cash to you, I expect.'

'I'll think about it. How's Carmel?'

'She'll be here tonight. She was looking after AIDS children in Zimbabwe the past two years. The Bishop's offered her Mother Superior. She's thinking about it. Where are you going to live? You can't stay here. I've got a full house coming. Three priests and two nuns. I need your room.'

'Passion Dale's for sale. Needs a lot of money spent on it apparently, but someone should keep it in the family.'

Jerry doesn't like sleeping in the kitchen. Mum's given him an old blanket in a corner by the window for which most dogs would be grateful, but he's Prussian aristocracy. His ancestors were fondled by Bismarck's wife. I can tell what he's thinking as he emits a Teutonic grunt: kitchens are for servants.

'*Finde dich damit ab!*' I tell him. But he just gives me his sneer. 'I'll give him a black sausage in the morning. That might work.'

'You care more about that dog than you ever did about a human.'

Carmel and I are sitting at the kitchen table after dinner. Mum's in bed. We dined beneath a heavy cloud, and the depression remained during the washing-up. Carmel's fervent prayer of Grace was interminable and included a plea to bring my errant soul back into the Catholic fold. I'd missed Agnes's wink of complicity, the nudge of her foot against my ankle which had once made Carmel's Graces bearable.

Our family seems to have been savagely pruned. Dad and Agnes, Uncle Tommy and Aunt Bridie. One day there'll be just Carmel and me, and then . . . Dank Void.

'That's not fair. I've always loved my family.'

'You've a funny way of showing it, Johnny.' Carmel's ice-blue eyes hold mine and there's no warmth in her face. 'You ran away from Maria Santos Almeida with a lie about becoming a priest. You rejected Frankie when you thought she'd been promiscuous. You took Agnes's money to chase Frankie halfway across the world and only came back for a couple of days when Dad died. Mum's hardly heard from you since. You ran from Cheryl rather than confront her about her past. The most successful relationship you've ever had is with Laura Friday, a woman of your own creation. Who goes around killing people. And you didn't even have the guts to use your own name. Now you're getting rid of her, too. What is it with you?'

'It's all Laura's fault.' I drain the dregs from the dinner wine and open another bottle. Carmel covers her glass with the palm of her hand. 'She was only meant to be a catharsis for Frankie. She's blighted my life.'

'That's ridiculous.' Carmel tosses her head in scorn. 'How can you blame a fictional character? I could just as easily say Laura made you rich. Who're you going to blame once you've killed Laura off? The dog?'

At which Jerry stirs and fixes Carmel with a malevolent stare. She stares right back and he's the first to falter. He rises from his blanket, comes across the kitchen and licks her hand.

'Strength and discipline, Johnny.' Carmel pats Jerry's head and points to his blanket. Jerry returns and goes back to sleep. 'It's the best thing for the dog. Perhaps it's time you applied a little of both to your own life.'

'What do you mean?'

'Decide where you want to spend the rest of your life. How you want to spend it. And who with. It's not too late for children. Settle down. Grow up. You might wake up one morning and realise you're happy.'

Chapter 49

The following morning no white smoke rises from the BWC plant on Back Bullock Road to signal that all is well. The main building and its attendant outbuildings remain locked and silent, surrounded by yellow tape.

When I tune in to Radio Bullock, Hutch Scandrett's doing his best to play the situation down. He makes no further mention of his encounter with the Bullock Five as he gives the prices for sheep meats, wool, beef, skins, grain and stock feed. '... *Hoggets no change, two-tooths no change, forequarters up one, hinds down two ...* 'Then he launches into his Earlyday Talkback and music segment. *'Hutch, whaddya reckon to these new mobile phones?' 'C-c-c-can't stop progress, Boyd. Good question, though. Now we've got Linda on line one who wants to tell us about all the things you can do with garlic, after which we'll pause and think about the wisdom of John Rowles as he sings* "If I Only Had Time".'

At first, when there's no Bullock Lite delivery on people's lawns in time for breakfast, Hutch fields a few calls but there isn't too much concern. BWC deliveries are notoriously haphazard. But once the news spreads about the BWC shutdown, his phone lines begin to glow. People have never had to face a weedless Bullock. They don't know what to do. They wander around aimlessly, go down to the local dairy, and when they get there, forget why they went. It isn't so much that people are addicted, simply that a Bullock Gold or a Bullock Lite is as much a part of people's lives as their track pants or their lawnmower.

When Jerry and I walk into Murray's Barber Shop, we enter a hive of consternation.

'Tea's got the law on his side.' Murray's trying to keep things on an even keel. 'But weed's done a lot of good for this town.'

Things are certainly on an even keel with Big Andy. Ensconced in his seat against the window, a bag of doughnuts at his feet, a milky coffee, three sugars, in his right fist. On the other hand, Lloyd Webber looks as if a platoon of army ants is gnawing at his vitals. As well as being addicted to nicotine, he's been a Lite smoker for as long as anyone can remember.

'Plus the Council gets a good return from its share of profits,' he says. 'Keeps the rates down. If Tea shuts the plant for good, a lot of people could suffer.'

'Tea hasn't thought this thing through, Lloyd,' says Murray. 'Strategically, he's astray. Bullock Weed Cooperative sponsors the Dog Show. BWC people sit on the judging panel. Tea'll have to make a decision. Continue to deprive the town of its weed means he'll risk pissing the judges off. Could lose the Cup for the first time in four years.'

This keeps Lloyd quiet. Military strategy has never been his strong point. Famous murder trials are, but right now there's not much demand for a discussion about Crippen or Jack the Ripper. He sips his coffee.

'You guys mind if I language something?'

This from a guy in the corner. Murray picks up my puzzled frown.

'Johnny, this is Stan Cullis. Stan runs Cullis Heating and Ventilation on Orinoco Street. Knows more about air conditioning than the rest of Bullock put together. He's just back from an ExecutiveSpeak course.'

We wave to each other across the shop.

'And this is Jerry,' I say, pointing beneath my bench.

Stan waves, but Jerry's morose. He still hasn't forgiven me for making him sleep in the kitchen.

'Go ahead, Stan,' says Murray.

'Don't undervalue the quantum of the impact capability of Tea Nelson's mission statement. He could effectively implement a constraint model within the parameters of the legal paradigm.'

Everyone takes this in by staring at their coffee, or at the amputated hair lying around the floor. It's some time before anyone's able to formulate an appropriate response, and the person who eventually does is Murray.

'I hear where you're coming from. But Tea's made a pre-emptive strike.' Murray snips and considers, snips and considers. 'Tantamount to a declaration of war. You remember what Clausewitz said about war, Stan?'

Stan purses his lips, shakes his head.

'I'm out of the loop on that one, Murray.'

'War is a fascinating trinity. What he called a *"wunderliche Dreifaltigkeit"*. An unstable interaction between emotion, chance and calculation. Cool heads. That's what we need right now. If everyone starts jumping up and down, Tea's going to think he's winning. Look at it this way. The closer it gets to the Dog Show, the more worried Tea's going to be, because he's going to realise he's risking the loss of his precious Cup. Of course, Tea won't lose. There's no dog in Bullock can beat Tea's Red Setters. But how about if we let him think there is? That's what this is all about.' He looks at Big Andy in the mirror. 'Never lose sight of the objective, Andy.'

But Andy has lost sight of his brown paper bag, and that's of more immediate concern. He shuffles around with his feet, tries to bend over but comes up red-faced. Without any signal from me, Jerry gets up from his bed, goes across the shop, gets down on his haunches, takes the bag in his teeth and brings it up from beneath Andy's midriff.

There's an awed silence.

'Would you consider entering Jerry for the Dog Show, Johnny?'

Murray's stare is directed beneath my bench, where Jerry has resumed his sleep.

'I could think about it. But we don't know each other too well yet.'

'Haven't bonded is what you're trying to language, I think,' says Stan Cullis. 'Proactively taken the relationship to the next level. You require more bandwidth.'

Meanwhile Murray's been snipping and thinking, snipping and thinking.

'Andy?'

'Yeah, Murray?'

Big Andy looks up from his doughnut.

'How about you go along to the police station? Talk to the Bullock Five. See how they're feeling.'

'See if I can get 'em out on . . . what's it called?' Big Andy snaps his fingers, releasing a spray of sugar. 'Boil?'

'Think you mean "bail", Andy,' says Murray. '*Habeas corpus*. Set the body free.'

'Gotcha!' Andy hands his mug to Merv the Mink, who's on his way to the coffee table for a refill. 'Maybe I'll have another coffee first. Couple of doughnuts. Build up my strength. The usual, Merv. Milk, three sugars. Heaped.'

Chapter 50

The following morning, between doughnuts, Big Andy reports on his meeting with the Bullock Five.

'Spirits were high. Lester had found a ukulele and was singing show tunes. *Oklahoma! West Side Story. Oliver!* Red Setters providing backing vocals from the kennels. Lois and Jill were playing *Scrabble.* Jill had just scored two hundred with *zygotics* across two triples, so she was feeling pretty good although Lois was glum. Sunny and Thunderclap were playing *Name That Poem.* That's where someone quotes the first line and you have to—'

'Name the poem.'

Lloyd Webber sits back with a smug look. But Big Andy is undeterred.

'Thunderclap had just said, "*I went out to the hazel wood*"—'

'"Wandering Aengus".' Everyone grudgingly admits Lloyd knows his poetry, but that doesn't make him popular. 'Yeats. Everyone knows that.'

'Well, Sunny didn't.' Big Andy's face is firm, his sugar-coated lips a thin pink line. 'And I'd appreciate it if you'd let me finish, Lloyd, if it's all the same to you.'

'Sorry.' Lloyd shrugs and looks offended. 'Just trying to help.'

'So Sunny made coffee and I gave each of 'em a doughnut and we talked about that thing . . . bail. Sunny said Tea was going to let 'em all go home in the morning anyway, so he could get back to his hideout behind the rhododendron bush, so there was no need. Then we talked about ways to keep supplies going.'

He turns to me.

'Sunny said there's an old drying barn out at Passion Dale your grandfather used to use after he got back from the Great War, Johnny. If you buy the place, maybe we could use that?'

'Fine by me.' I feel partly responsible for this mess, and I'm happy to help in any way I can. 'But I haven't even seen the place yet. I can't make any promises.'

'There's no machinery there. Each cigarette would have to be hand-rolled,' says Murray, 'so Sunny'd have to ration supplies. But it should keep everyone going until Tea comes to his senses.'

I look around the shop at the staunch, determined faces. Eyes are hard. Jaws clenched. Lips pursed. I can sense the feeling. Yes, it will be tough. Yes, people will suffer. But sometimes, when right is on your side, you just have to make a stand. It's a proud moment. A moment everyone who's there that morning will always remember. Even Lloyd Webber is moved.

'We few.' He takes a sip of coffee, pauses for effect. 'We happy few. We bond of brokers.'

'I think you mean "band of brothers", Lloyd.'

In his inimitable way, Big Andy celebrates his small victory.

Chapter 51

As Sunny and I drive into the hills behind Bullock, we pass rank after rank of vines and orchards heavy with fruit. After a while we turn onto a gravel road and drive until we reach a pair of gates flanked by a thick hedge. Sunny finds the key to the padlock and chain, forces the gates back against calf-high grass until there's room for the Land Rover to squeeze through. Then he drives up an overgrown gravel track to an old homestead set on a promontory overlooking the town.

'Welcome to Passion Dale. Nice name. Has a kind of rustic feel to it.'

'Sean had a good war.' I look up at the creeper-covered walls and rusted guttering. 'Enjoyed the trenches. Said they were more comfortable than where he grew up in the bogs of Ireland. He was a *spalpeen*. Lowest of the low. Went over the top in 1915 and spent the next three years in a no-man's-land bomb crater. Renamed it Kennedy's Pit Stop. Dispensed coffee and snacks to whichever side happened to be attacking. Emerged in November 1918 unscathed, rich, with the Iron Cross and the Military Medal. When he died, my Uncle Tommy inherited. We used to come out for poker nights and weekends. I lost track of what happened when I went overseas.'

'Tommy's wife Bridie died in the early 'nineties.' Sunny pads across the gravel to the front door. Jerry and I follow. 'Tommy died earlier this year. Never troubled the place with a paint brush or a hammer all the time he lived here. Refused all offers to sell. Tommy's four kids inherited, but they all live overseas so they put it straight on the market. Lawyer in Gundry's got power of attorney.'

We stand in the hallway and crane our necks to look at the carved plaster ceiling, sagging and damp, with a patch near the door where the plaster has crumbled leaving the rafters showing. We wander from room to room, admiring the handmade wallpaper in the living room which flows from the frieze up the wall and across the ceiling. There's a stove in the kitchen, and a rustle among a pile of old newspapers nearby that excites Jerry. He dives and emerges with a rat between his teeth.

'Lass' es!'

Jerry drops the rat, which scuttles away. Jerry gives me a dirty look, but I get no thanks from the rat.

'There's five hectares altogether,' says Sunny.

We've gone outside and are wandering through the long grass.

'Soil's ideal for anything. If it was me, I'd grow grapes. Pinot noir's in great demand. Make it yourself if you have the time, or let someone else do it. Your Aunt Agnes used to grow a premium varietal weed, didn't she?'

'Yeah.' I remember the first time I tasted it. Sitting in her bedroom, trying to work out how to get out of the mess I was in with Maria Santos Almeida and her family. *'Human waste, pet. After I've said a prayer over it. Next time you need to go, I'd be grateful if you'd use the bucket provided.'* 'Pot of Gold.'

'Paddock out the back'd be ideal. BWC could market it for you. To discerning clients.'

I shake my head.

'It'd just be a labour of love. Keep it for my own use, and for appreciative visitors. I could probably get a few cuttings from Agnes's old plot at Wey Street.'

Then something strange happens which makes up my quavering mind. Behind the drying barn, there's a paddock filled with vintage farm machinery. Rusty old harvesters and tractors, steam engines, ploughs and hoes, dibbles and forks, balers and binders.

'Sean must have been a collector,' says Sunny. 'Some of this stuff's worth a lot of money now.'

But it's not so much the sight of the machinery that's knotting my gut as the atavistic desire to take it to pieces, clean it, polish it, and put it back together again. Sunny senses my excitement.

'You want to make an offer, Johnny?'

'Let's get back to your office and do the paperwork.'

Sunny has trouble finding reverse so we use the four-wheel-drive to cross a boulder-strewn rose garden and eventually return to the driveway near the gate. As we drive back into town I reason that buying Passion Dale would not necessarily be a permanent commitment. If I decide to go back to London, I can sell the place, perhaps even make a profit once it's been restored. Then I wonder who I'm kidding. There's nothing in London for me to go back to. Everything I need is right here.

Chapter 52

My offer is accepted and I give Sunny a cheque for the entire amount. A week later, Sunny hands me the keys and I drive out to Passion Dale with a blow-up mattress from Meggett's department store. Jerry's travelling light, too. Just his food bowls and twenty-four hours' of dog roll in a canvas backpack. When we park on the overgrown driveway, Jerry leaps out to establish his territory.

The back of the house is a lean-to with the house's only toilet. A door leads to a 'seventies kitchen in brown and yellow, cabinets lined with sticky plastic and yellow newspaper. The room looks old and tired. Worn lino, doors askew, a cheap lampshade covered in dust. There's an ugly cupboard which contains the hot-water cylinder with a dead rat on top.

The dining room was where Uncle Tommy and Aunt Bridie had their Sunday evening card sessions and probably every other social event. Being next to the kitchen it was a natural enough place to sit, but there's only one window. Draped with a net fabric it's difficult to see through, but there's a tall hedge outside so there's no view.

The house is a maze, rooms leading left and right, walls where there should be doorways, different carpets in each room, different wallpapers: striped, Regency flock, shiny vinyl.

There's a bedroom in the centre of the house, papered in violent yellow with a sculptured carpet and built-in wardrobe. A window looks out to a porch at the front where there are stunning views of the town and Apprehensive Bay. I draw the porch's net curtains aside. It's a perfect summer's day, a few high clouds, clear blue sky, the sea deep green.

The porch walls are lined with weatherboard, the ceiling with acoustic tiles. The floor is an off-white carpet. I picture glazed tiles, strings of dimmed halogen lights, a candlelit dinner, The Carpenters on the stereo, the lights of the town twinkling below, Jerry slumbering in a corner.

I go from room to room trying to work out how the house is organised, but it's obvious the layout is all wrong. Although the dining room was a popular place to gather, it's in the gloomiest corner. The sunniest side is occupied by the lean-to toilet, a bathroom and a bedroom. The central bedroom makes no sense. The entire house will need to be gutted.

Tommy Kennedy's kids took what they wanted before Passion Dale went up for sale. The furniture, carpets and curtains that remain are falling apart, but there's no point in buying new until the house has been restored. In any case, I need time to get the feel of the place. Plus there's an email from Helen asking how I'm getting on with Laura Friday, and five hectares of land waiting for me to show an interest.

I establish my office at an old school desk in the spare bedroom overlooking the back garden. The desk carries the primitive carvings of one of the Kennedy clan. It's stained with ink where nibs have rested and bottles leaked or spilled, and there's a ring from a coffee mug. The room is decorated in pink and pale blue paper, so I suspect Ella Fitzgerald Kennedy, the youngest of Tommy's children. The desk becomes a repository for my laptop. I plug it into the mains, find an old office chair with a torn seat, and settle down to begin my last Laura Friday story.

I'm not one of those writers who has the whole book in his head before he starts. I'm an organic writer. I allow the story to develop in its own way, giving the characters the freedom to do and say what comes naturally. Somehow or other it seems to work. Laura and I have been together for so long that I know her as well as I know myself — what she'll think, do and say in any given situation. I have to be careful these days. Laura has fan clubs all around the world. Vigilante websites run by strange people with sad, empty lives. If I make a mistake, I get abusive emails from Wyoming or Wigan.

Sometimes the idea can take days or weeks to develop. This time it comes as soon as I open the file. An old flame arrives in town. Someone Laura hasn't seen for twenty years. She thought she was over him, but when she hears his voice on the phone, she knows she'll never be. It's still like melted caramel. Her favourite flavour. Always was, always will be.

I begin to write.

'Been a long time. What are you doing back here?'

Laura stroked Pavarotti's feathers, watched the sign across the street flicker off and on, off and on, poured another shot of Jack Daniel's. The heating was on strike, but JD was the kind of scab who wouldn't think twice about breaking it.

'I'm in big trouble.'

'What sort of trouble?'

'I killed a reporter. Frank Carpetta.'

'I know Frank. We used to be close.'

'There's a woman on my back. She was Frank's but she was part-timing with me. She said if I killed Frank we could get together full-time. Now she wants a grand a week or she'll go to the cops. I need you to rub her out. For old times' sake.'

'Old times were long ago, sucker. There's been a hundred guys since then. A hundred bars. A hundred bottles of JD. A hundred one-night stands. Get lost. Go break someone else's heart.'

Laura reached into a drawer, took out a peanut, held it in front of Pavarotti's beak. The bird rocked from side to side on Laura's shoulder.

'Rich man's world! Rich man's world!'

'Damned right it is, Pav.'

The following morning I go into Bullock, tie Jerry to a parking meter outside Meggett's department store, and go up to the first-floor balcony for coffee and Bullock Cake. Mum used to make Bullock Cake on Saint Paddy's Day, but she'd often have been at the Bushmills and would sing lachrymose Irish ballads as she mixed. Meggett's is drier, and has a better balance of ingredients.

I sit at a balcony table overlooking Thames Street. The balcony is busy with ladies who do morning coffee. They chatter like starlings, their Meggett's shopping bags scattered between the chairs. The spoils of war. None of the faces is familiar. I guess these must be New Bullockians, attracted here by the lifestyle.

The balcony's not my scene, so I ask for a doggy bag and go downstairs to collect Jerry. He's looking forlorn. As I approach I can see why. There's a parking ticket attached to his collar. I untie his leash. He picks himself up and mooches beside me. That's one of the few things I don't like about Jerry. He bears a grudge.

'Let's go and see Murray. His ambience is better and so's his coffee.'

Big Andy's there, clutching his white, three sugars. George and Merv the Mink are in their usual corners. I bed Jerry beneath the coffee table, fill a stainless-steel bowl with water. Then I pour a coffee and settle down next to Merv with a well-thumbed *Psychology Today*. Merv puts down *Julius Caesar*, reaches beneath his chair and produces a square-shaped cake box.

'It's my birthday,' he says. 'Thought I'd wait to see if Johnny and Jerry came in before we got stuck in.'

Murray takes a cut-throat razor from his bench and slices the cake.

'None for me, thanks,' says George. 'I'm in training.'

'I'll have George's piece,' says Andy. 'Hate to see good food go to waste.'

The customer rises from the barber's chair, removes his smock, and holds up a restraining hand.

'Isn't there something we're forgetting?'

'Sorry, Father Connolly.' Murray bows his head. 'Go ahead.'

The priest makes the Sign of the Cross.

'Bless us, O Lord, and these Thy gifts which we are about to receive from Thy bounty, through Christ our Lord. Amen.'

Everyone except me makes the Sign. The priest gives me a filthy look.

'Are you not One of Us?'

'I was, Father. But I lapsed.'

The priest resumes his seat. He has very little hair. If Murray drops crumbs amid the wisps they'll stand out like rocks among dried grass, so he keeps well clear.

'God loves a challenge. Were you ever at Benny's?'

'I was, Father. I'm Johnny Kennedy.'

'Ah, so you are.'

Big Andy's shifting in his seat, which means something's bothering him.

'Murray, can we talk in confidence?'

'Andy, everything we discuss here is confidential. Right, lads?' Everyone murmurs their agreement. 'See that plaque on the wall? That's the Barber's Oath. We swear it when we qualify. What seems to be the problem?'

'I'm worried I might be impotent. I can't get it up the way I used to.'

Murray snips and considers, snips and considers.

'This is a very common problem, you know, Andy. If we're honest, every man here has probably suffered from it at some time or other. Except Father Connolly, of course.'

'No, no,' says the priest in the chair, 'I've had my problems with it, too. I'll be as interested in what you have to suggest as the next man, Murray.'

'Let's be clear about definitions. We're talking erectile dysfunction, not impotence.'

There's a whiteboard parked where the second chair used to be before Murray decided to downsize to a less pressured lifestyle. He takes a black felt pen and draws a flaccid penis.

'An erection occurs when impulses from the brain and local nerves cause the muscles of the *corpora cavernosa* to relax, allowing blood to flow in and fill the empty spaces.'

He switches to red for the inflowing blood.

'I get mine whenever I think about Sharon Pollock.' George rests his *Architectural Digest* on his lap in an inverted V.

'The *tunica albuginea* helps trap the blood,' Murray continues, 'and when the muscles contract, the erection is reversed.' He switches to blue for the outflowing blood. 'It's a complex process, Andy. It just takes one thing—'

'Like she looks at it and laughs,' says Merv the Mink.

Murray gets busy with red, blue and black felt pens.

'An erection requires nerve impulses to fire *here . . . here . . . here . . .* the brain, spinal column, and around the penis . . . and a response from muscles, fibrous tissues, veins and arteries in and near the *corpora cavernosa.*'

'Makes you wonder how it ever happens at all,' says Merv.

'Diseases account for about seventy per cent of ED cases.' Murray stands back and admires his work. 'Smoking, being overweight, and avoiding exercise are also common causes.'

'Well, I don't smoke,' says Big Andy. 'So it can't be that.

Except Bullock Lite, of course.'

'Are you on any blood-pressure drugs, Andy?' Murray pours himself a coffee and takes a short break. 'Antihistamines, antidepressants, tranquilisers, appetite suppressants?'

'I don't have an appetite to suppress.'

Big Andy finishes his doughnut with his right hand, reaches into his brown paper bag for another with his left, never missing a beat.

'In that case we may be talking psychological factors,' says Murray. 'Stress, anxiety, guilt, depression, low self-esteem, fear of failure.'

'So what do you recommend?'

Merv has been taking a big interest in Murray's exposition.

'One of the new wonder drugs. Viagra, Cialis. You take one forty-five minutes before sexual activity. With Cialis you've got a thirty-six-hour window of opportunity.'

'I'm not sure I'd need that much time,' says Andy.

'It's not obligatory.' Murray returns to work on Father Connolly's sideburns. 'What about the diet?'

'I'm on low-fat milk. If you're getting another coffee, Johnny . . . '

Big Andy holds out his mug.

'Usual three sugars?'

'Got to keep my strength up. Don't want to send the body into shock. You know anything about this Atkins Diet, Murray?'

Murray finishes with the sideburns and begins to shape the nape.

'There's not a major governmental or non-profit medical, nutrition or science-based organisation in the world that supports the Atkins Diet.'

'Yeah, but what do you think?' asks George.

'Can't see how I can recommend it either.'

'That's the clincher. I'll just take it slow and easy.'

Andy stirs his coffee and reaches into his brown paper bag.

'How are the *Swan Lake* rehearsals going, George?' asks Murray.

'Sharon came up with this great idea the other day. I lift her above the stage where there's a rugby ball on a ledge. Sharon takes the ball, comes to ground and we form a ruck with the *corps de ballet* coming in behind with good body position.'

'Sounds impressive,' says Merv. 'What are the arrangements for Saturday night? Andy, you going with your latest fling? What's her name? Monica?'

'Yup.'

'Murray?'

'Wouldn't miss it for quids.'

'What about you, Johnny?'

'I'll be there. But I don't have anyone to take. Jerry's not a great ballet fan.'

'We'll have to find you a Bullock girl,' says Murray.

The door opens and Tea Nelson walks in. The ensuing silence is as if Billy the Kid had entered the Dry Gulch saloon. He sits but doesn't make himself or anyone else a coffee and keeps his cap on. He glares at me.

'Hear you're entering your dog for the Show, Kennedy.'

I look up from my *Journal of Cardiovascular Medicine*.

'Thought I'd give it a whirl. Just to see how he performs. Doubt he'll be much competition for your Red Setters, though. Wouldn't worry about it if I were you.'

'Worry?' Tea frowns. 'I'm not worried. Why should I worry? Just wondering why you can be bothered, that's all. Lot of work, getting a dog ready for the Show. You coming along to the club tomorrow night? Put your dog through its paces. Familiarise it with the arena. Get it used to crowds.'

'I'll just take Jerry along on the day, have a look at what he has to do, give him his instructions. He's pretty bright.'

'He understand English yet, Johnny?'

Frank Wright has a yellow moustache and a hacking cough. Sure signs of a tobacco smoker.

'Refuses to learn.'

I lean down and stroke Jerry's thick fur.

'Got a stubborn Teutonic streak. Do anything I tell him in German, though. Watch this. *Jerry, gehen Sie zum Bord und finden Sie mich eine Kopie der* Architektur Heute *Zeitschrift.*'

Jerry pads across the shop to the bookshelves, nuzzles along until he finds an *Architecture Today* magazine, pulls it out and brings it back to me. I pat his head.

'*Guter hund!*'

Everyone in the shop except Tea Nelson applauds.

'Now watch this. Jerry, go to the shelf and get me a copy of *The Lancet.*'

Jerry gazes at me, the merest hint of a sneer flickering around his lips.

'See? Either doesn't understand English, or thinks it's beneath him.'

A frown of concern has creased Tea Nelson's brow. He gazes at Jerry, now slumped once more at my feet, then reaches for his cap.

'That's a smart dog you've got there, Johnny. I'd keep a close eye on him if I were you. Wouldn't want to see him get into any trouble.'

As the door closes behind the Bullock cop, the shop lapses into an unaccustomed silence.

'Tea's upset.' Big Andy inhales a doughnut. 'That trick got him worried.'

'Achieved our objective, though,' says Murray. 'The pressure's on him and his Red Setters now. Won't be worrying too much about the Bullock Five from now on. It was a good idea to lace that *Architecture Today* with beef extract, Johnny.'

Chapter 53

I'm in my shed tinkering with an old horse-drawn plough. I've detached the blade and I'm giving it a polish with an old pot of Dad's dentist's rouge when I hear the crunch of tyres on gravel. It's Mort Sorenson with a Toyota Hilux and a double-axle horse box.

'Hi, Mort. What can I do for you?'

Mort nods towards the horse box.

'Got a hundred kilos of Special Curler in there. Missus and me picked it ourselves. Heard you were running an emergency plant.'

I smile at the sound of a faint whinny.

'You got a horse in there, too?'

'Tempest. My eldest daughter's black stallion. Got a bit of toothache so I'm taking him to the vet.'

'How are we going to get the weed out, then, Mort? Stallion with toothache. Don't like our chances.'

Mort laughs, walks to the back of the horse box, presses the button for the hydraulic tailgate. It whines down to reveal Tempest's rear end.

'Before we started we spread weed all over the floor, mixed some in his feed. On the way over here we played a continuous loop of Gilbert O'Sullivan on the horse-box stereo. Be sweet as a lamb by now.'

Mort unbuckles the straps, climbs into the box alongside Tempest's gleaming black flanks and reverses him down the ramp. The horse stands still, his head down, eyes heavy.

'He looks depressed.'

'So would you be, Johnny, after thirty minutes of "Alone Again, Naturally".'

Mort points to the thick pile of weed covering the floor of the horse box.

'You want to give me a hand to unload this stuff? Looks like Tempest's given it a good trample.'

'Be a bit of piss and dung in there, too, I should think.'

'Might enhance the flavour,' says Mort. 'You never know. Sometimes things like that can start a whole new trend.'

By the time we've shovelled the weed out of the horse box, into the trailer attached to my 1928 Fordson tractor, and transported it to the drying shed, the Bullock Five have arrived. Sunny Kennedy in his old Land Rover with Thunderclap beside him, Lester, Lois and Jill squeezed into the back beneath the torn tarpaulin.

'Any sign of Tea?' I look towards the front gate. 'Did you make sure you weren't followed?'

'We staged a diversion,' says Sunny. 'Just as we were leaving the cop shop, Merv the Mink shot through the stop sign in a hot V8 with a flaming muffler. Tea took off after him. Gave us time to get well clear.'

'A noble sacrifice.' Lester exhales towards Tempest's nostrils. Tempest buckles at the knees. 'Merv deserves a medal.'

Thunderclap looks beyond Apprehensive Bay, her eyes as misty as the far horizon. 'There'll be a lot more medals, a lot more sacrifice before this war is over.' She turns. 'Let's get to work.'

As news of the processing plant at Passion Dale spreads on the

Bullock grapevine, supplies begin to arrive beneath trailer-loads of rubbish ostensibly destined for the tip, between bales of hay, and in one case inside the huge revolving bowl of one of Dan Ogilvy's bright red Ready-Mix trucks. Tea knows something's going on so he establishes a block on the only road out of town, causing a jam several cars long, but Sunny's Secret Army knows every farm track, every forest road, every private driveway that has a front entrance and a rear exit.

Tea has his share of success, though. I hear this story from Sunny.

Ella Marjoribanks has always been one to push her luck. She and her husband, Carl, were among the last of Bullock's Catholics to practise *coitus interruptus*. Carl hated condoms, had no faith in the rhythm method, and was an assistant manager at the Bullock Savings Bank. There'd been three kids in four years and it was while attending to Jason, her youngest, that Ella ran into Tea's road block instead of diverting down Wey Street and through Roy Calloway's carport.

'I see you're not wearing your seat belt, Ella.' Tea leaned on the Commodore's roof. 'Any particular reason for that?'

'Jason was pissing about with the radio, Tea.' Ella ruffled Jason's hair. 'Had to give the little bugger a bit of gentle counselling. Every time I stretched round, the belt jammed. Sorry. Won't do it again.'

'Mum's got some weed in the back.' Simon was Ella's second. Rumour had it that he was the result of a cleaning cupboard encounter with a persuasive priest during a Knights of Saint Columba Christmas Party. 'We're taking it to the secret plant.'

'That so?' Tea looked towards the boot. 'Mind stepping out of the car, Ella?'

When Tea threw back the old blanket and gazed at the bright green Crackling Rose, neatly bundled with elastic bands, Ella knew what she had to do. She'd negotiated the same deal with the builders who'd worked on her new Les Cuthbert Executive Home, and ended up with a thirty per cent discount.

'Look, Tea.' She laid a hand on the cop's left forearm and moved in close. 'Can't we work something out? We're putting in a pool and sauna, so my diary's pretty chocker, but I can fit you in Wednesday afternoons. Before I pick the kids up from school.'

Tea's eyes narrowed. He surveyed Ella's ample frame, thought for a while. He liked ample women. But he had a job to do.

'Sorry, Ella. No can do. You'd better follow me back to the station.'

But mostly the weed got through.

Chapter 54

We gather at Murray's place for pre-ballet cocktails. Murray's wife, Janice, runs the distaff side of the business, *Hair Today, Gone Tomorrow*. Murray and Janice look startlingly similar, both tall, both quietly confident, both with short hair, parted on the right, although Janice wears a pink knee-length dress whereas Murray's in a Macdonald clan kilt and matching bow tie, so there's no confusion.

Although there are plenty of nibbles to go with the champagne, I can't help noticing that Big Andy has brought his brown paper bag.

'Got to keep my strength up, Johnny. I'll rest it on my lap during the performance. In case I get a sudden hunger attack. Open it during the loud bits so I don't bother anyone.'

Merv the Mink's in Big Andy's shadow. He's wearing white silk socks and white shoes that go nicely with his white tuxedo and white bow tie.

'Fitz, this is my wife, Betty.'

I'm sure I've seen the heavy woman by Merv's side before, but I'm getting used to that feeling. Everywhere I go around Bullock I see half-familiar faces, twenty years older than my memory recalls. Merv sees my puzzled look and helps me out.

'Used to be Betty Rice.'

He gives me a big wink. Betty and I make small talk about the good old days when she used to serve us ice cream, then Murray suggests it's time to go so we pile into our cars and head for the Bullock Weed Cooperative Little Theatre. This is on Thames

Street opposite Meggett's and alongside Paddy McGinty's Irish Pub (*A hundred thousand welcomes! Last orders 9 p.m.*), Sherry's wine bar (*Happy Hour 5–5.30, try our Sheet Stainer*), and the Ritz cinema, which is now part of a chain. I smile when I see they're showing a Laura Friday movie. *The Parrot's Not for Plucking*. It came out in London twelve years ago. The sign outside says there's a Stay All Day concession, but there's no sign of a Ritz Little Cracker.

The foyer sparkles beneath a huge crystal chandelier, and it's obvious that the town's glitterati are making this a night to remember. Diamond necklaces and tiaras have been retrieved from the Bullock Savings Bank's vaults, duty-free perfumes applied, and for the past week Janice and Murray have been keeping late hours to cope with the demand.

Murray points out the town's celebrities.

'Remember Septimus Punch. Just been re-elected for the seventh time.'

Punch is a small man who seems burdened by his Chain of Office, whereas the woman by his side looks like a galleon under full sail.

'And his wife, Miriam.'

'Stuttering' Hutch Scandrett's beside the Mayor. Hutch is wearing a hairpiece which has slipped to his left.

'*He's bald now,*' whispers Murray. '*Comes into the shop to keep up the pretence.*'

'Scandrett's all pretence.'

I remember his performance outside the hospital when Dick Worth lost his penis.

A whistle blows for the start of play. We file into the theatre, settle into our seats, the only problem being the small lady immediately behind Big Andy who complains that she hasn't paid good money to watch someone's back for two and a half hours. Andy good-naturedly offers to exchange, but then the person in the next row raises a similar fuss. Andy plays musical chairs until he arrives at the back row.

When the curtain rises, George as Siegfried comes on with his best friend, Benno.

'*That's Ray "Piranha" Dobson,*' whispers Murray. '*Loose-head prop for Bullock the past sixteen seasons.*'

George and Ray leap about the stage touch-tackling each other, then gather the party together for a rolling maul. One of the party emerges missing an ear lobe, which he playfully retrieves from Ray's teeth.

The queen arrives with the evil Count von Rothbart's daughter, Odile. Murray whispers. '*Erin Childs, captain of the Bullock Women's Softball team.*'

Unhappy with her performance, Siegfried dismisses her with a yellow card.

The queen makes it clear that Siegfried must marry Odile by passing the family ring back and forth in a dazzling three-quarter line movement. They pause for breath while a tutu'd physio attends to a feigned injury to one of the *corps de ballet*.

Siegfried sits with Benno, contemplating the loss of his youth. Two tragic, lonely figures, a flagon of beer between them, concealed in a brown paper bag. Odette comes on and performs the traditional thirty-two *fouettés*, following which Siegfried prevents her from staggering around the stage by hugging her to his chest.

Odette and the Bullock Silver Ferns then dance an intricate movement, each remaining within her defined part of the stage before passing an imaginary ball to Odette, who scores after being awarded a penalty for interference. This ends Act One.

As the lights come up, I turn to Merv.

'The Royal Ballet would never put on something like that.'

'They're only part-timers,' says Merv, 'but you'd never know.'

For Act Two the curtain rises on an exuberant party, with the females on one side grouped around a pram, the males on the other around a crate of beer. Benno introduces several princesses who surround the prince, tearing at his tights, but, even when half-naked, Siegfried maintains his *sang froid*. He is not interested in anyone but Odette.

The princesses then vie for Siegfried's attention by forming a ruck which circles the stage until the whistle blows. The audience sighs. One of the princesses has dived over the top and killed a promising movement.

In the final scene, Odile disappears into the lake, smacking her fist into a softball mitt. The flock of swans embrace their beloved captain Odette as she, too, dies from a broken heart, their hands outstretched towards the basket in a touching tableau.

As the curtain comes down and the music comes to its crashing finale, the sobs and gasps of the audience bring the evening to an emotional conclusion. I reach for the hand of the person sitting next to me.

'You need a woman in your life,' says Merv the Mink, as he gives my hand back.

Chapter 55

'So.' Laura turned, her eyes hooded. 'Did you mean what you said just now? Or are you just like every other man I've ever known? A liar, a cheat and a heartless bastard?'

'What did I just say, Laura? Remind me.'

He dragged on the post-coital joint, gave it to Laura, blew smoke at the ship's wheel above the bed.

'About loving me. You forgotten already, you creep?'

'Oh that.' He took another long drag, drew it down into his lungs, let it swirl, not giving a damn about the risk, because why should he — he was a dead man walking unless Laura played ball. Released it in a long, slow expulsion through both nostrils. 'Sure. Of course I love you. Why? Don't you believe me?'

'You were humming "The Dying Swan". What am I supposed to believe?'

I sit back, stretch, and gaze bleakly through the spare bedroom window at the sun dappling the trees. It's eleven already and I've been working since five. Feeling like good coffee and good company, Jerry and I drive into town and park outside Murray's.

We get our usual warm welcome. Big Andy and Merv the Mink are there, but there's no sign of George, who's presumably sleeping off the effects of the First Night Party. There are no customers, so Murray's in his chair browsing the *Telegraph*.

'I see they're reporting slow but steady progress on the new airport. Can't say we don't need it. Current runway's down the racecourse finishing straight. Control tower doubles as the commentary box. Fine most of the time, but the punters got a bit confused at the last New Year Carnival when Clear To Land was declared the winner of the 3.30.'

'When's it going to open?' asks Merv.

Murray searches the report.

'Some time within the next ten years. There's a photo here of the paddock that'll become the new runway. It's carrying two hundred head of Friesians although they were away being milked when the photo was taken so it's lost a bit of its impact.'

'Anything there about last night's ballet?' asks Big Andy.

'Too soon for that,' says Murray. 'Harry Squire usually writes his review on Sunday after bowls. Good or bad write-up can hang on whoever wins the last end. Gets printed on Monday, delivered Tuesday.'

'Given any more thought to finding yourself a woman, Johnny?'

Merv the Mink has been browsing through *Romeo and Juliet*, which he casts aside.

'Carmel's been asking the same thing.'

I go over to the coffee table where the sign still says *If you're getting one for yourself, ask others if they'd like one, too* and refresh Andy's at the same time.

'I've been weighing up the pros and cons. I think she's right. A woman would be good. Jerry gives me love and loyalty, but even a German Shepherd has his limitations.'

Murray nods.

'There are some things only a woman can do.'

'I don't know where to start looking, though. There's Meggett's café but I don't care for the look of what's on offer there.'

'What sort of model would suit you best?' Merv the Mink's face is eager, as if he's warming up a prospect. 'Age, condition, mileage? Family or sporty? Colour? Full service history?'

'Interested in the same things as me. Movies, music, food, wine, books. She'll be bright, funny, well-travelled.'

'You could advertise in the *Telegraph* Classifieds,' says Big Andy as he munches a doughnut. 'I found a great lawnmower there once.'

'What about the internet?' Murray folds the paper and stares into space. 'Dozens of dating websites. Thousands of women. Must be someone there from Bullock who'll catch your eye.'

Chapter 56

That evening I register with a dating website. I post a recent photograph and fill in the profile, omitting all reference to my former life. The next day my page is bombarded. I draw up a shortlist and, after a few emails and phone calls back and forth, set up a batch of meetings.

On a fine but cold Saturday morning I head for my first appointment, which is coffee with Gretchen on Meggett's balcony. I've printed the profiles of each person together with their photos and notes from our phone calls.

I arrive early and stand around the bookshop, watching new arrivals and checking against the photo. This shows a woman in her early forties. She has a pretty face, framed by blonde hair, with a Mary Quant fringe covering her forehead. She's from a German family but was born in Bullock, has a PhD in Psychology, and is a child behavioural therapist.

I see her approaching the café, and walk towards her, my smile fixed.

'Hi, Gretchen. I'm Johnny. Sorry if I kept you waiting.'

'Time is of no importance.' She's wearing sunglasses which she removes from her nose and rests on her head. 'As Freud said, *"the goal of all life is death"*.'

'Sure, of course.'

I puzzle over this as we look for a table. Most are occupied by couples engrossed in their Saturday papers, distractedly stirring lattes and double espressos. But there's a place in a corner. We squeeze into it.

'What would you like?'

'A decaf latte, please.'

I order Gretchen's decaf and a long black for myself, plus a slice of carrot cake with yoghurt on the side. There's something strange about this woman, and I can't figure out what it is. When I return to the table, Gretchen has taken a small leather-bound notebook from her bag, flipped it open and has a pen poised.

'I always take notes. Wasn't it Nietzsche who said, *"I have done that, says my memory, I cannot have done that, says my pride, and the memory yields"*?'

'Was it? I'm not sure. It's years since I've read Nietzsche. How long have you been using the website?'

'Ah. You wish to establish whether this is a routine encounter, or something special.' Gretchen nods pensively. 'Utterly logical and reasonable, if demonstrative of a slight insecurity. Wasn't it Fromm who said, *"The psychic task which a person can and must set for himself is not to feel secure, but to be able to tolerate insecurity"*? But to answer your question, I've been on the website now for . . . ' she flips through her notebook ' . . . five months, during which time I've met . . . thirteen men. Eight for only one meeting, three for a second, and two for several more. I've slept with . . . three people, but only one more than once. And you?'

'This is my first time.'

She laughs and shows two rows of large teeth. She has long fingers and nails with which she encircles the coffee cup, holding it close to her mouth, which is wide and full.

'A virgin. Who said, *"Virginity is like a bubble — one prick and it's gone"*?'

'I don't know.' My cup is empty. I catch the eye of the girl behind the counter and mouth my need for a refill. 'Who?'

'I don't know either.' Gretchen laughs with her throat, a hard, rasping sound. 'But I like it, anyway.'

My refill arrives. I use the caffeine buzz to fight a lethargic *ennui*. I worry. Maybe it's me. I've been away for twenty years. Maybe this is how urbane Bullockians converse these days. I nod and suppress a yawn as Gretchen tells me about her job, her past experiences with men, her house where she is building a rock garden. She scatters quotations like confetti, and each time I speak makes cryptic notes in her little book.

There's a clock on the back wall. At eleven-thirty-five I decide I've had enough.

'Well, Gretchen, it's been terrific meeting you. But I have to go. I'm meeting someone for lunch.'

'Not a problem.' She snaps her notebook shut, drops it into her bag, stands and gathers her coat. 'I like you, Johnny. When shall we two meet again?'

'I don't think so.' I see no point in dissembling. Jonathan Hess has said I must not avoid confrontation. 'But it's been . . . interesting.'

We stand outside, ready to go our separate ways. I offer my hand. She leans forward, kisses my cheek. I feel faintly patronised.

The lunchtime rendezvous is a wine bar called Waterside on Nile Quay. It's a busy place on a Saturday, with several dozen tables inside, a wine bar, and outside tables. The photo is of an attractive face, slightly round and fleshy, but with wide dark eyes which look interesting, and a sexy mouth. It's a close-up mugshot, so I have no idea how tall Tania might be, or what sort of figure she might have. I find an inside table for two, order a glass of red wine, and wait. Several attractive women come in, but none of them is Tania.

Then I see her. There's an icy wind blowing from the water, and most people are well wrapped up. Tania is wearing a fur coat, the collar turned up to shield the lower half of her face, and a Russian fur hat. My first impression is of a very large brown bear. Beneath the layers of protective clothing she is pear-shaped. Her legs are immense. I feel overwhelmed. I panic, look for an escape route. To reach the front door I will need to pass her. But the men's toilet is at the rear.

I find a twenty-dollar note. I toss it on the table and rise. It's too late! She's seen me. She's navigating like a supertanker between the tables. As she brushes past an unfortunate couple, a plate and glass crash to the floor. I point towards the toilet, wave my arms in a milling motion which is meaningless but impressive, and rush to the back of the room. She follows, leaving a trail of destruction in her wake.

There's a small corridor with two doors, one for the men's toilet, the other for the women's. She could park outside and starve me into submission. The kitchen is at the end. I push through the door. Steam rises from several stainless-steel saucepans. It's very hot. A girl in whites is stirring something. There's a guy placing things on plates. Another is yelling into a cellphone. A radio blares. No one takes any notice as I head for the back door, which is closed but unlocked. I push the emergency bars. The door swings open. Someone behind me yells, *'Hey! Shut that fucking door!'*

I run up Thames Street and into Paddy McGinty's, order a pint of Guinness and a packet of crisps, and find a hidden corner behind a fruit machine.

It's six-thirty before I emerge and set sail for my final appointment, drinks in the house bar of the Shipwreck Arms, with a lady called Harriet.

'My friends call me Harri,' she'd said when we first spoke on the phone, but the idea leaves me dubious. In moments of passion I can't hear myself murmuring *'Oh Harri, Harri, Harri...'*

If we hit it off, we'll go somewhere for dinner. If we don't, we won't.

The fresh Bullock air induces the need to pee. I look back at Paddy's and wonder whether to beat a retreat. But the facilities are basic, whereas at the Shipwreck there'll be hot towels and little soaps and luxury urinals where you can stare at a wall of *Playboy* bunnies in Santa suits, fingers in their mouths, pointing.

Although the glow of the Guinness provides inner insulation, the shortest route to the Shipwreck is an exposed one. As I hunch my shoulders and fight the wind past locked and dark buildings, the need grows ever stronger. I'm about halfway there when I know I'm not going to make it. I find a doorway, unzip and relax as the warm flow trickles towards the welcoming sea. Comfortable again, I hurry on. Harriet will be waiting. I must hurry for Harriet. I take the hotel steps two at a time and enter the reception area.

'Your house bar, young man?'

A suited person behind the desk points to a wide spiral staircase.

Harriet is as I'd hoped. Unquestionably, indubitably attractive, her face a perfection. Her hair is dark, long and straight, French-polished and well cut. A very fine nose. Goodness, it's fine. It's very, very fine. Blue, blue, sea-blue eyes which wash over me when I wave. There's a hovering, uncertain smile as she toys with an empty wine glass.

'Harriet! Harri! Hi!'

Overwhelmed by aspirates, I slump into a tub chair. Topple. Hit my right knee against a low glass table but feel no pain.

'I'm Johnny. So, so, so, so very sorry I'm late. Have you been here terribly, terribly, terribly long?'

'We said six-thirty.'

Her voice is manuka honey. Smooth, very sweet. I loved it on the phone. In person it's even better.

'It's now ten to seven. So I've been here twenty minutes.'

'Yes, well . . . '

What can I say? That I've been hiding from a brown bear in a mock-Irish pub? That I was delayed by the need to pee?

'Can I get you another glass of wine?'

'That would be nice. Thank you.'

A waiter hovers. I ask him what Harriet is drinking.

'A Bullock Reserve Pinot Noir, sir. It's twelve-fifty a glass.'

'Another for the lady, then, and the same for me.'

Our wine arrives. I raise my glass in a toast.

'So,' she says, 'what have you been doing today?'

'Oh.' I wave a blithe hand. 'I met someone for coffee this morning. Didn't hit it off at all. Can't even remember her name now. Like a Canadian town. Alberta? Winnipeg? Saskatchewan?'

Harriet's laugh is crystal streams over rippling stones.

'This person's name was Saskatchewan?'

'No, no, no.' I wave my hand again. 'Gretchen. That's it, Gretchen.'

'And what was it about this Canadian town called Gretchen that you didn't like?'

'She kept throwing quotations at me. As if what other people have said and thought was more important than what she had to say and think.'

'I can see how that would be a problem.' Against all odds Harriet seems to be enjoying herself. I begin to relax. Maybe this is going to work out after all. 'Any others?'

'Well . . . '

I tell her about my aborted lunchtime meeting with Tania, my escape through the kitchen, and hideout in Paddy's.

'That was a shitty thing to do.' Her eyes grow cold. She puts her glass down on the table. 'All you had to do was say, "Look, I'm sorry, this isn't going to work." Running away from situations doesn't solve anything.'

'That's what Jonathan Hess says.'

'Who's Jonathan Hess?'

'My analyst.'

She wrinkles her forehead, her eyes wide and deep. 'You're in therapy?'

'Have been for years.'

'Why, for God's sake?'

'To try to discover why I'm always running away from situations.'

Unexpectedly, Harriet laughs. Her anger has faded.

'So I'm the third today. Any more?'

'Three tomorrow. And that's it. If nobody works out, I'll have to do it all over again some other time.'

'Well,' she says, 'I'm not sure how to feel. It's like I'm being interviewed for a job.'

'It's a two-way street. I'm under scrutiny, too. What about your day?'

'Saturdays are my busiest day. I've been teaching since nine this morning.'

'What do you teach?'

'I told you on the phone. I work at the library during the week and teach singing during the evening and on Saturdays. I perform now and then. With the Bullock Choral Society. We're doing the *Messiah* next Sunday. Do you like classical music?'

'Play it all the time.'

'Who's your favourite?'

'Abba, The Carpenters, Bananarama, Dire Straits, Elton John. All the greats.'

'No, I mean older, more formal music.'

'I've never got into it. I was brought up on Irish folk music and John McCormack. "I'll Take You Home Again, Kathleen" was about as close as we got to formal.'

'Do you play a musical instrument?'

I show her my fingers.

'Mum said I should have been a pianist. But I always wanted to be a writer.'

'Thousands of people want to be writers. Very few ever make it.' Harriet signals to the waiter. 'Could we have two more glasses of wine, please? You could have done both. Played the piano and been a writer.'

'I could have. But I didn't. How old were you when you started to sing?'

'Seven. I left Bullock when I was eighteen. Went to a singing teacher in New York.'

'What happened after that?'

'I did a couple of competitions. Went on the road. But I didn't really enjoy performing. Got very sick beforehand. Had to be helped onto the platform. As soon as I started to sing I was fine, but before and after . . . eventually it got to me. So, like you, I came back to Bullock. Teaching's always been my first love. Watching talent bloom. The library job just pays the rent.'

The drinks arrive. I offer to pay. Harriet waves me away.

'This is fifty-fifty. I'm running a tab.'

'What about relationships? Have you been married?'

'I was once.' She takes a pensive drink, as if wondering how much to tell me. 'But singing's death to anything else. You have to love what you do more than anything. Or anyone. Then there's the travelling. We hardly saw each other for weeks on end. And the cocktail parties. And the constant temptation.'

'You mean you had affairs?'

Harriet's head snaps up and her eyes go cold again.

'Not me! My husband. He was a conductor. If I'd been older I might have known better. They're notorious philanderers. All that power plus immense creative energy. If you're good-looking as well, it's just about the sexiest combination you can think of. And Anton was very good-looking.'

'How long were you married?'

'Three years. He fell in love with a cellist.'

'Any kids?'

'We were planning a family once things settled down. They never did. And I've recently—'

A shadow falls across our table.

Harriet's eyes flick away. I follow her gaze. A woman in her mid-forties, with dark brown hair, cropped above her ears, heavy make-up, a round, chubby face, is standing between us. She's wearing tight jeans and a loose floral blouse, a painted wooden necklace. I've seen her face before, but can't recall where. She's clutching a piece of paper.

'Are you Johnny?'

The woman looks nervous, as if it's taken a huge effort to approach the table.

'I'm sorry, but . . .'

'I'm Hazel. We arranged to meet here at seven-thirty. Drinks. And maybe dinner later. I've been sitting over there for the past half-hour.'

'Hell, Hazel, I'm here with Harriet.'

'I've printed out the email you sent me.'

She thrusts a piece of paper. I read: ' . . . *looking forward to seeing you in the house bar of the Shipwreck Arms at 7.30 on Saturday.*'

I look at my watch, as if this will give succour. The time is seven-forty-five.

'I wrote that to everyone. You're supposed to be Sunday. It's a typing error.'

'It says Saturday.' The woman is standing her ground. 'I've made special arrangements. A babysitter I can't afford. I drove all the way from Gundry. I had to pay someone to do my shift. What do you mean it's a fucking typing error?'

'Look,' Harriet is standing, gathering up her stuff, 'I'll go. Have a nice time, Hazel. But don't believe a word he says. He's all wind and piss. Quite a lot of piss as a matter of fact. And to think I was beginning to like you.'

'No, please.' As I stand I hit the glass-topped table with my shin. *'Shit!'* There's a satisfied smirk on Harriet's face as she goes to the bar to settle her tab. Hazel sits in Harriet's tub chair.

'So, Johnny. What have you been doing today?'

Chapter 57

According to Friday's edition of the *Bullock Telegraph*, the Bullock Orpheus Choir, together with the Bullock Philharmonic Orchestra and a trumpeter from Gundry, will perform Handel's *Messiah* in Saint Andrew's Presbyterian Church at two on Sunday. I've never seen or heard the oratorio. All I know is the "Hallelujah Chorus" and I've read about the quaint tradition of standing for it, so I decide to broaden my musical knowledge. It's also the only way I'm going to see Harriet again.

I join the crowd shuffling into the church. The women are mostly white-haired, in floral dresses and sensible shoes. The men look as if they'd rather be anywhere else. To my right is an elderly guy in a dark grey suit, with a hearing aid. To my left is a rugby type who eyes me as if he'd enjoy an encounter at the bottom of a ruck. We're surrounded by lavender, eau de cologne and carbolic.

To scattered applause, the orchestra walks in in single file from a side door. I count eighteen violinists, one viola, an oboe and a cellist. The choir follows the orchestra. There are thirty-two members, twenty-three of them female. The men stand in a thin row at the rear and look at each other as if seeking reassurance.

The applause increases when the conductor, a nervous-looking guy with a beard and a stoop, marches to the front, stands on a box, bows to the audience, then turns and raises his baton. After the overture, a tenor comes to the front and sings, *Comfort ye, comfort ye my people.*

It's Merv the Mink. Merv's voice is a little thin, but he gains confidence when he sings *Make straight in the desert a highway* ... Merv is succeeded by a short, well-constructed woman with red lips and a new hairdo. She sings *Ev'ry valley shall be exalted* in a faltering, flat soprano and misses several cues.

The conductor's style is unusual. His head is bent over the score, his baton above his head, waving about like a willow in a breeze. From time to time he makes gestures with his left hand from which the musicians select at random.

A soprano in a long black skirt and high-necked white blouse comes forward to sing *He shall feed His flock like a Shepherd.* Her voice is superb. It soars above us, diamond-bright. Pure, beautiful, and utterly captivating. It's Harriet. I feel a knot in my gut that I haven't experienced since I first saw Frankie.

When she resumes her seat, the conductor pauses, as if to savour the moment, and gives Harriet a special smile before leading the choir into 'Unto Us a Child is Born'. I remember what Harriet said about conductors. And feel as if Laura Friday has just thrust her Bowie knife into my heart.

At the interval I walk outside and stroll the church grounds. I chide myself for my jealousy. I hardly know Harriet, and I'm hardly likely to. I've fallen at the first hurdle. And yet I haven't stopped thinking about her all week and wishing I hadn't made such an idiot of myself.

In the second half I carefully follow the programme. I don't want to miss the 'Hallelujah Chorus'. In fact I might even score a few Brownie points with Harriet if I pre-empt everyone else by a second or two. As the conductor raises his baton, I rise and fix Harriet with a kind smile. She stares blankly back. I hear no rustle behind me. I look around. I stand my ground. The rugby type is tugging at my jacket. Merv the Mink comes forward and sings *Thou shalt break them with a rod of iron; thou shalt dash them in pieces like a potter's vessel . . .*

I sit. I shrink. I see grins from the corners of my eyes. A smile plays at the edges of Harriet's mouth. Or is it a sneer?

When the oratorio ends, I shuffle into the afternoon sun. In a feel-good Hugh Grant movie, Harriet would come dashing up, say something funny, and I would go *'gosh, ah, well, um,'* and after that everything would work out fine. But this is real life. I watch her get into the passenger seat of a Volvo. Watch the conductor fasten his seat belt and lean across to help her with hers. Watch white smoke drift from the car's exhaust. Hear its tyres' derisive hiss.

Merv joins me by the kerb.

'Well, you really made a prat of yourself in there. I wouldn't have missed it for quids. Laughing so much I nearly missed my cue for the aria.'

'I was trying to impress the woman I was telling you about. The one I met on the internet.'

'Which one's that?'

'Harriet. She has the voice of an angel.'

Merv's jaw drops.

'Harriet Poynter?'

'Yeah. You know her?'

'She's been engaged to Tea Nelson for the past three years. She's just dumped him. She's the reason why he's running around like a bear with a bullet up its arse. Oh, man! Are you ever in big trouble!'

Chapter 58

The restoration of Passion Dale is complete. Tiles cover the porch floor and flow into the new kitchen, which looks sleek in its grey and black livery. Massive windows give a panoramic view of the town and Apprehensive Bay. The old dining room and kitchen are now bedrooms. The builders have filled three jumbo skips with rubbish.

As I sit outside with my coffee and toast and watch the sun's rays come over the hill, I experience my own slow dawn as I realise that I feel more connected to Passion Dale than to any house I've owned, even Barton Lodge. As if by giving it a new lease of life I've become part of it. For the first time since I left Wey Street, I feel as if I belong somewhere.

The phone rings. I go inside to answer it.

'Johnny? This is Roy Calloway. What are you doing for lunch?'

We meet at the Bullock Workingmen's Club. Roy now has a hearing aid and carries a stick, but otherwise looks spry for someone in his late seventies. We sit at a table by the window and drink pints of Special Curd while we wait for our order of fish and chips. I tell him he's looking well.

'Takes the old body a while to get into gear in the mornings. Creaks and groans like a rusty gate until I've had a whisky with my morning coffee. Good to see you. You want your old job back?'

'I was wondering if you'd be interested in selling the paper.'

Roy nods, as if he's been expecting the offer.

'Your mum suggested it. I said we should wait and see. Come back to the paper first, get back into the swing of things. Take it from there. How's Passion Dale coming along?'

'House is finished. I'm starting to think about the land now. Sunny Riverbank reckons I should plant grapes.'

'Could do worse.' Roy sits back as the waitress brings our lunch, the cutlery wrapped in white paper serviettes, tartare sauce in little pots. It's a huge piece of crumbed fish, a pile of chips, another of peas. 'Long-term project, though, Johnny. Need a lot of cash to get started. You won't see much return for four, maybe five years. Longer if you plant red grapes. You prepared to wait? You prepared to stay in Bullock that long?'

'Carmel said it's time I put down some roots and I agree. I think I'm here to stay.'

'What about a family? Got any thoughts in that direction?'

I smile, liking Roy's direct questions.

'Haven't found anyone to have kids with. I guess I'm just not cut out for it.'

I tell Roy about my escapade with Harriet and Hazel at the Shipwreck, and about the 'Hallelujah Chorus'. I make it sound funny. He nearly chokes on his fish.

'Harriet's a nice lady. Fantastic talent, too. When she started out we ran a fundraising campaign in the *Telegraph* for her to study in New York. She starred at the Met, you know. Got her big chance as Mimi in *La Bohème* when the diva got sick. Got rave reviews. She recorded with Plácido Domingo, José Carreras. Take a look in Meggett's music department some time. Classical section. Get her recording of "Norma". It'll blow you away.'

Roy's enthusiasm makes me feel even more depressed.

'What's the use? I fucked things up. Twice. She's probably been snapped up by some other guy from the dating website by now. And she and the conductor seemed pretty close.'

'Another little tip.' Roy waves away my objections with his knife, spraying crumbs of fish across the Formica table. 'She runs along Bullock Beach every evening about six with her spaniel bitch. Take your dog. Make it look casual. You've got nothing to lose.'

'Thanks. I'll think about it.'

'Don't take too long. What was it our man said?' Roy looks up at the Club's nicotine-stained acoustic tiles as he searches his memory. ' *Go and love, go and love, young man,* | *If the lady be young and fair . . .* | *There is nobody wise enough* | *To find out all that is in it,* | *For he would be thinking of love* | *Till the stars had run away* | *And the shadows eaten the moon. . . .* | *One cannot begin it too soon.*'

I remember summer evenings reading Yeats on the lawn at Wey Street as Dad polished his ports, Mum made dinner, and 'I Cain't Get No Satisfaction' blasted from Agnes's open bedroom window.

'I've still got that book of poems you gave me, Roy. "Brown Penny" was one of my favourites. *I am looped in the loops of her hair . . .* That's me, for sure.'

'Something else.' Roy nods his remembrance but seems preoccupied. 'Your mother asked me to talk to you. You know, I've been her friend for sixty years. We were at school together. Well, not exactly together. She was at Bernie's, I was at Benny's. She was three years behind. I saw her over the fence one day. My mates and I used to climb onto the cricket pavilion roof, hide in an oak tree, and watch the girls play netball. I loved her the minute I set eyes on her. But she took no notice of me. She was my Maud Gonne, Johnny. Looked like Maud, too. Same determined mouth, same wild hair, same big, penetrating eyes. I was nineteen, she was sixteen when I asked her to marry me. She just laughed.'

Roy toys with his fish as he gathers his thoughts. I recall something he said to me long ago. *'The loss of love can be a terrible thing, but it can also provide the spark for great creativity.'* Roy's creative spark was sheep-shearing; mine was Laura Friday.

'Go on, Roy.'

'When I left school I went to work on the *Telegraph*. My dad was running the paper, I was learning the ropes, and it was expected that I'd take over one day. Marge came to work there as a typist, proofreader, you know, general dogsbody. We saw a lot of each other. Started going out. Irish Night each Friday here at the Club with Marge's family and mine. They lived here then, moved over to Gundry a few years later. I used to see Moira Kennedy across the room. She'd smile and wave, but that was as far as it went. Then your dad came back from dental school and started to play with the band. He was a good-looking man. I never blamed your mother for choosing him. Love takes many forms, Johnny. Our man Yeats knew that better than anyone. Marge and I loved each other. But I've always been *in* love with your mother. She doesn't love me in the same way. But she does in her own way. If we don't do something about it now, we never will.'

'How do you mean? Do something about it? In what way?'

'How would you feel if we got married?'

Now it's my turn to choke.

'Married? You? And Mum? But—'

'We're too old?' Roy bridles. 'Is that what you're thinking?'

It's exactly what I'm thinking. Carmel would have said it and given Roy her Look. All I can say is, 'Are you sure?'

'Johnny, I'm seventy-eight. Your mum's seventy-five and she's got cancer. Neither of us knows how long we've got. How sure do we need to be?'

'She's never said anything.'

'That's because there's a thing between you two. I've done

my best to bring you together but I know you were always closer to your Aunt Agnes. That's why your mother wanted me to talk to you.'

I push my empty plate aside, point to Roy's Special Curd glass.

'My shout. Same again?'

'Thanks, yeah.'

On my way to the bar with the empty glasses I have a thought. When I return it's with an ice bucket, a bottle of champagne, and two fresh glasses. I pop the cork, fill the glasses.

'Here's to you and Mum, Roy. May you have many happy years together.'

We clink. We drink. We grin.

'One more thing, Johnny.'

'What's that?'

'About your Aunt Agnes.'

Chapter 59

It's early evening, the sun low over Apprehensive Bay. The time of day when sound travels far. I clearly hear the happy screams of two kids playing with a ball; a dog as it dashes into the water chasing a stick; the sound in the sky before I see the plane's approach, balancing on thin air like a trapeze artist on a wire. It zooms low over the beach and disappears towards the racecourse.

I see her running barefoot through the edge of the waves with a flop-eared spaniel loping by her side. They are fifty yards away when Jerry spots the spaniel and pricks up his ears. I unleash him and whisper.

'*Geh*, *dafür!*'

He dashes across the sand, splays his paws in front of the spaniel. The spaniel does the same. After a sniffing ritual they chase each other across the beach, Jerry taking it easy with the smaller dog.

'*Keine Gewalttätigkeit!*' I told him before we left Passion Dale, so he allows the spaniel to nip at his flanks and yap at him without his usual overpowering response.

Harriet runs on for a few yards then stops, turns back, stands in the shallows watching the dogs. By then I'm close. She looks at me for the first time.

'You never told me you have a dog. What's his name? I presume it's a he.'

'Jerry. What's yours?'

'Milly.'

'They seem to like each other.'

'First impressions can be deceptive. He's probably got another mate lined up if this one doesn't work out.'

'Several, I would think. There's safety in numbers. Do you come here every evening?'

'You know I do.'

'What do you mean?'

'Roy Calloway told you. He said you'd be here one evening and I should be nice to you, though I don't see why I should.'

'Look, Harriet, I'm sorry about that Saturday. I fucked up, OK? You can hold it against me forever or forget about it now. It's up to you. It's not as if we were on a date. We were meeting for the first time. If we'd been going out together, it would have been different.'

But Harriet doesn't concede the point.

'What happened to Hazel?'

'We had a few drinks. I took your advice and told her it wasn't worth going to dinner.'

'What did she say?'

'She called me an arrogant prick.'

'Pretty much spot-on, I'd say.'

Harriet gazes across the bay. The outlook doesn't look good. My only consolation is that although she's angry at least she's standing her ground. She could have walked away by now. In her shoes I would have.

'What about those other women on your list? Did you meet them?'

'I couldn't go through it all again. Anyway, once I'd met you I didn't want to meet anyone else.'

'Did you call them?'

'The next day.'

This isn't getting us anywhere, so I decide to try another tack. Contrition.

'Look, Harriet, I'm really, really sorry. I completely cocked things up. We were getting on so well. Please don't run from me. Please don't hide in the ebb and flow of the pale tide. People will think you were hard and unkind and blame you with bitter words.'

'That's Yeats. You think you can win me over with Irish blarney? You'll be singing "Molly Malone" to me next.'

'That would really drive you away.'

Jerry's very sensitive to moods. He and Milly have been playing in the sea. Now they slump side-by-side on the sand. Milly rests her jaw on Jerry's chest.

'Shall we walk for a bit?'

'I usually run.'

'I'm not into running.'

Harriet goes *'Huh!'* and stuffs her hands in the pockets of her shorts.

'Did you enjoy the *Messiah*?'

'Everything except the "Hallelujah Chorus". You have the most wonderful voice I've ever heard.'

'Thank you. That was very funny.'

'I'm glad you thought so. I tried to see you afterwards, but you disappeared in a cloud of white smoke.'

'I didn't want to speak to you. I might have said something I'd regret.'

'Like what?'

'Like I haven't stopped thinking about you since I walked out of the bar at the Shipwreck Arms.'

'Nor have I. Anyway you haven't exactly been honest. What's all this about you and Tea Nelson?'

'I was about to tell you when Hazel arrived. When he's off-duty and out of his uniform, Tea's actually a very nice man. He's funny, intelligent, well-read and good company. He never wanted to be the Bullock cop. He was working in London when his dad died. His mum was heartbroken, took sick. No one to look after her. He was the only child. So he came back. Cop's job had been in the Nelson family right from the beginning. That was five years ago. His mum's still sick.'

'But what about you and him?'

'I'm coming to that. We met at the dog club. When I came back to Bullock I didn't know anyone and I thought it might be a good way of making friends. I took Milly along. She got on well with Tea's Red Setters. And it kind of went from there.'

'And what went wrong?'

'If you give me a chance, Johnny, I'm coming to that, too.' Harriet stops and faces me, hands in her pockets. The dogs have been padding along behind. They stop, too. 'You're very persistent, aren't you? What were you doing in London?'

'Newspaper reporter. Criminal investigator. For the *Daily Chronicle*.'

'Ah.' Harriet nods. 'That explains it. And what brings you back to Bullock?'

'It's a dirty business. I'd had enough of it. I'm probably going to buy the *Bullock Telegraph*. Roy's ready to retire. Tell me about you and Tea.'

'He gradually became more and more possessive. Wouldn't give me time and space. Got jealous when I went to choir practice or had a singing student and couldn't go out with him. Wanted me to come with him to dog club every Thursday. Got pissed off if I didn't. Sulked. I got fed up with it. I need my independence, Johnny. I'd like a relationship with someone who's got a life of his own and is happy for me to have mine.'

'What did he say when you told him?'

'Hit the roof. Stormed off. He keeps coming in to see me at the library. Just won't accept that it's over.'

'Meanwhile the rest of Bullock suffers.'

'What!' Harriet scoffs. 'You think I should go back to him so that the BWC can resume normal service?'

'No, of course not. So why did you decide to go onto the internet?'

'To meet someone different. Interesting, funny. Someone who's well-travelled, has lived, suffered, learned from the experience. Come through it all with a positive view of life. Looks forward rather than back. Enjoys the same music as me. Opera, of course. I love church music. Oratorios. The Fauré, Bach, Mozart requiems. Foreign films.'

'Instead of which you found me.'

Harriet laughs.

'Yeah! Well . . . you're not so bad. Your taste in music's terrible. But at least you don't take yourself too seriously. I like that. So. What do we do now, Mister Crime Investigator?'

She looks up at me, her face alight with laughter.

'I think I'd better kiss you.'

'That's the most sensible thing you've said so far.'

So we do.

'Call me.'

And she's gone. Running away, her hair dancing in time with her feet, the dog at her heels.

As Jerry and I retrace our steps, the incoming tide washes them away.

Chapter 60

The dock was a ghost town. When Laura kicked a newspaper, a rat scurried but did not flee. Night was its time, these wet cobblestones its territory. She hunched her shoulders inside her belted Burberry.

On her left, Pavarotti stretched his claws and his wings. Using night-vision glasses she picked out a tramp in a sleeping bag, a tart on her knees giving a seaman a cheap thrill. And there, sitting against a container of nuts from Brazil, was a lone figure in a black wetsuit.

Laura gave Pavarotti whispered instructions, but he knew what to do. He'd been through the routine a hundred times. He launched with a rustle of feathers, was visible for a second as he flew across the sodium lights, then hovered a few feet in front of the figure at head-height, his wings outspread.

'Hallelujah! Hallelujah!'

The startled woman stood instinctively. Then met death without a sound. As the Bowie knife sliced through the wetsuit, Laura twisted the blade, cut the heart in two. The body fell. Pavarotti flew back to her shoulder.

'Never turn your back, Pav,' said Laura. 'And never flinch from a fight. Not if you want to like what you see in the mirror every morning.'

Coffee's hot when we get to Murray's. Big Andy, his brown paper bag, and Merv the Mink are ensconced. Father Connolly's in the chair for a trim, which seems strange since he only came in a couple of weeks ago.

Merv leans across and whispers.

'Your sister Carmel's still undecided whether to take the Mother Superior job. Connolly's wining and dining her tonight at the convent restaurant. He wants to look his best.'

As soon as there's a gap in the conversation, I bring the guys up to speed on my meeting on the beach with Harriet.

'She loves church music, you say?' says Murray as he gives one of the priest's hairs a judicious snip.

'She particularly enjoys a good Requiem Mass.'

This provokes a snort from the chair.

'You're not supposed to *enjoy* a Requiem Mass, Johnny. The Mother Church is not a place of entertainment but of Penance and Redemption.'

'Talking of which,' says Big Andy, 'I've been thinking about what you said about the Atkins Diet, Murray, and decided to lose a bit of weight. I've joined a club called Food Watchers. We meet each Tuesday evening in the Heavy Going Founders' Hall. Someone brings a plate of food.'

'And . . . ?' Merv the Mink leans forward. 'And?'

'We watch it.'

'Doesn't sound very interesting.'

'It is if you're a foodie,' says Andy. 'The tension builds until eventually someone cracks. Then it's every man for himself. Whoever's last gets a gold star.'

'How did you get on?' asks Merv the Mink.

'I won.'

'Congratulations,' says Murray. 'Didn't know you had that kind of willpower, Andy.'

'I don't,' says Andy. 'I made the first move, but I was slow getting up and crossing the floor. By the time I reached the table all the food had gone.'

'You won that gold star fair and square, Andy,' says Murray. 'That's all that matters.'

'There's something else.' Andy digs into his second doughnut. 'I met someone there.'

'You mean a lady?' Murray smiles into the mirror. 'That's great! What's her name?'

'Anthea. She's anorexic. Trying to put on weight but lacks the know-how. I said to her, "I know a thing or two about how to put it on and you know a thing or two about how to lose it, so why don't we get together?" I'm going to be her personal trainer and she's going to be mine.'

'Sounds perfect,' says Merv the Mink. 'What they call a win–win situation.'

'A gain–lose situation's how I'd describe it,' says Big Andy. 'Having a few people round for drinks tonight. Want to come, Johnny? Bring your new lady if you like.'

'Love to. Once we're all done here, I'll pop round to the library and ask her.'

'Take it easy with this new love of yours, Johnny.' Murray stops snipping and turns away, scissors a chrome cross between right thumb and forefinger, comb a natural extension of his left arm. 'Hate to see you get hurt. You need to keep a cool head and consider what's happening here. Let's look at this thing scientifically. Humans are highly evolved mammals. Darwin made that clear. Right?'

'Right.'

Heads nod in general agreement.

'Johnny has experienced what the French call *un coup de foudre*. Literally, "a bolt of lightning". Love At First Sight. The stuff of legend. Romeo and Juliet, Antony and Cleopatra—'

'George and Sharon,' says Merv the Mink.

'But let's strip away the emotional subtext, let's look behind the so-called mirror of love and consider what Johnny is experiencing from a purely physiological point of view.'

Around the shop people look at each other, and acknowledge the sense of Murray's approach.

'Male and female mammals are attracted to each other by smell.' Murray goes over to his whiteboard and picks up a black felt pen. 'When a bitch is on heat, male dogs can smell her from miles away. Though we may not be aware of it, humans are affected by smell too.' Murray makes notes on the whiteboard. 'Lemon increases health perceptions; lavender lowers mathematical ability; eucalyptus increases respiratory rate; rose oil reduces blood pressure.'

'Fried onions increases appetite,' says Big Andy.

'I think it's significant,' says Murray, 'that when Harriet and Johnny met the second time, which was when their love blossomed, Harriet had been running around Apprehensive Bay. Raising a sweat. Emitting heightened quantities of female pheromone and thereby making herself far more attractive to a male. Using the same hypothesis, they're currently conducting a study into the increased degree of coupling between males and females at the gym.'

As Murray drops this bombshell, there's a stir of consternation around the shop. I can sense the same thought going through everyone's mind: *When I first met my wife, had she been running? Or to the gym? Had I?*

Murray turns to me.

'I'm not saying you knew anything about this, Johnny. It's an unconscious process. And don't forget, the first time you met you'd been rushing from Paddy's pub, and the second time on the beach you'd been throwing sticks for Jerry. Both would have raised your own pheromone levels. When Harriet's and your olfactory senses collided . . . well, the result was inevitable.'

'Are you saying if I'd met Harriet somewhere else — the supermarket, for example — this wouldn't have happened?'

'That's impossible to say.' Murray strokes his chin. 'I'm no expert . . . '

People look at each other and smile. Murray's modesty is legendary.

' . . . but I'd say it might depend on where in the supermarket you'd met. Near the chiller cabinets— perhaps not. Around the checkouts, where things can get pretty heated at times — who knows?'

Chapter 61

The Bullock Library is funded by a bequest from the McCurdle Foundation. Over a century and a half, the McCurdle family have transformed a barrel, a jug, several glasses and a hose on Bullock Beach into a brewing and distilling dynasty. The Foundation is now dedicated to returning the family's fortune to the community. There's a statue of Arthur McCurdle outside in typical pose, polishing a glass with an old tea towel, and an Arthur's Bar at the back where you can read over a beer as long as you're over eighteen and quiet.

When I walk through the batwing doors later that morning, Harriet is behind the counter running returns through the barcode reader. She's wearing the library uniform. Black jeans, black shirt with double breast pockets and silver piping, a black Stetson hat. Her long black hair dances in the breeze from a rotating fan. I smile and nod at the books on the bench.

'Good clean stuff?'

She laughs.

'The usual. Joanna Trollope, Bryce Courtenay, Vince Humber. Not too much Proust or Turgenev. Most of our members prefer something light.'

'Humber's popular, is he?'

'Oh God, yes.' Harriet loads the books onto a trolley, tosses her mane and sets off across the library. 'I think we've got every Laura Friday that's ever been written. It's total rubbish, of course, but quite well-written rubbish.'

I follow her into the Philosophy section.

'Have you read them?'

'I haven't personally, no, but Tea's a huge fan. Got a shelf full of them. Belongs to some stupid fan club. They hold competitions on a website. Who was so-and-so, which book did he appear in, how was he killed? That sort of thing. Laura Friday and Red Setters — that's about the sum total of his off-duty life. That's one of the reasons we split up. Sometimes he talked about Laura Friday as if *she* was his girlfriend, not me.'

Harriet sticks her thumbs into the pockets of her jeans, rests a spurred heel against Heidegger's *Sein und Zeit*.

'I can see how that would be a problem.'

'Johnny, it's nice to see you. But I'm very busy. We're two short and Politics is a mess. Is this just a social call?'

'A friend of mine. Andy.' I toy with Sartre's *Transcendence of the Ego*. 'He's having a few people round for drinks and nibbles tonight. I wondered if you'd like to come.'

'Tonight?' She sets off again, this time into Travel, her spurred heels clicking on the polished lino, her Stetson at a jaunty angle. She doesn't look back to check if I'm following. 'Yes, I'd love to. What time?'

'Oh, about seven.'

'Will you pick me up?'

'If you insist.'

And I do. Arms wrapped around her torso, I lift her from the ground and kiss her lips, a long, sweet, luscious kiss, her arms around my neck. I drop her to the ground. She's giggling.

'You're crazy. I meant tonight. Now bugger off and leave me to get on with my work.'

As I turn to go I notice someone standing at the entrance to the section. It's Tea Nelson. And he doesn't look at all happy.

Coward that I am, I touch Harriet's hand, brush past Tea's unyielding body and leave him and Harriet to sort out their differences. I reason that it's not my problem. That a library is no place for a stand-up confrontation. That two men fighting over a woman is a terrible cliché of which even Vince Humber would be ashamed. That Tea has the power of the law on his side, and that he can, if he so wishes, make my life even more troublesome than it already is. That Harriet has it all under control. But beneath all that reasoning is the knowledge that even now, after all this time and so many lessons, I still haven't learned to stand my ground. To face trouble head-on.

As I unleash Jerry from his lamppost and walk up Thames Street I chide myself for a coward and a fool. What the hell am I doing telling Harriet I've been working for a newspaper? Playing games in the library with Vince Humber and Laura Friday? Why not tell Harriet who I really am? Trust her. Accept the same curled lip as I got when I told her about my musical preferences. If we're going to have any kind of a future, it's going to have to come out of the closet some time. And then there'll be even more explaining to do. Apologies. Backsliding. Oh yes. I'm very good at those.

I'm passing Meggett's and for something to do with my overheated brain decide to browse through the bookshop on the ground floor. I tie Jerry to a parking meter, pay for thirty minutes, and wander inside.

I never read my own books. Ever since *Fat Parrot* they've been a grind and a torment. As soon as I've sent the final proofs back to the publisher, I relish the interim between then and starting the next one. In the past I've taken a holiday. The Caribbean. Africa. Once to Saint Petersburg with a Russian supermodel named Balalaika. But now, maybe because I've just been reminded of them in the library, I go to the fiction shelves and look for their familiar covers.

I take a few from the shelf and retire to a leather chair where I skim through them. *'It's total rubbish, of course, but quite well-written rubbish.'* The backhanded compliment still rankles. I remember what Helen Valentino said, over that first lunch at Le Gavroche: no Laura Friday novel will ever win a Booker Prize.

But they've given millions of people a lot of pleasure over two decades. That's not a bad achievement. And, incidentally, made me and quite a few other people very rich. I can live with that.

I look at the inside covers. Check publication dates, dedications, epigraphs. It's been a long road. And whoever would have thought that it would lead me back to Bullock?

I return the books to their place and leave the store. And it's then, on Thames Street, unleashing Jerry, that the clouds part as I realise that Laura Friday holds the key to resolving all my troubles.

When I get back to Passion Dale I call Tea Nelson.

'Tea, this is Johnny Kennedy. I've got a proposition for you.'

Chapter 62

I fuss about what to wear, finally settle on a casual tan jacket, navy blue shirt, tan slacks and a pair of Lobb shoes. I drive up Wye Street, a switchback road where Bullock's accidental tourists sometimes go for a view of the town before leaving for Gundry. I park outside a two-storey house, knock on the front door. Harriet lets me in. She's wearing a wrap-around top, a matching pair of flared pants. Her hair is loose about her face and neck, a rough fringe flickering on her eyelashes.

'How do I look?'

A tentative smile hovers around her mouth as she asks me the question. I take her hands in mine.

You need but ... bind up your long hair and sigh;
and all men's hearts must burn and beat ...
Stars climbing the dew-dropping sky,
live but to light your passing feet.

'I'm beginning to think there might be some good points among all that bad.' She kisses me. 'Shall we go?'

Big Andy's house is a rambling structure with bits and pieces added at whim. He answers the front door in a bright blue top and track pants with a Nike swoosh on his left breast and a sweat band around his forehead. There's a glass of what looks like carrot juice in his left paw.

'Hey! Johnny! And you must be Harriet! Good to see you. Come in! Everyone's here, but we're waiting for Anthea. She's gone for a run. She's on cold-turkey, but she slipped out before I could stop her.'

'You're looking . . . well . . . '

'Feeling it, too.' Andy attempts a jog on the spot, but the floor's got borer and it's not worth the risk. 'Anthea's got me on vegetable juice. Feel like I've lost about three kilos since breakfast.'

We go through to the living room where there's a gathering of familiar faces: Murray and Janice, Merv and Betty, George and Sharon sitting together on a sofa. Sunny Riverbank Kennedy. Thunderclap Cornfield in Roman sandals, a floral skirt, decorative safety pins and multi-coloured hair. The air is heavy with weed, mainly coming from the trio in the middle of the room — Lester Judd, Lois Wilson and Jill Stubbings — although plenty more people are on Bullock Lite or Bullock Gold.

'Andy's a changed man,' says Murray. 'Anthea's obviously going to be very good for him.'

'Somehow I can't imagine him with a stick of celery and a carrot juice,' says Merv the Mink. 'Morning coffee won't seem the same without Andy's white, three sugars, and his brown paper bag.'

'Personality change is a worry.' Murray gazes at the rough-plastered Spanish arch leading through to the kitchen as he gathers his thoughts. 'You remember the work of Koeppl, Heller, Bleecker and others, Merv?'

Merv purses his lips, shakes his head.

'Sounds vaguely familiar but I can't recall the detail off the top of my head. Remind me.'

'Fifty-three overweight males went through a weight loss and exercise regime and were tested for personality changes. Results were significant.'

'I remember it now,' says Merv. '*Journal of Clinical Psychology*, July 1992 if I'm not mistaken.'

'Andy's weight's the foundation of his psychological framework,' says Murray. 'Change one aspect, you risk changing others. I just hope they both know what they're doing, that's all.'

There's a faint knock at the front door which can only be Anthea. A hush in the room as we await her arrival. The living-room door opens and Andy's standing there looking proud, filling the space. He moves aside and there she is, looking adoringly up at him. I can see the beating of her heart beneath her ribcage, the pulsing at her temples, and wonder if it's Andy or the run that's the cause of it. Her Food Watchers T-shirt (*Watching's calorie-free*) hangs limply from her coat-hanger shoulders. Andy brings her across to meet us.

'I'm looking forward to working with Andy,' she says. 'He knows so much about different kinds of cakes and doughnuts and what things to avoid and, oh, I don't know, putting on weight's something I've always wanted to do but I've just never seemed to have the incentive before.'

'You're in good hands,' I say. 'And so's Andy from the looks of things.'

When I'm sure everyone's there, I clap my hands and wait for the silence.

'Ladies and gentlemen, sorry to interrupt but I've got good news and I thought you should be the first to know. Tea Nelson and I had a bit of a chat this afternoon, man to man. And I'm delighted to tell you he's decided to drop the vendetta. BWC's back in business. Yellow tape can be removed. People of Bullock can look forward to getting their regular supplies of Bullock Gold and Bullock Lite again — not forgetting new Bullock White, mellow teeth not yellow teeth. As soon as Lester, Lois and Jill can get organised.'

The room erupts.

'That's fantastic,' says Sunny. 'How—?'

I hold up my hand.

'Haven't finished yet. He also accepts that it's over between himself and Harriet. We've shaken hands on that, and he's wished us both all the luck in the world.'

I can't resist a glance at Harriet. Her mouth is agape.

'But he won't back down on the Dog Show. So I've withdrawn Jerry's entry. Tea's got a clear field.'

'Two out of three's a pretty good deal,' says Merv the Mink. 'The woman and the weed. You'd be happy with that, Johnny.'

'You going to tell us how you brokered this settlement?' asks Big Andy, who's looking thinner by the minute as he crunches a carrot. 'What kind of road map you followed during the peace process?'

'Sorry, Andy. Tea and I have agreed to keep it confidential. Lips are sealed.'

Once everyone's lapsed into their own excited conversations Harriet comes up to me, stands very close. Our bodies are touching everywhere that matters.

'I know how to unseal them,' she says.

As soon as I decently can, I reach for the doorknob . . .

Chapter 63

A dog barks from a nearby farm, the sound carrying in the clear air. Jerry grunts in response but remains recumbent. Milly's by his side. I watch the room lighten as dawn breaks. I pick out shapes. The frosted glass lampshade. The open door to the en suite. The door leading to the passage and the living spaces I've created. The shape of the bed, and of my toes beneath the duvet. The mound of my erection. When I flex it, it works.

I turn and see Harriet. Facing me on the other side of the bed. Her body shape, one leg straight, the other crooked as if she's running along the beach. Her left hand flung across the bed, nearly reaching me, the other tucked somewhere. The etched outlines of her face. High cheekbones. Broad, high forehead. Soft mouth. Hair, tied back during the day, now everywhere. The sweet smell of last night's lovemaking. Her breath, still fresh. How does she manage that? My mouth is a cesspit. I must have uncovered her during the night. I lift the duvet, gently take hold of her fingers.

'Bugger off.'

'I thought you were asleep.'

'I was.'

'Sorry.'

'No, you're not. You're still horny.'

Her hand dives beneath the covers and takes hold of my mound.

'Piss proud. Go and get rid of it.'

I move closer, run a finger from her ribs to her toes, then

back again. Hitch myself onto an elbow and run the palm of my hand across her pillow-strewn hair. Kiss her forehead.

'Make yourself useful. Make some coffee.'

'What's it worth?'

'I'll think about it.'

When I slip from the bed, Jerry and Milly stir, watch me pad across the floorboards to the bathroom. I emerge wrapped in a white-towelling dressing-gown and follow a trail of clothes across the bedroom floor and into the kitchen. The tiles are cold on my bare feet. I put water to boil, crush a strip of dry leaf and spread it upon a paper bed. Roll, lick, roll again. Set a match to it. Inhale. The sweet aroma of Pot of Gold fills the room. I feel like some classical music. I hit a button on the stereo. Hot Chocolate. 'You Sexy Thing'. I do the *Full Monty* shuffle to get outside.

Across the lawn, wet between my toes, to an area of rough ground where Jerry and I stand pissing, our yellow streams steaming, while watching the goldening sea. Milly squats demurely. I throw a stick, which Jerry chases and brings back. He sits there, waiting for me to do it again. I don't. I'm tough. But fair.

Back inside as Jerry inhales his breakfast of black sausage and sauerkraut, and Milly dabs at a dog roll, I slice a baguette, toast the pieces, spread damson compôte and set them with coffee on a tray which I take back to the bedroom.

Harriet is propped on both elbows, face full of sleep.

'If I didn't know better, I'd think you were after something.'

'Who says you know better?'

'You want it now or after breakfast?'

I scratch my chin, pondering.

'I think after. Don't want the coffee to get cold.'

'Ha!' She scoffs. 'Don't kid yourself.'

I loosen my belt, let the dressing-gown fall to the floor.

'OK, you asked for it.'

'Well, I didn't actually, but . . .'

'You want foreplay or get right down to it?'

'I think get right down to it, don't you?'

'Literally?'

'Yes, please.'

We thrash the breadth and length of the bed. A fight for top dog, won by Harriet with my compliance. Her body is lithe and supple and warm and welcoming. She comes without warning. *'Oh Jesus fucking Christ'*, freely yelled with no one to hear but Jerry and Milly. And possibly the farm dog.

We lie side by side, sharing a post-coital joint.

'Lips unsealed yet?'

Harriet blows a perfect smoke ring. I wonder how many as yet undiscovered talents she possesses.

'There's much more to this than what happened between me and Tea. I guess this is as good a time as any to make my Confession.'

'I'm not your priest, Johnny. I can't offer you Absolution.'

'I need to make a clean breast.' Distractedly, I caress a nipple. 'If you're in love with me, you need to know who it is you're in love with.'

'You arrogant bastard! Who said anything about love? I've just been using you to slake my desires.'

'Are they slaked now?'

'Pretty much. For the moment.' She sits up, rests an elbow on the pillow, her head in the palm of her hand. 'You've got me worried now. You haven't done anything dreadful . . . killed someone or something? Have you?'

'Dozens of times. But only in fiction.'

Harriet frowns. 'Sorry. I don't understand.'

'I'm Vince Humber. I invented Laura Friday.'

'Don't be ridiculous. You're Johnny Kennedy. Used to be Fitz Kennedy. You were a reporter on the *Bullock Telegraph*. Then you went off to London to work for the *Daily Chronicle*.'

I twist around, pick up the phone receiver from its bedside cradle. Hand it to Harriet.

'Tea didn't believe me when I told him, either. You can do what he did. Call my agent. Helen Valentino. She'll confirm it. Or Solly Greenberg in Los Angeles, who produced Laura's movies. Or a dozen other people. It's true.'

Harriet's quiet for a while, although I can almost hear her brain working overtime. Then she says, 'I want the whole story, Johnny. The whole truth. And nothing but.'

Chapter 64

Thirty minutes later I've given Harriet the *Reader's Digest* version of my life story. She's puzzled by the last chapter.

'Do you mean to tell me that, in return, Tea said he'd drop all charges against Sunny and the BWC team? Drop me? Drop everything except his stupid Dog Show trophy?'

'Yep. He's on top of the world about it. Literally. He'll be the hero of all those nerdy websites.' We're on our third Pot of Gold, beginning to feel ultra-mellow. 'So you see where his priorities lie.'

'Are you OK with it? Creatively?'

I give a hollow laugh, verging on a scoff.

'I'm just happy that at long last Laura Friday's been able to do some good. If it hadn't been for the fact that Tea's one of her greatest fans, a lot of Bullock people — good people — people like Sunny and Thunderclap, Lester, Lois, and Jill — could have been in a whole heap of trouble. And a lot more people would have continued to suffer from weed deprivation. Quite apart from how it's worked out for you and me. I'm very OK.'

'This doesn't make any difference, you know,' says Harriet, 'you being Vince Humber and a multi-millionaire. I loved you before I knew about your bank account.'

'But you said you were just using me to slake your lust.'

'Yeah, well.' Harriet does something with her ice-cold fingers which provokes an immediate response. 'That, too. You can love and lust someone at the same time, can't you? They're not mutually exclusive.'

'I guess so. There's something else.'

'Oh shit. What now?'

'My mother was a nun.'

'*Wha-a-a-t!*'

Harriet's on her knees facing me. Hair awry. Face contorted. Breasts pert. They're at least as lemony as Maria Santos Almeida's, possibly even more so.

'I told you about Roy Calloway. The old family friend who's going to marry my mum.'

'Go on.'

'When he told me about that, he also told me about my Aunt Agnes.'

'The peripatetic nun. Always in and out of the convent.'

'I always wondered why she had an Irish accent and Dad didn't. Turns out she wasn't Dad's sister. She was a distant cousin from Blackjack. When she was seventeen she had an affair with the village priest and became pregnant. An Irish village can be a very spiteful and condemning place. Her parents and the Church sent her out to Bullock where people would be much more tolerant. Mum and Dad hadn't been married long. Dad was just getting his dental practice going and, apart from anything else, they needed the money. We had a spare room, the Church offered to help with Agnes's board and lodging, so she moved in with us. Carmel was about a year old. When she was born, Mum had nearly died. She couldn't have any more children. It seemed to make sense to make Agnes's baby one of the family.'

'So Agnes is—'

'Was. My mother.'

'How do you feel about that?'

'I always had a special affinity with Agnes. Always felt a bit guilty that I loved her more than Mum. Maybe this explains it. I don't know. I never felt that way about Dad. I just think it's very ironic that my birth father was a . . . well, a Father.'

'Have you discussed it with your mum?'

'No.'

'Are you going to?'

'Roy and I talked about that. She asked him to tell me because she couldn't face telling me herself. She knows I know. Dad and Agnes are gone. It might explain a lot, but it changes nothing. I don't think there's any point in stirring up a lot of emotion at this stage of our lives.'

'What about Carmel?'

'She doesn't know. Unless someone at the convent has told her. If she does know, she's never said anything.'

Harriet purses her lips, takes a drag, hands the roach to me.

'Seems like that's the way you do things in your family. Skirt around the big issues. I'm not saying it's right or wrong. Maybe it's a Catholic thing. Repression. Dank Voids. Hidden depths. White lies, black truths. If we're going to stay together, Johnny, that's not how I want things to be. I believe in fresh air and facing the truth of things. Can we agree on that?'

'It'd be a blessed relief.'

I say it, and at that very moment I mean it. But I don't know if I can do it. Not full-time. On an impulse I get out of bed, pad across to the tallboy, take a key from my key ring. Then I go to Harriet's side of the bed and get down on one knee.

'This is the key to my heart.'

'No, it's not.' Harriet giggles. 'It's the key to Passion Dale.'

'Same thing. Will you come and live with me here, and be my love?'

'If you insist.'

Chapter 65

'So.'

Laura stroked Pavarotti's feathers, allowed a thin smile.

'It's Tea time. I heard you broke out of the slammer, Nelson. What's that big thing in your hand? You'd better be careful. Might go off. Hurt someone.'

'You dumped me. No one dumps Tea Nelson and gets away with it, Laura.'

'Gimme a break! Who gives a shit, anyway? You shouldn't have tried to come back. You can never go back. Tell me, Tea, I've always wondered: why did your folks give you such a stupid name?'

'My Mom's name was Beveridge. She had a cruel sense of humour. It's blighted my life. That's why I became a cop. So I could work out my anger on innocent people. I've got a brother called Milo and a sister called Tina. Short for Ovaltine. But you don't care about that. Stalling's not gonna help you now, Laura. Never a day since they put me away I didn't dream of this.'

'That's a double negative, Tea.'

'Yeah? Well, here's another, Laura.'

Pavarotti squawked.

'Mamma Mia, here I go agai—'

The .38 spat twice. The first slug smashed the parrot's beak, ricocheted, took out the neon sign. The second took the top off Laura's skull. She went horizontal. Her hips twitched in a kind of hula before she lay still.

Tea Nelson blew smoke from the muzzle, turned to the Red Setter by his side.

'It's all over, Bruno. Let's get out of here.'

As the sirens wailed, Pavarotti lay on his back, claws up, his feathers fluttering in the breeze.

THE END